CHICAGO PITS

Also by Bill Walker

Skywalker—Close Encounters on the Appalachian Trail (2008)

Skywalker—Highs and Lows on the Pacific Crest Trail (2010)

The Best Way—El Camino de Santiago (2012)

Getting High—The Annapurna Circuit in Nepal (2013)

Tall Tales—The Great Talisman of Height (2014)

CHICAGO PITS

by
Bill Walker

ISBN-13: 978-1981143283

ISBN-10: 1981143289

Dedication

My younger sister, Kitty Walker Foster, for being as genuine as the day is long.

AUTHOR'S NOTE

This is a work of fiction. Names, characters, businesses, places, events, and incidents are either the products of the author's imagination or used in a fictitious manner. Any resemblance to actual persons, living or dead, or actual events is purely coincidental.

In a few cases, references are made to public figures. The Hillary Rodham Clinton cattle-trading story as discussed in this book conforms to the way it has been reported on extensively in the press. However, the one quote attributed to former President Bush is fabricated.

Please let me say in advance that I know of no way to authentically depict a trading floor without including graphic language. For adult readers only.

- Bill Walker

"Its gods were false. Its taste was bad. Its heroes were oafs and brutes and thieves and bullies."

- Thomas Frank, *Pity the Billionaire*

PART I

GLOSSARY

CCE: Chicago Commodities Exchange

Pit: Amphitheater-like arenas where futures and options contracts are traded

Locals: Independent traders for their own account

Brokers: Traders who execute customer orders for commissions

One contract: $100,000 face value in Treasury-Index futures (Bonds, Notes, Bills)

Price: Ex. 96-24 = 96 and 24/32 cents on the dollar

Sold: Shouted by traders to initiate a trade with another trader. Trades done on honor system

Chapter One

FEAR.

FOR THE HORDES hurrying through the spacious lobby of the Chicago Commodities Exchange (CCE) every morning at seven, fear ruled. You either struck it in others, or they stuck it in you. Many sported studied gaits and swaggers that seemed calculated to induce envy and resentment among their fellow-traders. The predominant din was the squeak of sneakers and coaching shoes. However, various stoic individuals clung to the fiction that working on a trading floor was a normal job. They were the ones wearing hard-soled wingtips, which added a crunch to the cacophony of steps.

Thirty-one-year-old Chris Parker was in a fearful state as he hurried through the revolving doors of the CCE. He had been lying awake since four a.m. in apprehension of the bedlam that lay ahead. Immediately Chris kept a lookout for *her*. As always, he was neurotic about the desirability of that. Squinting, he scanned the masses for a lithe female in her early thirties who barely cleared five-feet. So far, the coast was clear. Nonetheless, Chris kept his head down, not easy for someone who measured six-foot-ten inches in bare feet.

When he got to the coatroom, a skinny-black male in his late-teens spotted him. "How are we this morning, Mr. SKY?"

"Never as good as you, Curtis," Chris responded with a free-flowing smile. Lately, it had occurred to him that this youngster was the person he looked the most forward to seeing every day.

Curtis skipped to retrieve Chris's navy-blue trading jacket, which bore his appropriate trading acronym, *SKY*.

Chris suited up before taking the final escalator to where the action awaited.

***

THE MAIN TRADING floor of the CCE resembled a huge storage warehouse. It sure as hell didn't look like the single most important piece of real estate in the global financial markets. But that's what it was. Over the next several hours, $200 billion in contracts would change hands on a floor that measured little more than two basketball courts laid side by side. In fact, most market experts opined that the stratospheric trading volume in this drafty old room drove the level of interest rates the world over.

Several amphitheater-style trading platforms, all raised eight feet off the ground, ringed the floor. But the big-swinging dicks—and without question the truest dicks—made their living in the Treasury-Index Pit. That's where Chris was headed.

He slalomed his way around bodies swarming in all directions, before arriving at the base of the Pit. He then scaled a built-in wooden ladder reaching to the top step, from where he peered down into the cavernous arena. Tense, already perspiring traders in various color-coded trading jackets were wedged into steep stair-steps.

Again, Chris felt relief. *She* wasn't there.

"Good morning, fellow cocksuckers," Marty Allman greeted his Pit neighbors. When nobody responded to his standard morning salute, Allman asked, "Has anybody heard the call?"

"Almost a point lower," a nearby clerk answered, referring to the estimated-opening price.

"Wow, what happened?" Chris asked him.

"Some asshole from Japan said something that sent the market into the shitter."

Japan. The name struck fear deep into the minds of traders. The United States of America had become a nation of ill-repute in the financial markets because of its gaping budget deficits. It borrowed from the only country capable of lending such staggering amounts of money, the same nation it had dropped two atomic bombs on less than a half-century ago. Still, who could complain? Washington's reckless fiscal policies represented a bonanza for Treasury traders who craved *instability.*

However, according to the morning's news, the people funding the whole orgy—the Japanese—were showing lender fatigue. The Japanese finance minister's statement was displayed in radium-green letters on the trading room's east wall: "Our appetite for funding American spending sprees is limited." By the prophylactic standards of Japan-speak, that was a harsh rebuke.

Chris had a strong suspicion that many traders couldn't so much as have defined a Treasury Bond. Note, or Bill. All they knew was that they made their living off economic turbulence. However, as a broker of customer orders, Chris feared volatile openings.

A moment later, his stomach sank when monstrous Ray Malley rounded the bend in his black trading jacket. He bore through a crowd of clerks and ascended the ladder to the Treasury Pit, as Chris savored his last moments of physical integrity.

Speaking of someone who would not know what a Treasury security was, Chris suspected that was Malley. But Malley always seemed to remember two things. First, he was the biggest person in the entire Pit, a 290-pound former professional wrestler. Second, and more crucially, he could use his size to intimidate other traders. His main target was Chris Parker.

The last person on the entire floor that Chris would have chosen to stand next to was Malley. It was any trader's worst nightmare. But due to the CCE's notorious lawlessness, the two had ended up parked next to each other on the back row of the Treasury Pit since Chris's first day as a broker five years ago. He had been unable to escape from Malley ever since.

***

REAMS OF TRADERS and clerks were packed in penitentiary-style—rear-end to rear-end—a galling setup that had earned it the unaffectionate nickname, *Buttfuck Row.*

Malley inserted his bulging frame against Chris's backside, and took to rocking back and forth to clear bodies out of the way. Soon he had Chris's lean physique turned sideways and swaying over the Pit's dividing rail. Rolling his almost cruelly-muscled neck around in semi-circles with his eyes closed, Malley looked as if he might be preparing for another Saturday afternoon wrestling bout. But when he opened his eyes, he saw David Littler standing in front of him on the top step. Immediately Malley's face turned purple and his nostrils flared like a bull's.

"Hey, what are you doing here?" Malley barked.

Littler had once been a rock star at the CCE—the single biggest broker of customer orders. But then traders arrived one morning to hear the shocking news that he had been suspended for prearranging trades.

Littler was Jewish. Since his return a few months ago, he had been angling for various spots around the Pit, picking up the moniker *Shylock.* Not a few seemed to take pleasure in the misfortunes of this wandering Jew. This morning, however, he had arrived early and stationed himself in a coveted spot: front row of the top step of the Pit. Amazingly, eighty-six percent of the Treasury Pit's volume was traded on this one step. Those standing on the other five steps down below were left with the scraps. Getting—or not getting—a spot to stand on the top step routinely made and broke careers.

Littler turned and looked up at Malley, not able to hide his trepidation. "I've stood here before," he answered. But Chris noted it sounded like a prepared response.

"No, you haven't," Malley shot back, before lowering his pipe-sized elbows into Littler's shoulder blades and commencing a cleaving motion.

Chris had heard rumors that Littler was training intensively in kung-fu. Still, he knew from personal experience that Malley's massive girth was better suited to the tightly-packed Treasury Pit. Malley kept prying at Littler from above with what looked like a lever of incomprehensible power.

"You can't do that," Littler shrieked in ill-disguised horror.

"I'm doing it," Malley said matter-of-factly. Soon he had toppled Littler off the top step.

He began lunging back at Malley, reminding Chris of a fullback trying to eke out a first down on fourth-and-short. But the ex-Pit star's desperate attempts were greeted by Malley's club-like arms once more, hurtling him helplessly into a crowd of traders on the step below, and finally all the way down to the well of the Pit. *No Man's Land.*

Chris couldn't escape the thought that Littler looked like an animal in the wild that had lost a contest over food and sex to a superior predator. Even worse, and not for the first time, Chris noticed a disturbing homoerotic vibe wafting through the air among the large audience of alpha males at the naked display of violence.

Also, he dreaded that Malley might be readying to give another clinic in the very first minute of trading.

Chapter Two

"HEY, CHRIS. BUY a hundred on the opening," his assistant Danny shouted up at 7:14.

Chris's stomach tightened. At $100,000 face-value per contract, this was a customer order to buy $10 million worth of Treasury-Index Futures. Chris was the senior broker for *Elliott House*, an old-line Wall Street firm. He knew that opening ranges, which lasted the sixty seconds from 7:15 to 7:16 a.m., resembled a game of Blind Man's Bluff.

Meanwhile, Ray Malley heard the order and smelled blood. With fifteen seconds remaining to the opening bell, Chris raised his long, thin arms and began battling with Malley for wing space, the two of them looking like basketball players going up for a rebound. Chris's hands reached much higher, but Malley had them shoved laterally over the head of one of Chris's Pit neighbors.

Ten seconds left: hands were gyrating in all directions, indicating offers to buy and sell at various prices. The Pit was a sea of rapacious faces, as adrenaline pumped noticeably throughout the room. *Waves, waves, waves.*

7:15. The opening bell rang.

"Sell a hundred at 96-22," shouted Bill Perkins of *Hamilton James.*

Perfect! Perkins was selling just the quantity Chris needed to buy.

"Buy a hundred, Bill, buy 'em, buy 'em, Bill," Chris screamed at Perkins, hoping to get a quick fill on his order.

Unfortunately, Malley had Chris plastered crotch-first into the dividing rail, facing away from Perkins. He struggled to break loose. But when Malley saw him trying to buy the hundred contracts from Perkins, that was his cue to steal the trade. Chris felt a sharp jolt, as Malley used his right hand to pivot off his spine.

"Buy 'em, buy 'em, I said buy 'em, you fucking idiot," Malley thundered at Perkins.

Hamilton James' brokers were known for being innocent-faced cherubs laboring amongst savages. They were also considered the crappiest brokers in the Pit. Perkins was no different. He belatedly realized Chris had been first and turned to signal selling him one-hundred contracts. But then he spotted Malley bearing down on him, with bodies scattered in the former wrestler's wake, including two of Perkins' clerks. His self-preservation instinct took over.

"Sell you a hundred, Ray," Perkins said.

Stealing the trade put Malley in shoe shape. He was now *long* one hundred contracts from a price of 96-22. Better yet, he knew the broker right next to him—Chris—had to buy a hundred contracts in the next thirty seconds.

Chris was sure that Malley would try to squeeze him to pay up on his order. "96-23 bid for 100," he screamed, flailing his arms. His fabulous pit presence was reduced by Malley's elbow wedged against his vertebra. Finally, Chris spotted Jimmy Hawkins on the other side of the Pit, practically doing jumping jacks to accentuate his offer to sell at a price of 96-23.

"Buy 'em, buy 'em, Jimmy," Chris screamed at Hawkins. "Buy a hundred at 96-23."

When Malley saw Chris had located a seller, he reversed on a dime. "Sold, sold, sold," he shouted at Chris, while shaking him like a bush.

Chris became stubborn. Hawkins was the first sell offer, and he wanted to buy the hundred contracts from him, instead of Malley. "Jimmy, Jimmy, buy a hundred, Jimmy," Chris continued screaming for Hawkins's attention at the top of his lungs.

Malley began hacking at Chris's arms, impeding his access to Hawkins on the far side of the Pit. Meanwhile, Hawkins finally became aware of Chris screaming his name from afar. Sensing his desperation, Hawkins dropped his hands, and acted like he didn't see Chris.

And the split-second Malley saw Hawkins no longer wanted to sell, he also quit yelling, "Sold."

Chris was stuck. "96-23 bid," he screamed, his panic on full display.

He heard the phone brokers back at the Elliott House desk shrieking at his clerk.

"Just buy 'em, Chris," Danny pleaded. "I've got to give them a price." There were only twelve seconds left in the opening range.

"96-24 bid," Chris yelled at the top of his lungs, his trading jacket billowing in multiple directions. But the locals were all lying in the weeds, hanging him out to dry.

Finally, Chris heard a voice from his blind side, screaming, "Sold, SKY, sold, sold, sold." He attempted pirouetting to his left to locate the seller, only to have Malley smash him in mid-air, jackknifing his head over the rail.

"Sold, sold," Malley shouted at Chris.

"Have you bought 'em yet?" Danny screamed at Chris, echoing the furious shouts from the Elliot House desk.

Again, Chris became defiant: *anybody but Malley.*

"Groover, Groover," he yelled, while lunging at Dave Groover who was also offering to sell at 96-24. But Chris knew from hard experience that these were the situations where Malley dispensed with any vestige of civility. He proceeded to double Chris's waist over the rail. The rail-thin Alabaman was contorted in helpless fashion, his head hanging two feet over the rail and well below Malley's. The only trader in the entire Pit he could see was Malley screaming, "Sold, sold. I said sold, you fucking asshole."

"Buy 100," Chris gasped in capitulation.

"96-24 trade," Malley hollered up to the Pit reporter.

It was 7:16 a.m.

Chris had paid the highest price in the opening range for his customer. Worse yet, his nemesis Ray Malley had made 200 ticks in sixty seconds—$6,250—a dog's breakfast for the ultimate trading hack.

Meanwhile, Chris had an irate customer on his hands.

Chapter Three

"WHAT IN THE holy fuck happened?" screamed Mark McMann, a phone broker from Elliott House. McMann's voice carried over the clerks and phone brokers standing between him and the Pit.

"They want to know what happened," Danny called up to Chris.

"The Hamilton James broker pimped me when I tried to buy from him at 96-22," Chris explained to his clerk. Rolling his eyes, he thumbed back at Malley. "He stole the trade from me."

Chris tried turning his back away from the Elliott House booth, hoping the storm would pass. No such luck.

Danny relayed the news. "They want to talk to you."

"I can't get out of here," Chris shot back. Soon he heard more unpleasant rumblings coming their way.

"Mark says look back."

Chris turned back and saw a sour look on McMann's face, as he pointed at the phone in his left hand. This happened only a few times a year, a customer so pissed off that he demanded to speak directly to the Pit Broker who had purportedly screwed him.

Chris writhed to extract himself from the train of packed bodies. The split-second he was free from the body jam, he heard a thud as Malley smashed against the rail due to the relentless pursuit from behind. *Wow*. Chris lowered himself down the ladder and waded through a gauntlet of clerks to get back to the Elliott House desk.

The first person he passed was Hank Downey. "Hey, Chris, what happened on the opening?" Downey asked in a sympathetic voice that Chris had learned to dread. By the logic, Chris knew Downey couldn't have been happier that he had botched the opening. Downey had been with Elliott House for fourteen years and was a master at the blame game. The highlight of his day often came when something went wrong, which he could then leverage into larger controversies.

Mark McMann began waving the phone at Chris. "Come on. This is Keith, our biggest salesman. He wants to know what happened."

Chris had always thought explaining a bad trade to an angry customer was like discussing sexual inadequacy to a female. The broker had done his damnedest, only to disappoint. Likewise, he couldn't fire back too hard at the customer for fear of losing any repeat business. This conversation would be a no-win.

"This is Chris," he answered, trying to keep his voice low.

"Please tell me how to explain this terrible price to my biggest customer," asked someone in a Long Island accent. "Please tell me what happened in there?"

Chris found himself wishing the man had said anything other than *please,* given the acidic fashion it was voiced.

"The whole Pit turned into buyers at once," he offered, true as far as it went. Perhaps the worst thing: he could *not* tell the man the real truth. If the Elliott House higher-ups knew his geographical position in the Pit every morning was disadvantageous, to the point of disabling, they *would* have understood. But they would also take their business elsewhere.

"Something must have traded at 96-22 and 96-23," the salesman said. "Those were the first prints on the screen."

"It barely traded at those prices," Chris tried to assure him.

"I don't know what vantage point you had," the man shot back, "but the trader sitting three feet from me here on the 56th floor of the World Trade Center placed a buy order through Dean Witter. He bought his contracts at 96-22."

Ugh. Chris knew that was the oldest trick in the book, telling one brokerage firm that you got a better price from a competitor, in hopes of extorting a price adjustment. He held his tongue.

"You've got my word we will do better next time," he said, trying to cut his losses.

"Next time, huh?" the man spat before Chris heard a click.

That wasn't the last of it. The jerk immediately called the Elliott House floor manager, Jack Fitzgerald, demanding an adjustment of his client's price from 96-24 down to 96-23.

Fitzgerald's background was as a desk trader on Wall Street; Chris had long suspected he didn't understood the cutthroat dynamics of pit trading in Chicago. "Chris, I had to give him an adjustment to 96-23," he said upon hanging up. That meant Elliot House would write the customer a check for $3,125 from Chris's error account.

"Man, it must be nice," Chris muttered, aware that his year-end bonus had just taken a four-figure debit. He stood at the desk another minute, savoring the time out of the fray. The market appeared to have smoothed out after the herky-jerky opening minute. Sensitive to any time he tarried, Chris dutifully headed back to embed himself in the smorgasbord of male bodies.

A heated debate of some immediacy had broken out amongst several traders. But it centered around an age-old question: *who* had farted?

"I always own up when it's me," said a frizzy-headed trader known as *Batesy*, who had earned his label due to behavioral likenesses to Norman Bates in the horror-thriller, *Psycho*.

Batesy had been medically diagnosed with *meteorism*, the uncontrolled-farting disease that so embarrassed Hitler. However, Batesy suffered from no such timidity as the Fuhrer, regularly putting his malady on exhibition for his Pit neighbors. It was his other diagnosis, *onanism*, which had him bolting from the Pit with increasing frequency due to excessive-compulsive masturbation, that had begun eating at his income.

"Seriously," Henry Cash said with a sincere tone of annoyance, "somebody please go take a shit."

"Don't look at me," Batesy responded with a broad smile.

Chris quickly realized it was not a superfluous debate. Something that smelled on par with a dead animal was emitting a powerful stench that had traders wrapping their trading jackets around their heads. No relief was forthcoming. Finally, the avuncular figure of Jimmy Cain, at age fifty-three the oldest person in the Pit, stepped in with some Solomonic wisdom.

"It is you," he said to Batesy in a confidential tone.

Batesy gave him a serious look, but no response.

"For God's sake, go clean it up!" Cain urged him.

To everyone's relief, Batesy took the sage's advice and headed to the bathroom, looking like a kid being sent to the woodshed after dinner.

***

"HEY, BOB," RAY Malley called down to his trade checker, "you got those pictures yet?"

"Right here," a freckle-faced, all-American-looking kid in his late teens reported with a wide smile. Malley reached down to grab a large envelope from his clerk. Dark half-moons had already formed in the armpits of his trading jacket, despite the day having just begun.

Chris rolled his eyes; he had a good idea what was coming.

Malley reached into the envelope with his giant, hairy paws and plucked several photos. He started handing individual pictures to various traders. Each contained a graphic shot of a large male in the act of sexual intercourse with a dazed-looking young female. The male's head was not visible, just coffee-can forearms, as well as a bulging organ tightly sheathed in the woman's vagina. Everyone recognized the man. But Chris noted it was a different girl from last week's photos. Not a surprise since Malley had been on a winning streak of late.

"Hey, Marty," Malley yelled to Martin O' Reilly, the Bear Stearns broker, when the photos arrived into his hands. "You ever seen an Irishman with a cock that big?" Malley bellowed with a glow washing over a face that could only be described as deeply unlovely. These were the good ole days.

One trader who had been up to his office swore that Malley had shown him an alphabetized file of all the different females he had manhandled. But another trader told Chris, "He does it to impress brokers." Indeed, the more Chris had seen of the whole shtick, the more he suspected that analysis was true.

"Hey, wait a minute," Malley yelled down into the Pit, his grin having vanished. "Get those back up here." It wasn't that he had suddenly been afflicted with a case of modesty. Rather, there was a trader standing a few steps down who would not have been appreciative—the younger brother of Malley's wife. Malley repatriated his photos and began putting them away when Batesy returned from the men's room in a happy-go-lucky fashion.

His Pit neighbor Howard Kaner whispered something to him, at which point Batesy appeared to seize up. "Hey, come on, now," Batesy pleaded to Malley, looking like a kid who had had been deprived of cotton candy. "You know where I was." He reached over and began cuffing at the sleeve of Malley's trading jacket. Since Batesy was always one of the more appreciative viewers, Malley acceded to his wishes and handed down the envelope.

"Looka' here, we've got a live wire," Batesy said, brightening up.

Right then, Jimmy Cain jumped up like his hand had touched a red-hot stove. "Goddammit," he yelled at Batesy, "I still smell that shit." The way he said it indicated it wasn't a standard fart accusation.

Emboldened by Malley's exhibitionism, Batesy showed he was in a similarly transparent mood. He handed the envelope back to Malley, before reaching into his trading jacket and pulling out his boxer shorts. He opened them up to reveal a perfectly-formed bowel movement.

"Get the fuck outta here," Cain erupted, shoving Batesy as he jumped backwards like a grasshopper. Batesy's face was aglow despite being evicted from the Pit for the second time in fifteen minutes for hygiene reasons.

In the world's largest market—the U.S. Treasury-Index Pit, a local's job was to get noticed by brokers, hoping to get preferred trades on the broker's customer orders. By that standard, both Malley and Batesy had done their jobs well this morning. However, Chris knew neither one was as devastating as *she* was in accomplishing that task.

Chapter Four

"KAROL. WE NEED to see you right away."

A knowing smile crept across Karol Stanislav's suntanned face. It was the look of someone who knew he was good at something. Few would disagree. Stanislav was widely considered the most powerful member of the U.S. Congress. He was undoubtedly the most feared.

His favorite constituency had always been the commodities exchanges in his hometown of Chicago. There was just something Stanislav loved about the business. To be sure he was amazed at the brash way they asked him to deliver favors on various taxes, regulations, and special exemptions. But compared to all the other lobbyists, they had style. He certainly sympathized with the unabashed way they pursued money. "There are only three things that matter in politics," he was fond of saying. "Money, money, and I forget what the third one is."

However, this late February afternoon in Sarasota, Florida, Stanislav had received a different type of phone call from the Chairman of the CCE, Dean Beman. It had a sound of urgency that had never been part of any previous requests. The standard ingratiating tone of, *Wow, we really need this. Yeah, Yeah, that would be huge. Oh, and one other thing*, was absent. In its place was a more ominous note.

"Sure," Stanislav replied to Beman's urgent request for a meeting. "I'm down here playing golf with the oil and gas folks ... how about first thing Monday?"

"Actually," Beman said. "we were wondering if we could come see you tomorrow night after you get off the golf course."

"Gosh, Dean, I hate to see you folks come all the way down here," Stanislav responded, sounding surprised. "I'll go there."

Stanislav enjoyed every aspect of life in the arena—the five-star restaurants, luxury hotels, and plush golfing resorts. His common touch, if he ever had one, had long since deserted him. But at the end of the day, the thing he valued most was being the go-to man when the chips were down. The folks back home needed him.

"Dean, what time?"

"Could you make it tomorrow night at 6:00?"

"Is there really no way we can wait until Monday?" Stanislav asked. But then he remembered the new *family arrangement* they had made for him. "Forget it, Dean. I'll be there at eight tomorrow night. There shouldn't be much traffic on Saturday night in downtown Chicago."

Chapter Five

IN HIS ENTIRE career, only one person had been able to keep CCE Chairman Dean Beman on the defensive. That was the man he was waiting for this late-winter Saturday evening at the CCE in downtown Chicago.

Beman had made a fortune as a floor-trader despite lacking any discernible trading ability. The story of how he did it lay shrouded in dark tales lingering in CCE lore, and that had a disturbing specificity to them. Still, he never let the whispers hold him back, eventually slashing and clawing his way to become chairman of the world's largest futures and options exchange. Not bad for a former used-car salesman.

His 26th floor office had a floor-to-ceiling window looking out on the metropolitan area far below. Through the city lights, a sinuous blackness marked the Chicago River's winding path towards the vast emptiness that was Lake Michigan.

At 8:30, CCE President Mike Kilpatrick entered Beman's office to inform him their guest had arrived. Beman took to his feet. Soon the formidable figure of the country's most powerful Polish-American politician, Karol Stanislav, walked through the door as if entering his own home.

"Good evening, Karol. Thanks for being here."

"Dean," Stanislav said in casual acknowledgment, before plopping down in the same chair he had occupied during meetings with eleven CCE chairmen over the last thirty-five years.

Beman couldn't complain at such a spare greeting. Stanislav no longer took the trouble to learn the names of new members of Congress. Beman also knew he had better not beat around the bush. Stanislav was famous for walking out of meetings he saw as a waste of his time.

"Mr. Chairman," he addressed Stanislav in his Washington title of Chairman of the all-powerful House Appropriations Committee, "let me be clear. There would be no Chicago Commodities Exchange without everything you've done for us. Tens of thousands of Chicagoans who might otherwise be sweeping the street—and that includes myself—owe their livelihoods to you."

He stopped to let his words sink in. But the man sitting across from him was immune to verbal cues. Beman shifted restlessly in his chair and ruffled his hair, slick with brilliantine and parted high on his forehead. Kilpatrick stood by the door, looking more like a sentinel than the Exchange President.

"The FBI investigation has hurt us more than we were aware," Beman said, referring to the FBI sting operation of a few years back that led to dozens of indictments. The exchanges had vowed to change. But so far, the CCE's medieval-like politics had stifled any meaningful reforms.

"The Wall Street trading houses," Beman elaborated, "have been complaining for years about our open-outcry style of trading. They keep asking, 'Why do you keep doing business in this old-fashioned way? Our traders in New York feel like they're trading blindfolded.'"

Stanislav pursed his lips.

"They've been threatening the nuclear option for some time now," Beman said.

"The nuclear option?" Stanislav raised his eyebrows in apparent confusion.

"Yes. They're developing an electronic system to trade Treasury-Index futures. Our Washington liaison says the first test is coming this week when the Commodity Futures and Options Subcommittee meets on Capitol Hill to vote on approval." Beman dared to stare at Stanislav. He needed some buy-in.

Finally, Stanislav spoke up. "The obvious question is could such a system ever work?"

"I made myself clear on that last time I was down in Washington," Beman quipped.

That drew an appreciative laugh from Stanislav.

Beman was referring to the press conference he had given on the Capitol steps after a grilling by the House Banking Committee on the viability of electronic trading. " We grow risk takers in Chicago the way they grow corn in Nebraska and terrorists in the Middle East," he defiantly told the assembled Washington press corps. "There is no market—I repeat, no market—without us in Chicago."

Point well taken ... and tough luck for Wall Street customers forced to remain hostage to the anarchy of the Chicago pits.

Since then, however, the ground had been shifting against the Chicago exchanges. First the Germans had opened an electronic exchange in Frankfurt that was steadily eating away at market share. The Swiss followed with an electronic system that was drawing rave reviews. London was experimenting with automated trading. Only Chicago stood in the way.

That had all begun to change in mid-February—the 16th to be precise, when Beman received word from a confidential source that the heads of trading of the ten largest Wall Street firms had secretly convened at the Plaza Hotel in New York. They agreed, reportedly with enthusiasm, to develop their own electronic-trading system. It would allow them to place their bids and offers on an electronic screen and bypass the Chicago commodity cartel altogether. Beman had always been full of bravado. But deep down he knew a fundamental truth: the real market would be wherever the Wall Street customers took their business. Wall Street had the ultimate whip-hand, not Beman's trading cowboys in Chicago.

Beman personally owned around $2,000,000 worth of memberships in the CCE, and he had a partnership interest in one of the most profitable trade-clearing firms. His entire persona was wrapped up in the Exchange, a place where working-class boys like himself could hit it big. As best he could tell, there was only one man who could avert the catastrophe.

"Our sources tell us," Beman continued, "that the proposed electronic exchange will be ready by summer. And," he leaned forward with a squint in his eye, "the Wall Street firms are going to require that their traders start putting some of their orders on it."

Beman paused, wondering if Stanislav grasped the enormity of what he had just explained. "Mr. Chairman," he lowered his voice. "We've been trading commodities on these floors in Chicago since the Civil War. But if that Wall Street system flies, our doors could be locked by the end of the year."

He waited silently like a patient with cancer beseeching a miracle cure from a doctor.

The object of his plea, Karol Stanislav, tilted his head and let out a small chuckle. But it was not the laugh of someone trying to make those-not-in-the-know uncomfortable. It was at *himself*. He was caught between two powerful forces.

The Chicago exchanges had always been his most loyal supporters. He liked them. In Washington, Congressmen periodically approached him with mouths agape at what they had witnessed on visits to the Chicago trading floors.

The idea of the Midwestern swashbucklers taking on the New York elitists appealed to his Polish sensibilities. Often over his second or third martini, he had fantasized about how much money he could have made himself as a trader: *Nobody would have gotten in my way.*

However, there was one big problem. As a politician, Stanislav had to look after himself. As much as the Chicago exchanges strained to accommodate him, he received a lot more money from the Wall Street firms. Chicago could not possibly match Wall Street's political clout. The unwritten rule amongst the managing directors of the New York investment banks was to contribute the maximum allowable by law to Stanislav's campaign coffers. Sure enough, Stanislav had delivered for Wall Street as well, helping them chip away at the Chinese wall dividing investment banking and commercial banking. An objective analysis said he should back the proposed electronic-trading system, which would come under his subcommittee's jurisdiction.

Rarely was this most gifted of politicians playing the role of Hamlet. But now he faced the most agonizing of dilemma.

"You've always had the solutions that allowed us to prosper and grow," Beman continued. "We're wondering what can be done to cut this whole thing off at the knees."

Stanislav continued looking at the area around Beman's head. Another smile came across his face. However, this time it looked like a smirk. He knew exactly what to do. Recently, Stanislav had arranged for the subcommittee overseeing the commodities exchanges to be placed under the Appropriations Committee's jurisdiction. He occasionally referred to Lonnie Herbert, the acting chairman in his frequent absences, as *Dropshot*. With one hand tied behind his back, he could trump Herbert and crater the proposed system. But did he want to?

"How do you think such a system would work?"

"It can't work," Beman shot back. "You can't trade on computers. That's why we have locals trading for their own accounts here in our pits, to make markets for customers."

"Then why are you so worried about it?" Stanislav asked.

The bluntness of the question threw Beman off. His face rushed with blood, the look he used to get after selling a used car, only to have the customer return the next day to complain the car had already conked out. In reality, Beman didn't know much about electronic trading other than that it represented a mortal threat. At the recent CCE board meeting called to discuss the Wall Street electronic system, his old friend Larry Walsh had joked, "Kinda' reminds ya of the story about the two Indians standing on the beach in 1492, when up walks Christopher Columbus. One Indian looks at the other and says, 'Oh shit, there goes the neighborhood.'"

Beman splayed his hands awkwardly. "You see, Mr. Chairman, if there is an imbalance of either buy or sell orders on an electronic system, the whole thing will fall apart."

Stanislav stared back with a quizzical look. "Does that not ever happen in the pits?"

"Yes, sure," Beman replied with assurance. "But that's when the locals come in and Hoover up the balance."

"Oh," Stanislav responded, but he didn't sound satisfied.

Beman had just done something that Stanislav refused to permit in his fiefdom back in Washington—make a point that was partially true, but more misleading than enlightening. Everyone knew that order imbalances in the various pits were often met with anarchic price movements.

Beman sensed Stanislav was trying to figure out what to do. He decided it was time to be direct. "Mr. Chairman, do you think you can help us survive this threat?"

"I'm going to have to learn more about the proposed system," Stanislav replied in a flat tone.

"What do you recommend we do in the meantime?"

"One good thing is to firm up your support on Capitol Hill through our political-action committees. It always helps when we've got plenty of money in there to horsewhip the Committee Members."

"We'll double down on everything," Beman offered. Now though, it was time to play his trump card. Beman nodded at Mike Kilpatrick, the supernumerary who had been quietly standing by. Being a product of Chicago's old Riley political machine, Kilpatrick shared the same political DNA as Karol Stanislav. During the years of cutting his political teeth, he had learned one thing: timing was everything.

"Mr. Chairman, could I walk you down to my office?" Kilpatrick asked Stanislav. "I have something important to discuss."

"Sure."

Beman and Stanislav shared perfunctory farewells, at which point Kilpatrick and Stanislav headed off to Kilpatrick's hideaway office. And that's when the evening's real business began.

Chapter Six

"MR. CHAIRMAN," KILPATRICK said after they sat alone in his smaller office, "we think it would be a good idea for you to open up a commodities trading account."

Kilpatrick knew that like most politicians, Stanislav didn't like to look surprised. But his eyebrows knotted, indicating he was taken back by the suggestion.

"What makes you think that?"

"Because you'd do well."

"I'm too old to go down there and fight like a gladiator," Stanislav said. And too dignified, he might have added.

"No. Nothing like that ... you wouldn't have to leave your job in Congress. It wouldn't take any of your time once the account is set up."

Stanislav had witnessed every conceivable form of flattery by lobbyists, members of Congress, even presidents of the United States seeking to enlist his clout. But this seemed to be of a different flavor. He listened enthralled.

"I have access to a huge broker in St. Louis," Kilpatrick continued. "You invest in his fund, and he makes the trades for you."

"You mean like Bill Clinton's wife—uh, Hillary?"

"Yes." Kilpatrick looked him in the eye.

Arkansas Governor Bill Clinton was taking some heat in this year's Democratic Presidential Primaries over the so-called *Cattlegate* affair. According to *The Wall Street Journal* and other newspapers, soon after Clinton had been elected governor, a representative of the chicken industry had encouraged his wife to put down $1,000—a fraction of the amount required by regulations—in a trading account. Within a few weeks, she had reaped a $100,000 gain in cattle futures. Her broker in the transactions, a RefCo employee named Bo Dale, had since been fined the second-largest amount in CFTC history for a fraud known as *trade allocation*. The suspicion was that the winning trades were being allocated to the preferred customers, while less prominent investors were given the losing trades.

Stanislav looked interested. "How does one set up such an account?"

"I'll have the broker—Richard Sherry is his name—contact you."

"What kind of money would I need to put up?"

Kilpatrick couldn't help noting how Stanislav had lost his magisterial air and sounded as innocent as any other potential customer. But Kilpatrick gave him a different answer than most received. "Oh, something nominal, let's say five or ten-thousand dollars."

Stanislav stirred in his seat, a gesture out of character for one so comfortable in his skin. Suddenly he looked skeptical ... then stern. "Mike, you damn well know the *candy-boys* are looking to knock me down from my perch." Kilpatrick was familiar with that pejorative term Stanislav used to describe reformers, citizen-action groups, and the like.

Kilpatrick responded in a voice that sounded more like a plea. "Mr. Chairman, setting up a trading account is perfectly legal."

Stanislav was not finished. "Just remember, Mike. If my ship sinks, so does yours."

Kilpatrick nodded, but he didn't feel foolish. After all, Stanislav had recently begun making acerbic remarks to Beman and him about traders. Namely, that a bunch of kids who didn't look much beyond punk stage were sometimes having single days in which they made more than he did in a year. Kilpatrick and Beman had been delighted when they heard Stanislav's youngest daughter was marrying a CCE trader. That hadn't stopped his occasional references to *those damn traders making all that money.*

"Mike," Stanislav answered, his skepticism ebbing, "it does sound interesting. But how in the world am I supposed to know what trades to make? I've always heard the investors in those funds get murdered."

"That's what this broker does. He handles all that."

"You're telling me it's that easy."

"Trust me," Kilpatrick said, "I have it from reliable sources that this broker Sherry is a homerun hitter. You won't be disappointed."

"It sure as hell worked for Hillary Clinton," Stanislav acknowledged with a laugh.

"You can be confident you will do better than the Arkansas first lady," Kilpatrick said, peering into the veteran congressman's eyes.

Stanislav caught Kilpatrick's stare and swallowed hard. "You know, maybe it would be worth giving trading a try." He added, "And we'll have to take a closer look at that electronic-trading system they're ginning up in New York."

Chapter Seven

CHRIS WALKED THROUGH the studio door of *Seifu Martial Arts* and placed his right hand over his left to cover his knuckles. The gesture demonstrated he was a friendly fighter.

The instructor, Master Tan, reciprocated. "Good evening, Chris," he said in a formal manner.

"Hello, Master."

Chris had been introduced to this martial art—*wing chun*—by one of his former clerks, who became tired of watching his boss getting shoved around in the Treasury Pit. For the last two years, Chris had faithfully attended class twice a week.

He removed his jacket and began the pre-class warmup regimen. While practicing double-punches, he felt a tap on the shoulder. Turning, Chris looked down at the smiling visage of Batesy, who made a show of covering his left knuckles.

"Christopherrrr, how are we?" He couldn't resist adding with a knowing look, "Keeping it stiff, are we?"

Chris groped for an answer. "Haven't checked in a few hours."

Batesy nodded with appreciation. "Love it!"

Chris had been taken aback the first time he entered the studio; seemingly half the people there were traders. He normally would've enjoyed some towel-snapping banter with Batesy, but at his side stood a mum David Littler. Chris had not seen Littler since his humiliation at the hands of Ray Malley in the Treasury Pit a couple weeks back. Littler had since been AWOL, which had tongues wagging.

"Hey, David, how are you?"

Littler's eyes dropped for a couple seconds before covering his left knuckles. "Hey, Chris."

Chris remembered his first few lessons when the Master kept repeating that wing-chun was designed to teach a weaker person to defeat a stronger person. He wondered if that explained Littler's presence.

When Batesy and Littler headed off, Chris began warm-ups. After a half-hour, the Master called him over to *the vortex*.

"Chris, we will practice circle-stepping today."

Reluctantly, Chris voiced his concern. "Master, combat on the trading floor is close quarters. There is no room for circle-stepping."

The Master looked at him intently. "Okay, we will work on close-range strikes." He proceeded to lead Chris through a series of chops and thrusts. Chris felt adequate, but not powerful.

"Chris," he said in a low voice, "you must deal with people on your own terms."

"Yes, Master. But I have a very powerful man that stands right behind me; he manhandles me through sheer body mass."

The Master's eyes lit up at that remark. "Can you please describe his exact build and style?"

Chris did his best, offering visual cues of Ray Malley's signature grinding motion with his elbows.

"Has anybody ever struck him in the center?"

Chris hesitated. "I don't believe so."

The Master continued asking probing questions in a way he had never done before. Chris found it odd, because the Master had made it clear from the first lesson that he did not do mercenary work. Apparently, he was bombarded with such requests. However, Chris began to wonder if the Master wasn't making an exception in the case of Malley, as revenge for humiliating one of his students.

What a damn business, he couldn't help thinking. Instead of studying the markets to improve their incomes, everyone's trying to get ahead by taking kung-fu lessons.

When the ninety-minute lesson was over, Chris was drenched with sweat and headed to the locker room to wash his face. Heading out the door, Master Tan gave his standard salutation. "Remember—all you have to do is breathe."

Chris bowed. The lanky southerner knew he lacked the pugnacious nature necessary to be a good fighter. Still, if nothing else it was better than a gym workout. Better yet, it got his mind off *her*.

He left Seifu Martial Arts and began skipping up Wells Avenue toward Lincoln Park in the cool night air. It felt bracing. Lately, Chris had begun to wonder how unhealthy it was working at the most crowded place in the city—if not the entire country—along with living in a high-rise apartment building and not leaving the city for months at a time.

When he got to North Avenue, he decided to continue a couple blocks to Arby's where he often wolfed down two roast-beef sandwiches after class. Just as he was about to enter, he heard a vaguely familiar voice call out, "Hey, Chris. Chris Parker!"

Turning, Chris looked across the street and exclaimed, "No way!"

"Yes way, dude," a man with a gliding athletic figure said as he strode in Chris' direction.

Chris had a WASPY aversion to hands-on displays of affection. But he immediately threw his left arm unabashedly around Skip Slider, a friend he hadn't seen in years. "Congratulations, dude. Honestly, man. I can't tell you how moving it was when your brother gave me the news."

"Thanks," Slider said with uncharacteristic meekness.

"Dude, forget the commodities business. You made it up Everest. Better yet, you made it down!"

"Making it down was far less important," Slider chortled.

"You obviously haven't changed," Chris said, nodding appreciatively.

"Are you still down at the Exchange?"

Chris shook his head. "Yep. It's an addiction." He knew he could be candid, given how poorly Slider himself had fared as a trader. "You back in town for good?"

"Yeah, looks like it," Slider said with a palpable sigh. Then looking embarrassed, he said, "I have a job interview tomorrow."

He didn't ask where, but Slider supplied the answer. *The Windy City Times.*"

"Hey," Chris said, trying to put a positive spin on it. "There's gotta be room for a maverick there."

"Hope so."

"Outdoors section?"

"Nope," he answered with a twitch. "The business section."

"Oh, okay," Chris said, not hiding his surprise. He found it disappointing, given Slider had been a success in the outdoors, but a failure in business.

"Let's get together sometime," Slider said. "You've got Fred's (brother's) number. I'll be there."

"Yep."

Chris started to walk away. Then he heard Slider again. "If I get the job, I'll be expecting you to give me the inside scoop about the trading floor."

"Sure thing," Chris said, before heading on into the foggy night. But after about ten steps he stopped and turned back. "Hey, that ain't such a bad idea."

"Any time, man," Slider said.

Chapter Eight

CONFIDENCE.

BARBRA LASKY had long since gotten her act down, as she strutted into the Chicago Commodities Exchange one early March morning. It was 7:00 a.m., yet here came the first *bro' pack* of the day.

"Hey, Barbra, where you headed?" one weenie mouthed over the head of several moving bodies. That proved to be a blunder, as the four guys in his group also spotted her and had the inside track. In monolithic fashion, they moved straight at her.

"Morning, Barbra," the closest to her said with a flush smile.

Noting him scanning her immaculately-shaped *derriere,* she shot back, "My eyes are up here."

His smile drained so fast he looked like Mike Tyson had just smacked him.

"I saw you in your new Porsche last week," a burly male in a denim jacket said, "and you didn't even offer me a ride."

"Why should I?" she shot back. "You never trade with me anyway."

"C'mon, it would take pom-poms to get your attention where you stand over in that corner."

"Oh, so I'm invisible, huh?"

The aspirant went mute.

"Look," the closest one said, wedging his way back in, "Elton John is coming to town next month."

"I've already got my tickets," the husky one on the outside interrupted.

"Sorry, no hay for the horses," Barbra said, dismissing all five weenies at once. Her well-honed brushback did the trick and they slinked away. Besides, they were all locals trading for themselves, just like her. That made them the enemy.

"Hey, Barbra," a soft-spoken man called from behind. She didn't hear him, so he reached over and tapped her shoulder. Barbra turned to be greeted by a smiling, early middle-aged man, who happened to be the RefCo broker that stood directly behind her in the Pit. "How was the concert Saturday night?"

"Cracking," she answered, looking fresh and alert. "I can't wait to see Seinfeld this weekend."

"Have you already got tickets?" he asked.

"Yes. Good thing, too. Those 96-18s you sold me late yesterday destroyed me."

"Oh," the man smiled in recognition. He could have pointed out how all the other locals had wanted to buy from him at that price, but he had chosen to sell to her, only to see the market turn sharply lower. However, he let her comment stand uncontested.

"I mean, what's with this?" she gibed. "That's like three days in a row you've buried me."

"Aw, you'll get it back."

"I hope so," she said, feigning a forlorn tone. In reality, she had made money all three days. But never mind.

"Good luck today," the broker called out to her receding figure as she cut away. It sounded odd, given that Barbra's firm backside would be situated directly in front of him all day.

She headed to her personal locker and pulled off her fur coat, changing it out for a baby-blue trading jacket with her trading acronym *BAB*. A muscle-bound male in his early thirties approached from behind and swooped her up in his arms. "My favorite jacket!" he exclaimed, his eyes bright and face aglow.

"No, let me down," Barbra demanded, escaping from his bear hug.

He appeared surprised. "You know how to ruin a person's day, don't you," he spluttered, attempting to save face.

"Look who's talking. You don't even know I exist in the Pit."

"We'll have to do something about that."

"Yeah, right ... I'll be lucky to get a trade from you before New Year's."

"My customers trade so big, it's tough to break it up into small sizes."

Barbra rolled her eyes. "I've got to go check the charts," she said before walking off, leaving the big-swinging dick high and dry.

Just before entering the technical room to check out the daily-market trends, she spotted *him* in his navy-blue trading jacket at the end of the hallway. In fact, she caught him gazing dumbly at her—not hard to do considering he was the tallest guy on the floor, if not the whole world. But like a scared rabbit he accelerated away from her.

At least he's different, she thought.

***

AT 7:12 A.M. BARBRA burrowed her way into the biggest bro' pack of all, the teeming United States Treasury-Index Pit. She stood surrounded by at least five-hundred alpha males, whose feral capacities were balanced out by approximately four females. Barbra wedged into the spot where she had stood every day for six years, in the far northeastern corner of the huge Pit.

Like every local, she had spent her first years in the Pit inveigling to secure a spot as close as possible to the brokers filling customer orders. That was where the cream lay. However, this area was known as *Coffin Corner* due to the high-casualty rate of the traders who stood there. Since it was the least physical part of the Pit, Barbra had chosen by default to place herself here.

Her stomach sank. Jay Rickey, who usually stood to Barbra's immediate left, was there. He was the last remaining pocket of resistance for Barbra in this isolated section of the Pit. The obsequiousness she was accustomed to being showered with was replaced by brusque interactions. Rickey had sensed from the beginning that it was all about intimidation. He always appeared like he was getting ready to rip another trader's eyeballs out. *Sturm* and *drang*. Other than when making an actual trade with Barbra, he had not spoken a civilized word to her in years, despite standing elbow-to-elbow. Actually, it was more like elbow-to-head—him standing 6'4" to her 5'1" on tiptoes.

Knowing she couldn't let this hostile competitor dent her confident pose, Barbra flicked her long brown hair back, while maintaining the erect posture of a stage actress. She went to her default position, chatting up the brokers behind her.

"Hey, Jerry, when are you going to get over your vendetta against me?" she jabbed at the broker behind her.

His eyes widened in what appeared to be legitimate befuddlement. "Vendetta?"

"I screamed *sold* at you three times on those 96-18's yesterday afternoon. But you bought 'em from somebody way over there." Barbra kept her tone conversational, but it had the right punch.

"I don't know," Jerry responded in tepid defense.

Jay Rickey rolled his eyes.

***

7:15 A.M.: OPENING BELL RINGS.

"96-23 for 500," cried out the Goldman Sachs broker.

"96-23 for 10," Barbra shouted, joining in.

"Hey Barbra, sell you ten at 96-23." Jerry Freed called down to her.

"Buy ten," Barbra nodded. "96-23 trade," she hollered up to the Pit reporter. Barbra had her first *edge* of the day.

"Fucking asshole!" Jay Rickey uttered his first expletive of the day. "I was bidding 96-23 before her," he fired at Freed.

Sure enough, the Goldman Sachs broker soon began paying 96-24.

Barbara needed to sell out the ten contracts she was long. "Sell ten at 96-25," she cried out.

Her timing was propitious. The RefCo broker Danny Blake came in to buy fifty contracts.

"Sell 'em at 96-25," the locals around him all screamed.

"I'll buy twenty Allen, twenty Jerry, and yeah, Barbie, you, ten."

"Sell you ten," Barbra shouted back to Blake, before calling up to the Pit reporter, "96-25 trade."

"You make it look easy," Blake exulted to Barbra.

The day was two minutes old and Barbra was up twenty ticks—$625. She decided to wait out the next thirteen minutes until the U.S. Labor Department released its closely-watched monthly unemployment report.

Chapter Nine

News Flash:
7:30 a.m. CST
U.S. economy added 412,000 jobs in September

THE MARKET CONSENSUS had been for the U.S. economy to only add 135,000 jobs. The stronger-than-expected economic report came across as bad news, stoking fears of inflation.

"Sold, sold, sold!" Barbra screamed and waved her hands in a swatting motion, indicating she wanted to sell. It was useless. Brokers, locals, everyone raced each other; no one was buying. The market plunged two full points—over two percent.

I'll try to buy the bottom. Barbra knew the brokers would sell at any price they could. She stood poised to uncoil at the right moment.

Finally, the Merrill Lynch broker on the far side raised both hands high, "94-26 bid for 500."

Now! Barbra leapt like a kangaroo. "94-27 bid for 10," she shouted in mid-air, making a pulling motion with both arms indicating she was a buyer.

Jay Rickey bid 94-27 a split-second later.

Jerry Freed of RefCo had been frantically trying to sell 100 contracts all the way down. Everyone in Coffin Corner began braying at him, thinking Freed was offering up a red-light special. "Sell you fifty, Jay, ten, Barbra," Freed said, before doling out the balance to nearby traders. For once, both Rickey and Barbra were satisfied. It made Barbra long ten contracts; Jay Rickey was long fifty. Better yet, the market began to jump.

"94-28 bid," shouted the Merrill Lynch broker. Nobody would sell to him. "94-29 bid, 94-30 bid, 94-31 bid."

Barbra had a chance to ring the cash register right here for a forty-tick profit in twenty seconds, which was $1,250. But the ambitious female chose to hold her hands close to her chest, waiting for a higher price to sell out.

However, the Goldman Sachs broker came crashing into the market, "Sell 500 at 94-31." The whole Pit turned from buyers to sellers on a dime. Barbra lunged to her left. "Sell ten at 94-31," she screamed. "Sold, sold, sold." No luck.

"Sell 500 at 94-30," the Goldman broker shouted.

"Sell 10 at 94-30," Barbra screamed.

"Sell 50 at 94-30." Jay Rickey joined in.

Tough luck. No buyers.

"Sell 500 at 94-29," Goldman continued offering... still no buyers.

"Custer, Custer, watch out Custer," squealed a gleeful Mitchell Kay, the resident Pit clown. Like most such harlequins, he rarely traded much himself. He was enjoying the spectacle of his nearby colleagues helplessly trying to sell out their long positions. "Last stand, Custer," he kept screaming. "More Injuns coming over that hill." He was right. More sell orders came crashing into the Pit.

"Sold, sold, sold," Barbra shouted valiantly at anyone who had their palms inward, indicating they were buying. But the few buyers were on the far side of the Pit, with hundreds of bodies between her and them. Nobody looked over at Coffin Corner.

"Sell 'em at 94-27, sell 'em at 94-26, sell 'em at 94-25, 94-24, 94-23..."

I'm screwed.

Barbra had spent her entire career trying to avoid getting caught on the wrong side in a one-way market. Now, she faced the possibility of losing $10,000, if not $20,000, in the next minute, which would be her worst loss ever on one trade.

"Sell 10 at 94-22," she shouted while at the top of her vertical leap. Suddenly, she spotted a hand lifted above the crowd on the far corner of the Pit. It was him, SKY. He had one finger pointed in toward his forehead, signaling to buy ten contracts. *Both* she and Jay Rickey signaled to sell 10 contracts to SKY.

"Me?" Barbra screamed, pointing at her head.

"No, that was me." Rickey said while looking straight ahead.

"He looked at me!" Barbra contested Rickey.

"SKY, SKY," she shouted, which was a sure sign of an emergency. Both had been secretive about their trading with each other. But she couldn't get his attention as the pack of traders to his rear had him colliding into a Pit-dividing rail. *Why doesn't he push them back?*

Jay Rickey continued frantically trying to sell out his remaining long position. "Sell 'em at 94-20, sell 'em at 94-19, sell 'em at 94-18....", he screamed. But he couldn't find any buyers and the market continued to careen down.

If I didn't get that trade from SKY.... Barbra held her hands as high as her five-foot physique would allow. "SKY, SKY, Hey SKY," she screamed.

Finally, SKY was able to shove himself off the rail and look her way. "Checking, I sold you ten," she shouted, with her hands raised in an arc to indicate a higher level. "Ten at 94-22."

He appeared to be straining to raise his hands in acknowledgment, but was unable to lift them. Instead, he nodded.

Barbra felt relieved. She had lost $1,537.50 on the trade. Meanwhile, several others in Coffin Corner had losses running into five-figures and were still bleeding.

"Sell 40 at 94-15, sell 40 at 94-14, 94-13, 94-12...." Jay Rickey raged, desperately trying to sell out.

Barbra stood in rapt attention, watching her Pit neighbor bleed his position. *Wow, he's down $30,000 just like that.*

Like any other trader, she delighted in seeing one of her colleagues get crushed. But there was something about Rickey that said *caveat.* His bellows held a certain angst to them.

Finally, J.P. Morgan came in to buy way down at 93-26; the market hit a floor.

"Sell you forty," Jay Rickey shouted at the Morgan broker in capitulation.

Why did he only sell forty? Barbra knew he had bought fifty contracts earlier. She suspected the worst and peered out the corner of her eye to see Rickey's trading card.

Rickey pounded his fist on his trading card before writing down:

Sell:10
Price: 94-22
Buyer: SKY

No. Barbra tensed up when she saw Rickey had recorded the same trade with SKY as she had made, knowing there was going to be hell to pay.

"Hey, hey, tall guy, you," Rickey hollered at SKY. "Check your trades, how 'bout it. I sold you ten...." he looked at his card to remember the price, "sold you ten up at 94-22."

SKY was being jostled in all directions. But when he saw Rickey trying to check a trade with him, Barbra thought he looked like he had been struck by a bolt of lightning.

"No," he screamed in horror, his long frame appearing to vibrate.

"What?" Rickey shouted at SKY. "What are you telling me? You signaled buying ten from me."

SKY proceeded to make a pronounced checking symbol to Barbra. "Checking Barbra, I bought 10 at 94-22."

Rickey looked down at Barbra to his immediate left as if she were some kind of urine specimen, before focusing his gnarled face on SKY. "What the fuck are you talking about? You were looking straight at me."

"No. I was looking at her," SKY protested. "She offered to sell first."

"She offered to sell first," Rickey screamed back in a mocking fashion. "Don't go trying that shit on me." There were hundreds of bodies between them, but Rickey's voice carried over them.

"She offered to sell at 94-22," SKY yelled back. He began imitating Barbra's hand signal to sell at that price. "I bought 'em from her."

"Yeah right, and fuck you too. You signaled buying ten from me. We're splitting the error."

"I'm not splitting a damn thing," SKY shouted, surprising Barbra with his vehemence. "I made the trade with her. You should have checked it before now."

"Hey, listen up, too-tall little-boy," Rickey shouted back. "I'll take it to arbitration if you try to welsh out of the trade. Arbitration! You hear that?"

Barbra knew that so far both SKY and Rickey were following a standard template for out-trade arguments, one asserting they had looked straight at each other and done the trade, and the other categorically denying it.

Next, Rickey decided to go deeper. To everyone in his immediate vicinity he began yelling, "That SKY asshole over there is trying to do all his trades with this little girl here and screwing the rest of us."

Barbra took pride in the number of catfights she had had in the Treasury Pit. Now, though, she looked uncharacteristically timid and took to shuffling her trading cards.

"Arbitration," Rickey continued shouting, "Arbitration. You hear me, SKY? We're going to arbitration over this." He stopped for a moment, allowing a nasty smile to break out on his face. "Is there something we don't know about," he called out. "What is this all about? Huh?"

"I traded with her, and we checked it right away," SKY tried reasoning. But explaining was losing.

Barbra's innate instincts told her to lie low. However, a worrying thought crossed her mind. *Have I made my last trade with SKY?*

Chapter Ten

HUMANS COPE WITH crises in various ways.

Chris barreled through the revolving door leading out of the CCE. He had been waiting all day to escape the stench of thousands of tightly-packed human bodies and hit the fresh air. Without hesitation, he crossed over Madison and onto LaSalle Street, barely looking in either direction.

For years, he had waited out in front of the Exchange to catch the city bus home, until he finally realized he could out-walk the bus through the immediate downtown area. Recently, he had found the walk to be such a tonic, that he had begun covering all four miles to his Lincoln Park neighborhood on foot. Rain, shine, sleet, or snow, walking home was now his favorite part of the day.

Perhaps most important, it gave him time to clear his mind and think.

Chicago, what a vast topic. Norman Mailer had once described Chicago as the last of the great cities. Indeed, there was a certain x-factor about this Midwestern metropolis that had long entranced mortals. Chris was no different.

One glance at the downtown area revealed a city that had never given up its romance with *big*. Chicago had been the birthplace of the skyscraper. Gleaming steel and glass towers now lined both sides of LaSalle Street, leaving those passing through mildly claustrophobic. Just one block over from where Chris was now loping stood the tallest building in the world, eternally swaying in the wind howling off Lake Michigan.

The entire downtown area had been incinerated in 1871 by the Great Chicago Fire, which the city famously blamed on a cow. Nonetheless, by 1893, Chicago was ready to host the World's Fair. The city threw everything at its disposal to showcase *Paris on the Prairie*. A man named George Ferris designed a giant spinning wheel to give visitors hysterical delight sailing through the air in its attached cars. Word of Ferris's magnificent delight spread like wildfire throughout the land. By the end of that summer, over twenty-seven million people had come from all over the country to the fair, marking it as one of the seminal events in American history. Only New York stood in Chicago's way.

However, despite the gale-force winds at its back, something dogged the city. From its inception, Chicago had fought a reputation for being dirty, dark, and dangerous. Just a few miles southwest of the downtown area had stood the infamous Stockyards. At the height of the industry, fourteen-million animals per year were slaughtered in their yards, immortalized in Upton Sinclair's 1906 novel, *The Jungle*: "Tens of thousands of frantic beasts, cattle, sheep, pigs, and animals in an orgy of gorging and dropping, and wailing, and smelling blood."

Rudyard Kipling, who had taken a tour of the stockyards, remarked of Chicago: "Having seen it once, I desire to never see it again. It is inhabited by savages." Such sentiments had left Chicagoans with a subtle uneasiness that the city, in its rush towards wealth and commercial success, had failed to cultivate some of the finer human traits. The yards were finally shut down in 1971, but remained embedded in the city's subconscious. Had the city's largest employer for more than a hundred years left behind a character defect? Chris caught himself wondering this on occasion.

Now dressed in his familiar brown storm-trooper's jacket, Chris strode up LaSalle Street, the main artery connecting downtown Chicago with the near north side. On this late-winter afternoon, the sky was a heavy pewter with a cutting-edge wind coming off the lake. The sidewalks had a chalky residue from the salt dumped after the latest snowstorm. Seemingly half the people at work had shown up with hacking coughs—many Chris suspected, hoping to get others sick.

It would be a cliché to say the weather matched Chris's morale. But the weather was merely a lead-gray, while his mood was black from outside to inside.

He considered himself fortunate it was a four-mile sojourn. It usually required the first three just to emerge from the vise-like grip that *she* held him in. The deliverance was always followed by a certain solemn clarity, *My God, what hath I wrought?* The juxtaposition seemed all the starker when compared with the trip downtown. Each morning, he caught the bus at 6:30, always sitting in the very- back with his eyes closed, practicing deep breathing. His single-minded focus was directed on finding the will to STOP. He couldn't rid his mind of a haunting line he had recently read in Shakespeare's *Macbeth*: *Stars hide your fires. Let not light see my black and deep desires.*

The opening bell was at 7:15. Habitually, by 7:30 she had already shattered his willpower. *No, no, that's wrong, Chris. She hasn't done it. You are doing destroying yourself.*

Chris thought back seven years to when he had left behind a promising track as a bank-trainee in Montgomery, Alabama. He headed off to the Chicago commodities business immune to any voice of reason. "Is this what you want to do, Chris?" his father had asked in disbelief.

He felt great sympathy towards his father that night. How many people make the overwhelming sacrifices of parenthood with hopes of their kid ending up on a trading floor, yelling and screaming like a chicken with its head cut off? Then there was the final straw with his girlfriend back in Montgomery, when he showed her a picture of the smocks traders wear. "Those look like what people wear at bowling alleys," she had snorted with her nose curled in disgust. Not long after, she married Chris's boss from the bank.

None of those objections had blunted his blazing juggernaut north at age twenty-four towards that great temple of finance: the Chicago Commodities Exchange. The saying was correct: *He whom a dream hath possessed, knoweth no more doubting.*

Now, seven years later, Chris was in the middle of the fray. Because of his unusual height, he had been able to get preferred jobs as a clerk, followed by a quick promotion to leading broker for a Wall Street company. Better yet, he had justified their confidence by getting off to a lightning-quick start, drawing raves at his ability to make fast numerical calculations. All the smart money had tagged him for stardom status. Yet now he was weighed down with enough grievances to make a Third World Revolutionary blush.

Chris crossed the bridge over the gray waters of the Chicago River, less than a half-mile from where it flowed out to Lake Michigan. He was out of the immediate downtown area and felt lighter for it. *Are humans meant to live so close together?*

His daily life on the trading floor was all about disaster prevention and self-preservation. So far, he had pulled it off. Still, there was a certain sub-rosa feeling, just a matter of time. This morning, the whole Manichean drama had entered a new and more dangerous phase. The hounds were baying in the distance.

If any clarity was going to seep into him, it would be out here on foot. As he neared the end of his long trek up LaSalle Street, the outlines of the most unlikely solution began to materialize out of fresh air and enter his fragile psyche: Master the daily grind of intimidation, corruption, and implacability that were the daily fare of a trading floor? Forget it.

No, his plan would transcend all that. It would play to his strength—the penchant for the big play, the bold move. He desperately needed to go on offense.

To be sure, his trading career may get sacrificed in the process. Six months back, Chris would have considered that catastrophic. No longer. One way or another, his bizarre Dantean dance was nearing an end.

PART II

Chapter Eleven

THE LONG HAND of fate had played a critical role in Chris Parker's current plight. It went back more than six years to a meeting held on a bitter-cold January afternoon in Chicago.

Jack Fitzgerald, Elliott House's CCE floor manager had been depressed all day. But when he looked outside the long windows at the south end of the trading floor, his spirits surged. It was a Chicago-style whiteout. The snowstorm gave him hope the managers meeting would be cancelled.

In colloquial terms, Fitzgerald didn't give a shit. Actually, he did care—about his own personal trading. Preston Beatty had been impressed with his Wall Street background and allowed him to trade his own account. Other Elliott House floor staff periodically griped about the favoritism, noting that Fitzgerald's personal trading occupied 80% of his work hours. Worse yet, it consumed at least 50% of his healthy salary.

Lately, however, Beatty had shown signs of becoming less enamored with his Wall Street refugee. "You haven't signed a new customer in over a year," Beatty complained at their last meeting.

"I'm in touch with several people I used to know in New York," Fitzgerald claimed.

"Didn't you tell me that at the last meeting?"

Fitzgerald had left that meeting moping and proceeded to make a $90,000 error the next day by double-entering a customer order. He could feel his star waning at Elliott House and dreaded the annual managers meeting. Alas, at

1:59 the phone rang. Preston Beatty's secretary told him to be at headquarters in twenty minutes.

Grabbing his briefcase, he went downstairs to get his heavy Swiss-hunting jacket, and headed out into the winter storm. Fitzgerald decided to cut up LaSalle Street, giving him some cover from the westerly current. But when he turned onto Monroe Drive, icy-cold channels of wind clobbered him. He reached for his black face mask to cover everything but his eyes, and continued boring head-first into the storm.

As he continued up Monroe he periodically jerked up his head and squinted to get his bearings. Fitzgerald knew he needed to turn left when he got to the Chicago Mercantile Exchange. Like many of the Irishmen who dominated the CCE, Fitzgerald had always been reluctant to treat the *Merc Jerks* as equals. His mind went to the last meeting of Elliott House floor personnel, where he sat behind the tallest guy he had ever seen. That would have been no big deal except he had to listen to Johnny Carlucci, the floor manager at the Mercantile Exchange, preening about his new prize recruit. Just the thought of hearing Carlucci's voice again this afternoon made him nauseous.

Wait! Hold on, Fitzgerald emerged from his misery and realized he was standing in a snowdrift in the middle of Wacker Drive. He needed to take a left here. But now Fitzgerald had the *mojo,* because he also had a grand new idea.

***

"EVERYONE CALLED THEIR architects in Florida and told 'em to go with the hurry-up plan?" Beatty joked to open the meeting.

"Architect, forget it," Johnny Carlucci piped in. "I want an agent to find me a home by this weekend."

Their humor wasn't far off-base. Seemingly, every successful trader had a second home in Florida. The whole topic made Jack Fitzgerald sick. He was further away from his dream of a Florida-golfing home than ever, due to his daytime habit. Today he had lost another $2,300 of his own money. If he didn't quit, or get better but that never seemed to happen—he was looking at having to jerk his two children out of private school in Evanston and subject them to the tender mercies of the Chicago public school system.

Fitzgerald felt like the odd man out. It was time to spring a surprise. "Preston," he said in a low voice. "Johnny." He looked down to indicate seriousness. "I've been thinking a lot about our marketing strategy. As you know, I've always emphasized my technical analysis skills to potential customers." He shrugged. "That's my background, going back to Wall Street days. However, lately I have been bowled over by how critical execution in the Pit has become to clients."

Beatty gave a motion of assent while Carlucci added an emphatic double nod.

"The Treasury Pit is a war," Fitzgerald continued, feeling a gathering momentum. "It's the single highest-stakes financial conflict in the world. Every trader on Wall Street knows it. When they come visit us on the floor, they always ask: *How does anyone know what's going on?* Which brings me to a proposal I've been carefully considering for some time now."

So far ... so good. Beatty and Carlucci seemed genuinely curious about what he had in mind. Still, Fitzgerald knew he had to deliver on the money.

"Johnny," he lowered his long frame and put his elbows on the table to look Carlucci in the eyes, "at that meeting in November, you piqued my interest. You said how helpful it was having a big man in the Pit watching our phone brokers." Stopping for effect, he started in for the kill. "Chris is the guy's name, right?"

Carlucci gave an uncharacteristically terse answer. "Yes, Chris."

"Chris Parker," Beatty added.

"I've come to the conclusion," Fitzgerald said, swooping his head down and back up, "he is the missing piece we need. If you send him to the CCE," he looked at Beatty, "I can market that to customers. We can sell execution. Customers will take one look at him and say, Yeah, I want that guy doing my business in that gigantic Treasury Pit."

Carlucci sat with his mouth half-agape, while Beatty tilted his head back in executive thought.

"How about lending him to us for a month?" Fitzgerald said eagerly. "If he's as good as you said at that meeting, we'd probably want to promote him to broker soon. Again, we can market this."

Carlucci jumped in. "Hey, he's our point man ... watching all the different phone clerks in both the deutschemarks and Swiss francs. Preston and I've already discussed making him a broker there." Turning to Beatty, he said, "It does no good robbing Peter to pay Paul."

"Who do you think we would replace him with?" Beatty asked.

Carlucci's bowling-ball-shaped head turned a flush color. "I don't know."

"Johnny," Fitzgerald said, clasping his hands together. "I applaud you for your hire. But," he turned to Beatty with his head tilted, "in my heart of hearts, I think his maximum value to Elliott House is in the Treasury Pit. He'd have a huge advantage in that vast Pit. I can't wait to begin touting him to customers."

Fitzgerald was surprising even himself.

Beatty relaxed his initial neutrality and seemed to have swooned. Raising his eyebrows at Carlucci he said, "Damn,

Johnny. It's gonna be hard to pass this up. After all, we are a team. We'll find someone else for you over there."

"How will I ever find anyone like that?"

Chapter Twelve

"HERE," CHRIS SAID, lofting a $5,000 check over the table to Frankie Hope.

Hope grunted.

Even though the check represented over half of Chris's net worth, it didn't bother him that Hope did not thank him ... he never did. Still, he always repaid Chris, usually offering to pay back double whatever he had borrowed. The last time he did it, Chris had briefly considered taking the extra five-thousand, knowing Hope might be borrowing again within a couple months.

There was one thing that did grate on Chris. "How 'bout Brian and John? Or those two spongers, Jake and Lennie? Anything from them?"

Again, Frankie mumbled. Chris knew what that meant. All the weasels who borrowed money from Frankie when he was flush knew that beneath the hard-shell exterior was the biggest soft touch around, who would never ask anyone to pay him back. One scoundrel after another came to Frankie hat in hand, only to never be able to look him in the eye again. Despite looking tough, Hope was shy to the point of disabling. Besides, Frankie was that rare trader who *knew* he could make money when his back was up against the wall.

The minute Chris had met him upon his arrival in Chicago a couple years back, he noticed Frankie was different. He possessed the intense eyes of a Las Vegas card-counter and had an uncanny ability to step foot in a commodity trading pit and read everyone's mind—their hopes, their fears, what positions they were carrying. Like so many little guys, the 5'6" Frankie Hope's mind was whippet fast. He always seemed to be a step or two ahead of everyone else.

Perhaps best of all, Chris had never been jealous of Frankie Hope in the least. He considered their close friendship an opportunity to witness rare talent at close range.

"I've got some news," Chris said.

No response. Frankie was playing hard-to-get, despite being a borrower.

"They're transferring me to the CCE." He hesitated, before adding, "They say they're gonna make me a broker by the end of the year."

"Broker," Frankie muttered in acknowledgment.

"Is it really as crowded as they say in that huge Treasury Pit?" Chris asked sincerely. "Or, is that just another thing everybody exaggerates?"

Bad question. They were hovered over a chessboard in Frankie's sixteenth-floor apartment. Chris had seen Frankie looking disheveled like that on many occasions. It usually meant one thing—he had been sitting right there since that morning. The stark fact was that Frankie Hope hated the Treasury-Index Pit.

Barely weighing 125 pounds soaking wet, Frankie was useless in shoving matches. He got jostled, hacked, and clubbed mercilessly in the Pit, and couldn't get over the people doing it. "Those people never trade," he repeated time after time in disbelief. "They just stand there, making all this noise and throwing their lard all over the place."

Every time his account jumped—which was any time he spent two weeks straight in the Pit—he would lapse into staying at home. That's where the trouble started. He traded as much as ever from his high-rise apartment on

Michigan Avenue with its brilliant vista of Lake Michigan. But rather than his purposeful maneuvering in the Treasury Pit, he phoned in wildly speculative trades in the likes of the cotton, soybeans, gold, silver, cotton, and Japanese yen markets. Those orgies of speculation always ended the same—with him gambling away his entire account and being forced back into the Treasury Pit.

Frankie had the burning eyes and razor-sharp instincts of the outcast. Those who watched him closely never ceased to be amazed at the college-dropout's ability to read the market's direction. He had a virtual license to print money. Yet he still despised it in there. Now, after another disastrous run in the cotton market, he was going to have to return to the Pit. That explained his sullen mood tonight.

Frankie pulled his head up from the chessboard and looked at Chris. "Why do you want to be a broker?" His question was sincere.

"I'm a Calvinist," Chris responded.

Frankie looked at Chris as if he was some kind of alien.

"I was raised that you get up in the morning and head off to do a day's work," Chris explained.

That didn't draw a response either.

"Heck," Chris continued, "a lot of brokers make big money, especially in the Treasury Pit."

"Yeah," Frankie acknowledged, as if halfway in comprehension.

"With a big company like Elliott House behind me, they've got to give me a decent spot to stand, right?"

Frankie's eyes narrowed.

"If you're filling customer orders, you gotta stand on the top step," Chris continued to argue.

Frankie shook his head, still looking wary. He and Chris discussed every trading topic under the sun. However, that had begun to change since Frankie became a local in the Treasury Pit. A couple months ago, Chris had spent several days trying to contact him with no luck. He finally became so concerned he took the bus to Frankie's apartment. After knocking on the door for a few minutes, Frankie opened it wearing sunglasses.

"Going to work for Capone," Chris joked. But then he saw the welt under Frankie's right eye which the shades only partly covered. Sensing the topic was off-limits, they had never discussed it.

"It doesn't look good on that top step," Frankie finally said. He added, "You're not gonna believe some of the idiots camped out up there."

Despite being opposites in basic ways, they trusted and cared for each other. Still, Frankie couldn't fathom why anyone would want to be a broker. He had inherited his father's attitude that you should never work for another person, no matter what deprivation it entailed. You always shot for the brass ring. Chris's stated goal of making a million dollars a year as a broker simply didn't register with Frankie.

"Just promise me this." Frankie finally looked up from the chess board. "If they do put you in the Treasury Pit, that you become the biggest broker in the whole business."

This time it was Chris who did not respond.

Chapter Thirteen

"TRAINED APE ALERT!" Chris heard a voice call from somewhere on the top step of the Treasury Pit.

"Monster from the Deep!" a second voice followed.

"No, Dude," a third wannabe comedian argued. "That's Big Foot Itself We're Looking At!"

Chris continued walking until he heard someone scream, "Tiiiimbbber!" The phony lumberjack call was followed by the sound of a tree crashing. The anonymous voice-over artist ended his ditty with a horse laugh, indicating great self-appreciation. Chris knew from long experience to keep moving. However, an unknown male parked himself in his path. "Dude, we're having a bet." The guy was wearing a smug look, and glanced back at a group of onlookers with a mischievous smile. "How tall are you?"

"Six-foot-ten and nineteen sixty-fourths," Chris answered in a monotone as he veered to the interrogator's side.

"Are you walking on stilts?"

"Nope. You're standing in a hole." The answer served as his getaway line and Chris continued around the arc of the Pit looking for anything familiar. He heard a voice from behind.

"Hey, Chris, where you headed?" Jack Fitzgerald joked.

"Home."

"Come on, follow me." He led Chris to a booth along the southern wall of the trading floor, ringed with phones and surrounded by almost a dozen people in Elliott House jackets.

Fitzgerald was a Princeton alum, as anyone who talked to him was destined to quickly find out. "Chris, a couple yokels from Yale here," he pointed out. "Andy and Henry."

"A pleasure," Andy responded, offering his hand to Chris.

"As well."

"Likewise," Henry said, repeating the gesture.

"And here," Fitzgerald continued, "is our resident Harvard scumbag, Blake Evans."

Chris smiled. "Hello, Blake."

"I take it you're another of Jack's elite Princeton corps?" Evans inquired.

"Try University of Alabama—The Harvard of the gridiron."

"I like it," Evans said with approval. "We're looking forward to having you up there."

"Bringing in a ringer," Fitzgerald added with an emphatic nod.

This Ivy League Mafia looked impressive at first glance, and far too polished to engage in personal interrogation. Chris couldn't help but note they stuck out like French virgins in the grubby atmosphere of a trading floor.

Fitzgerald ushered him to another phone broker for a toned-down introduction. "Chris, Mark McMann."

"Hey, Chris!" McMann showed a healthy smile. "What brings you here?"

"Unbridled greed," Chris deadpanned.

McMann laughed before a question hit him. "I've gotta ask. Did you play basketball?"

"You don't recognize me?" Chris feigned dismay.

"No." McMann looked enthused. "Who'd you play for?"

Chris filibustered. "Did you say basketball?"

"No, really," McMann persisted. "Which team?"

Chris noticed Fitzgerald giving McMann some negative body language, before moving away. But McMann was irrepressible. "Dude, you're gonna be dominant in there. You've got *can't miss* written all over you. This is gonna be unbelievable."

"I expect it to be challenging," Chris responded.

"Don't worry," McMann said, shaking his head as if in disbelief. "Lemme tell you, one way or another, you're gonna make a fortune."

Chris found the guy likable, but the subject matter uncomfortable. He had learned on the junior-golf circuit in Alabama the advantage of low expectations.

Next, Hank Downey introduced himself. With a pockmarked face, drinker's nose, and a jelly belly, the man had *holdover* written all over him. Downey confirmed Chris's suspicion. "Wish I'd had your height when I was in there."

"Oh, you traded?" Chris asked.

"Yeah." Downey did not provide any details, although Chris would later hear horror stories of Downey's error-prone tenure in the Pit for Elliott House. "They say every inch over six-feet is worth a quarter of a million dollars," Downey added.

Chris raised his eyebrows in recognition, although it sounded like the kind of story that was the product of an after-work drinking session. Downey looked as if he'd been in a few of those.

It seemed clear there was a cultural divide at the Elliott House desk between the elites and the Chicago natives. The natives craved an opportunity to get in the Pit and mix it up, while the Ivy Leaguers wouldn't get near it.

Fitzgerald led him to the far end of the desk. "Okay, Chris, why don't you hang with us back here for an hour to see how things are working, and who is who. Then when you're ready, we'll send you up to the Pit."

Chris nodded, his insides stirring. He gazed up at the top step of the Treasury Pit, where he would spend his next several years. Some formidable characters were lining up. Not one of them appeared to bear the slightest resemblance to him.

Where in the world am I gonna stand up there?

Chapter Fourteen

TWENTY-YEAR-OLD Tripp Cole normally showed off used cars at the BMW dealership in Wrigleyville. But one early spring afternoon, two salesmen were out with viruses and Tripp was put in charge of flashing the newest BMW models.

It was heady stuff for Cole who came from a working-class family in the hardpan just west of Wrigley Field. It was taken for granted that a person would work until old age or sickness, whichever came first. College was for *them*; the rich was *them*. Still, Cole felt content; if nothing else, he was better off than the White Sox fans on the South side.

Around 4:00 that afternoon, a fortyish male in a tight-fitting jacket turned up unannounced. The man approached Cole and asked, "Could you show me the latest models?"

"Sure." Tripp led him over to a cluster of shiny-new BMWs.

"Hey, Hank," the man called across the showroom to a customer he obviously knew. "You've already got enough cars."

"Ah, Drew," the other man responded with a good-natured laugh. "You've gotta see these new 316i's ... High Performance."

"Whatever you say," Drew gibed.

A few minutes later, Hank drove off with the latest BMW. Meanwhile, Tripp's customer took one look at a different model and cracked, "Hank doesn't know shit about cars. This is the one I want."

They walked into the office where a very short closing process occurred.

"Drop that price by $300," the manager called over to Tripp.

"Awful nice of you," the buyer responded without a twitch. He wrote a check and rode off as if he had just left the grocery store.

Tripp quickly scanned the purchase form to find the key items:

Name: Drew Solly

Place of Employment: Chicago Commodities Exchange

The Chicago Commodities Exchange? Tripp had heard of it. A couple of his friends had gotten jobs down there as clerks. That night Cole called one of them and told the story.

"What was the man's name?"

"Drew Solly."

"Hell, yeah!" the friend exclaimed. "He's a god down there."

The next afternoon Tripp walked into the world's largest commodities Exchange, hoping to find Drew Solly. He took the elevator up to the visitor's gallery, where he was immediately staggered at the chaotic mess he beheld. To think that the man he had sold a car to the day before was one of the biggest traders in that gigantic melee!

His friend had advised him to wait for Solly at the trading floor exit after the two-o'clock closing bell. Sure enough, Tripp spotted Solly in a cluster of people engaged in verbal swordplay as they left the floor. Tripp didn't want to interrupt, but chose to follow the group. When they got to a row of offices, the group split, and he continued to track Solly.

"Excuse me, Mr. Solly."

"Drew," Solly corrected him.

"Drew, I'm Tripp Cole, the guy who showed you the BMW yesterday."

"How bout that," Solly responded, brightening up.

"I was wondering if you could give me a quick idea how to apply for a job down here."

Solly surprised him. "I can offer you a job as trade checker." Cole's heart skipped a beat. But then he said, "Starting pay for a new trade checker is $200 per week."

That seemed incongruent. But Tripp would find out that evening it was standard-starting pay at the CCE. "Everyone's trying to get in the business," his friend explained to him.

***

TRIPP HAD ALWAYS seemed ordinary to others. He had never distinguished himself as an athlete or student. Nor, did he have a way with the girls. Nonetheless, since he was a little kid Tripp had harbored a secret about himself. Namely, he was a *sharp cookie*, more alert than everyone else.

The minute he set foot on a trading floor, Tripp realized he had found his métier. In the midst of all the yelling, screaming, and chaos, he had the uncanny ability to stay focused, regardless of how frantic things got. Wow, did they. Seemingly everyone wanted Solly to broker business for them. Trying to match up Solly's trades with all the different customer orders was like a game of Chinese arithmetic.

Tripp also had a more important realization; *I am better than all the other clerks.*

Word filtered back to Solly. Within three months, Solly promoted Cole to broker's assistant and raised his salary to $500 weekly.

Now, Tripp was the man standing next to Solly all day, whispering customer orders into his ear and reporting the prices back to phone brokers. Again, Tripp excelled. For the first time in his twenty-three years, Cole felt the wolf rising inside him. *I can make it big.*

There was one speed breaker on the horizon.

"Height is a big help down there," several people had told Tripp before he even started. And the Treasury Pit was the largest pit in the entire business. For the first time in his life, 5'7" Tripp became intensely concerned about his height. *What a stupid thing.* Half the tall people he had ever known came across as clueless. Nonetheless, lots of companies seemed to have been tempted by that fetish; parts of the Treasury Pit already looked like a tree farm.

Height became Tripp Cole's silent obsession.

***

SPEAKING OF STUPID, the tallest person Tripp had ever seen walked out on the CCE floor one morning. While everyone kept staring at the giant, Tripp became alarmed. The guy wore a navy-blue Elliott House jacket; that was Solly's biggest customer.

Worse yet, at around 10:00 that morning, the Elliott House floor manager began pointing in the direction of the Pit. Rivulets of anxiety coursed through Tripp's normally imperturbable demeanor, as he watched the Cyclops-like character lope over to the edge of the Pit before hoisting himself up the ladder to the top step. He made his way next to Tripp.

"Hi, I'm Chris," he said in a horrible southern drawl before proffering his hand.

"Hey, Chris," Tripp mouthed, meeting his stare up to the guy's neck.

"And your name?"

"Tripp."

Tripp had never traveled out of the Midwest. His first thought went to the *Andy Griffith* and *Gomer Pyle* shows.

"Jack Fitzgerald wants me to stand here and watch the Elliott House desk."

Newcomers to the Treasury Pit were often met with wanton acts of violence, especially on the top step. *Better yet,* Tripp's legs resembled tree-trunks, perfect for shoving matches. But because the guy worked for Elliott House, Tripp couldn't follow basic instinct. The freak took his place in front of Tripp in the mass of packed bodies, turned sideways on the back row. It was even worse than Tripp had imagined. His eyes were staring at a point not even halfway up the guy's back.

"Hey, see if you can climb to the top of him," one phone broker called up to Tripp. Others doubled over in laughter.

The giant was leaf-thin, causing him to pitch back and forth with the press of bodies. Tripp had to restrain himself from firing an elbow into his back.

"How bout' if I watch Mark and Bob," the guy called down over his shoulder, "and you get Joe and Blake."

Tripp didn't respond. So the idiot repeated the whole thing. And it took him twice as long to say as a normal person because he talked like he had two tongues and a ball of cotton in his mouth.

"Yeah, I'll take the two," Tripp finally answered in a clipped tone.

"What? What?"

"I'll take the other two."

"Okay, so I got Mark and Bob," he tried to confirm.

No response. Tripp already had him on the defensive.

Soon the giant got an order from the Elliott House desk. "Me, me?" he asked doing a double-take. "Was that me?" Tripp didn't answer so he whirled down to give the order to Drew Solly with a jerky motion. The crush of bodies sent his long physique crashing into several traders. Solly had to help haul him out of the Pit before he received a further mauling.

The market slowed down. Now, Goliath, he of the southern graces, wanted to chat.

"So, Tripp, are you from Chicago?"

"Yeah."

"What part of town?"

"Uptown."

"How long have you worked down here?"

"Two years."

"How'd you meet Solly?"

"At work."

"Oh yeah, where'd you work before here?"

Another member of the Solly group piped in, "Dude, what's with all the questions?"

Dead silence.

Tripp had always insisted on taking the last break of the morning among Solly's clerks. But he whispered to the other assistants that he wanted the first break and hurried down the Pit ladder.

"Hey, Tripp," a phone broker called over. "How fucking tall is that guy?"

When Tripp didn't respond, another phone broker chimed in, "You should have seen it, man. You barely cleared that dude's waist.

Tripp moseyed away. Two more times before he could even get to the men's room, people came up with looks of glee to tell him how much they had enjoyed the whole thing. But he didn't respond; it cut too deep.

***

TWO PROPITIOUS THINGS happened to Tripp over the next couple months. First, the tall guy got called out of the Pit one day. Tripp watched closely as he walked back and stooped to speak to Jack Fitzgerald. It appeared to be more than an idle conversation. Soon Tripp overheard someone say, "They're transferring him to the Board of Trade."

A smile began to purse Tripp's lips. Just like that, the thing that had haunted him was no longer. He watched as the dope shook hands all around, while making his way through the masses and off the trading floor. Tripp could not contain his joy. *I never want to see that human abomination again.*

All that afternoon Tripp felt a lightness-of-being, laughing and clowning it up with the other clerks. Better yet, the momentous event of the day had yet to come.

After the close of trading, Solly called him over. "Hey Tripp, we're getting awful busy."

Tripp looked him in the eye.

"Do you think you're ready to start brokering the small orders for us?"

After a split-second's hesitation, Tripp nodded. "Sure, I'd love to give it a try."

"All right, we'll get you started with the application process."

Chapter Fifteen

TRIPP'S INCOME SHOT from $500 a week to $10,000 a month. He bought a Porsche and reveled in tearing through the old neighborhood, offering rides to friends. Not surprisingly, they all wanted in on the action. But the theretofore affable Tripp drew a firm line on any friends at work.

He also began taking a harder line with other traders. "Wake up," he found himself snapping at Pit veterans. Unlike most newcomers, nobody picked on Tripp. Any slight would bring retribution from Solly, masterful in rewarding locals with good trades and punishing them with bad ones. Soon Tripp ruled the back row of the top step. It could only be a matter of time until he made it to the front row, where he would have a chance to make the kind of money that until recently had sounded like stories from an alien world.

Then one morning, Tripp took his position in the Pit and looked out towards the Elliott House desk. There *he* was again. Worse yet, he was wearing a member's badge, meaning he had been cleared for trading. *SKY* was his acronym.

Before the opening, he took a place on the back row of the top step, right up against Tripp. SKY had now morphed from someone Tripp couldn't stand to a mortal enemy.

***

TRIPP DID SOME quick arithmetic: every contract of business brokered by SKY was $1.25 of commission out of his pocket. SKY was already costing him a hundred dollars per hour, more than his father ever made in a day. That was just from small orders.

Then one day, Mark McMann of Elliott House flashed an order into the Pit to buy two hundred contracts, $20,000,000 face value. Tripp pointed at himself. SKY also appeared unsure. But McMann confirmed the order had gone to SKY. Anger steeled across Tripp's face. *Let's see if this guy even knows how to count to 200.*

"95-17 bid for 200," SKY began to scream in his slow-as-molasses voice.

Tripp's heart leapt in anticipation when an obnoxious neighborhood local named Marc Pinto sold SKY 9 contracts. That will screw up his count, Tripp figured.

"95-17 for 191," SKY continued shouting

Another local sold SKY 25 contracts.

"95-17 for 166," he continued bidding.

All at once, everyone screamed, "Sold, sold, sold," selling SKY ten or fifteen contracts at a time.

What an amateur, Tripp thought. Solly would have shoved the whole thing down one person's throat. But SKY stood there acknowledging the odd quantities sellers were throwing at him, trading with a dozen different people.

"Filled, I bought 200 at 95-17," SKY shouted down to his clerk. "Checking, I bought ten Batesy, fifteen Arnie, nine Pinto...." he called out to every person he had traded with, before handing the card to his clerk.

Tripp's slit-like eyes practically poked out of their sockets scanning SKY's card. *No way, he bought the right quantity!* Surely, somebody in Elliott House's trade-processing department would come rushing back with an alarmed look, reporting an error.

To Tripp's disappointment, nothing happened.

Later that afternoon an Elliott House phone clerk flashed in an order to buy 300 contracts.

"Buy 300," whispered one of Solly's clerks.

"No." Tripp stopped the clerk and cocked his head upward. "It went to him."

"95-18 for 300," SKY screamed, bidding out into the open market.

Idiot! Tripp thought. *Solly wouldn't have bid the whole order like that ... scaring sellers away.*

Only one local on the far side of the Pit offered to sell SKY 25 contracts.

"95-18 for 275," SKY continued bidding.

Locals from around the Pit began selling him odd quantities, which SKY acknowledged. Then the biggest trader in the Pit, Don Guritz, leapt into the air in his signature style. "Sold! Sold! Sold!" he shouted at SKY.

"Buy 138," SKY responded to Guritz. "Filled, I bought 300 at 95-18," he yelled back to his clerk.

The bothersome thing was SKY did not seem to be sweating the quantities he had bought and sold, like most brokers.

Right before the 2:00 close, Elliott House flashed another order to SKY's clerk. "Sell 200, Chris."

"Hey, Sammy," SKY called out to a nearby trader who had his hands up bidding 95-18. "Sell you 200."

"Buy 200," Sammy signaled back with two fingers pointed inwards against his forearm.

Bam! Just like that, SKY had sold 200 contracts, $20 million of futures contracts.

Solly jerked his head back. "What the hell is going on back there?"

Tripp had no answer.

Often Tripp did so many trades in the last couple minutes, he found himself recording trades until well after the 2:00 close. Now it was SKY writing down reams of trades. But instead of calling out, *Who did I buy from? Who did I sell to?* as most brokers did, he just kept on writing and handing cards down to his trade checker.

What's the deal with this guy?

The coming days and weeks brought more bad news. He and Solly weren't imagining it. The human skyscraper next to them really did have a knack with numbers. Tripp began to worry that he was some sort of mathematical freak, as well.

Tripp had even seen signs that SKY was competitive. Despite all those Sunday manners that seemed so out of place in downtown Chicago, he wasn't budging. He kept leaning back and relaying market information to the Elliott House desk, before Solly's group could get it out. He even had a certain loose-jointed grace about his movements that nagged at Tripp.

How could a carpetbagger from Alabama walk in and take business away, not just from him, but from Drew Solly?

Lèse-majesté.

Chapter Sixteen

"WHAT DO YA' say about tonight?" Chris asked.

"C'mon, that's a no-brainer," Ron Hughes chided in his best wise-guy's voice.

"What's your bet?"

"Yak-Zies in a landslide."

"That easy, huh?"

"Ducks in a barrel."

For twenty and thirty-somethings, Lincoln Park on Chicago's near North Side was one of the great locales in America. Nobody fit in better than Chris Parker. He loved the scene of wandering along the bars, grills and shops lining the northern and western edge of the park. Better yet, he and his friends were very single.

One Saturday night not long after Chris had been promoted to broker, he and two of his mates entered a popular chicken wings bar named *Yak-Zies*. The scene wasn't outright raucous, like the infamous Division and Rush Street Bars often satirized as *the Crab Trap*. Nonetheless, most of the males and females were in play; everyone in Chris's group had the swivel head. Worse yet, Hughes couldn't quit asking girls, "Haven't we met? Don't we know each other?"

Chris stood by sipping a draft beer, intermittently fielding questions about his height. His answers were noticeably less attitudinal when the questions came from females. However, the first two he chatted with appeared to tire of craning their necks and fled to the bathroom.

A group of four ladies in their early to mid-twenties walked in and began looking around. The bowling-ball shaped Hughes struck first, approaching the tallest one for what ended up being another foul ball. Another of the ladies looked at Chris. "I've gotta ask. How tall are you?"

"Almost as tall as my little sister."

"Nuh, uh," she responded with a look of horror. "How tall is she?"

"Who knows?" he threw up his palms. "I haven't seen her since Christmas."

"He's lying," said a third female in the group.

"I'm from the South. I don't know how to lie."

"That settles it. You're definitely lying."

Curiously, Chris chose to wind down the towel-snapping with the two interrogators. His eye was on the fourth and shortest member of the group, who had been listening without comment. Something about her had caught his eye. "Ma'am," he spoke to her, "how tall do you happen to be?"

"Me?" she looked surprised. "You want to know how tall I am?"

"Well," Chris tilted his head, "how tall is your boyfriend?"

That question turned her eyes wide as saucers.

"We don't have boyfriends," her friend broke in to say. "Why do you think we're here?"

That broke the ice and gave Chris license to ask, "Would you ladies fancy one of these beers?"

Looking at each other with indecision, the shy one said, "Yes, that would be nice."

After handing each one a glass, Chris looked at the far corner of the bar. "Maybe we should grab seats at that table opening up over there."

Everyone headed to an elevated wooden table against the wall, while Chris stole more glances at the short one with the willowy features and feminine mannerisms. He made sure to get seated next to her. During the first few minutes, he strived to maintain the fiction that he was talking to everyone. But he was burning with curiosity about the girl next to him.

"Mam, what is your name?"

"I'm Shannon," she answered in a pillow-soft voice.

"Aw, yes, Shannon. What part of Italy are you from?"

That drew a spontaneous laugh. Over the next three hours, while her friends scattered into the crowd, Chris would find out Shannon was *different*. She had grown up in a strict Roman Catholic family in the northern suburbs of Detroit and attended a Catholic girl's school. In the big social event of the year, the St. Pius girls had a dance party with the St. Gregory boys. The girls typically spent the entire evening blushing on the far side of the gym ... as far away from the males as possible. After graduating from a Jesuit college, she joined the ranks of young Midwesterners flocking to Chicago.

The back and forth with Shannon felt so natural, Chris had no hesitation asking, "Shannon, would you be up for going out to dinner one night?"

Although the momentum dictated a quick yes, it was not forthcoming. After discreet questions aimed at his exact plans, she looked him in the eye. "One thing I should tell you; I have *never* been with a guy."

Chris had been on his A-game all night, but suddenly he found himself groping for a response.

She added, "Do you understand?"

He looked at her in deafening silence, before remembering to affect indifference. "Yeah. I mean, sure. It's really not important."

She regained her friendly voice. "Yes, I would like to go out with you."

Chapter Seventeen

DREW SOLLY HOISTED his bantam frame up the ladder and assumed a position on the front row of the Treasury Pit. He stood in the same spot he had occupied for the past fourteen years, always projecting a statesmanlike aura. However, this morning he was prepared to cast that above-the-battle pose aside.

He turned to his top backup, Tripp Cole. "We draw the line here," he whispered before giving a veiled look behind at the improbably tall broker who had begun to shadow his brokerage group. "We don't lose the cash," he said, looking Cole in the eye. "Got that?"

Cole nodded, wearing a grim look.

Solly was a long way from his former station in life. For thirteen years after high school, he had been content working at his uncle's pizzeria in East St. Louis. But then one day, based on a lone twenty-five-minute conversation with a customer about the Chicago commodity business, he decided to up sticks.

"Uncle Tizzie," he said, "I'm leaving to go trade in the Chicago commodity markets."

"Why?" asked his dumbfounded uncle.

Solly stood silent in his messy bib.

Uncle Tizzie asked. "Do you know how to win?"

"That's what I'm going to find out."

The lean, thirty-one-year-old Solly arrived in Chicago on a dusty summer afternoon. The fledgling Treasury Futures Market had a California gold-rush atmosphere at that time. Within a few days, he had a runner's job at the CCE paying $75 a week, plus bartending at night for survival money. Four weeks later, he was promoted to broker's assistant and soon after his employer sponsored him as a broker. Solly was customer-oriented, dating to his years at the pizzeria. With dexterous hands, he thrived in fast-paced markets. It paid off in spades. Within two years he was making $500,000 a year; two more years and he was the largest volume broker in the entire Chicago commodities business.

On the surface, Solly remained humble and unassuming. But he couldn't get enough of being a rock star, as traders all day screamed, "Solly, Solly, hey, Sol," trying to get his attention to make a trade. East St. Louis was a long way away, and he wasn't going back.

Even at forty-five, it was difficult to imagine anyone challenging Solly. He was stationed at the epicenter of the Pit, with Tripp Cole and two more junior brokers standing right behind him, followed by a whole army of clerks a step down. A challenger simply wouldn't be able to field the necessary infrastructure to challenge their veritable Berlin Wall.

But now the most unlikely of scenarios had begun to unfold. His biggest customer Elliott House had sponsored that ghastly tall employee of theirs to come into the Pit and start brokering orders. Despite being stuck on the back row and pinned sideways up against a rail, SKY had begun firing large trades all over the Pit, while Solly sat there stewing. For the first time in his storied career, the momentum was in tidal shift against him. Still, he had a couple aces to play against the rookie. Elliott House's biggest proprietary trader in New York was an *arbitrageur* who had made hundreds of millions of dollars trading spreads between Treasury Futures in Chicago versus the

Treasury Cash Market in New York. That huge client represented Solly's firewall.

This morning before the opening bell, Solly had looked back at the Elliott House desk and noticed SKY leaning down and having an animated conversation with Blake Evans, the phone broker who handled the arbitrageur's orders. SKY had then called over his clerk and brought him into the discussion.

A few minutes after the opening bell, Solly heard SKY scream over his head, "Sell 68 at 95-12."

"Buy 'em," Batesy screamed to SKY over Solly's head. "Sixty-eight."

"Sell you sixty-eight," SKY shouted back at Batesy, completing the trade. "95-12 trade," he hollered up to the Pit reporter.

Two seconds later, SKY was again shouting, "Sell 68," before spotting Don Guritz to his far-left bidding 95-12. "Hey Guritz, Guritz, sixty-eight," he shouted, giving him the hand-signal for selling sixty-eight contracts, which Guritz acknowledged. "Sold 68 more at 95-12," SKY shouted down to his clerk.

Sixty-eight. That number filled Solly with dread. He knew the arbitrage orders came into the Pit in odd quantities. His last line of defense against SKY's insurgency was being breached.

He turned around to Tripp Cole and whispered, "Now."

***

THE YOUNG-MAN-On-The-Make has always been a primal force. Chris Parker had *that* quicksilver feeling again on this May morning. His clerk, Danny, continued calling up one order after another to sell sixty-eight contracts. The last dam was breaking in the Solly imperium. *If this business keeps up, they won't be able to deny me a spot on the front row.*

It was only 9:00 and he had already cranked out 4,000 contracts, three thousand coming straight from Blake Evans. Better yet, it had gone off efficiently. He even summoned the gumption to turn around to Ray Malley and shout, "Get the fuck off me, asshole. You're barely even trading."

Malley growled, but loosened his hold on Chris.

The only glitch came when he traded with Drew Solly, himself. Each time Chris had been forced to call out, "Solly, Solly, checking?" But Solly wouldn't acknowledge him, forcing Chris to spend valuable time peering over Solly's shoulder to spy what he had written on his card.

"Don't let your eye off Blake," Chris called down to his clerk.

"Sell 68 more," Danny called up for the fourth time in a minute.

Even with his great height, Chris had to spring to his toes from the back row to get everyone's attention. "Bobby, Bobby," he shouted at the Merrill Lynch broker and flashed a signal to sell sixty-eight contracts. "Filled, I sold 68 at 95-12," he called down to Danny who reported it quickly to the Blake Evans.

Chris held his cards above Tripp Cole's head to write down the trades. Therein lay his vulnerability. The pursuit from the subterraneans packed behind Chris sent him flying into Cole, who fired his left elbow into Chris's wide-open gut.

"Uuh!" Chris let out a guttural sound. He knew any retribution was hopeless, so he kept his arms raised and continued writing down trades. Soon the pressure from behind sent him sailing into Cole again, who lowered into a crouch and cleared Chris backwards.

"Stay the fuck off us," Ralph Molina shouted from behind.

"He pushed me," Chris said.

"Who gives a shit. Hold your ground," Molina said before shoving Chris back into Cole, who fired another elbow at him. This time Chris swiveled enough to make it a glancing blow.

"Chris, sell 68 more."

"Sold, sold, hey, sold you," Chris began screaming at a local bidding 95-12 on the far side of the Pit. With precise timing Tripp Cole lowered his butt and drove Chris into the crowd of traders behind him. They pummeled Chris's backside, sending him sailing into Drew Solly, himself, on the front row.

"Get out, goddamnit," Solly yelled back.

"Have you sold 'em yet?" Danny yelled up.

"No," Chris screamed at his clerk. Right then, two more bodies smashed into Chris from behind. He went careening into Tripp Cole, with his trading cards splaying in all directions. Chris dug into a crouch to stabilize himself and find his lost cards.

"Blake says he needs a fill right now," Danny shouted.

"One sec," Chris called back, anxiously rummaging the area beneath his feet for his trading cards. Fearing getting trampled, he jerked back up.

Danny screamed, "You're off the order!"

A second later Chris heard Tripp Cole lean over to Drew Solly. "Sell 68."

Solly filled the order with dispatch. A slew of 68-lot sell orders followed from Blake Evans to Solly's group.

Chris continued trying to reconstruct his trades. He remembered trading with Solly but couldn't find the card, so he wrote it down again. "Who else did I sell 68 contracts to?" he called out. "Solly, I didn't sell you two 68-lots at 95-12, did I?"

"I've got one," Solly said.

"I've got it written down twice." But then Chris corrected himself. "Oh, it was you, Darren, right?"

"Yeah," Darren McDuffie responded. "I bought sixty-eight."

The market began to rally. Soon it was trading 95-13, then 95-14.

"Hey, what happened to that second sixty-eight lot you sold me?" Solly asked.

"I did it with Darren."

"You said you sold me two sixty-eight lots," Solly contested.

"No. I lost some cards when I went down. I double-carded the same trade."

"So what? You come to me saying we've made two trades. The market rallies, now you tell me you only want to sell one sixty-eight lot?"

"No. I was checking with you to make sure we didn't do two trades," Chris protested.

"Doesn't matter," Solly dug in, raising his voice. "Win, lose, or draw, we're supposed to split the error. You owe me a check for the difference."

Meanwhile, all the Elliott House orders were being fired to Solly's group. Phone brokers were calling up to Danny to ask what was going on between Chris and Solly.

The next day, Solly dropped his demand that Chris owed him a check. Nonetheless, he had gotten his most loyal customer back.

Chris's juggernaut had been kneecapped.

Chapter Eighteen

"ALWAYS REMEMBER, IT'S just as easy to marry a rich one as a poor one," David Lasky was fond of repeating to his four children. It was the type of message a child could understand. And it was his youngest daughter, Barbra, who took her father's advice to heart unusually well.

The snickering always started at the Lasky household when dinner broke up. Fourteen-year-old Barbra and father would head into the den where they would begin dissecting the fine print of the *Wall Street Journal* stock-market page.

"Is he creating an Einstein?" Barbra's older brother wondered aloud.

"No. A Frankenstein," her older sister replied.

Barbra had always looked on academics the way some view a root canal. When a teacher assigned her to do a book report on *The Great Gatsby,* she couldn't believe her eyes. On the first page, Daisy expressed hopes for her infant daughter: "I hope she'll be a fool—that's the best thing a girl can be in this world, a beautiful little fool." Barbra shouted to her mother it was the stupidest thing she had ever read, before tearing the book into pieces. She repeated the same sentiments on her one-line book report, for which the teacher promptly gave her an F.

However, that stock market business that her father kept going on about had immediately seemed relevant. Everything she coveted—clothes, records, skates, a car— could be had simply by buying shares of a company in the stock market, then turning around and selling them at a higher price. At school, Barbra began regaling friends with her father's latest machinations in the stock market. All she received was mystified stares.

"Wow, I've gone through some phases myself," her close friend Eve told classmates. "But this stock market thing of Barbra's takes the cake."

The Laskys lived in the predominantly Jewish suburb of Skokie, located directly north of Chicago. The American dream had an especially alive feel in the upwardly-mobile community of 30,000. Most had lifted themselves from their ancestors' humble environs in the city. Few hid their aspirations to continue further north or east towards the leafier suburbs of Evanston and Highland Park. Being sandwiched between a large metropolis and lush affluence gave the village of Skokie a bittersweet feel.

Barbra and her cousin, Trixie, had always planned on having their *bat mitzvahs* together. When Trixie was thirteen, her family's helicopter-parts business suddenly boomed and they upped sticks to Highland Park. Trixie was now planning to have her party at the prestigious Highland Park Country Club, while Barbra's celebration was relegated to a more pedestrian affair at the municipal hall in Skokie. When Trixie turned sixteen, she made a rare appearance back in Skokie to show off her new 280-Z sports car. The Lasky family stood outside, everyone shuffling their feet and looking at the ground. Barbra turned sixteen a few months later, but was still forced to catch rides to school. Her relationship with Trixie was now a relic, victim of the economic caprices of two different families.

***

BARBRA LASKY HAD grown up fearing she was ugly. Being very short with large pop-out eyes, she was subjected to cheap commentary—"Hey, I thought only owls had eyes that big"—that sent her into spasms of tears and self-doubt.

"I don't think I'm ever going to get married," she confided to her parents.

But as the clock kept ticking, the playing field inexorably began to change. For Barbra Lasky was gifted with some exceptionally good genes. Her Hungarian immigrant mother had spent her entire youth in the ballet. Barbra inherited her eyes, the burning, alive eyes of a Nazi refugee. However, looking at a photo of the Lasky couple, it was her father, David Lasky, who struck the pose of a Hollywood matinee idol.

The jocks and studs who had given Barbra short shrift began paying close attention to the blushing new beauty walking the halls. Barbra never grew over five-feet and a fraction of an inch. But she was destined to be renowned for having a perfectly taut physique that left males prostrate. And her prominent eyes that had humiliated her now gave her an aquiline profile, only adding to her devastating effect.

Barbra basked in the newfound spotlight. She also began to discover a profound truth about human beings of the opposite gender. At age fifteen she had watched the actress Cybill Shepherd in a television interview. "I have a body that men will do absolutely anything to get their hands on," Shepherd unabashedly proclaimed. "It gives me power over them."

Barbra wasn't as brusque as Cybill Shepherd. Not quite. Still, she became increasingly aware of her raw sexuality.

In most families, it was up to the eldest son to achieve the unfulfilled dreams of the father. In the Lasky family, the task would fall to the youngest daughter.

***

UNLIKE MOST COLLEGE graduates, Barbra was not indecisive. She knew exactly where she wanted to go. A male friend got her an interview at the world's largest futures and options exchange.

In the interview, Barbra's was clicking on her A-game, fielding an array of questions that became increasingly personal. *Does he really need to know my favorite style of dance?* In the middle of her interview with the Exchange functionary, someone walked in and announced, "President Reagan has been shot."

"What's gonna happen?" Barbra asked.

"Let's go upstairs and see," he suggested.

When Barbra walked onto the main trading floor of the CCE for the first time, she couldn't believe her eyes or ears. All around the large wooden room, white males were baying for money with a Muslim-like religiosity.

"Is it always like this?" she asked the man.

"No, everyone is buying Treasury Bonds as a safe-haven in case the President dies."

Barbra's natural doe eyes became the size of silver dollars. One thing became immediately apparent; this was a man's game. Barbra immediately cottoned on to the type. These were *hero males*—yelling, berating, and strutting. They had egos the size of airplane hangars, which meant they were vulnerable to the likes of her.

When the man offered her a job later that day, Barbra accepted on the spot.

***

BARBRA ARRIVED EVERY morning at 7:00, and could feel the juices flowing. Just as she had suspected, the trading floor was a hotbed of alpha males and fast-money, along with gossip, drama, sexual tension, and guile ...plenty of guile.

She fancied herself as having acute antennae as to the best bets. Soon, she began to hang around a group of four whiz kids in their mid-twenties known as the *Flaming Ferraris*. All four drove Ferraris and each one was on a fast track. It was a well-established fact that sixty-percent of new traders were gone within a year. However, this foursome had defied the laws of gravity; each was making well into six-figures. One of the four, however, had begun to show he marched to a different drummer.

"He's like Hank Aaron with a baseball bat." Barbra overheard two aging traders saying on an elevator one day. "A natural." They were speaking of Thomas Krone.

One Friday night she was at a nightclub with all four of the Flaming Ferraris. Their table was littered with empty and half-empty bottles of a half-dozen brands of whiskey. Barbra had been listening for hours to their tales of derring-do in the Pit that week. Krone, the least extroverted, sat to her right.

She elbowed him in the ribs. "Thomas, you haven't said much."

He looked bashful. "It hasn't happened yet."

"That's not what I'm hearing."

"Yeah," he leaned forward and squinted, "but I mean, if you look closely, the market sometimes screams out loud telling you what to do."

Barbra stared at Thomas to the exclusion of the rest.

He began elaborating on his trading style. "Everyone is just trying to scalp ticks out of the market, darting in and out, trying to buy at the Bid Price, sell at the Ask Price all day. But the real money is catching the big moves. Take small losses like mosquito bites. When the market goes your way, let it cannonball for all it's worth."

She decided to keep a closer eye on Krone.

Soon after that conversation, in one of her frequent forays down to the CCE trading floor, Barbra noted commotion in the Treasury Pit. Deciding to saunter over, she perched herself on the edge of the Pit. The first thing she saw was a red-faced Krone screaming as if he was having a conniption fit. It looked as if he was selling to every buyer he could find. Barbra's eyes were transfixed on the scene. She couldn't help but notice most of the other traders wore petrified looks. Turning to look up at the board, Barbra saw why; The Treasury market was plummeting!

By the time Barbra left work that day, word of Krone's dazzling success in short-selling the Treasury market had made it upstairs to the CCE offices. Various accounts had the twenty-four-year-old bagging $300,000 in the last hour of trading, accompanied by bloody stories of all the money veteran traders had lost from trading with Krone.

She ran into him the next day in the hallway. Her gaze of awe at the new Greek god of the Pit was reciprocated by his look of blazing delight.

"Would you be up for dinner?" he asked with intensity.

"Sure," she answered, beaming back.

His courtship proved equal to his trading style. He played for keeps, throwing the full-court press on her. Quickly the couple became a *fait accompli*. But that wasn't even the most exciting thing for Barbra. Thomas Krone also had vision.

"I honestly think you can carve out your own winning formula as a trader," he said one day.

"Me, as a trader?" Barbra clarified.

"Yeah, why not?"

"Look at how short I am."

"Let me tell you something," Krone explained, looking deep into Barbra's dark eyes. "I heard that all the time when I first got down there. Being only 5'8", I halfway believed it myself." He stopped to wince at his own naiveté. "Look around in there," he added to her surprise, "most of the best traders are on the short side. When you get in there, you will see why."

"But Thomas," Barbra said, hanging on to him, "there are hardly any women trading in the pits."

"Let's change that."

She quickly became entranced with the idea. What neither of them could know was that, in the manner of Hollywood, this plan would eventually doom their courtship.

Chapter Nineteen

"WHAT THE HELL is Viviani doing back there?" Chris muttered to his clerk, who had free motion of his limbs because he stood a step below.

"I swear he's got his body parallel to the ground, pushing off that rail back there," Danny reported up to his boss, whose body was being thrust into the Pit-dividing rail.

"It's wrenching my fucking back."

"Hey, you're lucky we even let you in the Pit today," said Mickey Molina, "after you fucked us on those 95-18's yesterday."

Chris maintained both hands locked onto the rail, trying to keep his back at an angle in case a sharp blow materialized from behind. He stared sullenly into the Treasury Pit. Since being thrashed a couple months ago, his volume had returned to pre-insurgency levels. He remained isolated on the back row of the top step of the Pit, while Drew Solly and the big guns cracked out huge trades from the front row.

Chris had been looking forward to this week, knowing Ray Malley was on vacation. But he also knew that was no great cause for joy because of *the Sleazebags*, a group of stocky, thirtyish males—Molina, Grutzkis, Mutley, D'Abruzzo, along with the CCE chairman's son, Benjie Beman —who operated in something akin to a shadow market on Buttfuck Row. The whole throng survived off the teat of a deck of customer orders the chairman had arranged for Benjie. As a matter of *modus-vivendi*, Chris grudgingly paid the Sleazebags their daily ransoms. But he rejected altogether their omerta code and was determined to set himself apart.

Chris heard the Sleazebags get a customer order to sell twenty contracts. Benjie Beman executed the order, selling five contracts to each of his four fellow Sleazebags at a price of 95-02. It looked like it might be a good trade for them, as the Treasury Pit was a sea of traders holding two fingers up facing inwards, signaling they wanted to buy at 95-02.

Like automatons, the four Sleazebags began screaming, "Sell five at 95-03,", hoping to take a quick profit of $157.50 each

Chris rolled his eyes.

Danny yelled up, "Chris, buy ten."

The Sleazebags heard the order and immediately lunged at him. "Sell five at 95-03, sell five at 95-03," they all shouted.

"I seen it first," Mickey Molina yelled back at his fellow Sleazebags.

"No. I seen it before," Mutley rebutted.

"So what if you saw the damn order," Chris yelled over his shoulder in protest.

"Fuck you. Sell five at 95-03," Mutley shouted up.

"No, goddammit. Divide it up," a Sleazebag four bodies back yelled up at Chris.

Chris rolled his eyes at these *bottom-feeders* he knew all too-well. He briefly considered selling to the locals who stood in front of him. But they were the same locals preventing him from escaping Buttfuck Row. No, not them.

"What da fuck're you doing?" Molina demanded, when he saw Chris staring out into the Pit.

Chris was looking for a face-saving way to cough up the trade to the Sleazebags. The stark fact was that he had to exist with this group of flatfoots every single day, the way Taiwan lives as an eternal neighbor of mighty China.

Right then, though, he spotted a pert female in a baby-blue trading jacket on the far side of the Pit jump on the ledge of the Pit-dividing rail. It was the same girl he had seen flitting about the Exchange, networking, chatting, and trading, always with seeming purpose. *Damn, she's acrobatic.* She was accentuating her offer to sell at 95-03.

Chris discreetly waved his hand at the girl and caught her attention.

At first, she looked puzzled. Then he made a summoning motion with his fingers, indicating he was buying the ten contracts she was offering to sell. She returned a Sell-Ten signal, before hopping off the rail.

Molina craned his neck to look up at his foot-and-a-half taller Pit neighbor. "What'da fuck you just do?"

"What happened?" asked another Sleazebag three bodies back.

"He bought 'em from some asshole on the other side of the Pit."

"Jagoff!"

"Who was it, Parker?" Molina demanded to know.

Chris didn't respond and discreetly went about checking the trade with the girl. Since it was the first time they had ever traded, both pulled off their trading badges to show their acronyms. She gave a brief laugh when she saw SKY inscribed on his badge.

Her acronym showed as *BAB.*

"Who the hell did you do it with?" Mutley demanded to know.

"He did it with somebody he doesn't even know," Molina reported over his shoulder to his compatriots. "He had to show his badge."

"Who was it?" Molina kept demanding. "Who did you trade with?"

"Some local over there I was chatting with this morning," Chris lied.

Soon Dean Witter came crashing in with an offer to sell at 95-02.

"Sell five at 95-02," four Sleazebags screamed in unison, desperately trying to sell out their long positions. Luckily for them, the group received an order to buy twenty contracts, which Benjie Beman used to purchase five contracts each from his fellow Sleazebags, allowing all of them to scratch the trade. But they weren't close to mollified.

Molina looked ready to explode. "You think you can fuck us just like that, huh?"

"I don't have to trade with you," Chris shot back.

"You buried us on that shit sandwich you sold us yesterday that went straight against everyone. Then you have a chance to come back to us on a good order today, and you give it away to some asshole on the other side of the Pit."

"Hey," Chris protested. "I don't know what's gonna go the customer's way and what's gonna go your way."

"You just wait, what goes around comes around." Molina's hand was balled up in a fist.

Chris blew off their anger and gazed at the girl he had just made a trade with across the Pit. The impressive thing was that she didn't start screaming like a hyena to cash out for the smallest profit like the Sleazebags always did. Instead, she hoisted her gazelle-like figure back up on the rail and tried to sell more contracts at 95-02.

"I need the card for those ten contracts you bought," Danny called up to Chris.

Chris continued dragging his feet, but finally wrote down the trade. Dick Grutzkis, the Sleazebag two rows back, was the first to spot it.

"BAB," Grutzkis exclaimed. "Who the hell is that?"

"That's the girl over in Coffin Corner—you know, the one Mutley's always saying has a nice ass." Molina looked confused. "Why?"

"He did the trade with her."

"Get the fuck outta here," Molina said in disbelief to his colleague. He turned his attention to the culprit. "What da fuck you'se think you're doing?"

Chris strained to act like he didn't notice.

Later that day, Danny shouted up an order for Chris to sell thirty contracts. The majority of traders throughout the Pit were bidding 95-12.

Again, the Sleazebags heard the order coming in. "95-12 bid," they shouted in unison at Chris. "Come on, Parker."

Emmet and Tommy. The two nearby locals had gotten hurt on trades with Chris earlier in the day. Chris decided to play the game and give them a get-well trade.

"Hey, Emmet," Chris called out. "Sell you 10 at 95-12. Tommy, sell you ten."

The girl in baby blue was also bidding 95-12 for ten contracts when she spotted Chris selling at that price. Raising her forehead in recognition, she gave a quick blip up with her arms. Chris flashed a sell-ten signal at her, which she acknowledged with an inward-facing index finger touching her forehead... easy as pie.

Molina saw it. "He did it again," he tattled to his comrades.

"Who? the girl?"

"Yeah."

"Hey Parker, what do I have to do?" Grutzkis shouted. "Wear a wig?"

"And don't forget a skirt," another Sleazebag added to the great appreciation of his colleagues.

"Hey, hey! Parker, listen up, you hear me?" Molina berated him. "Why don't you go stand over there if you're gonna trade with her."

97

But for the second time that day, Chris felt an inexplicable high from trading with BAB, offsetting the depression of an afternoon spent seesawing on the back row of the Treasury Pit with the sweaty bodies of characters who could have been extras for *The Dirty Dozen*.

Chapter Twenty

CHRIS AND SHANNON walked in heavy jackets through the March fog.

"Dammit, I'm telling you, the azaleas are already blooming in Alabama."

"In March?"

"Yes," Chris maintained. "Remember. Chicago is closer to the North Pole than to Alabama."

Shannon did not respond to this dubious factoid. It was Friday night and they were trooping towards the neighborhood pubs in Lincoln Park West, Shannon in a light mood, but Chris feeling crabby.

When they had first started dating, Chris planned something different every weekend. Despite Shannon's rigid adherence to Catholic catechisms, she was full of Irish. He still remembered the freezing-cold January night when they had gone to a bonfire party thrown by a group of girls in her neighborhood to celebrate serial rapist Ted Bundy's execution. As the execution hour approached, the girls began a countdown, while the guys lay strewn across the yard pleading mercy for their hero. At the stroke of midnight, the females erupted in a collective shout of ecstasy. Chris cherished the memory of Shannon sprawled out on the ground in helpless laughter.

In recent months, Chris's mood swings had become increasingly erratic as he began to realize he was destined to be a journeyman-backrow trader. "I'm trying to get my full range of motion back after being pinned up against the rail by Malley all day," he said in a pained tone.

"I'm sorry."

"Honestly, if you saw it," Chris went on, "you'd wonder if there isn't a sexual element to it. Isn't that what Freud said?"

Ignoring that last part, Shannon asked, "Have you tried talking to him about it?"

"I don't speak caveman."

She didn't respond.

"I mean," Chris continued protesting, "it's like being in kindergarten again, fighting over who gets to put their foot or arms here or there all day, every day."

"I'm sorry," she said again.

"I'm sorry for complaining."

"No, I understand."

"How was your week?" he remembered to ask.

"Let's see. Harry and Elsie assigned me to put together a list of distributors to send publicity about our upcoming discount on the magazine."

"Sounds like you have a real job."

"I like to think so."

"Commodities traders should make ten times less than you, instead of ten times more."

"I'm just glad to have a job," Shannon said.

They reached Lincoln Ave, which ran diagonally going out of the park.

Chris shivered. "God, I hate walking in this cold wind," he groaned, "especially after being on my feet all day."

His last bitch was true. However, the diminutive young woman alongside him got up early every morning and walked three miles to the Wrigley Building on Michigan Avenue, and the same mileage home, earning her the label *the Roadrunner* by a group of construction workers she whizzed past every day.

Her rosy face looked up at Chris. "Which restaurant would you like to go to?"

"Whichever one offers the greatest damage limitation," Chris answered without hesitation.

Finally, he spotted a lit-up awning over a wooden building that perhaps signified respectability. "How 'bout that one over there—*Shamrock*?"

"Okay," Shannon answered, but with a rueful smile, "The Irish aren't known for their food."

"What are they known for?"

"Maybe drinking."

They entered *Shamrock*, which was packed wall-to-wall. "Oh no, this reminds me of the trading floor," Chris observed. "I hope everybody in here isn't sick, also."

"Let's get our name on the waiting list," Shannon suggested. She approached the maître'd to inquire. "Twenty-five minutes," she reported back to Chris.

He said nothing.

"Hey," came an inebriated-sounding voice in their direction. "Hey!"

Chris tried acting like he didn't notice. But it became too much to ignore. "Hey, hey," a rotund mid-thirtyish male at a table full of guys and empty shot glasses bellowed in a hoarse voice. "Hey, you. Yeah, you. We've got a bet. How fucking tall *are* you?"

In what was by now a well-honed routine, Chris turned in a pronounced fashion and looked down at 5'3" Shannon. Without flinching, she eyed the interrogator and answered, "Five-feet one."

"Oh, funny, honey," the man blasted in return.

"Bathroom," Chris whispered. They escaped through the mass of heavily-jacketed customers in that direction. "Nice getaway," he shouted into Shannon's ear. "I've seen louts like that want to fight when they come away empty-handed."

In the smoke-filled men's room, Chris was queued up trying to remain anonymous when he heard a voice from by the sink. "Hey, thanks for that trade today."

Chris looked over at a stocky, thirtyish male with bleached-blond hair. "Oh yeah," he responded to a man he recognized as a trader who stood on the far side of the Treasury Pit.

"Remember it?" he asked.

"Uh, yeah, we traded this morning, didn't we?"

"Yeah, you sold me 96-11's. I sold 'em out at 96-08."

"Oh dear," Chris commiserated, realizing the guy had a purpose. He was lobbying for a get-well trade from Chris in the future. "Better luck next time."

When Chris started urinating, he heard the door behind him open. "Holy shit," an alcohol-drenched voice called out, "how fucking tall are you?"

Chris jerked his head around in midstream, glad to see it wasn't the CAD who had interrogated him near the entrance.

"6'11", he coughed up.

"Who did you play basketball for, man?"

Chris zipped up his fly and scurried out, not even washing his hands.

Shannon stood against the wall, peering at the back of a boisterous group of males.

"Let's find somewhere to put our coats," Chris suggested.

They moved again towards the door, but not before another sauced male grabbed him on the arm and slurred, "Hey, dude, how tall are you?"

"Uh," Chris grunted, making it sound like he was giving an answer without doing so.

He leaned down with his back almost at a ninety-degree angle. "Shannon, how 'bout if I go outside until they call our name, and you stick your head out and tell me." Chris strained to hear her amongst the din. He assumed she was in agreement and headed out the door to commence a series of stretching exercises in thc frigid air. Ten minutes later he heard the warm inflection of her voice. "Chris, they're ready for us."

They made it to their seat unscathed. The waiter, a ruddy-faced male with a handlebar mustache, approached and bent down on his left knee in front of Chris. "I saw you come in."

"Oh yeah, big crowd tonight," Chris responded in neutral fashion.

"How's it going?" the guy asked, seemingly with great interest. "Still down there?"

"At the Exchange, you mean?"

"Yeah."

Chris angled his head as he looked over the man who appeared to be about his age. "Oh, yeah. Rusty."

"Uh, huh. Been a couple years," Rusty answered. "Are you still a broker in the Treasury Pit?"

"Still on the salt lines," Chris answered in a weary voice, before turning to Shannon, who was listening closely. "Shannon, this is Rusty Sabich, my ex-bus-riding mate on the #156 La Salle."

"Oh, were you down at the CCE?" she asked.

"Go ahead and tell her," Rusty said in a matter-of-fact way.

Chris angled his head. "He tried trading."

Shannon absorbed the words without reaction.

"You know," Rusty said, leaning closer, "I've thought a lot about the conversations we used to have. You were right; I should have gotten a job as a broker's assistant first, instead of diving into that huge Treasury Pit to trade with my own money."

"I couldn't say for sure," Chris responded, taking a different tack from their spirited early-morning debates a few years back. "It's still a nightmare up on that top step."

"Is that big ol' guy who you were always going on about still there?"

Chris sighed. "Take a guess."

He turned to Shannon. "You're not the only person I complain to Malley about."

"Chris," Rusty said, getting closer as he lowered his voice a couple octaves. "I've been working two jobs to save up enough to get back in the Pit. But I'm wondering, would there be any way you could hire me as a broker's assistant? I'd love to be up there near where all those customer orders are flowing and learn how everything works."

"I would," Chris said, throwing up his hands, "but we've got one right now that's pretty good, except when he's threatening to quit."

"Well, look," he said, rifling through his pocket and pulling out a pen. "If something comes up, I'd really appreciate it if you gave me a heads-up." He wrote his number on a napkin and handed it to Chris.

"Will definitely keep you in mind." Chris folded the napkin.

"Thanks," Rusty said, the enthusiasm draining from his voice. He proceeded to take their orders.

After he left their table, Chris turned to Shannon with a faint smile "You know what they say—that's show business."

"I guess so," Shannon responded with a shrug. Like most people, she didn't quite know what to make of that strange business her boyfriend worked in, that happened to be Chicago's largest industry.

***

CHRIS AND SHANNON returned to her loft apartment on a side street off Lincoln Park's main thoroughfare and scaled the winding staircase.

"Where's Kaylina?" he asked of her roommate.

"She has a date tonight."

"Same guy as last week?"

"Thankfully not."

"Have you ever noticed the guys always seem happier about their dates than her?"

"Kaylina says she's never going out with another trader," Shannon reported with embarrassment.

"I hope she didn't get the idea from you."

"No. She says they're so obnoxious and aggressive it's easier to just go ahead and have sex with them, instead of trying to explain why she can't."

"I've seen the type," Chris said with a knowing smile.

Shannon placed her hand lightly on his forearm. "Hot chocolate?"

Chris gave a crucifix sign and she headed off to the kitchen. He entered her living room and did a slow dive onto the rug. This was where he typically spent the last two hours of every Friday night. After being cramped all week, he finally felt comfortable in these spacious surroundings with high ceilings.

Shannon returned with the mugs. They both took a couple swallows before putting them aside and embracing each other in passionate hugs and kisses, punctuated by intermittent gulps of hot chocolate.

Chris pulled away abruptly and looked at her. "How do you do it?"

"Um," Shannon murmured, her face blushing. "Sorry?"

"How are you always so pleasant?" But then he added, "Of course, you would quickly turn into an impossible harridan if you worked at the Exchange."

"I hope not," she responded, her eyes affecting horror.

"I want your honest opinion on this," he said in a sincere tone. "Do you think the type people who work on trading floors are screwed up to begin with, or is it the place that messes them up?"

The flesh over her cheekbones welled up into two pillars of warmth as she pondered the question. Finally, she threw her head back. "What do you think?"

"In the case of me, both," he responded.

"Stop," she said with a light slap.

"Consider this. I had a broker's assistant a couple years back who could have been called *HopSing*, he was so on his toes. But next thing I knew he was nothing but trouble, full of specious tales, scurrilous gossip, and skipping down the street to a gambling hall to lose all his money, and anybody else's he could get his hands on."

"What do you think happened?"

"That's what I want to know."

Chris continued massaging her, as she purred with low-level pleasure. For a virgin, maybe even because of her virginity, she was especially arousable; tickling never failed to double her over helplessly. "This is as good as it gets," he exulted in droll fashion.

"You should be a piano player," she observed.

"Wow, that's the most erotic thing a woman has ever told me," he said, drawing another laugh. Prim as she was, Shannon enjoyed his offbeat humor, and began stroking his face with her smooth fingers, her tongue running circles around his lips as he moaned softly. Slowly she removed herself from his embrace, before proceeding to mount him.

Chris lay in Dionysian pleasure, at blissful ease, while his hands explored her ribs and spine and shoulder blades

underneath her blue turtleneck. Given her impeccable
hygiene and soft scent, he could stay locked with her in
fully-clad coitus for hours on end, giving full berth to his
moans of pleasure. After a half-hour of mid-level passion,
his groans began surging. He flipped Shannon, placing her
head on his heavy jacket and crushed her soft body to his,
writhing in pleasure at a mock-feverish pace. "Stop it, stop
it, more, more," he bellowed, feigning chewing on her neck.

Shannon tumbled over in laughter. "Shhh, Chris; the
landlord is on the next floor. He might think I've got a billy-
goat loose in here."

"So."

Her cheeks were flushed, hair mussed, and lips parted.
Her eyes gazed at him with adoration. This *pas de deux* had
been their predominant cold-weather routine for almost
three years now. It wasn't euphoria, by any means,
although Chris had reached climax on several occasions.
But it did lift him out of the here and now.

At 12:30 he bid her farewell.

"Night," she said in a voice as soft as the fallen snow.

They performed an assymetrical kiss, both leaning at
perilous angles, a technique they took pride in. When he
finally hit the freezing-cold air, he skipped the half-mile
home, feeling lighter than at any point since the previous
Friday night at this same hour.

Chapter Twenty-One

"BUSTED YOU AGAIN," one Sleazebag after another taunted Chris every time somebody spotted him trading with Barbra Lasky. "Whad'ya think, you're gonna get laid or something?"

Chris didn't respond, hoping to avoid further ribald commentary from the peanut gallery. No such luck.

These high-school rejects ferociously protected their $100,000 incomes. As far as they were concerned, Chris's trades with BAB represented money directly out of their pockets. Then it became more than that, an assault on their pride, seeing he could trade with a tiny female on the far side of the Pit every bit as easily as with them.

As for Barbra, Chris was impressed that she wasn't error-prone like the Sleazebags; she recorded the correct quantity and price on her card, and quickly checked them with him by hand signals across the Pit. Soon the trades became a daily occurrence. Then an hourly one.

"I'm telling you, Parker, you ain't gettin' shit, kissing her ass like that," Molina said.

The rear Sleazebag added in his most assuring tone, "He has more chance of his penis ending up in a pickle jar than in her vagina."

"It's like when I trade with anyone else," Chris protested.

"Why can't you just do it right here with us?"

"I sold her 95-16s earlier this morning," he fictionalized, "and it went straight down against her."

"I didn't see it," Molina contested him.

"So what if you didn't see it."

All his defiance earned him was another plastered crotch against the rail. After he had made one especially juicy trade that immediately went her way, Dick Grutzkis burst out, "Bonnie n' Clyde are alive and well here in Chicago." After the laughing died down, Jeremy Mutely asked in his best wise-guy tone, "Hey Parker, do they know about the whole thing back at the Elliott House desk?"

Get away.

"Danny, let's take a break," Chris instructed his surprised clerk. "Be back in twenty."

Chris hurried off the trading floor, planning to wander around the downtown area to clear his mind. He chided himself for letting the Sleazebags get to him. Yet trading with Barbra Lasky was one of the few things he found to look forward to each morning when he inserted himself in the crush of bodies. The odds were that more tension lay ahead.

As he was hurrying down the hallway, he froze in his steps. Twenty feet in front of him was BAB herself, latched onto a well-chiseled trader in a purple jacket who was talking on a telephone. Right then, she turned and spotted Chris. Like a scared rabbit, she hopped away from the guy, leading him to open his empty hands at her as to say, "what gives?"

Her quick retreat made for two hares. For Chris, with his southerner's sense of place, darted left like a coyote into the men's bathroom. He barely avoided colliding with the janitor as he rushed to the nearest stall, where he sat on the toilet for several minutes trying to regain his composure. *The Sleazebags and getting bent out of shape over some girl I don't even know.* Ironically, the only thought that brought any serenity was the man he had just avoided crashing into, the janitor. *He's got a real job, for Christ's sake. No wonder he always seems so pleasant.*

After several minutes of staring sullenly at the wall, he got up and left the bathroom from the other exit. By ten o' clock he was back in the Pit, with the Sleazebags packed up against him. A few minutes later, Barbra slithered into the Pit on the far side.

Soon Jeremy Mutley returned from a break. "Hey, Parker," he said in a surly tone that Chris knew to take umbrage from. "I've got some news. A few minutes ago, I'm walking down the hallway and who do I walk right past?"

"Elvis Presley," Chris shot back.

"Barbra," Mutley pronounced in an arch tone for his fellow Sleazebags to enjoy. "And guess what," his voice rose with deliciousness, "she was hanging on to some guy in a purple jacket."

"And?" Chris answered in his best standoffish voice.

"I'm sorry, Parker," Dick Grutzkis said, making a show of patting him on the shoulder. "You gave it your best effort, including losing any friends you might have had."

"Wait," Mickey Molina jumped in, "does he wear a purple jacket, about my height?"

"Yeah," Mutley said, nodding.

"I've seen her with that guy, too. Who is he, Parker?"

The Sleazebags looked at Chris, waiting for a reply.

"Oh, that guy?" he answered in as carefree of a tone as he could muster. "Haven't you heard? Has far and away the biggest dick on the floor."

"Is that so," Molina muttered.

Chris made a show of staring into the Pit, hoping it would shut the Sleazebags up. But he couldn't get over the poke in the gut from his misfire in the hallway. About all he knew of Barbra's personal life was she had had a high-profile fling with one of the biggest traders on the floor that had flamed out.

A couple minutes later, Molina tapped him on the arm in an uncharacteristically gentle fashion. Chris turned back warily at the squat trader. "You've got company," he said, pointing down.

Chris looked at the bottom of the Pit ladder where *Barbra* stood staring up at him. "Have you got a minute?" she asked.

Chris started to respond but nothing came out.

"Yes, Parker," came an elated Sleazebag voice from three bodies back. "Finally."

Chris remained in virtual stasis, as her eagle eyes were trained on him.

"It will just take a minute."

He tried tarrying for a few seconds to save face.

The Sleazebags weren't buying it, though. "Jump, jump, jump," Mutley said in a delicious tone. "She'd better have a good way to say thank you for all those trades."

Chris looked back at the Elliott House desk where everyone was occupied with a game of liar's poker.

He handed the deck of orders to Danny. "Let me know if the market gets near any of these orders," he instructed his clerk, before shimmying down the ladder to the ground floor where he stood staring almost two feet down at Barbra. He couldn't help his eyes from wandering helplessly to her lower extremities. The light-green skirt she was wearing hung about three inches above her knees, revealing ballerina legs the color of café au lait.

Everything about the situation bespoke long shot. He decided to open with a *Hail Mary*. "Gosh, you look much taller up close."

"Is that so?" She cracked an obligatory smile. "I hope I didn't get you at a bad time."

Chris defaulted to modesty. "No, our business has gone kaput."

"Not true," she rebutted. "But I don't understand why you have to stand back there where the clerks are supposed to be."

He threw up his hands. "I guess it's Darwinian or something."

Right then, Dick Grutzkis called down, "Parker, get down on your knees."

Joe D' Abruzzo piled on. "And don't forget to bark."

"Just so you know," Jeremy Mutley contributed, "it's illegal to make trades down there."

Barbra turned and cast a cutting eye in their direction, causing the white noise raining down on them to go mute. Chris couldn't help but notice the way her back tapered sharply to a small waist.

As if remembering an errand to run, Barbra said, "By the way, I haven't had a winning trade with you in a week."

Chris stood hunched over her, rendered temporarily speechless. If he had been more ruthless, he would have called up to the Sleazebags and quoted her to bring on their derision. Instead, he temporized, "Oh, you'll get it back."

Is that why she pulled me out of the Pit?

"I have a question." Barbra stood firm.

Chris looked around to see how many observers there were to this conversation. Runners, trade checkers, and clerks were whizzing by as he sidestepped back and forth.

"6'11", he sallied.

"Not that," she said with an offhanded smile. "I wish I had some of it."

"Well," he responded, stringing out the vowel and drawing a spontaneous laugh. Chris was starting to get in the flow. But not for long, before she rocked him again.

"I have a tall girlfriend I'd like you to take on a date."

Chris stood flat-footed. Again, he tried deflection. "You mean like 6'9" or so?"

Barbra cocked her head. "No, but she's at least 5'9"."

Chris was apoplectic. His every desire was to accommodate the tiny woman in front of him. But some stubborn instincts kicked in. *Dammit. I've ruptured relations with everyone around me and may be endangering my career. Now she's relegating me to Johnny Sidekick.*

Chris firmed up. "That's nice of you," he spoke softly, "but I'm dating someone."

Her blazing eyes temporarily lost their high-wattage gleam, making his stomach sink. He had disappointed her. Even worse, he detected surprise in her eyes that he had a girlfriend.

"How long have you been dating her?"

"Almost three years."

"Does she work down here?"

"No, she has a real job."

Barbra turned her head to the side at that response, the look of someone used to moving in a straight line to get what she wanted. Spinning around to retreat. "Okay, just asking. I'd better go back and try to make back all that money I've lost to your customers this week."

Chris tensed up straining to find a witty reply, but it eluded him. He observed her as she sashayed off with a bit of extra hip-roll through the crowd.

Once again, Chris felt like escaping outside. But he had just been on break, so he climbed up the ladder.

"Okay, Parker, tell us," Mutley cranked up before Chris had fully wedged his way back onto Buttfuck Row, "why did you look so nervous?"

"Because I'm not half as cool as you are."

"Are you gonna tell us what you two talked about?"

"Sex," he replied, but chided himself for lacking the necessary impudence.

For the second time in fifteen minutes, he was so down in the mouth that he was magically immune to the Sleazebag's blather.

Chris had disciplined himself to not stare at Barbra in the pit. But he couldn't help intermittently peeping at her, usually ending in her busting him. That was exactly what happened now, as she walked back into the Pit on the far side. Their eyes locked and Chris jerked away. She bolted out of the Pit again, leaving him feeling like a potted plant. And marooned on the backrow with the Sleazebags, clinging to him like vermin.

He couldn't help but think of one of his father's favorite sayings: "This is not going to end well."

Chapter Twenty-Two

"BARBRA COULD I have a word with you?"

"Sure." Like most locals, Barbra dreaded being called into Herman Mann's office. His summons usually had one theme: you're trading too large given the amount of money in your account.

Mann was the owner of *Vortex Trading*. The firm stood out for its WASPY character in a city and business that was an ethnic goulash. Mann himself had harbored some anti-semitic sentiments early in his career, but had long since become a fan of Miss Barbra Lasky. And there being no fool like an old fool, the jolly old man couldn't get enough of harmless flirtation with his dynamo trader.

He had been skeptical five years ago when Thomas Krone had brought this diminutive girl in for an interview. "Why do you want to trade?" he asked.

"To make money," she answered plainly.

"How are you going to deal with that Pit full of bigger men?"

"I'll take care of them."

"She will," Krone added with a laugh, which Mann joined in on. He agreed to clear her trades, which meant he was her ultimate guarantor in case of financial disaster.

"Introduce yourselves formally to the brokers," Mann often counseled his locals. "Buy them beers. Take them to lunch, to the golf course, whatever. They'll eventually trade with you." Being a WASPY firm, he always added, "Be a gentleman." None of that was Barbra's style. She had her own way.

At first Barbra had barely eked out a living, always laboring under Krone's shadow. But since their sudden breakup, she had steadily made her way from survivalist to something of a cash cow.

Mann watched his business like a hawk, staying after the closing bell each day to review every single trade that his fifty-nine locals had made that day. Most were having terrible years up to this point; some were facing their first-ever losing year. Meanwhile Barbra's volume had ratcheted up fifty percent and her income had more than doubled from the previous year. Mann was getting increasingly curious about his newest shooting star.

"Barbra," he inquired, "this SKY that I've been seeing on your trading cards lately—a helluva' lot, actually—uh, who is he?"

"He's the tallest guy in the Pit."

"You're not talking about that really tall guy?" he asked, holding his right hand as high as he could reach? "Like the tallest guy I've ever seen?"

"Yes," Barbra answered, beaming.

Mann was a skeptic. He knew three out of every four of his traders would go broke, which would require him pulling the plug.

"But why," Mann asked, "why do you think he's trading with you so much all of a sudden?"

"Because I'm the shortest person in the Pit."

Mann gave her a sly smile and responded with his favorite line. "Is that so?"

"He just started trading with me one day," Barbra explained with sincerity. "Most brokers can't even see over to our area. But I can trade with him like he's standing right next to me."

"I just want to make sure everything is okay with it."

Barbra walked out, wondering what he meant by that last line. Like all Vortex locals, she had listened to Mann's exhortations that a local's main job was to bid and offer all day in hopes of getting the Bid-Ask edge off brokers. Now that she was getting more edges, he was questioning her.

***

MANN LIKED TO amble into the Pit himself in the middle of the day and discreetly watch his *Vortex* locals make trades. That afternoon he waded into the giant Treasury Pit to keep an eye on SKY. Like most tall guys, he appeared to have a laid-back style. One look showed the results: SKY was standing back where all the broker assistants were stacked up, curled sideways to the Pit. Yet Mann had also seen him filling large orders from way back there. But none of this explained how he ended up trading so frequently with Barbra Lasky on the opposite side of the Pit.

Mann watched SKY closely. He was craning his neck in various directions to scope out what was trading around the Pit. Yeah, he is easy to see from afar, Mann agreed. He also noticed two of his *Vortex* locals, Barbra, as well as John Weakley, were bidding 95-16. Weakley was a local from the Deep South, who until recently had been getting a lot of trades from SKY. But Mann had noticed from reviewing his trading cards that the faucet had suddenly been turned off.

Mann turned back to SKY whose eyes narrowed, followed by a furtive glance around the Pit. Next, SKY flashed a signal to sell ten contracts to *someone* on the far side of the Pit, before parceling out batches of ten contracts to the locals right around him. He then looked up at the Pit reporter's stand and gave the signal to record a 95-16 trade. Who did he trade with?

Mann saw Barbra writing something on her trading card. He then looked back at SKY, who glanced over in

Barbra's direction and made a discreet checking, *sold-you-ten*-sign with his index finger.

Wow, they are good at this!

Meanwhile three other Vortex locals in baby-blue trading jackets had been unable to buy any contracts at 95-16, and were now bidding 95-17 with grim looks on their faces. One of those was John Weakley, supplanted by tiny Barbra Lasky standing just a few feet away.

When Barbra ran into Mann the next day he said, "Golly, you and that SKY work together like Fred Astaire and Ginger Rogers."

"Thank you," she said with a buoyant smile.

"How did you first meet him?"

Barbra would normally deflect such a line of questioning as having malevolent intent, probably for hallway gossip. But this grayhead had never had anything but her best interests in mind.

"I haven't," Barbra said, sounding amazed herself. "I've hardly ever talked to him other than some brief chit-chat outside the Pit." She neglected to mention that she had tried to set SKY up on a date.

"How did it start?" he asked in authentic confusion.

"I noticed him looking at me one day," she said.

"And he just started giving you the edge?"

"Some of them are bad trades for me," she reminded him.

"I'm sure."

Mann had always cautioned his traders, "Remember, a lot more bad than good things can happen to you in there."

Meanwhile, Barbra decided Mann's instincts were worth considering; it was time to learn a little bit more about the poker-faced individual on the other side of those trades.

Chapter Twenty-Three

THE LIFESTYLE WAS what it was all about as a trader. Nobody played that game better than Barbra Lasky. She had taken her new exalted status as a trader and run with it. Often ahead a few thousand dollars by ten in the morning, she usually left, for shopping, pedicures, massages, a nutritionist, or to the swish East Bank Club. It was difficult to not cast a disapproving eye at those who still populated the Pit in the late afternoon. *Losers.*

On this Friday morning, Barbra hankered to make some quick money and take off. Later that day, she was heading to the tony Wisconsin resort of Lake Geneva with her boyfriend and another trading couple. The U. S. government was scheduled to release its estimate of GDP (Gross Domestic Product) at 7:30 a.m. Chicago time. Until recently, Barbra had heeded Herman Mann's warning:

"It's a snake Pit before those reports," Mann always forewarned. "Stay out of harm's way."

However, she had noticed that the market was so inefficient in those first fifteen minutes that there was easy money to be made. Indeed, this morning she skillfully swapped buys and sells with the surrounding brokers and one long-distance trade with SKY. By the time the bell rang at 7:30 for the government's report, she was already up $1,500 for the day.

At that point, everyone on the trading floor looked at the huge screen covering the west wall of the trading floor. The consensus market forecast was that GDP would increase by 2.4% quarter over quarter. At exactly 7:30, the board flashed the report; GDP had grown by 3.9%. Treasury Bond Prices began to plummet on fears of an overheated economy.

Almost every broker in the Pit received hot orders to sell Treasury futures. But there were no buyers and Barbra joined the rest of the locals in racing the market lower. By 7:31, the market had already lost over a full point. She lay in the weeds waiting for the perfect moment to pounce, knowing brokers usually sold the lowest price for their customers. She began to train her eye on SKY, who was part of the herd furiously attempting to sell.

Suddenly, Goldman Sachs's broker came in at the dead-low of 95-26. "Buy 'em, buy em," he screamed. "95-26 bid."

That was Barbra's cue.

"95-26 bid," she hollered at the top of her lungs. "Buy 'em, buy 'em, buy 'em." She lunged to her left, and then back to the right. But none of the brokers in Coffin Corner had anything for sale. She quickly glanced across the Pit at SKY who was beginning to dole out his sell order to the vultures around him. Barbra raised her hands like a referee signaling a touchdown, which caught his eye; she made a pulling motion with her arms, indicating she wanted to buy what he was selling. Unfortunately, right that instant, gigantic Ray Malley hurled himself onto SKY.

"He's the ugliest man I've ever seen," Barbra told fellow traders who insisted on regaling her about Malley's sex photos. "I hope he goes broke and can't afford any more women."

The former wrestler had a *trader's hold* on SKY, sending his top half careening over the Pit-dividing rail. That old violated feeling—that she was not getting trades she deserved—returned to Barbra. However, this time SKY shook loose from Malley and looked out at Barbra. He put one finger pointed outward on his forehead to signal selling her ten contracts. She responded with two fingers pointed inward on her forehead, signaling she wanted to buy twenty. After a split second's hesitation, SKY flashed back the signal to sell her twenty contracts—their largest trade so far.

Now Barbra was playing for $625 per tick. Given the market had just moved thirty-five ticks, this was hyper-risky. Within fifteen seconds, the market was four ticks higher; she had a $2,500 winner on the trade. Given how contorted SKY had been, she decided it was necessary to check the trade. She began waving both hands over her head to gain his attention. Finally, SKY regained his balance from Malley's pummeling and gave her a quick checking motion; trade confirmed. She was long twenty contracts.

If she sold out now, she would be ahead almost $4,000 for the day, which would be plenty for most. There was one problem: this was David Lasky's daughter. Not only that, she was Thomas Krone's ex-girlfriend. Barbra couldn't stand being another member of the pack. Instead of selling out, she raised both her hands in fists signaling a 96-30 bid, hoping to help goose the market to an even higher price.

Suddenly, however, Chase Manhattan came in with a huge institutional sell order. Like a thunderclap, the Treasury Pit turned on a dime from all buyers to everyone selling. The market dropped six ticks in thirty seconds down to 95-24; Barbra's $2,500 winner was now a $1,250 loser. Like most traders, she harbored a perennial faith the market would come back, so she waited. Unfortunately, the Goldman Sachs' broker swatted down all the bids for 95-24, and offered to sell more at that price. Goldman then sold everything available at 95-23. Finally, there was a large bid available at 95-22. If Barbra sold out here, she was looking at a $2,500 loss.

One of those bidding 95-22 was SKY, who was trying to buy thirty contracts. She eyed him closely.

Wham. The Merrill Lynch broker came crashing into the market with a sell order. The nearby locals began waving the SOLD sign to SKY. Barbra gave her maximum leap while signaling to sell him twenty contracts. Right then, Mr. Assassin, Ray Malley, practically garroted the human skyscraper. SKY appeared to be struggling to acknowledge Barbra's sales, as they had come first, but Malley had him locked down. Finally, SKY relented and bought twenty contracts from Malley, who then gave his limbs enough freedom of motion to signal purchasing the remaining ten contracts from Barbra. That left her still long ten contracts. The market continued falling and she sold the remaining ten contracts at 95-19. Her total loss on the twenty contracts was $3,937.50. That put Barbra down just over $2,400 for the day.

Almost as grim, the market died, and the Pit began to thin out. Those who were ahead went home. Barbra yearned to be in her sports car headed back to her Evanston condominium before continuing north to Wisconsin. But now she was surrounded by a bunch of trading drones in a slow, sweaty market. As was always the case, the temperature in the old warehouse room rose steadily; fetid gusts wafted at random throughout the Pit. Worst of all, seemingly everybody still there was down money on the day. Many looked like desert troops who had gone too long without water; tempers were short. These occasions called for sharp elbows. Barbra had them.

"Sold," she shouted at Ron Steele, standing a few feet away. He tried dropping his hands and denying her the trade.

"Steele," she called him out, despite his being fifteen years her senior.

He turned red. "My hands were down."

"What was that I saw in the air? Your feet?"

He caved and agreed to buy ten contracts from Barbra, as humiliation shone across his face. Barbra turned the trade into a $500 winner. She had also filled in all the brokers in her neighborhood on her morning's mishap. They became like members of her team, giving her practically any trade she wanted from their customer orders. She also got a few key edges from SKY on the far side of the Pit. By the end of the day she had clawed her way back to a loss of just under $200 for the day.

After the 2:00 close, traders mingled in an area called *the T*. Conversation featured the good, the bad, and especially the ugly. Barbra was rarely on hand for these occasions, having long since split. But now she was there, along with her companion in the purple jacket, when SKY came loping along. It was time to heed Herman Mann's advice.

"Hey, you," she called over. "Where do you think you're going?"

SKY froze in his tracks and looked over. With male escort in tow, Barbra walked up and planted herself in front of Chris Parker.

***

CHRIS HAD ALWAYS considered his principal task as a futures broker to be disaster-avoidance. Friday afternoons were sweet; the pressure was off until Monday morning. But then he heard the confident voice of Barbra Lasky.

"Chris, do you know Tim?"

"No," he answered, proffering his hand. They shook, then waited for a cue from the woman standing one and two-feet respectively below them.

"Go ahead and make that call," she said with a dispatching motion. Tim headed off to the bank of telephones, effectively banished from the conversation.

She commenced her first full-set conversation with Chris, starting with her bread-and-butter topic. "Is there some reason I don't know about that your customers are always right, and I keep getting crushed?"

Chris began to speak as well as gesture.

She continued. "That twenty-lot you sold me this morning was a death sentence."

"Oh, did that not work out for you?" Chris responded, as if in surprise. In truth, he had watched her flailing away helplessly to sell out her position amidst the mayhem.

"Work out?" Barbra bore in. "Your customer should send me to the Red Cross."

"You and the rest of the locals I sold to."

"Oh, you're classifying me with the rest of the them, huh?" Barbra fired back.

"Well, . . ." Chris faltered.

Round one to Barbra.

"Chris, tell me. Where are you from?"

"Manhattan."

"Is that so?" she responded, playing along.

"Very southern tip of it."

"Pretty good."

"Actually, Montgomery, Alabama," he said, coming clean. "I'm sure you know it well."

"Can't say I've been there," she said. "What brings you all the way up here?"

"The northern charm of all you Yankees."

"Oh yeah," Barbra said. "Seriously, how does a person from Alabama ever end up at the Chicago Commodities Exchange?"

"I said Alabama, not Antarctica." He grinned to soften the retort, but Barbra didn't react. He continued. "No, I started studying the financial markets in college."

"Where did you go to college?"

"University of Alabama. I was there for Bear Bryant's last four years."

"Okay."

Chris launched into a tale about how he used to wear a tie to the football games, while the girls wore skirts and carried their dates' bottles of bourbon into the games in their pocketbooks. But Barbra didn't seem curious about southern university life, so he took a different tack. "Anyway, after college I worked for a bank; they reprimanded me for reading the *Wall Street Journal* the first hour every morning. Finally, I decided I wanted part of the gig."

"Do you like the business?" she asked.

"Oh, you know," Chris said with a sigh. "It was the best of times. It was the worst of times."

Barbra didn't acknowledge his literary reference and continued honing-in with her roving sapphire eyes. It was not an endearing look. Rather it bespoke confusion, *why are you trading so much with me?* Especially ironic coming from a trader who, from what Chris had heard, had spent half her career badgering brokers for not trading more with her. But then basic instinct appeared to take over again. "So why won't anybody ever trade with us over in our section of the Pit?"

"Because you are on the far side of the moon," Chris offered.

"You can say that again."

"Have you always stood in the same spot?"

"Yes," she said. "It's too physical anywhere else."

The way she slacked her shoulders in frustration briefly goaded Chris's animal instincts. *How could people not look!* The irony was that he had barely noticed her during his first three years as a broker, either.

The guy in the purple jacket returned as if on cue. He stood at her side taking it all in. Surprisingly, he didn't shift his weight restlessly from one foot to the other. He appeared comfortable in his role as the supernumerary.

"Is it done?" she asked without looking over.

"Yes," he answered. "We're booked for the fourteenth."

Rogue volts of envy shot through Chris. *So, this is the gig, huh. My role is to give her the edge on my customer orders, bringing on verbal and physical abuse from my neighbors in the Pit. This other guy's job is to kowtow to her, as well as the less humiliating task of fucking her brains out.*

"What are your plans this weekend?" Barbra asked.

"You wouldn't be impressed."

"Do you have friends up here?"

"Besides you?"

She received his awkward joke with a satiric smile. Her dark pupils were trained on him like radar. "Where do you live?"

"Lincoln Park."

That brightened her. "Oh. I dated a boy who lived in Lincoln Park. I loved roller blading all around there."

"You and John Kennedy Jr. and Darryl Hannah."

She lit up. "I heard about that. Have you seen them?"

"Yeah, they've whizzed by a few times." Chris thought to add, "Why wasn't he with you?"

"His loss," Barba said without self-consciousness. "You'll have to invite me sometime."

That brushed Chris back for a second, hyper-aware as he was of a male standing by with at least some sort of special status. "But there's a height-limitation for renting roller blades," he stammered.

'Stop it," she said in a reprimanding tone that he liked.

Fearing the conversation would turn boilerplate, Chris decided it was time to cut out. "I had better get going on my walk home."

"You don't walk to Lincoln Park in this weather, do you?"

"Anything to not have to take the bus." Then Chris's contrarian instincts kicked in again and he raised his eyebrows. "Besides, they just raised bus fares by ten cents, each way."

He could see the dubious tactic briefly throw Barbra off balance.

"Well, have a nice weekend," she said.

He nodded and started walking away, before turning back to the other guy. "You too, Tim."

Chris felt high from the conversation as he left the CCE and began his long trek up LaSalle Street in the freezing temperature. However, he also knew the fundamentals were not fortuitous. She had been interrogating him.

Chapter Twenty-Four

"MY GOD, THERE'S the Treasury Pit," Chris exclaimed to Frankie Hope.

His good friend said nothing, leaving Chris wondering what he was thinking.

It was Opening Day at Wrigley Field. Seemingly every trader who was ahead for the day had taken off the afternoon to make the pilgrimage to the famed ivy-covered ballpark. Chris could see that hot dogs and beer were already flowing among his colleagues even before the opening pitch was thrown.

But he knew that wasn't really the point. It was who *bought* the refreshments. And who you were hanging with —the bigger the trader, the better. And most importantly, how much you bet.

As usual, Chris tagged behind Frankie, wondering where they were gonna sit.

Not there! Scott Worshell was standing in the aisleway like a leprechaun with a wide grin as they approached. He slapped Frankie's back. "With or without chili?"

Recently, Chris had made a trade with Worshell, only to have his trade checker report a few minutes later that Worshell had recorded a different price. He hurried out of the Pit and over to Worshell to explain that he had traded with nine other people at the same price. However, Worshell took the time-wretched tack of acting like he was too busy to discuss it, and Chris had been forced to split the error. Ever since, they had circled each other warily like sharks.

But now Worshell couldn't ignore him. He shot Chris a quick look. "Hot dog?"

"Pass."

Frankie had a coltish stride and whizzed past Worshell, with Chris on his heels. Since he had been red-hot lately in the Pit, lots of traders threw high-fives at Frankie. "Ooo-wee! Hotter than this dog here!" one trader exclaimed, motioning to the chili dog in his left hand.

Fortunately, Frankie was still plenty happy to hang with backbenchers like Chris, even since catapulting into the top-rank of traders. But who could completely resist the narcotic of adulation?

Chris was happy when they found seats next to Foggy Ash, once a rising star himself, as well as intolerable egomaniac, before imploding in spectacular fashion. He had recently returned as a smaller trader with a sense of humor.

"Gentlemen, I'd love to purchase your first hot dog," Foggy said, "but they've raised the prices a quarter from last year."

"Well, in that case," Frankie said.

Their timing was perfect. The opening pitch was a minute away. Chris looked around and saw the usual signs: *This is Next Year.* Having gone almost a century without winning a World Series, Cub fans never lost hope.

"Jimmy, Jimmy," Sandy Lovett called three seats down to Jimmy Yopp, capturing everyone's attention. "We on again?"

"Sold," Yopp fired back in trader parlance, signifying that he was accepting Lovett's bet that the opening pitch of the season would be a strike.

"Supposedly Lovett hasn't won in ten years," Foggy informed Chris and Frankie.

Everybody turned their attention to the diamond. If nothing else, Lovett had made himself the crowd favorite. "Come on, Sandy," traders were shouting, "This is next year for you, too. Straight into the mitt."

The Cubs pitcher wound up and fired. Even from the stands it was immediately clear he had yanked it. The left-handed batter jumped back to avoid the ball scorching his ankles. The catcher jerked to his right, but the ball eluded him and sailed all the way to the backstop. The collective groan of the crowd was matched by delirium amongst the traders, all directed at Sandy Lovett.

"You should have to wear a dunce's cap after that," Worshell exulted.

But it didn't dim Lovett's enthusiasm. He took to his feet in front of the impromptu audience and shouted, "Cubs —live or die."

As he was reaching into his pockets for money, Ron Gaffney screamed, "Sandy, that sucked. You should have to pay double for a passed ball." Others agreed. "Hell, yeah. Do the honorable thing."

This left the crowd-pleasing Lovett in a conundrum. He held up his hands in confusion, before settling his eyes on Drew Solly, sitting two rows back. Solly, the grand statesman of the Treasury Pit, motioned with one hand down the middle of his arm, indicating a split. Lovett nodded in agreement at the resolution, before pulling out a wad of bills, looking like a stadium ticket-master. He counted out fifteen hundred-dollar bills and passed them down through three different traders before they arrived in Yopp's hands.

Chris couldn't help but think Lovett was being a fox. Solly's favor alone was worth a lot more than the $1,500 he had just peeled out. Better still, the story would make rounds the next day on the trading floor.

The annals of renowned CCE bets was long. One loud-mouthed trader dubbed *Tuna,* due to his relentless efforts at becoming a big fish on the trading floor, kept claiming his trade checker had the largest breasts on the trading floor. After days of increasingly heated debate with a neighboring trader who also had a well-endowed clerk, they decided to bet $5,000 on whose trade checker was the more buxom. They agreed to poll fifty traders; Tuna lost two votes to 48. The other guy then decided to give him a chance to recoup his money. Tuna was infamous for spewing traders with spittle; nonetheless, his pit neighbor wagered Tuna couldn't go outside and keep spitting for ninety seconds. Hundreds of traders gathered around them on the sidewalk outside the CCE. All kinds of side bets were flowing, Tuna being a 4:1 favorite. Unfortunately for him, an ice-cold cold wind was howling through the open passes in the downtown area. Tuna began spewing in different directions, as audience members simultaneously jumped back and howled with glee. To the shock of anyone who had ever stood near him in the Pit, his saliva glands went dry—even quiet—after thirty seconds. Boos began cascading at Tuna, along with ridiculing laughter. He sulked away and refused to pay the second bet, claiming the other guy had tricked him.

Here on Cubs Opening Day, nobody wanted to be left out of the action. It sounded like the trading floor, as traders barked the name of their colleagues. But instead of buy or sell, it was ball or strike, at $100 a throw. The key was to affect insouciance when losing; the loser usually took the hundred-dollar bill and mailed it as a paper airplane to the winner. Better yet, when the recipient missed the bill, the loser got the pleasure of watching the winner having to grovel to pick it up.

Chris noted Frankie was keeping his hands put, despite having no small chops himself as a gambler. This wasn't his scene either. Nonetheless, traders gathered to big traders like moths to a flame, and Chris was not surprised that various people began finding ways to plop into the chair to Frankie's left to try to engage him in conversation. Chris sat by idly, wishing he were elsewhere. His thoughts drifted.

Shannon.

Wrigley Field had never failed to bring the best out of her. The whole game-day scene, from walking two miles up Clark Street to the ballpark, the shouts of surrounding fans, the cotton-candy, Chris's off-beat commentary, and finally the walk home along the lake back to her apartment, kept her cheeks beaming all day, affecting Chris himself through osmosis. He missed her today.

Chris kept trying to focus on the game, but the clatter from inebriated traders distracted him. He found himself gazing blankly at the crowd. Suddenly, though, in one split second his whole being was seized.

She was sitting just above the Cubs dugout. Even worse, she was with *another* man. This new guy was big and curly-headed; Chris recognized him from the trading floor, but he had never seen him talking with Barbra Lasky. Right this minute, though, he had her bare-left shoulder cupped with his meaty hand, and was firing away as she laughed on cue. Chris had almost gotten used to the guy in the purple jacket on the trading floor, but seeing Barbra with another man overpowered him. *Keep your damn hands off her*! He became concerned somebody would notice him staring, and strained to divert his attention to the outfield. But it was useless; his eyes wandered helplessly at them. The only consolation was she wasn't providing any reciprocal contact, even as the guy kept yakking and boring in.

It was the sixth inning and Chris was looking for a face-saving way out. *Harry Caray!* The famed heavy-drinking announcer for the Cubs always rollicked *Take Me Out to the Ball Game* at the top of the seventh. That's when Chris would make a break. But in the bottom of the sixth, Barbra jumped out of her seat and began walking up the aisle. Will she see me? Chris decided the scenario was a no-win and laid as low as he could in his seat. She got to the body of traders and flashed passing salutes to a couple people. As she was passing, without even seeming to notice, she suddenly looked down at Chris. "Why didn't you come talk to me?"

Chris inhaled. "I'm not allowed in the VIP section."

"I'm down there," she scoffed, before resuming her eye-opening march up the steps.

Chris's mood shot from despair to disillusion. He wondered if Frankie noticed. They had discussed everything under the sun, except Barbra.

He desperately wanted out of the ballpark before Barbra returned, and wondered what to tell Frankie. One of the first things Chris had learned about Frankie was he spotted fakery quicker than anyone he had ever met. Finally, he just looked at his friend and asked, "Can we get out of here?"

Frankie's eyes flashed a quick sign of recognition before he gave an *out* sign with his thumb and leapt to his feet. Better yet, he economized on handshakes, patting the guy next to him, before leading their way to the exits.

For Chris, the afternoon at the ballpark had been no better than a day on the trading floor.

Chapter Twenty-Five

IT WAS SHANNON'S twenty-sixth birthday and Chris was dreading it.

On his four-mile walk home, he had spotted a shop on LaSalle Street and popped in to buy the first couple things he saw. For dinner, he took her to a restaurant in Greek town that was a step above their normal Friday-night fare.

The most special thing about the occasion was they were traveling in a Cadillac, instead of by foot. Frankie Hope had taken his wife on a tour of national parks while holding a highly-leveraged silver position. The market had sharply reversed as the Hopes crisscrossed America in a RV, sending his account from flush to debit. Upon returning, his clearing house informed him he couldn't trade any longer without putting up some cash. Only a few months before, Frankie had bought a brand-new Fleetwood. Chris agreed to purchase the car from him, with the understanding Frankie could buy it back any time. So instead of trudging the streets as was their wont, Chris and Shannon were traveling in style. Nonetheless, the mood was foreboding.

They got back to her apartment where Chris assumed his usual sprawled position on the floor and Shannon served up a mug of steaming cider.

"Kaylina wants to know if I'm going to sign the lease for another year," she said. The sound of her soft, yet brave, voice caused torrents of guilt to wash over him. She had recently let him know the three-year mark was make-or-break. He was suddenly overcome with a compulsion to spit out not just the simple-truth, but the whole tale.

"Shannon, why am I such an idiot?"

"Chris, don't say that?"

He hesitated. *Do the right thing.*

"There's something I need to tell you," he finally mouthed. But the words didn't settle well, and Chris felt himself getting short of breath. Still, he continued. "That girl down there at the Exchange I've mentioned to you a couple times, the real short, Jewish girl?"

Shannon gave a short but determined nod, looking like a young child listening to her parents break bad news to the family.

He blurted, "I've developed a fixation on her."

Her mouth formed a silent-O, as she stared at Chris in shock. Worse yet, the ball remained in his court.

"You remember," he explained, "I've told you how independent traders make their living off brokers filling customer orders."

"Yes," she quivered, her lips parted and tremulous.

"I trade with her all the time, almost like I'm helpless."

"Oh God," she gasped, sounding like they were falling into a twilight zone.

"No, no," Chris corrected, "it's not illegal. I mean, I have orders to make those trades for my customers. I would do them at the same price with another trader, if I didn't do them with her."

Great birthday discussion, Chris thought, Rodney Dangerfield on steroids.

Shannon appeared to be struggling to hold her core faith intact. "Why don't you take her out on a date?" she asked in plain-tone fashion.

"No, no, Shannon, the whole thing is irrational," he rebutted. "It's nothing like the authentic feelings I have for you."

Confusion stole across her face of love and wonder. It was the stunned virginal silence of a woman whose heart was being crushed by the only guy she had ever loved. *Pieta.*

"I've screwed up all kinds of things in my life," Chris continued, "but I've always done the right thing at the end. The last six months I've been telling myself, 'You know what to do—propose holy matrimony'. My parents and friends are all crazy about you. But now, God forbid, it looks like I'm headed the other way."

His soliloquy wound down. Shannon didn't feel the need for any outbursts or guilt-mongering drama. A lone tear rolled down her face. She found the courage within to say, "Don't be too hard on yourself."

"I'm planning on going to a psychologist," Chris offered up.

She didn't comment.

This was going to be that rare night she didn't send him home rejuvenated. He grabbed his coat and left her neighborhood apartment for the last time, tears streaming down his face on the twenty-five-minute walk home. Chris was to see Shannon Daly only one more time, a chance encounter on the sidewalk. After chatting freely for a few minutes, he asked, "So are you dating anyone?" In a meek voice, she answered, "I'm not comfortable answering that question."

Forever after, he would periodically find himself on his knees praying that she would find a husband to give her the children that she so deeply sought.

Chapter Twenty-Six

"IS THIS 116 MICHIGAN Avenue?" Chris asked in a voice just above a whisper.

"Yes," a corpulent black man in a brown suit answered. "These old buildings are confusing. You need to walk through that corridor and you will arrive at a bank of elevators. That will take you to #116."

"Is it an office building?"

"Yeah. Actually, it's a bunch of psychiatrists and all that up there." The man looked at Chris confused. "Are you sure you're in the right building?"

"Yeah, I guess." Chris hurried off. He remembered his mother telling him as a young boy that ladies often towed poodles along to disguise visits to psychologists. Now he understood why, petrified as he was of being spotted walking into the office of a *nut doctor*, a label his father gave them. Word traveled at the speed of light at the CCE.

When the elevator arrived on the sixth floor, Chris tiptoed off and was relieved to find the name he was looking for—Dr. Gary Kater. Moving tentatively, he opened the door.

A middle-aged woman sat at a desk. "Can I help you?" she asked in an upbeat voice. The look on her face was sympathetic.

"Yes, I have an appointment with Dr. Kater at 3:30," Chris said in a grave tone.

"Your name?"

"Chris Parker," he answered, lowering his voice even more.

"Yes. You called the other day. How did you get our number?"

He shrugged. "I found it in the phone book."

"Good. Please have a seat."

Chris walked behind a dark-wooded panel and looked for a place to sit as shielded from the entrance as possible. He pulled a copy of *LIFE Magazine* off the glass table and tried reading. His concentration was marred by fears he would know the person who popped out. Soon he heard the door open and a light voice. "Goodbye."

Chris caught a hind-side view of a woman who appeared to be in her thirties, rushing out the door.

A few minutes later, the secretary came around the panel. "Mr. Parker, you can come in."

Chris got to his feet and walked into a room done up in beige hues and lit by dimmed lamps. A nondescript middle-aged man whose predominant feature was a bald dome of a head, just like that of the television character, Bob Newhart, got up from his desk.

"Good afternoon, I'm Dr. Gary Kater."

"Chris Parker."

Dr. Kater pointed to a brown sofa on the far side of the room. Right away, Chris felt at ease.

After eliciting some background information, Dr. Kater asked, "Chris, what is on your mind these days?"

Chris launched into a tour-de-force of his tenure at the CCE, including a simplified sketch of the byzantine logistics in the Treasury Pit. His monologue was fluent; this was the same narrative he had presented to friends, family members, and anybody else who seemed interested.

"Well, Chris," Dr. Kater said, "just from listening, you sound good."

"But I haven't gotten into the most immediate reason why I'm here."

Dr. Kater acknowledged his remark with a blink.

Chris took the non-verbal cue and veered into theretofore forbidden terrain. A palpably different tone took over. His voice became sorrowful, even wounded-sounding, as he tried to explain the intricacies of the Barbra Lasky imbroglio to this man who had been a total stranger only a half-hour before. Talking from the heart, Chris began to realize how lonely he had been. He hadn't revealed any of it to his closest friends, because they were all traders. One night at a pickup bar on Rush Street, he had chatted with a drunk lady who couldn't quit raving about his height. For two hours, Chris had poured out the details of his strange relationship with Barbra Lasky in a way that surprised even himself. "Why don't you just quit doing it?" the lady kept asking.

Chris was hoping to get a more professional response from a trained psychotherapist. Dr. Kater listened without interrupting until Chris wound down.

"If we could go back to the beginning," Dr. Kater said. "What do you think caused you to initiate this trading relationship—am I correct in saying you initiated it?"

Chris nodded. "Yes, it was me, alright."

"Have you given any thought as to what caused you to take that first step?"

"Yes." Chris shook his head and sighed. "Let me say, sooner or later even the most servile masochist would become deeply unhappy standing all day in a crowded place where everybody can shove him at will, but he can't push anybody back."

Dr. Kater looked confused. "Why is that?"

Chris answered without hesitation. "Look, I'm not complaining about being this tall. But height, especially when you're as thin as I am, ain't any good in any shoving contest."

"Oh, okay." Dr. Kater sounded as if he were learning something new. "What do you think about working at a place like that?"

Chris spoke softly. "After all the big things you hear about the commodities business, I move here from Alabama and end up doing something all day that makes first-graders look magnanimous."

"And these people on the other end of all this, do they seem happy?"

Chris curved his mouth in a pensive manner; his forehead wrinkled. "Of course, they're thrilled to be making a lot more money than their parents ever did. Can't blame 'em for that. And obviously, you can't expect Marquess of Queensbury rules with so much money at stake." Chris opened his hands. "But, you've gotta ask—can somebody really be deep-down happy engaging in debased behavior all day?"

An incredulous look came across the psychologists's face. "Are there not exchange officials who regulate that kind of thing? Those are huge markets down there from all I've heard."

Chris gave a cold laugh. "Honestly, for somebody who worked at a bank, it's amazing." He shook his head while staring at the rug. "I've tried explaining it to all kinds people. But, no, it really does seem like you can get away with almost anything down there, especially in that huge Treasury Pit. *Better* still, you will be respected for it."

He stopped, and Dr. Kater let him process his thoughts. "One eerie thing is watching the glow going out of people's eyes, and everybody becoming more suspicious of everyone else. Heck, even the more bloodthirsty ones take on a hunted look after a while."

Dr. Kater took a minute to absorb those words. But then he honed in. "Chris, do you think this is a good career path for you?"

Chris tilted his head, searching for the right answer. "Despite everything, I still can't say for sure it's a mistake. I get to live in a cool city and work in a storied business. And I make pretty good money." Chris checked himself and swallowed, before continuing. "To tell you the truth, and maybe this is the latent Christian coming out in me, I grew up living in the big plantation house, so to speak. All day long as I'm being jostled, shoved, dissed and the like, I try to tell myself that it evens out over the long run and builds character."

Chris couldn't help but notice the number of times he found himself saying *honestly*, making him think he should have made this appointment a few months earlier.

"What about this girl, Barbra?" Dr. Kater asked. "What are your *true feelings* about her?"

Chris breathed deeply and looked out the window at a nearby skyscraper, trying to summon his deepest emotions. "No two ways about it, she gives a clinic when it comes to manipulating males. No crime there." He paused to take a deep breath. "There is one other thing that I guess is significant. The male attitude towards females down there, it's medieval. Women are viewed as depreciating assets from the first day they step on the trading floor—almost like models, or even strippers. But this little woman, she takes that equation and seemingly reverses it." After another hesitation, he lifted his eyebrows, seemingly struck by a realization. "Who knows? Maybe that's why I began trading with her in the first place."

Chapter Twenty-Seven

CCE PRESIDENT MIKE Kilpatrick was not disguised. On second thought, maybe he should have been. Kilpatrick could feel the sleaze emanating from all around as he hurried past cubicles of salesmen leaning forward into their speaker phones, peddling investments in commodity funds to anyone gullible enough to listen.

"Eighty-nine percent return in six months in the Japanese yen," a man with his tie pulled loose shouted at a balky customer. "Yeah, yeah, no; you heard it correctly. Six months. You will double your money in six months." Just behind him, a hungry-looking salesman with curly black hair had taken to his feet as he spoke in virtual ecstasy to a potential customer, "This latest news on inflation is huge, huge, huge. The returns on investing in our gold and silver funds are going to be stratospheric."

Kilpatrick wanted to cover his ears. He was all too aware of the sordid history of these funds; 98% of their customers lost money. But he also knew, or at least he had been assured through winks and nods, that the person whose money he was getting ready to plow into the market would not meet such a dismal fate.

He kept his head down as he was led to the back-corner office by a secretary. The young woman, who looked like she might double as a pole-dancer on the side, opened the door to Sherry's office without knocking. "Richard," she called out to a man who looked to be double her age. "This is Mike Kilpatrick."

"No introduction needed, Dana," Sherry said with a wide grin. "We'll be awhile." He winked at Dana, who blew him a kiss back.

Kilpatrick had to steel himself to not rush to the bathroom and vomit.

"Mr. Kilpatrick, do have a seat," Sherry said in expansive fashion.

Kilpatrick had never been comfortable being addressed as mister. But he decided it was better to keep this man at arm's length, so he did not correct him. A member of the CCE Board of Directors had given him Sherry's name, describing him as a virtual magician in the commodity-investment-fund business, despite Sherry's numerous run-ins with regulatory authorities. Kilpatrick had instructed their intermediary that he wanted to avoid specifics as much as possible.

"I am representing someone who would like to open an account," he said with formality. Sherry nodded; Kilpatrick was relieved to see had a businesslike side. "What steps does he need to take?"

"Tell me what you've got, and we'll work from there."

Kilpatrick handed Sherry a form with Karol Stanislav's personal data, along with a check from Stanislav for $10,000. Sherry scanned the data as Kilpatrick watched intently. The CCE President noticed a smile begin to break out on Sherry's face, before he was able to squelch it. Their intermediary had told Sherry it would be a big fish. But he hadn't informed him it was the *Big Kahuna*, himself. Kilpatrick knew that, like anybody else in the commodities business, Sherry would do anything possible to curry favor with Karol Stanislav. He could look at Sherry's bulging eyes and feel him making calculations as to how much future business it would mean for him, if all went well.

"Can we expect this money to be invested prudently?" Kilpatrick asked.

"That and then some," Sherry answered in full-throated fashion. "Our funds have got trades going in so many directions, in so many different commodities, I cannot wait to see how much money your man makes." He hesitated a split-second and added, "He's gonna make Hillary Clinton look like a piker."

"No," Kilpatrick threw up his hands in protest. "Enough. I'm just facilitating this client setting up an account."

"No worries," Sherry responded in a chortling fashion that only made Kilpatrick more nauseous.

I've gotta get out of here. First, he had to nail down some details.

"When will Mr. Stanislav learn the results of his investment?"

"Ninety days."

"I would like a copy of the statement sent to my office at the CCE."

"Done."

"You got everything you need?"

"Absolutely everything," Sherry said. His oily smile broke out again as he reached for the phone to call Dana.

"No, no," Kilpatrick said, throwing up a hand and taking to his feet. "I'll show myself out." He shook Sherry's hand, avoiding eye contact, and bolted out. All he could think of was he never wanted to enter another place like that again.

Chapter Twenty-Eight

THE FOUR-MILE-WALK home up LaSalle Street and through Lincoln Park usually took Chris about sixty-five minutes, maintaining a brisk pace. The early spring draft off Lake Michigan made the weather tolerable, if not pleasant. It never failed to amaze him how dramatically things could change in the Windy City in such a short distance. Along the way he skirted the lush *Gold Coast*, which was bordered by the renowned *Cabrini Green Housing Project*, considered by experts to be the single worst place to live in the United States of America.

This April Fool's Day had turned out to be a normal one for Chris; the market was dead and the trading floor emptied out by afternoon. The biggest surprise turned out to be in his mind. Throughout the day, his thoughts were dominated by a short verse of poetry he had recently read, written by John Barrymore:

Only the days are long
The years have hidden wheels

At first glance, it had seemed nothing more than clever commentary on an existential human dilemma. But since then at spontaneous times during trading hours, Chris had caught this verse echoing in his memory. Days like today often felt like an eternity on a trading floor. Yet mortals clung fiercely, even helplessly, to the place as the years flew by. *Am I wasting my life?*

He reached the northern end of Lincoln Park and crossed Diversey Street, before entering the old high-rise he had been living in since abandoning the rat-infested dungeon apartment of his first year in Chicago. The postman was making his afternoon delivery.

"Hello, big fella," he said in jaunty fashion. "Good timing."

Chris responded in kind. "Any time you run into the postman, it sure is."

The man pulled out a large-rectangular envelope. "Mr. Parker, I need you to sign here."

His formal tone was unsettling. "What is it?"

"I couldn't say. Please sign your name here?"

Chris saw the delivery slip for registered mail, and the CCE logo on the package. "Thank you," he murmured in anxiety. Instinctively he felt the outdoors was a better place to read what could be a pivotal letter; he rushed out of the building. Once on the pavement, he glanced at the statue of *Goethe* at the edge of the park and decided to go there.

Chris began deliberately opening the envelope, before tearing off the end. The first thing he saw was the letterhead from the CCE. What made him shudder was the sub-title: **Trade and Dispute Department**

The letter began: "This is a demand to Elliott House Incorporated from Kite Trading for arbitration..."

Kite Trading was Jay Rickey's clearing house. The letter was addressed to Chris as a representative of Elliott House. Therein lay the larger issue. $10,625 would be Chris's largest error yet and deducted from his annual bonus. But the greater issue—the more ominous thought—was *Elliott House*. At some point, his company would get involved in this.

Would Rickey bring up Barbra? Chris knew company politics was fraught; he needed to act fast.

***

"CHRIS, I UNDERSTAND you've got something to show me," Preston Beatty said, dropping his voice.

"Yes, I'm afraid so."

Chris handed over the arbitration letter from Jay Rickey. "A lot of traders threaten to go to arbitration," Chris said, explaining why he hadn't brought the matter to Beatty's attention before now. "I didn't think he would actually do it."

"I see." Beatty began perusing the letter demanding that Elliott House split a $10,625 error because of a trade Rickey said he did with Chris.

They were sitting in Beatty's sinecure office on the 26th floor of the Prudential Building, with Lake Michigan visible in the distance. Like every trading company, Elliott House had suffered disastrous errors. In fact, that was the main reason Chris was the company's senior broker. Beatty and Jack Fitzgerald had found themselves marveling at Chris's pinpoint ways in the Treasury Pit, jokingly nicknaming him *Windows*.

Beatty himself exemplified a curious aspect of the Chicago commodities business. Traders were considered the breadwinners, while managers were looked on as pantywaists, if not outright losers. Beatty felt this mockery keenly. He had been a college running back at Navy and had the gregarious personality of a trader. Nonetheless, both his stints in the Pit as a floor trader had been execrable.

Fortunately for him, the blue-chip Wall Street companies were diving head first into the financial futures markets at that time. Better yet, they didn't understand the business. Pin-striped bankers from old-line firms would fly in from New York to visit the trading floors in Chicago and

147

return to New York dumbfounded. "You wouldn't believe it. They're a bunch of animals," was the universal assessment.

Nonetheless, financial futures were the fastest growing part of their business, so they hired people like Beatty at handsome salaries to run the trading floors.

"So, Chris." He clasped his hands together. "Could you go over the scenario in the Pit that led to this letter?"

Chris gave him a pedestrian summary of the trade in dispute and Jay Rickey's disaster off the unemployment report four weeks before.

"What is this Rickey's reputation?"

"A hothead."

"There's no shortage of those in there."

"Yeah, and this is probably the worst loss he's ever taken. It feels like he is asking us to participate in his disastrous trade."

"That's an old trick," Beatty said knowingly. "So, what do you suggest?"

"We should deny his claim and contest him in an arbitration hearing."

"What is he likely to say?"

"He'll say the exact thing everybody always says in out-trades," Chris said. "That I was looking straight at him. That's why you check a trade right away, instead of letting the market run wild first."

"Okay, I'm with you," Beatty concurred. "We can't let him do that to us. We'll contest him in arbitration."

Chris gave a firm nod, trying to project a confidence he did not feel.

Almost as an aside, Beatty asked, "Who did you do the trade with?"

Just like that Chris felt himself at the precipice. Here was a loaded question that could snowball nine different ways. He had been wondering if he was digging his own grave by contesting Rickey.

Chris opted for vagueness. "I did it with one of the Vortex locals on the far side of the Pit."

Beatty drew the logical conclusion. "We'll need *him* to testify you did the trade, right?"

Chris nodded, before putting his hands on his knees to get up. Prolonging the meeting was a no-win situation. But Beatty wasn't finished.

"Chris, there's one other thing I'd like to ask you about." His face turned a dark red, which Chris knew from previous experience was not Beatty's preferred look. Chris's heart pounded. "It has come to my attention," Beatty said with formality, "I'd rather not say how, uh, that you have been trading a lot, an awful lot, with a girl that stands on the other side of the Pit."

Cash.

Chris's mind shot to Henry Cash, an aging trader who stood a few feet away on the top step of the Treasury Pit, and happened to be a close friend of Beatty's. Cash loved new brokers whom he could rape mercilessly on their customer orders. Indeed, Chris had played the game for a couple years. The small trades of five and ten contracts he made with Barbra Lasky were right in Cash's wheelhouse. It appeared that Cash had gone and tattled to Chris's boss.

Sitting perfectly still, he watched Beatty's mouth complete his remarks.

Chris's preferred *modus-operandi* was to acknowledge merit in someone's remarks, even if ultimately disagreeing with the person. Partisanship bored him for its sheer predictability. But attempts at reasoning had never done him any good in Pit arguments, which were all about offense. Now his entire career had a dagger to its throat, and he opted for demagoguery.

"Let me guess, that crybaby Henry Cash told you that," Chris shot back.

Beatty appeared taken aback by Chris's haughty response. "Well, I do talk with Henry from time to time," he said in a defensive tone. "But somebody from our desk also mentioned it."

Ignoring that latter point, Chris went on the offensive. "I've been making a sustained effort to avoid trading with locals like Cash who won't take anything but layups."

That brightened Beatty and a glimmer of his becoming Irish smile emerged. "Oh yeah, Henry's the best in the business at that."

Chris bore in. "Everybody knows he doesn't deserve being on the top step. He's holding back my career."

"Yeah, Henry knows his career is over the minute he loses that spot," Beatty agreed.

Chris decided to continue along this line. "I've been trying to trade more with the locals off the top step; they appreciate it and will help me sometimes when I really need a trade." This was true. But in the case of *her,* it was a dubious assertion.

The meeting tapered off and they shook hands, before he departed.

Chris remembered the headiness of his first years as a broker, when he was greeted like a returning warrior-hero every time he walked into Beatty's office, the gladiator successfully doing battle in the Big Arena where others feared to tread. But now the luster was off his rose.

Things had changed faster than he could have imagined. *He* had changed.

Chapter Twenty-Nine

CHRIS SPOTTED BARBRA standing in the hallway. For once she wasn't surrounded by grasping males. He gingerly approached.

"Barbra, could I show you something downstairs?"

"Yes, sure."

Without hesitation, she followed him down the escalator. Chris decided against another shoestring conversation and stayed quiet.

This time he had more than scattered verbal jump shots to offer. When they got to the coatroom, he reached over the counter and retrieved two photocopied sheets of paper from his notebook. Each contained the copy of a trading card. One sheet had a copy of Chris's card showing him buying ten contracts from Barbra on March 3d at a price of 94-22. The second was Jay Rickey's card recording him selling those same ten contracts to Chris. He handed the two pages to Barbra.

"Do you remember this trade?" he asked.

She trained her luminous eyes on the two cards for less than a second before gasping, "Oh my God, am I being investigated?"

"No."

"What is this?" She wasn't trying to hide her panic.

"Remember Jay Rickey claimed I bought ten contracts from him off that unemployment report, when I really bought them from you?"

"Yes. Why are you showing me this?"

"Because he's taking me to arbitration over the trade," Chris explained in a businesslike tone. "He wants me to split the loss with him."

"How much does he say he lost?"

"Over ten thousand dollars on the ten contracts he is out with me. Fifty thousand on the whole trade."

"What do I have to do with this?"

"I went upstairs to the trade-dispute office and talked to the lead arbiter. He says standard procedure is to have the person you did the trade with testify in confirmation of it."

"No, I can't do that," she shot back, looking like a cornered animal.

"But it's just a routine stating of the facts," Chris explained. "I'm not asking you to advocate either his position or mine."

"I've got to ask Herman about this," she insisted.

Their eyes locked on each other for a few moments, before Chris fidgeted. "Well, on a happier note, that out-trade we had the other day when I thought I had bought two contracts from you, but you didn't have the trade."

"Yeah, what about it?"

"You saw what happened. Those jerks cracked me from behind right when I was selling you two contracts. I thought you saw me make the signal to you before I went down."

"You didn't check it with me for almost five minutes?"

"I couldn't. I was trying to gather all my cards and orders off the ground."

"What does that have to do with me?" she shot back in knee-jerk fashion.

"I made eight ticks on it. Comes out to $250. I'm supposed to give you half of it."

Barbra wasn't yielding. "I've got to ask Herman."

"Again, it's simply standard procedure," he said. However, Barbra's face appeared to be morphing from fear to suspicion.

"I'm going upstairs to ask Herman. Where are you going to be?"

"The cafeteria."

***

CHRIS HAD ALWAYS thought the CCE cafeteria was a shining example of one of the things wrong with the whole place. The food selection was much greater than the surrounding restaurants, and the prices were lower. But because it was primarily populated by clerks, most traders wouldn't be caught dead in there.

He went through the line, selecting beef stew, whipped potatoes, cabbage, and carrots, before heading to the far corner.

He heard a meek-sounding voice. "Hey, Chris."

It was Jimmy Gault, one of the first people Chris had met at the CCE; his first job with Elliott House had been working as Gault's broker assistant. Alas, the customers had complained so much about Gault's execution of orders, Preston Beatty had been forced to fire him. Out of necessity, Gault had become a local.

He had a ferocious work ethic in a business where such a mindset was virtually frowned upon. From opening to closing bell he faithfully bid and offered, with the simple hope of buying at the bid price and selling at the ask price from brokers. But the tag...*too-nice-of-a-guy-to-make-it*...hung on him like a scarlet letter. His first couple years he barely made enough to cover his $3,500 per month lease for floor-trading privileges. But in a business full of bad surprises, Gault had gotten a good one. Elliott House had promoted his old assistant, Chris Parker, to broker. Soon

Chris learned to fend off the neighborhood toughies and begin filtering some trades to Gault on the far side of the Pit. Gault's income had almost doubled, and he and his wife saved up enough money for a down payment on a house. Gault was forcing himself to trade larger sizes himself to accommodate Chris's customer orders.

Then it had all changed again. Out of nowhere Chris commenced trading with Gault's Pit neighbor, Barbra Lasky. At first, Gault thought every trade Chris did with Barbra had gone to him, until Chris sheepishly pointed to the diminutive girl to Gault's immediate left. Once, in a busy market he had been unable to check a trade with Chris for a few minutes. When he finally got his ex-clerk's attention, Chris pointed to Barbra, leaving Gault out $1,800. Any time after that, Gault had to take the humiliating step of checking with Barbra to see if the trade had gone to her or him. Ninety-five percent of the time it was to her and his income fell back to the survival line.

"What's happening Jimmy?" he greeted Gault in the awkward way he had recently. He slid his tray down to eat with his ex-boss.

"Having lunch before those economic reports come out at noon," Gault answered. "I saw you doing some big orders off the opening this morning."

"Easy come, easy go," Chris responded.

Gault would have been the perfect soulmate for Chris, having worked for the same company and with an obvious distaste for the egomaniacs who dominated the Pit. Better yet, he was one of the few people, along with Jay Rickey, who didn't desire jumping Barbra's bones, proximity apparently being the enemy of lust. But unable to broach the five-hundred-pound elephant in the room, the conversation turned banal.

Chris heard a hurried voice from behind.

"Hey, Chris, Chris. I need to talk with you."

He turned and looked at the whippet figure of Barbra Lasky. "Oh," he said, holding his breath. "Okay."

"Hi, Barbra," Gault said.

"Hey, Jimmy."

"How's it going?"

"Oh, you wouldn't believe it." She started in on her day's crisis. "I was trying to buy 94-19s off that report this morning. I was the first bid in the whole Pit by three seconds, but didn't get anything. I ended up paying 94-25. Cost me two-grand."

"Sorry," Gault said, sounding sincere.

She turned her prominent eyes to Chris. "I just talked to Herman. Come over here."

With a sheepish look, Chris uprooted himself from Gault's table. "See ya' up there, Jimmy."

"Yeah."

Chris transferred to the table that Barbra had picked out and plopped down on the other side.

"Herman says I can't testify," she said before he could get seated.

Chris's stomach sank, and he forgot about the food on his tray. "But Barbra, I'm not asking you to advocate my position," he said in as close to a combative tone as he dared adopt with her. "The arbitrator told me all he needs is a simple statement of fact that you did the trade with me. It's standard in every arbitration hearing."

"Herman told me not to."

Starting to feel panicky because a third party was involved—namely, his employer—Chris held out both hands and adopted a pleading tone. "Barbra, golly, couldn't you at least make a photocopy of your trading card for that day showing the trade with me?"

"I'll have to see," she said, her head shaking and voice trailing off.

Until this moment, there had been a fiction that theirs was a relationship of give and take. But now Chris couldn't even get her to provide the most elementary courtesy? A pall was cast.

They sat wordless for a few moments until Chris broke the silence. "Oh, and the error we had, again, that's just basic procedure to split that."

"Herman says don't take any check."

"But it's yours."

This was surreal. Traders fought like cats and dogs over out-trades, demanding a share of winners and refusing to split losers. Chris tried reasoning. "Barbra, if the market had gone the other way then, I would have expected you to split it with me."

Barbra's prominent doe eyes appeared hooded. What's going on here? Then, out of the blue, *it* happened.

"How do I know you're not setting me up?" she blurted.

At the sound of those words, a scalding feeling swept over Chris's brain. He sat frozen, looking at the healthy young woman sitting across from him.

"Setting you up?" he repeated in dazed fashion. He tried to act dumbfounded. The stark fact, though, was he knew exactly to what she was referring. Three years back, the FBI had responded to reports of rampant fraud in the Chicago commodity markets by placing undercover agents in various pits as traders. Indeed, they had scored indictments in every pit, but one, the gigantic Treasury-Index Pit. FBI plants returned to headquarters in amazement at the bludgeoning they had received from attempting to move near the top steps of the Pit.

Officials back in Quantico, Virginia, had received these reports dubiously until one agent returned with a big scar across his face from being slashed with a pencil. Another had been cracked in the jaw by a wrecking ball named Marc Willingham, who made a career out of harassing new traders. The net result was that they had nailed a few marginal traders down in the well of the Treasury Pit who agreed to go undercover and be wired for sound while trading. A witch-hunt atmosphere ensued, with feverish speculation as to who was a mole. Suddenly these blackballed individuals couldn't get anybody to trade with them; every one of them was gone from the Exchange within a few months, reaping the most bitter fruit.

Chris remembered how in college the easiest way to destroy someone socially was to say they were either homosexual, or had venereal disease. Fingering them as an FBI plant was the professional equivalent at the CCE.

He felt his jaws tighten as he stared at Barbra. *This is what I get out of the whole thing—a McCarthy-like slander?* He spread out his palms in entreaty. The only thing he could articulate sounded like a plea. "But, but all I'm trying to do is handle these trades. I mean, Barbra, I'm supposed to split a winner with you. And the thing about showing your trading card, they told me in the arbitration office that's just routine procedure."

Barbra had gone quiet. Chris looked at her burning eyes and again his big-picture instincts kicked in. *Jewish paranoia.* Having been victims of police-state tactics for thousands of years, they were ultra-sensitive to the heavy hand of the state. Barbra's high-wattage eyes had morphed from burning to suspicious in a nanosecond.

Chris couldn't stand arguing about small things. He found zero-sum, beggar-thy-neighbor thinking dehumanizing, and had a long history of falling in love with grand ideas and different people. He was the most unlikely romantic. But like most romantics, he was prone to walking off ledges.

Chapter Thirty

THIS TIME, CHRIS enjoyed his walk to 116 Michigan Avenue. It was a sunny spring day, although a stiff breeze off Lake Michigan required him to stay bundled up in the same heavy grey jacket he had been wearing every day since November. Nonetheless, the air was bracing.

He was no longer paranoid about going to see a psychiatrist. "They're great BS sessions," Chris told one friend. To absolutely no one, though, would he divulge the explosive central topic. Today he had the most bizarre turn of events imaginable to report.

"She thinks I'm a FBI agent," he opened to Dr. Kater.

"Barbra?" he clarified. "Barbra thinks you're an FBI agent?" He referred to Barbra like she was somebody he knew well.

"That's what she insinuated today," Chris said.

"What in the world?" Dr. Kater looked incredulous.

"You remember the FBI investigation down there a few years ago?"

"Some traders got in trouble, right?"

"Yep. There was a hot rumor mill about which traders had turned state's evidence."

"And she thinks you might be doing that?"

With hurt slipping into his voice, Chris answered the question. "I guess there's no other way to interpret that. She's refusing to testify for me in an arbitration case confirming a trade that I did with her, but another trader claims I did with him. Saved her a lot of money."

Like most good psychiatrists, Dr. Kater had been spare in offering solutions. But now he saw his opening. "This Barbra, she sounds like one of those people that's just trouble."

"No, no," Chris protested, splaying his hands at Dr. Kater. "I mean, yeah, she may be greedier than any other three people put together, but not a troublemaker like that."

"Is that okay?"

"God knows, greed isn't a crime in that place." He began to speak, before stopping. Then, almost as if speaking to himself, he added, "I've done this to myself."

"Have you ever considered asking her out?"

"It's not possible," Chris said, which drew a blank from Dr. Kater. "She's a main-chance player. That kind of person isn't gonna go out with me."

"Have you ever considered an experiment, like not trading with her for two weeks?"

"I tried that when I broke up with Shannon. I couldn't even make it through the morning."

"But you must feel you've got to quit?" Dr. Kater bore down with unusual severity.

Chris came right back. "Doctor, isn't it true that there is no rational stopping point for all addictions—drinking, drugs, gambling, whatever? Have you ever seen an addict decide to just quit without it first destroying them?"

"Is that what this is going to come to, Chris?" Dr. Kater bore down with unusual severity.

"I'm just trying to be realistic."

Dr. Kater stared at Chris in a way he hadn't before. Chris derived a small measure of pride that he had been more ruthlessly objective than his own shrink.

The feeling was different when they shook hands to depart. As Chris headed out the door he felt the need to turn back and say, "Dr. Kater, just in case you were worrying, this is not a crime in any way—compulsively trading with her. Everything is perfectly legal."

"Oh. Okay, Chris."

Chapter Thirty-One

CHRIS LOWERED HIMSELF from the Pit and walked back to the Elliott House desk after the 2:00 close, trying to maintain a low profile. His arbitration hearing was scheduled for 2:30 and he didn't want to arrive early on the 21st floor and end up in awkward chitchat with Jay Rickey. There is only one way this can go bad, he thought. *Elliott House.* In that eventuality, he could lose a lot more than ten-thousand dollars.

A few days back he had visited the arbitration office to nail down the exact procedures. The arbitration administrator had told him, "Just make sure you have the person you did the trade with testify for you." Chris rifled a series of questions at the man about how essential this was. "At the very least, *he* should submit a simple written affidavit."

Chris had gone downstairs to Barbra's locker and inserted a note asking for an affidavit. But the next day she appeared spooked in the Pit and had gone out of her way to avoid looking at him. She had not come in at all today, which Chris figured was no coincidence.

He loitered around the desk, waiting to inconspicuously head upstairs. To his surprise, Jack Fitzgerald, who usually coyoted at the sound of the closing bell, was one of the stragglers. Just as Chris exited the Elliott House booth, he heard Fitzgerald's voice. "Hold on a minute, Chris. I'm going up there with you."

"Oh? Okay."

Chris's insides stirred, sensing his task had just gotten more complicated. He knew company politics was a zero-sum game; Fitzgerald could turn a debacle into his own gain.

"So, what's our strategy?" Fitzgerald asked Chris once they got in the elevator.

Chris decided on preemption. "Just remember one thing, Jack. The facts are damning to his case, so he's bound to get nasty. You should see all the errors and shouting matches he's in with people all over the Pit."

Fitzgerald said nothing.

When they got off the elevator, the first person they came upon was Jay Rickey. A deadly silence ensued. But when Rickey saw Fitzgerald in his Elliott House jacket, he wasn't able to withhold a gotcha look. *I've got to change strategy.*

The previous night at dinner, a friend who also traded in the Treasury Pit had told Chris, "They're gonna split it, no matter what."

"But he never checked the trade until the market had fallen a full point," Chris had protested.

"Dude, they always split it up there in arbitration."

The conversation had left Chris peeved; but it also gave him an idea for the hearing.

***

THE ARBITRATION COMMITTEE consisted of floor traders from every pit but the Treasury Index. At least they got that right, Chris thought.

The committee members motioned Jay Rickey and Chris to two chairs next to each other, across the table from the arbitrators. Fitzgerald sat to Chris's immediate right.

"Mr. Rickey, would you present your case?" the lead arbitrator asked.

His argument was straightforward. "On March 3d, I had my hands up offering to sell at 94-22. Chris Parker of Elliott House, now sitting to my right, looked straight at me and gave me a hand signal to buy ten contracts. When I tried to check the trade, I learned we were out the trade. It's a basic out-trade. We're supposed to split it, but he refuses. I demand he cover half of my $10,625 loss on those ten contracts I thought I had sold him."

"Mr. Parker," the arbitrator asked, "how do you respond to that?"

Chris quickly went on offense. "This case seems very important," he said without hesitation. "Because the stark truth is that this committee is considered by most floor traders to be a rubber stamp." He looked up at the arbitrators, whose eyes seemed to have narrowed at that opening salvo. "Everybody thinks you automatically split everything, which makes the system rife for abuse. All anybody needs to do is claim they are out a trade with someone and they can get a split. In fact, I suggest to you that is the reason we are here today."

"That is dead wrong," Jay Rickey said, sounding like he was in another Pit-screaming match. "You looked straight at me, and I wrote the trade down. That's an out-trade and an honorable person would cover his share of the loss."

Chris felt warmed up. "Case in point," he came right back at Rickey. "Let me give you an analogy—in golf the joke is that 99% of putts that are short don't go into the hole. But in arguments over out-trades, fully one-hundred percent of the time the person who didn't get the trade claims the other person was looking straight at him. The argument is simply meaningless."

Rickey's fist landed on the table. "I don't know where this guy comes from. Actually I do know, but he is ruining his reputation by trying to welsh out. And that's before we even get into *who* he claims he did the trade with. We'll see how the committee reacts to that whole issue in a minute."

He is going to do *it,* Chris thought. *Preempt.*

"This brings up the fundamental problem with his entire case," Chris stated with as much certitude as he could muster. "Jay Rickey sitting to my left made a disastrous trade and he's trying to get me to participate in his huge loss. Think about it for a second—if he tries to check that trade immediately, I just correct him and point out the person I did it with. That happens all the time in the Pit, and nobody considers it an out-trade. But by not checking it until the market has moved sharply, he says that's an out-trade I have to split with him."

That was a frontal-attack on Rickey's argument. But what Rickey was getting ready to uncork could ruin his career. *Preempt.*

"And . . ."

"Whoa, hold on," Rickey interjected

"No, I'm still talking."

"No, I'm rebutting."

"He cut me off," Chris said, scanning the arbitrators. "I haven't made my most important point."

The arbitrators all looked at him instead of Rickey. He had the floor and heard Jack Fitzgerald shuffle in his chair.

"You've got locals who check their trades, and those who don't. I do my damnedest to trade with those who do check them, people like Barbra Lasky, who I did this trade with. It's crazy," he stopped to look around in disbelief at the committee, "this macho attitude on the CCE floor that diligently checking trades is for wimps. But guess what. When those same gunslingers have errors, they demand you split it with them, regardless of who's at fault."

Rickey pointed his finger at everybody around the room. "He gives all his lay-ups to this little girl at my waist, and I have to stand there watching it all day long. I'd like to ask him in front of the committee, as well as a representative of his own company," Rickey nodded at Jack Fitzgerald, "what in the world is this all about?"

"It's about boring the committee," Chris fired back. "Folks, you were just forced to listen to the kind of partisan lobbying that every single local, including Barbra Lasky by the way, does, always claiming I'm not trading enough with them. But heck," Chris said, deciding to go contrarian, "I trade with Barbra Lasky regularly. Yet she still checks her trades right away with me. Mr. Rickey and I rarely trade at all, yet he lets the market move sharply before attempting to confirm the trade. Effectively, he's trying to socialize his losses."

"Socialize? Hey, listen you," he said, practically bowing up. "You sit there and do half your trades with that b—-," Rickey caught himself, "with that little girl, while I'm standing next to her trying to make a living. All I'm asking is for the committee to acknowledge this is a basic error and he needs to man up for his half of it."

"No-fault out-trades are a terrible precedent," Chris said, staring at the committee. "That would serve as a disincentive to check your trades immediately after making them." Chris finished with an aside that seemed to strike dead center. "If you think about it, sloppy trading is what could lead to our downfall to electronic trading."

The flash points had been played out. They finished up with some questions on the exact details and timing of the trade. Chris was feeling good. But then the arbitrator on the far end of the table said, "It is standard procedure to bring the person you did the trade with to verify that fact."

"He doesn't object to my statement that I traded with Barbra Lasky," Chris said. "Just the opposite."

"He does everything with Barbra Lasky," Rickey sneered.

"No, but I did that trade with her."

All Chris could think about was the man sitting to his right, Jack Fitzgerald. *Is it possible both Rickey and I could walk out of here losers?*

The committee wrapped up with a promise to deliver a decision within two days. Chris sprung to his feet and spontaneously thrust his hand down at Rickey who was still seated. "Jay, Jay," he said. Rickey seemed confused at first, but then shook Chris's hand without looking him in the eye.

On the elevator leaving with Fitzgerald, silence reigned. Chris decided to break it. "So, Jack, do you wish you had gotten in the pit-trading side of the business instead of working the phones?"

A wondrous look came across Fitzgerald's face. He shook his head. "Damn. That was something in there."

Two days later, the arbitrators delivered a unanimous decision: Jay Rickey had to eat the entire error.

Chris found himself not so much exultant as relieved by the verdict. Preston Beatty called to offer congratulations, as well as say he would nominate Chris for Elliott House Vice-President at the end of the year. Any suspicions had vanished in the glow of victory. In a business where bad endings were the rule, his trading career was intact.

Chapter Thirty-Two

RICHARD SHERRY'S CIGARETTE hung out, his sleeves were rolled up, and his tie knot hung almost halfway down his shirt. He had decided a raw veneer was best for this make-or-break meeting. He could not leave Karol Stanislav's investment to chance.

His appointment was with Joel Barret, the administrator of *Brubaker Brother's* commodity investment funds. When Sherry had been a rookie broker, he often heard people refer to fund administrators as *Santa Claus*. Soon he realized they weren't joking. Brubaker Brothers claimed a specific formula determined each customer's gains or losses. But Sherry knew the truth was more complicated; certain salesmen had more brawn and their clients got allocated better trades from the fund.

Sherry had struggled in his early years in the business. But then he hit upon a sales stratagem so brilliant he still marveled at it two decades later. Before big, market-shaking economic reports were released, Sherry would call up potential investors with hot news, telling half of them he had reliable information the report would be better-than-expected, and the other half the exact opposite. During these calls, he would periodically snap a stapler close to the phone receiver to impart a sense he was receiving breaking news. Upon release of the report, he would call back those prospects to whom he had given a correct prediction to remind them of his brilliance. He threw away the numbers of the other half. This tactic, which he considered so valuable he never shared it with other salesman, had helped him survive in a business with a frightful attrition rate.

The cigarette was spilling ash when he entered the room to meet Barrett. As usual Barrett had on a brown suit and dark tie, along with hair combed over to cover up his bald head. This guy should have been a librarian, Sherry thought. *I'll make short work of him.*

"Hello, Richard," Barrett said.

Sherry stood still, looking Barrett deep in the eye. "Joel," he uttered in a solemn fashion.

"We need to go over your accounts," Barrett said, adopting a businesslike tone.

"Joel," Sherry again spoke in a momentous tone. "This is a big day for both of us."

Barrett looked taken aback and Sherry wasn't going to let him regain the tempo. "Joel, it's time to take it to the next level."

"Well, sure."

"Joel, look at me." Sherry drew his head close to Barret's, looking like a concerned parent examining a child. "If we take care of the right customers, we—you—are going to have more business than you know what to do with."

Barrett squirmed before making a visible effort to regain his official tone. "Yes, of course. We are all hoping for more business at Brubaker Brothers. Let's look at your current accounts."

Barrett went through a list of Sherry's customers. One customer had a quarterly gain of 8% and another of 13%. Three of his bigger clients had losses allocated of 36, 39, and 47%. There was one account, however, that stuck out like a sore thumb and that was Sherry's smallest client, Karol Stanislav. His original investment of $10,000 had jumped to $16,500, a quarterly gain of 65%.

Right here, Sherry thought. *Make your move.* Despite his lack of formal education, he had quickly honed-in on the single most important fact of the futures and options business, namely that it was a zero-sum game. One man's gain was another's loss. Trickery, guile and deceit were necessary evils.

Sherry focused on the three clients that had been allocated losses of greater than 35%. Together they totaled several hundred thousand dollars. Sherry knew from experience that these clients would close their accounts, especially considering that he had assured them of doubling their money in six months. So why not flush them out completely?

Sherry pointed at the printout. "I'm surprised Karol Stanislav only made $6,500."

Barrett looked surprised. "Yes, but he only invested $10,000."

"Joel," Sherry said, tilting his head in a knowing way, "Karol Stanislav is one of the three most important men in the United States, and vastly underpaid as it is. On a slow day in Congress he's making decisions worth hundreds of millions of dollars. I would be embarrassed to even call him up about $6,500."

Barrett peered through his coke-bottle glasses at Sherry, unable to form a viable response. Sherry stared back, determined to make him speak up.

Finally, Barrett blinked. "Okay," he said. "Alright. Everybody has been marveling about Hillary Clinton's big gain in cattle futures. And we've got some winning trades in Japanese yen futures that have not yet been allocated. That would get Stanislav up to a hundred percent return."

The jugular, now.

"Joel," Sherry said, furrowing his brow to denote reasonableness, "look here. These folks, our clients, that lost 36, 37, and 47%. Frankly, I'm surprised they didn't do worse. A lot worse, in fact."

"But they've already lost hundreds of thousands of dollars as things now stand," Barret responded in dismay.

"Yes," Sherry acknowledged with a grim nod. "All three had the hots for gold and silver when I first talked to them. They jumped on the bandwagon too late. To be honest, I thought you were gonna tell me their losses were at least double that amount—in the 80-90% range."

Sherry couldn't help but think that he was the first salesman to ever approach a commodity funds administrator and lobby to allocate worse trades for some of his clients. Did Barrett understand where he was going with this? Sherry continued peering into Barret's eyes.

Suddenly, like a night owl, they flashed in recognition.

Sherry knew the job was mostly done. "Trust me," Sherry said to Barrett in his most assuring voice. "You are doing the right thing. Karol Stanislav never has let us down. And we're not going to let him down."

Chapter Thirty-Three

CHRIS ARRIVED AT 6:59 a.m. at the Elliott House desk, a bit more anxious than normal.

Before leaving the previous day, Jack Fitzgerald had said, "Chris, we've got a Potemkin village tomorrow morning. Be in by seven."

This was a company-wide joke that wasn't really a joke. *Potemkin* was the name of the Russian village in the middle of nowhere that Josef Stalin had constructed in the 1930s to impress foreign visitors with the miracle of the Soviet communist experiment. In Potemkin, factories measured up to western standards, roads and bridges featured newly-poured concrete, and all the houses had modern appliances, along with two cars in the garage.

On Potemkin village days at Elliott House, Preston Beatty was usually on hand to introduce a big-fish customer. Elliott House personnel went through various gyrations to wow the unsuspecting person. Chris Parker, all 83 inches of him, was always a big part of the façade.

At 7:10, Beatty arrived bedecked in his finest blue carapace, with a nattily-dressed visitor in tow. Chris had noticed New York traders visiting the CCE trading floor liked to affect a studied nonchalance, as if they had somewhere more important to be, even if the person was defecating in his pants. This man appeared to be no different. Beatty went around introducing Max Garnett, a hedge-fund manager in his early forties who specialized in handling Middle Eastern petrodollars. This was Beatty at his best. "Here Max is Blake Evans, or *Mr. Cash Arbitrage* as he's known to everyone. And please meet Jack Fitzgerald, *Mr. Charts,* which we hope you'll get a chance to hear more about." It was wide smiles all around.

Then they got to Chris. "Max, you were talking about the importance of following the market action in the Pit," Beatty said. "Here is our not-so-secret weapon. We receive and report to our customers every morsel of information from all corners of the Pit before anybody else." Beatty beamed, while Garnett appeared engaged.

"I see," he said, his mask vanishing as he looked Chris over. "I see." An inquisitive look came over his face, followed by a sheepish smile. "I've gotta ask. Did you play basketball?"

"It's not a violent enough sport for me," Chris joked, giving a glance towards the Pit.

Garnett returned a confused look.

Enter Beatty in jovial fashion. "He gets to play something similar to basketball every morning in the Pit."

"I can't wait to see," Garnett gushed.

Chris never minded playing the game. What worried him was that guests typically visited in mid-day when the Treasury Pit had thinned out. But this particular trader was said to be execution-oriented and had asked to see an opening. Chris had long been wary of openings anyway. Worse yet, as he climbed the ladder up to the Pit, he saw that all his hospitable neighbors—Malley, Tripp Cole, the Sleazebags—were on hand. Chris fastened both hands to the Pit-dividing rail. *Don't get thrown over.*

The opening bell rang. What ensued could have passed as a skit from a rubber room; Chris got bitch-slapped around like a beach ball. Three different times he tried pushing back, which only caused him to lose all purchase and end up in the clerk's box next to Danny.

"They want to know which companies are buying in there," Danny kept calling up. "Lemme know."

When Chris snuck a look back at the desk, he saw a sea of waving hands; everyone was putting on a dog-and-pony show for the visitor. The alarming thing, though, was what he caught out of the corner of his eye. Max Garnett, standing next to a concerned-looking Preston Beatty, had his hands open and mouth agape as he stared at Chris.

By the time Garnett departed the trading floor at 7:45, Chris was drenched in sweat and wondered if had heard the last from that visitor.

***

"DAMMIT, CHRIS. I'M sick and tired of watching those assholes shoving you all over the lot," Jack Fitzgerald said.

"*You're* sick of it," Chris concurred with emphasis.

"I mean, I'd really love it," Fitzgerald said, his face reddening, "if you could just take one of those pricks and throw him out of the Pit." This Vince Lombardi act rang with the conviction of a man who would never entertain the possibility of stepping foot in any futures pit. Even worse, the conversation was taking place in Preston Beatty's office, right in front of their mutual boss.

"Chris," Beatty opened up in an uncharacteristically grave tone, "we've seen enough of this abuse in the Pit. The whole way back to the office I had to convince Max Garnett that what he had just witnessed wouldn't affect the execution of his orders through Elliott House." He swallowed. "It was a tough sell."

Chris nodded.

"Bob Rooney," he said, then looked at Chris. "You know Rooney, right? Over at the Merc."

"Yes."

Rooney was one of those guys in the business Chris periodically envied, even if he didn't care for his type. He had been with Elliott House for two years as a broker assistant. In that short time, he had become the toast of after-work drinking. His forte was thrashing broker assistants of other companies.

"He just got suspended for a week from the Merc trading floor for punching another clerk," Beatty said. "I'm moving him to the CCE in the Treasury Pit with you."

There wasn't much Chris could say.

"I want our broker standing on the front row of the Pit like everybody else," Beatty continued, as if the idea had just suddenly occurred to him, compared to Chris who had spent years obsessing over that one issue.

"Okay," Chris said. "What, uh, what role do you foresee for Bob?" *Is he gonna be a broker or a broker's assistant?* Chris left the thought unspoken.

"We're gonna put him on one of our memberships so he can broker, along with you."

Like most tall, thin people, Chris had a tendency toward the *ostrich complex*—excessive laid back. But he realized he could be facing a de-facto demotion. "Let me ask, Preston," he said in an inquiring tone, "How do you envision us dividing the orders?"

"I'm telling you, we're coming in with some muscle," the former Navy running back dug in. "I'm not showing up to a heavyweight bout with a welterweight." Beatty flicked his fingers away as if not wanting to be bothered by the details.

Chris nodded, despite the insinuation he was a welterweight. He headed for the door, feeling old for the first time in his life.

Chapter Thirty-Four

BOB ROONEY AND Ray Malley could have been mistaken for professional boxers. It was 7:00 in the morning and both were rolling their necks as if in preparation for a heavyweight bout. Rooney's prizefighting frame and shock of black hair looked evenly matched with Malley's upper-body, which resembled the stern of a battleship.

This was Rooney's first day as a broker for Elliott House, but he had already earned his spurs in six weeks as Chris's assistant.

"Hey, no, you can't put your arms there. They're in my way," head Sleazebag Mickey Molina had reprimanded him on his first day as a clerk. Rooney had immediately assumed a guerilla pose with his limbs fully extended, while Molina stood there looking vexed.

Solly's assistants had been policing standing rights and wingspans for the last dozen years. But the first time one of them complained to Rooney, he silently drew an imaginary line from his eyes to his penis.

"We're doing a lot of business," Tripp Cole complained to him.

"Who are you?" Rooney responded.

"We have the right to fill our orders," Cole protested.

"We'll see about rights," Rooney shot back. "The clock is ticking, nancy-boy."

Cole had been unable to turn away before worry had protruded across his face.

Chris had stood by during these confrontations, his emotions oscillating erratically between gleeful at Rooney voicing his own long-held grievances, as well as a sense of inadequacy. However, the Elliott House phone brokers appeared little shy of ecstatic watching their new man taking on these untouchables. The only hiccough occurred when Rooney botched the count of orders coming in, causing Chris to buy an extra hundred contracts, which led to a $10,000 error. But everyone quickly forgot it; morale seemed better than in ages.

On Rooney's first morning as a broker, Jack Fitzgerald sidled up to Chris. "Why don't the two of you switch after a couple hours."

Chris pursed his lips and gave a quick assent.

At 9:30 he leaned down to say, "Bob, you ready to come up?"

Rooney nodded, and they changed positions. Chris stood on the clerk's step for the first time in five years, facing out at the Elliott House desk. He became self-conscious, as nearby traders and clerks looked curiously at him. Even stranger, he turned and saw Rooney squared up to the Pit. Ray Malley had a frown on his face and was turned sideways to accommodate Rooney's extra territory.

An Elliott House phone broker flashed Chris an order to sell 25 contracts. "Bob, sell twenty-five," he whispered.

Ray Malley heard it.

"95-12 bid," Malley shouted in Rooney's ear. "Come on, Twelve bid, Twelve bid for 25."

Rooney called forward to another local, "Sell you 25 at 95-12."

"What the fuck," Malley protested. "Can't you hear?"

"Wipe the tears," Rooney shot back.

Malley responded with a deep sigh and soon left the Pit looking disillusioned. This left the Sleazebags positioned right onto Rooney. Immediately they drew his ire.

"Hey, jagoff, can't you see I'm standing here," he reprimanded Mickey Molina, pressed like a wet sponge against his back.

"I've gotta watch the Chase Manhattan desk."

"Get the fuck off."

Molina put some light pressure on two of his fellow Sleazebags as he tried to back up a half-step. But the pursuit of bodies from behind thrust him into Rooney. Like a fastball thrown to Hank Aaron, Rooney struck a sharp blow, sending Molina and three other Sleazebags careening backwards, causing the people behind to push him back in Rooney's direction.

Realizing what lay in store, Molina leapt off the top step into the clerk's box, where he found himself snuggled up against Chris.

"Miss me?" Chris jibed.

"This sucks," Molina said. He called up to his comrades that he was going on break.

After just a half-hour as a broker, Rooney's prison-cell strategy was showing results.

***

THE BREAKING NEWS flashed across the board: Clinton had drawn even with Bush in the presidential race. Elliott House phone brokers took to their feet and began flashing orders to Chris, who fed them to Rooney.

He could hear Rooney banging them out in machine gun-like fashion around the Pit. "Sell you 50 Mick, yeah, yeah, you, fuck-head, that's who," he called out executing one order. "Sell 200, sell 100."

Basic physics dictated there would be some intercourse, with so many bodies packed together. Soon the bulkiest of the Sleazebags Dick Grutzkis collided into Rooney. What ensued sounded like a clap of lightning it happened so fast.

Rooney fired a punch into Grutzkis's solar plexus. The sound reverberated over the market bedlam.

"For Christ's sake," Grutzkis cried out.

"Too late, asshole," Rooney shot back.

"But."

"Buttfuck," Rooney cut him off.

Next, Sleazebag Jeremy Mutley got bounced harmlessly into Rooney. Without a word, Rooney grabbed him by the neck and pointed out of the Pit. Mutley, who claimed to be a descendant of Al Capone, knew what authority was worth obeying and stepped out of the Pit.

After the market calmed down, Chris called up to Rooney. "Bob, one of us usually goes on break about now. Wanna' go first?"

"No, you go."

Chris's mood was volatile. Worse yet, just as he got into the narrow hallway leaving the trading floor, he ran into the very last person he wanted to see at this moment.

"Chris, Chris, what's his name?" Barbra Lasky asked before reaching him.

"Who?"

"The guy, you know, for Elliott House doing all those orders."

Chris swallowed. "Bob Rooney."

"Where did he come from?"

"The Merc," Chris answered, trying to sound offhanded.

"Why did they put him in here?"

"We're adding some muscle to the lineup," Chris said, coming clean,

"Why didn't you do that? He just tossed those guys right off him." She looked besotted. Then she threw the bumper jack at him. "Can you introduce me?"

Chris felt like running into the bathroom to cry. "Yeah, sure," he said tossing his hand away as if nonchalant, before moping to the escalator which took him downstairs to the clerks' cafeteria.

***

THE NEXT MONTH was like a netherworld for Chris. Seemingly everybody wanted in on the Rooney-mobile. Elliott House personnel fawned over the new star. By the law of the jungle, Chris was now second-string broker.

However, unlike most upstart traders, Rooney didn't preen. Twice Chris walked up on Barbra trying to schmooze Rooney. Both times Chris accelerated past, and neither time did she salute him. But each time Rooney called for Chris and used the diversion to break away from her.

Meanwhile, Rooney proved brutal to the point of maniacal about meting out punishment to anyone infringing on his space. He and Ray Malley circled each other like a tiger and a bear.

One afternoon, the Elliott House trade checker called up, "Ray Malley says the price was 95-15 on that fifty-lot you sold him." Rooney whirled around and stuck his finger in Malley's face. "What the fuck is this shit? The price was 95-16."

Malley was taken aback. "We're out the price," he explained. "I thought the price was 95-15."

"You lying piece of shit," Rooney cut him off. "You wrote the wrong price on purpose."

"Cool down," Malley said. "If we've got a problem, I'll change it." He called down to his trade checker and told her to change the price on his card. Then, adopting a tone of magnanimity, he said, "Okay, I took the error."

"You didn't take shit," Rooney fired back. "You're a scumbag."

Malley feigned like he was drawing back. But before he knew what had happened, Rooney nailed him in the stomach, with the sound reverberating all the way back to the Elliott House desk.

"Heaargruyuu," Malley grunted, emitting what sounded like some indigenous sound as he doubled over. Everyone in the vicinity looked stunned. He tried to recover by straightening up and demanding, "What the fuck?"

"Don't 'what the fuck' me," Rooney shouted from a boxer's stance, his face a purple rage.

Malley shook his head, but looked ashen-faced.

Chris had always found violence abhorrent, but couldn't help feeling jubilant at seeing the King-Bully himself get his comeuppance. However, that was marred when he glanced back at the Elliott House desk. From the floor manager down to the lowliest runner, they looked like religious fundamentalists in various states of rapture at the sight of their broker nailing the Pit Leviathan. They began waving at Chris to get Rooney's attention and throw mock high-fives at him. Rooney took it all in stride as if he had just eked out a first down.

He had achieved his *raison d' etre* of gaining Elliott House space in the Treasury Pit, along with renewed respect. Who could argue with the whole thing?

***

IRONICALLY, THERE WAS one person who did not seem convinced he had made it, Rooney, himself. As the days went by, Chris became subtly aware of the brawler's self-doubt.

He noticed Rooney staring at his cards for long periods, trying to add up his trades. His visage morphed from confident, bordering on bloodthirsty, when dealing with other traders, to dubious and troubled. Several times Chris leaned over his shoulder and saw he had purchased or sold the wrong number of contracts.

"Hey, Bob, you need to buy twenty more. Hey, Bob, you oversold by fifteen. Hey, Bob, ..."

"Oh yeah, right," Rooney would say and quickly correct the imbalance.

He also had trouble remembering who he had traded with. Chris took to whispering various traders' names over Rooney's shoulders to help him reconstruct his trades. A couple times, when nobody was within earshot, Rooney murmured an embarrassed, "Thank you."

Why am I bailing him out?

Nonetheless, Rooney's halo continued. Almost all of Ellliott House's business was going to Rooney, with only crumbs falling to Drew Solly's brokerage group.

Chris found himself becoming more withdrawn. When he passed Barbra Lasky in the hallway, she looked on him like he was some sort of handicapped person.

Should I get out of the business?

Chapter Thirty-Five

ROONEY'S JUGGERNAUT LASTED six weeks. His destruction took less than a half-hour.

Less than a half-hour before the close, a Gallup Poll was released: Clinton 45, Bush 41. Clinton had his first lead of the campaign. Given Wall Street's natural predilection for Republicans, cascades of hot sell orders came from New York, London, and Tokyo. Four Elliott House phone brokers flashed orders: Sell 50. Sell 200. Sell 100. Sell 300. Chris relayed the orders to Rooney.

"Sold, Sold," Rooney started screaming in all directions, while throwing elbows to clear his wing-span. He continued shouting, "Sold, sold, sold." But Chris noted he sounded shrill.

94-23, 94-22, 94-21, 94-19... the market was in freefall.

The Elliott House phone brokers stood with their palms open, looking at Chris. "Are we filled yet?" they asked, pleading and demanding at the same time.

Chris leaned over Rooney's shoulder. "Sold 'em yet?"

"No," Rooney shot back.

The market plunge hesitated a second. Chris could hear it trading 94-14 and 94-15; but Rooney appeared to be having trouble selling over 25 contracts to anyone.

Suddenly, Elliott House phone broker Bucky Avant called out, "Hey, there's an *uptick* from 94-14 to 94-15."

All the other Elliott House phone brokers turned and pointed at the board. Chris knew what they meant. By CCE rules, Rooney could not give the customer a price any lower than 94-14 because of the uptick in price to 94-15.

"Hey, Bob. There was an uptick from 94-14 to 94-15," he quickly informed him.

Rooney didn't respond and now the market was falling again, 94-13, 94 12, 94-11.... He continued flailing away trying to sell.

Two more Elliott House phone brokers picked up phones and flashed in orders to sell 150 and 100 contracts. Chris had no choice but to give the orders to a panicked-looking Rooney, who now had a total of $100 million of futures contracts to sell.

"Give it away," Rooney called back, sounding helpless.

"I'll try," Chris said and turned to arch-foe, Tripp Cole.

"Hey, Tripp," Chris asked, "can you sell 250 contracts for us?"

"We're full," he shot back. This rejection would prove to be infinitely more Machiavellian than any violence he had ever meted out to Chris.

"Bob," Chris said in a sympathetic tone, "sell 250 more."

Rooney did not acknowledge him. "Repeat, sell 250 more," Chris said.

Again, no response from Rooney.

The phone brokers kept screaming at Chris to report prices on their sell orders. Finally, he had no choice but to give them a confirmed trade at the uptick price. "You're filled at 94-14," he reported to four different phone brokers, and could read their lips reporting that price to different customers.

"Bob," Chris said, "I had to give them fills on those first 800 contracts of sales at 94-14."

Rooney looked frozen and said nothing, focusing on his trading cards instead of the Pit. In the middle of it all, Mickey Molina lost his balance and went stumbling into Rooney.

"Sorry, sorry," Molina said, holding up his hands like he was under arrest. "He pushed me."

Rooney ignored him, a surefire sign things were terribly amiss.

An Elliott House phone broker picked up a phone and fired another sell order for 500 contracts to Chris. He had no choice and dropped the sympathetic tone. "Sell 500," he shouted to Rooney. *I'm just doing my job.*

Rooney appeared in outright paralysis. "Anything?" Chris asked after a half-minute. "The customer needs a fill."

Suddenly Rooney turned to Chris. "You."

"Me?"

"Do it," he said, pointing to his spot in the Pit.

Chris squinted at Rooney, trying to read his face.

Rooney made the first move, brushing past Chris off the top step.

Chris took a step up to plant himself in his old spot. Quickly he saw what had been troubling Rooney; the locals appeared spooked and were shying away from taking any big trades. Chris commenced firing trades across the way, trading with eleven different people around the pit to sell 500 contracts. Meanwhile, the market kept tumbling.

When the closing bell rang at 2:00, the Elliott House trade checker rushed up to Rooney. "Do you have the cards for these orders?"

Rooney said nothing.

Chris became worried Rooney might take the time-honored tack of blaming the broker's assistant—himself—for not feeding him all the sell orders. Was Rooney's terrible inclination to violence matched by dishonesty? He would soon find out.

Jack Fitzgerald had packed his briefcase and headed for the exits when Chris called over, "Jack."

Fitzgerald gave him a quizzical look.

Chris bent his head toward Rooney and whispered, "Looks like he might have undersold."

"By how many?"

Chris shook his head. "Maybe a lot."

Chris and Fitzgerald looked at Rooney who was shouting, "Who did I sell 75 at 95-07 to? Hey, hey, guys. Come on, who was it?"

Chris knew this was a fool's errand. Even a trading *naif* could see Rooney was lost and simply erase any buy trades with him from their card.

Chris tried assisting. "Hey, Bob, you were yelling 'Sell you 75' to somebody in that corner over there." But the clock kept ticking without any buyers turning up for Rooney. "Let's see what you've got for sure," he finally suggested.

Rooney handed off his cards, and Chris added up Rooney's sales which totaled 850 contracts. Then Chris added up the sell order slips—1,400 contracts. He had undersold by 550 contracts. Given that the market had moved two full points, this was a loss of $2,000 loss per contract. The error had reached into seven-figures.

The Sleazebags looked on. "Did he find everything?" Mickey Molina whispered, trying to feign sympathy.

"I don't know," Chris dissembled.

Thirty minutes later no other buyers had appeared. Fitzgerald tiptoed over to Chris. "How bad does it look?"

Chris shook his head.

"Give me a ballpark," Fitzgerald said.

"Hold on." Chris walked over to the trade checker and began comparing Rooney's trading cards with the order slips. Five minutes later, he handed Fitzgerald a slip of paper. It read, $1,032,175.

Chris knew this was when Fitzgerald was at his best. Having once traded on Wall Street, he had seen his fair share of disasters.

"Okay," he said, "we've got to get rid of this tonight. Can you do it?"

The CCE had added a night trading session, to correspond with the next morning's opening in Tokyo.

"Yeah," Chris answered. "But you know night trading. It's easy to get whipsawed."

"Hide it as best you can," Fitzgerald said.

Five hours later, Chris stood in the mostly empty Treasury Pit. Word had it that Treasuries had responded to the big selloff in Chicago and New York by continuing lower in early Tokyo trading. The 7:00 p.m. bell rang. The market opened at 93-21, a half-point lower than the 2:00 Chicago close. Rooney's error had metastasized by another quarter. Worse yet, in the thinly-traded night market, it was difficult to imagine being able to sell 550 contracts without crushing the market even further.

One broker was bidding for 45 contracts. Chris elected to sit tight like a poker player, not wanting to set off a selling stampede. Everyone in the Pit knew he was a daytime broker in the Treasury Pit; there was only one reason he could be here.

Suddenly the Merrill Lynch broker bid 93-21 for 500 contracts.

"Sold, Sold, sold" Chris erupted in Vesuvian fashion. The Merrill broker looked at him with surprise, before acknowledging, "Buy 500."

"This truth is out," Mark Lato cracked and rumors of a big loss began reverberating around the Pit. Chris easily sold another fifty contracts before stepping out of the Pit to begin the four-mile twilight walk home. But before he left, he added up Rooney's error. It had increased by another $250,000 just from the afternoon to the evening session. The final tally was $1,282,175.

The old CCE saying that there is no substitute for violence had finally met its match. Rooney's brains had not proven equal to his brawn.

Chapter Thirty-Six

IT WAS A no-brainer for Chris to show up early the next morning. However, Rooney was already stationed in the Pit, looking like a running back raring to bounce back from a bad game.

Jack Fitzgerald came in a minute before the opening bell, and immediately motioned for Chris with his index finger. On the way back to the desk, he passed the Elliott House buzzards.

"Hey, Chris," Hank Downey whispered, "how big was the error?"

Chris shrugged at the voyeuristic Downey and continued toward Fitzgerald.

"Chris," Fitzgerald said in a low, controlled voice, "tell Rooney to meet me in Beatty's office in twenty minutes. You take back over."

He did a beeline for the Pit, where he leaned over to whisper to Rooney. However, the Sleazebags were in their own throes of voyeurism, attempting to eavesdrop, so Chris decided to write the message on a trading card and fold it up.

Rooney stared at the card. His hard face, which had never betrayed fear, was etched in depression. He wordlessly handed off the deck of customer orders to Chris, before stepping out of the Treasury Pit for the last time, a perp-walk many a mortal had taken before him.

When Chris ran into Fitzgerald at lunchtime, the floor manager informed him that Rooney had been transferred back to the Chicago Mercantile Exchange.

"As a broker?" Chris asked.

Fitzgerald shook his head. "Clerk."

"How did Beatty take the error?"

"Hey, it was his idea to bring in a bruiser," Fitzgerald said defensively.

An idea came to Chris and he leaned forward. "Listen, Jack, one quick thing. Those assholes behind me."

"Yeah, those assholes," Fitzgerald noted with mirth. "The Sleazebags."

"Yeah," Chris said intently. "Look, since Rooney was in there, they haven't been near the dicks."

A knowing smile broke out on Fitzgerald's face. "At least we got something out of it."

"Let's act like Rooney is sick, but will be back in the Treasury Pit soon."

"Yeah, okay, you deal with it," Fitzgerald said, before making a pushing motion with his arms and walking away.

When Chris got back into the Pit, he decided to preempt the Sleazebags, who had already asked twice that morning about Rooney. Looking at three of them, he asked, "Any of you guys got fever?"

"No. Why?" Molina asked.

"Bob Rooney's been diagnosed with the Hong Kong flu."

"What the hell's that?" Mutley asked.

"Beats me," Chris said. "But they told me to get my fever checked down at the infirmary."

The Sleazebags looked confused. The next few days Chris kept reminding them to get their fever checked. Dick Grutzkis did and reported back with relief that he did not have any symptoms. But the longer Rooney was gone, the more the Sleazebags began encroaching and pressuring him crotch-ward into the dreaded rail. The interrogations became more aggressive. One day, out of the blue, Molina said, "You know, I stayed after the bell that day. And I'm telling you there's no way he got everything filled and carded up right."

"Would you like his phone number to tell him that?" Chris kept his eyes on Molina.

"I'm just saying."

The next day Mutley announced, "Parker, this has all the earmarks of a cover-up."

"You'd know something about those."

"Trust me," Mutley said in his most confident voice, "if we decide to cover something up, there wouldn't be any questions."

Chris still had a syrupy tone left over from the Rooney era, but he could feel the walls closing.

***

JEREMY MUTLEY LEFT the CCE at 11:30 to go meet one of his Cicero mates at *Rostofino's*, a greasy spoon on Wacker Drive. The Chicago Mercantile Exchange was across the street and clerks frequently popped in for lunch.

Mutley arrived first and decided to order a meatball sandwich before grabbing an empty table. A few minutes later his friend Johnny Veckione showed up in a red Mercantile Exchange trading jacket.

"Hey, Veck," Mutley greeted him with his mouth so full it looked like a baby pig had been stuffed in there.

"What's up, Mut?"

Veckione ordered and hurried to the table, where Mutley had already demolished most of his sandwich.

"How're things over at the CCE?" Veckione asked.

"The Irish are teaching me how to drink," Mutley answered.

"How about to trade?"

"Oh, you know. There's plenty go around," Mutley answered with a smile.

He looked off to the side when his posture suddenly became rigid. Bob Rooney had walked in. What piqued his interest even more was what Rooney was wearing: a puke-yellow Chicago Mercantile Exchange clerk's jacket.

"Hey, Veck, hey," Mutley lowered his head. "Hey, Veck."

"Yeah?" Veckione looked confused.

"Veck, hey, Veck. Listen up, Veck," Mutley whispered. "I want you to slowly—very slowly—look over to your right. See that guy standing in line, dark hair and a scar on his face?"

Veckione took a glance and turned back, shaking his head. "Him!"

"You know him?" Mutley asked.

"Hell, yeah," Veckione muttered. "Well, actually no. And I ain't looking to get to know him either."

"Why, what's up?"

"He's a clerk in the Eurodollars," Veckione said. "Danny Cicco—you remember Cicco from Alexander IV elementary?"

"Yeah, Cicco."

"Remember how Cicco was always the badass? Yesterday he and that guy over there got into it over which one was crowding the other. All of a sudden that guy rips him in the gut. Man, you should have seen Cicco afterwards. I mean, this dude hadn't lost no fight since grade school."

Mutley leaned forward. "You're telling me he works at the Merc now?"

"Yeah, he works there. Look at that jacket."

"You're absolutely sure," Mutley pressed him. "I mean a hundred percent sure he's working on the Merc floor now?"

Confusion was writ over Veckione's face. "Hell, yeah, I'm sure. I see him every day."

"Veck, look, sorry, but one more time," Mutley continued bearing down. "He is a current employee right now, as in yesterday, today, and tomorrow."

"What the fuck?"

Mutley jumped to his feet. "Veck, I gotta hop." He patted his friend on the back while hurrying out. As the door was closing Mutley snagged one last view of Rooney, who was stuffing a Philly cheese steak in his Chicago Mercantile Exchange clerk's jacket.

He hurried back across the river and down Madison Street. Within four minutes, Mutley had entered the CCE building, another minute-and-a-half up to the trading floor, and less than sixty seconds to climb up into the Treasury Pit. He filed in behind three of his fellow Sleazebags, who stood watching Chris Parker offering to sell 300 contracts at 94-14.

Mutley could not cover his excitement. "Guys, listen up. At lunch, guess who I seen in a Merc clerk's jacket?" Before any of them could venture a guess, he supplied the answer. "Rooney."

"Rooney?" Molina repeated. "You mean," he added, pointing to the spot where Rooney had enjoyed his moments of fame.

"Are you a hundred-percent sure?" Grutzkis asked, looking him in the eye.

"Yes," Mutley assured them. "I seen him at Rostofino's. A friend of mine at the Merc told me he's a clerk over there. And listen to this: yesterday he clocks some moose from my old neighborhood."

There was a brief silence, before Grutzkis said, "So Parker was lying."

"Of course, he was lying," Mutley said, his voice regaining its old menacing tone.

"Yep," the other Sleazebags said, their cheeks flushing with elation. High-fives broke out. Then in unison, they turned to Chris Parker. It was time to dispense some village justice.

***

CHRIS FIRST FELT the hand, Mickey Molina's mitt placed on the small of his back. He had not felt the hand in several weeks. But now it had him corseted again.

"Hey," Chris erupted at Molina, "I've got a big order." He tried wiggling out and squaring up as he screamed, "Sell 300 at 95-14."

"Hey, Parker," the rodent-faced Mutley called out, his eyes gleaming like a werewolf's. "How's Rooney coming along with that Hong-Kong flu?"

"How long did you think you could hide it from us?" Molina asked, comfortably back in wise-guy mode.

Chris strained sideways against the rail trying to maintain focus on the market.

"So, Parker, tell us," Mutley asked ravenously, "was the whole thing your idea?"

"Sell 300 at fourteen," Chris continued shouted with extra vehemence.

Mutley yelled up, "Haven't you heard what happens when the *capo* is gone?"

When Chris acted like he didn't hear, Mutley spat, "Doesn't look like you'll be eating spaghetti tonight." He followed it up with a hideous laugh that sent chills through Chris.

"That asshole cost me $1,800 the last day he was here," Joe D' Abruzzo spat.

Chris continued with his Statue-of-Liberty pose. From four Sleazebags back, he heard another voice. "By the way,

Parker. Thanks for just standing there while your man was firing bombs at everybody. I've still got a welt from where your assassin slugged me."

Chris finally realized his above-the-battle pose was hopeless. "What was I supposed to do?" he protested.

"Oh, okay," said Molina in a voice dripping with derision. "You had nothing to do with it."

"What gives you the right to be here without him?" Grutzkis demanded to know.

Don't overdramatize it, Chris told himself. *This is just a bunch of bullies on a trading floor.* "Sell 300 at fourteen," he continued shouting, hands held high as lactic acid coursed through his arms. Finally, it began trading 93-14 around the Pit. "Sell 300 at fourteen," Chris screamed, jumping to his toes to accentuate his offer to sell $30 million of bonds. Molina began kicking violently at his feet.

Chris bounced laterally off the rail, then up against Molina, who shouted, "Get the fuck off."

Suddenly, Chris heard the big local Gary D'Arco scream, "93-14 bid.".

"Sold, Gary. Sold, sold, Gary," Chris yelled, still bobbing. "Sell you 300." But D' Arco was to his left, and the Sleazebags stood in his way.

"Stay the fuck off," Molina berated him.

Suddenly Chris felt a sharp knee jab just below the groin. The last thing he saw was D' Arco looking at him quizzically, as Chris signaled selling him 300 contracts while crashing to the floor at the foot of the Sleazebags.

"Get outta' the pit," he heard Grutzkis shouting down at him as he lay in the fetal position. "You're gone. Outta here."

Chris tried edging forward along the floor, but the traders in front had him blocked off. Fortunately, he was able to reach up and grab the rail to pull himself to his feet

The slim Alabaman had tasted physical freedom the last several weeks; modus vivendi was no longer enough. He was irate at being beaten roughhoused in the world's largest market by bunch of guttersnipes. In a flash, he remembered the words from *The Master*. "Your power, Chris. It all comes from the center. Let 'em have it from the center."

Out of the blue, Chris launched his best center-line punch at Molina's chest. It made a resounding thud that carried over the roar in the Pit. Molina was staggered and fell to his knees.

What have I done? He soon found out.

Sounding like a pack of dogs attacking a car, the other Sleazebags lurched in unison at their wide-open target. Grutzis latched on to Chris, allowing Mutley open season to fire punches at his rib cage. Fortunately, they knocked Chris loose just as the blows were becoming unbearable. Like a dying walrus, he heaved himself into the clerk's box and managed to scrum down the Pit ladder as the closing bell rang. Despite bearing sharp pain, he raced through the slalom course of clerks to find Gary D' Arco on the far-left side of the Pit.

"Gary," he called up to the huge trader in a winded voice, "did I sell you 300 at 93-14?"

"I couldn't tell," he answered. "Do you need the trade?"

"Yes."

"I'll buy 'em then."

I wish the hell I stood near him.

When Chris got back to the Elliott House desk, Jack Fitzgerald had his briefcase loaded on the way out.

"They got you again, huh," he said in a conversational tone.

"You might say."

"Those inbred assholes," Fitzgerald said with a look of annoyance. He started for the exits before turning back and saying, "Does this whole thing have to be such a shit show?"

PART III

Chapter Thirty-Seven

BY KAROL STANISLAV'S lights, he deserved to live large. Many agreed.

Rare did the week pass when he was in Chicago that Stanislav didn't step foot in *Morton's Steakhouse,* considered by many to be the finest in America. The lobbyists with whom he dined heeded his every whim, as he belted down three or four brandies with his salad, while waiting for the steak and potatoes to arrive. What bothered him was the caliber of the people treating him. They were all making several times his congressional salary and their lifestyle was handed to them. Yet every time he got in proximity, he had the same recurring thought: *I'd make minced meat out that guy, whether in a corporate board room or congressional committee hearing.*

Then there were those traders, which he had always viewed with avuncular amusement. The hard-drinking, colorful grain traders in the 1960s and 1970s at the Chicago Board of Trade (CBT) had been more of his type, whereas this new crowd of financial futures and options traders defied the imagination. Twenty-five-year old traders would come barnstorming into Morton's and sit down for a bout of eating and drinking that easily cleared a hundred dollars per person. He couldn't get it out of his head that, without his legislative sorcery, those same people would be sacking groceries and driving taxi cabs. In the last few years he would see some of them at the city airport loading up suitcases, skis, and golf clubs into private planes.

The part that bothered Stanislav the most was in the summer at Lake Geneva. He was exceedingly comfortable rubbing shoulders with the Wrigleys, Crowns, and Blaines that had patronized this tony resort for the past century. They showed class, whereas the newbies came off as punks. There were rumors of cocaine binges, which especially worried him because his youngest daughter had married a trader and his oldest hung out with them.

***

THIS MEMORIAL DAY weekend had a special poignancy for Stanislav. It was a glorious time of year in the Midwest and high-time to put the palace politics of Washington aside.

But on this occasion, the Stanislav household was in a fragile mood. His wife Sheila had called him in Washington two weeks before to report their youngest daughter had been diagnosed as a cocaine addict. Stanislav had to fork out $26,000 for her intensive rehabilitation at a getaway in Minnesota. The cost of care for his special-needs son was skyrocketing. Because he had also ponied up $10,000 for a commodity trading account, he had been forced to take out a loan against his assets. Stanislav's dream of his own Lake Geneva home seemed light years away.

He decided to take a low-key approach this weekend, staying in with family and having a barbecue. *This is the way Middle America lives, and that's the real me.* But such a thought left him in a subdued mood.

The phone rang. Being an old-school male, Stanislav walked by without picking up. However, when he glanced down he recognized the name on the keyboard: *Richard Sherry.* He had never met the commodities broker handling his money and decided to answer.

"Yes."

"Mr. Chairman, Richard Sherry at Brubaker Brothers Investments. How are you?"

"Tolerable, Richard. And yourself?"

"I just want you to know that we sent out your statement this morning. When it arrives, you will see your quarterly results."

On Capitol Hill, Stanislav preferred to let the counter-party show his hand first. But after a couple seconds of silence, curiosity got the best of him. "Anything I need to know?" he asked, feeling like a kid at a bingo game.

"Things are going well," Sherry answered with a southern drawl. "Very well, in fact."

"Is that so?"

"Let's see," Sherry said, seguing to a business-like tone. "Your initial balance was $10,000."

"Yes, I believe that is correct," Stanislav said, sensing the drama building.

"Well, your ending balance is $643,253."

"My what? Wait, repeat that," Stanislav demanded, but quickly got ahold of himself. "Repeat that figure please, Richard, would you?"

"$643,253," Sherry stated again.

"So, let me see," he probed a hair quicker than he wished, "what is my gain so far?"

"$633,253." "Six hundr..," Stanislav began blurting, before catching himself. He took a couple of deep breaths to corral his racing heart. *Act like you do in front of the Committee back in Washington.* Stanislav compressed his lips, but his entire body felt lit up like a Christmas tree. He realized he was breathing through his mouth and his throat was dry. Was this just dumb luck? In one stroke of fortune, all the things he had been worrying about: his daughter's treatment and his son's expenses, low congressional salaries, a vacation home in Lake Geneva, appeared moot. *Dammit, I deserve it.*

"Mr. Chairman, I'll let you get back to your family. We just wanted to give you an update on your account."

"Richard," Stanislav said, his chairman's voice returning. "Mike (Kilpatrick) told me you were a prudent manager."

"Thank you, Mr. Chairman. And let me say we have every confidence that we will be able to continue generating handsome returns on your investment going forward."

"Good. And, uh, Richard, one other thing," Stanislav said, fighting the feeling of overwhelming excitement. "The money in that account—how do I go about transferring it to my regular bank account?"

"Would you like to transfer it?"

"Yes," Stanislav said, feeling a twinge of embarrassment. He was effectively admitting he needed the money right now.

"Okay, we'll cut you a check today. It should be in your mailbox by next Tuesday."

"Good deal."

"Mr. Chairman. We look forward to continuing our successful relationship with you."

Stanislav hung up the phone before allowing himself a broad chuckle.

Chapter Thirty-Eight

LIKE MOST MORTALS, Jan Silverstein was a study in contradictions. For starters, she was a southern Jew. Despite her Yale education, she had never had allowed her innate sophistication to get in the way of loyalty to her native South Carolina. At age forty-two, she had rejected three marriage proposals, and seemed happy living an urbane lifestyle on the north side of Chicago.

There was the matter of her job. Silverstein worked in the executive offices of the Chicago Commodities Exchange. "I'm there to make a living," she stated plainly, although one couldn't help but notice a grimace. By conventional standards it was a good position, paying well and giving her access to all the top people.

The top people? That was what most people would call them. One thing was for sure; they were different from the erudite lady that was quartered up there with them. The great irony was that, like many Jews, she considered the naked pursuit of money an unworthy endeavor. Compared to music, the arts, the sciences, literature, and philosophy, it paled. On the forays she had taken to the trading floor, she noticed that many traders appeared to be of Jewish ancestry. It nagged at her conscience.

The other unusual thing was how the powers-that-be at the CCE had warmed up to her, enamored of Silverstein's worldliness and high-brow ways. But she also knew how to hold her ground. Once, when the inner circle began discussing a campaign to sexually smear a congressman who had been railing against special tax breaks for commodity traders, she snapped, "Oh, come on. Get off it." The executives went quiet before retreating to their offices, and the idea died a quick death.

Later during the FBI investigation, which had led to the indictment of thirty traders at the CCE, the exchange chairman Kurt Bowles decided to preempt it. He hired a private detective to find out which traders were facing indictment. When the detective returned with the names, Bowles saw an opportunity to make the exchange appear forward-looking; he had the CCE disciplinary committee draw up phantom charges against all thirty traders, along with a recommendation they be kicked off the floor. When Silverstein found out, she walked into Bowles's office and snapped, "Over my dead body with these fake charges." The dictatorial Bowles sat ashen-faced as she berated him. The plot was soon dust.

The current chairman, Dean Beman, had never known what to make of Miss Silverstein. She had a certain statuesque beauty about her that hadn't escaped his notice. Despite being gray-headed and well into his fifties, he routinely dated much-younger models and television personalities. But when he looked her in the eye and asked her to have dinner one weekend, she replied, "Thank you, but I'm attending a gallery showing." Beman sloughed away.

Nonetheless, Beman found himself confiding to her on occasion. "I have trouble clicking with Karol Stanislav," he lamented. "It bothers me. When Kurt was chairman, they were best pals."

"Why do you think that is?" she asked.

In a rare admission, he said, "We have similar ways. I don't believe I've ever met such an overpowering personality." He even seemed to laugh at himself, for once.

Silverstein consoled herself that she was sometimes able to steer these alpha males away from their worst impulses.

At least, so she thought. But then James Luxem, who was a special assistant to CCE President Mike Kilpatrick, walked into her office one Monday morning in late February.

"Hey, James," Jan greeted him. "How was your weekend?"

"Different," he said with a laugh. "I got called down here for a meeting."

"Down here? This weekend?"

"Yeah, Saturday night at 8:00."

"With Mike, or who?"

"Yeah, Mike. Also, Dean Beman and Karol Stanislav."

Silverstein didn't try to hide her dismay. "Dean Beman and Mike Kilpatrick met Karol Stanislav this past Saturday night? In these offices?"

Luxem was uncharacteristically mum.

"What in the world was it about?"

Luxem hesitated as Silverstein fixed her alert eyes on him, knowing he would soon crumble. "An electronic trading system they're planning in New York," he answered, coming clean.

"Oh," she said, bored as ever by the grubby details of trading.

"Well, one other thing. Stanislav is planning to open a trading account."

"A trading account—Stanislav? What is a politician doing opening a trading account?"

Luxem threw up his hands. "There's really no reason he can't trade just like everybody else."

She was having trouble believing him. "The Chairman and President of the Chicago Commodities Exchange meet with the most powerful member of Congress in downtown Chicago on a Saturday night to convince him to open a trading account. That's what you're telling me?"

"I guess so."

"I've heard enough," she said, rolling her eyes. What she didn't know was she hadn't heard anything yet.

Chapter Thirty-Nine

CONGRESSMAN LONNIE HERBERT scurried around the committee meeting room, in a hurry for the Commodity Futures and Options Subcommittee to convene.

He had listened to all the testimony, visited the trading floors, and read everything he could get his hands on. Six different European exchanges had already switched to electronic trading. Volumes and liquidity were increasing. Most tellingly, the customers overwhelmingly preferred electronic trading to open-outcry pit trading. It was faster, cheaper, and more transparent. They could expect better prices on their orders. Herbert stood ready to give approval to Wall Street's proposed electronic system.

"What about Stanislav?" the New York bankers, who were part of his congressional district, had been pressing him. "Doesn't he always protect the exchanges in Chicago?"

"No doubt about it," he acknowledged. "But he usually doesn't show up at subcommittees. "If we can get quick approval there, he will have a tough time blocking it."

That news had left them buoyant. Herbert's staff expected to get at least ten of the sixteen votes in sub-committee to support the new electronic trading system.

At five minutes before 10:00, committee members sauntered over to a long table and took seats in front of their nameplates. A quart bottle of sparkling water and a bowl of peanuts, compliments of the American taxpayer, were positioned in front of each of them. Herbert sat in the chairman's seat as the acting chair. Then the door opened.

It was Joe Wolf, Stanislav's executive assistant and a man widely feared in his own right. One national news magazine had recently rated Wolf the fifth most powerful person on Capitol Hill, despite not even being a member of Congress. It was said that Wolf handled the *m's* and Stanislav the *b's*, millions and billions.

Lonnie Herbert's stomach sank, because he knew Wolf wouldn't be here if someone else wasn't also going to be on hand. Indeed, Wolf formed the point of a triangular-moving formation known on Capitol Hill as the *Stanislav V*. Sure enough, embedded in the vortex was Karol Stanislav, Chairman of the House Futures and Options Subcommittee. Three serious-looking white males followed without expression in the path of the Chairman. The atmosphere in the room morphed from cool and businesslike, to electric, and then after a couple more seconds, fearful. What was *he* doing here?

The Chairman, tall, expansive, and gregarious, marched around the room pumping hands like he was at a class reunion. When Stanislav was looking away, Herbert hopped like a bedbug from the chairman to the co-chairman's seat.

"How are you, Lonnie?" he asked when he got to Herbert, now safely in his old seat.

"Good," Herbert answered, feeling uptight. "And you?"

"Fair to middling."

Herbert and Stanislav exemplified a Washington phenomenon, two people of diametrically-opposed backgrounds and temperaments being thrown together in the conduct of the nation's critical business. Herbert came from a middle-class Jewish family in Queens, New York and had earned a PhD in economics from NYU. With his thick spectacles, bald head, and pinched facial features, he didn't look or act like a superstar. He gladly took to the more toilsome aspects of being a congressman, earning him the nickname *The Inquisitor*, for his exhaustive examination of committee witnesses.

Stanislav sat next to Herbert, who felt overshadowed by the strapping man next to him. However, that was not the problem. It was the Chairman's unwavering policy of vicious retribution to anybody who opposed him. The committee members sat in chairs with rolling wheels. However, Herbert knew that was not always the case. Over the years a few of the more wayward committee members had arrived in committee after voting against Stanislav only to find the wheels had been removed from their chairs. But that was just temporary humiliation. He could also ruin a member's career by arranging with the Speaker of the House to have the member stripped of their prestigious committee assignments.

What is he going to do now? Herbert wondered.

Stanislav took his seat and went through the sub-committee protocol he had been observing for thirty-five years. "The issue before this sub-committee today is the proposed electronic-trading system of the New York banks."

Right away, Herbert got bad vibes, something about the way he said *the New York banks*. If it became a matter of New York vs. Chicago, he knew his goose was cooked.

For the next half-hour proponents gave detailed cases for the benefits an electronic system would bring in terms of increased competitiveness, deeper liquidity, and lower costs.

Stanislav sat expressionless until all the supporters had spoken. "Now we would like to hear the opposition."

"The Chicago commodity markets are the envy of the world," one representative from the western suburbs of Chicago said, with palpable hometown pride in his voice.

Again, the Chairman didn't move an eyebrow. When the dissenters had spoken, he announced, "The members shall recess until 2:00, at which point they shall report back for a vote on the issue at hand."

He banged the gavel and headed out the door with his staff in their V-formation. And that's when the day's real work began for Karol Stanislav.

***

BACK IN HIS cavernous Capitol Hill office, the chairman sat behind his desk waiting to hear the real story. Adorning the walls were photos of a beaming Karol Stanislav, with every president from Dwight Eisenhower to George Bush.

Jake Lipsky, who had been rummaging around the committee room talking to other staff members, walked in carrying a manila folder.

"How does it look?" Stanislav asked, sounding like a dentist debriefing one of his hygienists.

"We're down 10-6," Lipsky answered. "Here's the list." He drew a piece of paper from the folder and handed it to his boss. There were two columns of names. Stanislav focused on the one with ten names.

"Who are our three best lambs?" he asked.

"Perkins has got that oil-depreciation allowance thing up before Appropriations. Greenwald has been pushing hard for the pharmaceutical cap. And Blakely is live-or-die on agriculture price supports."

Stanislav nodded. "Get Greenwald first," he said. A staffer headed for the door.

Another staffer handed Stanislav a file on Greenwald with a list of his pet issues. Five minutes later Glenn Greenwald appeared in the doorway of the Chairman's office, looking like a schoolboy who had been summoned to the headmaster's office.

"Could I speak with Congressman Greenwald alone, please?" Stanislav said.

He had learned over the years that even loyal staff members couldn't resist bragging about the verbal thrashings they administered to members of Congress to get their votes. Recently, a staff member had crowed in the newspaper about how they had 'beat the shit' out of one congressman to get his vote.

Greenwald and Stanislav sat face-to-face. "Glenn, how do you plan to vote?"

"Mr. Chairman, as you know I'm a big believer that our financial markets need to be liquid to facilitate the flow of capital. The proposed electronic system promises to enhance that." Greenwald appeared to catch himself, and said, "Let me please say, though, that an electronic system in no way detracts from the markets already in Chicago."

Stanislav tilted his head back in a stately pose. "Congressman," he said, "I've talked with a number of industry leaders, as well as countless traders. They tell me in no uncertain terms that the New York electronic-trading system is fatally flawed. There is no substitute for having traders in the pits taking on risky trades like we've got in Chicago. If those New York banks start patronizing their own system, it's all over. The liquidity we've spent decades building up back in Chicago would vanish overnight and be replaced by a system that reminds people of a slot machine."

That was about as much detailed policy analysis as anyone was ever going to get out of Karol Stanislav. It was effective, leaving Greenwald apoplectic.

"Now, Glenn," Stanislav continued, "you've done a lot of work on the pharma-expense cap thing, right?"

At the mention of the issue that was his political lifeline, Greenwald's eyes took on the wide-eyed look of a kid at a horror movie. "Yes," he answered, as if coughing up a confession.

"Let me note," Stanislav continued, "all these issues fit together in our big, diverse national economy. And the last thing I am looking to do is to destabilize the pharmaceutical business in New Jersey." Stanislav paused to let the gravity of his words sink in, before adding, "Not any more than I'm sure you want to disrupt the liquidity of our markets in Chicago."

Greenwald looked stricken. "But," he stammered, as he drew his hands out in front. "Mr. Chairman, please consider this: Lots of people in the industry tell me that an electronic trading system will actually be synergistic with the open-outcry trading in Chicago."

"Then why don't you go out and purchase yourself a piece of the Brooklyn bridge?" Stanislav fired back. "This electronic thing isn't gonna do anything but destabilize what we've built in Chicago for the last 130 years. All those terrible things—bankruptcies, lost jobs—that you say are gonna happen in New Jersey if the pharma companies can't capitalize their expenses, they would be child's play compared to the catastrophe if we lose the most efficient financial markets in the world."

Greenwald didn't seem to trust himself to speak, so Stanislav continued. "Is that what it's gonna come to, chaos in Chicago and New Jersey? Or are we gonna work together like you always proclaim we should?"

"Yes, Mr. Chairman, of course we have to work together. What if we just voted to approve a prototype of an electronic trading system, and everybody could see how it works?"

Stanislav lowered himself to gaze at the congressman. "Look, it's not too much to ask somebody on the Commodity Futures and Options Subcommittee to gain a basic understanding of our nation's financial markets. I've tried to understand the pharmacy business, but you won't give me equal consideration. We've talked enough. At some point you've gotta play your cards. Are we gonna go forward with the pharma-cap provision or not?"

"Yes, Mr. Chairman. By all means," he croaked in answer.

"Do I have your word to not vote for this threat to us in Chicago?"

Greenwald sat glassy-eyed. Suddenly he blurted, "But Mr. Chairman, I have all kinds of buddies from college who trade on Wall Street. They're always telling me they get ripped off putting orders into the Chicago pits."

That did it. Greenwald had struck a live wire in Karol Stanislav, who had always been sensitive about not going to college, along with resentful of overpaid Wall Street traders. "Oh, ho-kay. Now you're gonna play your pink card, huh? Our job here in the U.S. Congress is to pamper a bunch of punks on Wall Street who never have had a real job. Is that what you're saying?"

"No, Mr. Chairman. I'm just reporting on what they say."

"Let me know when they quit whining, would you?" Stanislav rejoined.

Stanislav may not have taken any political science classes, but he was an expert on politicians as a species. What he knew most of all was they were creatures of survival. He held a sword of Damocles over Greenwald's head and fixed him with his full Torquemada stare, so infamous on Capitol Hill.

"Okay, Mr. Chairman, I'll vote no," he finally said with an air of resignation. Then his voice regained its strength. "Can we have an announcement that you will support the pharma cap when it comes up in front of the Appropriations Committee?"

"We'll get it out today," Stanislav said.

The two men stood to shake hands, and Greenwald left with no further ado.

Calling in Greenwald first served to economize on labor for Stanislav. Because he knew the moment Greenwald got back to his office, the first thing he would do is telephone Bill Perkins and Andy Blakely. Indeed, Perkins and Blakely both saved themselves the humiliation of a face-to-face backdown by sending a staff member to Joe Wolf, asking for a statement in support of the oil depletion allowances and agricultural price supports in return for their no votes on the proposed electronic trading system.

The final subcommittee vote of 9-7 against was anti-climactic.

CCE Chairman Dean Beman immediately issued the following statement:

"Investors, hedgers, brokers, fund managers, and end-users of CCE products from around the world can take heart from the subcommittee's action. This affirms the overwhelming evidence that our open-outcry style of trading in Chicago produces the most liquid, customer-friendly markets of any trading arena."

Chapter Forty

Oh no.

JAMES LUXEM STOOD alone in CCE President Mike Kilpatrick's office, gathering information for the next meeting of the Board of Directors. But when he looked down at Kilpatrick's desk, he saw an envelope with a *Brubaker Brothers* logo. He had recently spotted Richard Sherry slithering in and out of Mike Kilpatrick's office, and it stoked his ever-present curiosity.

Luxem's career was built on loyalty. But the off-the-record Saturday night meeting between Dean Beman, Mike Kilpatrick, and Karol Stanislav, and now the arrival on the scene of this shadowy character, Sherry, had begun to make him uneasy. He stared at the envelope. The seal had already been broken, and he was wondering whether to reach for it. The silence was deafening; Luxem knew this was a good way to destroy his career. Finally, though, he put his hand into the envelope and extracted the contents.

The cover letter read:

Dear Mr. Chairman,

It is a pleasure to report that our professional relationship—albeit only 90 days old—is off to a terrific start. You will see from the attached statement that the returns on your investment have been outstanding.

We at Brubaker Brothers look forward to helping you and your family reach its financial goals in the future.

Yours sincerely,

Richard Sherry

He turned to the next page where he saw the summary.

Summary
Beginning Balance: 10,000
Gains: 637, 494
Losses   4, 241
Ending Balance   643,253

Holy moly. Chills shot down Luxem's spine, as if he was afflicted with a rapid onset of whiplash. He wondered if his life had just changed on the spot.

Luxem knew Kilpatrick would be back from lunch in a few minutes. Nonetheless, he began poring through the details attached to the back of the statement. They included an itemized list of transactions in a variety of commodities, ranging from cattle, to pork bellies, corn, cotton, Treasuries, Japanese yen, Swiss francs, and stock-index futures, almost every one of them a winner. Finally, he saw a trade listed in red, a loss of $4,241 in the British Pound. *A token losing trade, to cover themselves.* It occurred to him that he should be wearing gloves. Too late. He reinserted the statement in the envelope, before darting out of the office and through the hallway, relieved that nobody was mingling about.

However, when he got back into his office he was overtaken with a compulsion: *I need a copy.* He poked his head in the hallway; still nobody out there. He rushed back into Kilpatrick's office and pulled the statement out of the envelope, before zipping over to the Xerox machine in the hallway. He made two copies and returned the originals to the envelope for a second time. Again, he hurried back into his office.

Luxem was a beta male of slight build and normally proficient at using the office technology. But suddenly a volt of horror surged through his being. He had left the last copy in the Xerox machine. He rushed out into the hallway where Dean Beman's secretary had arrived at the copier.

"Oh, Cathy, sorry, mine," he said breathlessly, before grabbing the copy from the tray.

"Sure," she said, giving the obligatory smile of someone you pass several times a day.

He was relieved to get back to his office a third time since spotting the envelope. Then he began to wonder if he had inserted the statement back in the Brubaker envelope properly. He heard secretaries chatting in the lobby; Kilpatrick would be back any minute. However, Luxem knew his psyche. He would writhe in a cold sweat all night, wondering if he had gotten it right. He rushed back into Kilpatrick's office and pulled the papers out, only to see that he had inserted one of the pages backwards. He corrected it and left Kilpatrick's office for the third and last time that day.

I have to tell somebody.

Luxem had eaten lunch many times with Jan Silverstein. But it was always hurried forays to sandwich shops and cafes in the downtown area.

At various times, he had mused about the possibility of asking her out for a more formal occasion. He felt attracted to her lissome figure and self-possessed personality. But his inner Hamlet had always contrived reasons to not stick his neck out.

The morning after his mid-day frenzy in and out of Mike Kilpatrick's office, he entered her office and closed the door.

"Hey, James, what's up?"

He felt self-conscious. "Jan, I know a Spanish *tapas* place on La Salle Street called *Café Iberico*. Could you meet me there for lunch on Saturday around 1:00?"

"Saturday?" She was caught off guard, but quickly recovered. "Sure, James. Saturday it is at *Café Iberico*."

***

LUXEM HAD ARRANGED a corner table when Silverstein arrived for their Saturday lunch date. A Spaniard came to the table where she did a serviceable job ordering for them in the waiter's language.

"I love the way these Latino people live for the moment," she said as the man walked away. "Sometimes I can't believe I work at a place like the CCE."

The waiter brought a whole delicatessen of delights— sumptuous yellow rices, herbs, spiced hams, and cheeses. *"Que disfruten,"* he said.

"Do you think he even speaks English?" Luxem asked.

"Who cares?"

"Look, Jan," Luxem said, adjusting his wire-rimmed glasses, "there's something I need to talk to you about."

Silverstein flashed her dark eyes at him.

"Do you remember the Saturday night meeting I told you about?"

"Uh-huh."

"And how I told you Karol Stanislav was going to start trading?"

"Yep," she giggled, not able to resist laughing with a mouth full of food.

"Listen," Luxem said in a quickening tone, "I happened to see his trading statement Wednesday."

"Where?"

"In Kilpatrick's office."

"What was it doing in there?" she asked, her eyes narrowing in confusion.

"Let me put it this way." Luxem spoke intently. "Stanislav started with $10,000 in his account three months ago."

"Yeah, $10,000," she acknowledged.

"Take a guess how much is in there now." He leaned forward on his elbows.

She stopped chewing and stared without venturing an answer.

Her silence gave him impetus to blurt the answer. "$643,253."

"What the f...!" Her mouth froze half-open. "What are you trying to tell me?"

Luxem stretched forward to a virtual crouch. In a near-whisper he eagerly began explaining the mechanics of trade allocation. "Remember, something like this recently came out about Hillary Clinton," he said.

"Yeah," she replied grudgingly, acknowledging fallibility of the feisty woman who had enthralled her in this year's presidential campaign. Here was a woman who valued her integrity to the extent that she even paid Social Security taxes for her maid. "How does something like this work?"

"It's called trade allocation," Luxem said, "Apparently, those commodity funds take customer money from different investors and pool it together to make different trades. They're supposed to allocate the gains and losses according to a formula. But from what I've heard—and now seen—they allocate the gains to the most important people. Everybody else gets screwed. I mean, heck, 98% of the people who invest in those funds lose."

"Those son-of-a-bitches," Silverstein intoned. "The sons-of-bitches. And you think that's what they did here—just gave, fuck, look at this, it's a bribe they're giving

Stanislav, so he'll take care of the Exchange's business? That's a bribe. Bribing a big public official with big money."

James Luxem, Mr. Calspar Milquetoast Jr., had known he was passing on more than standard office gossip. But her reaction indicated he had just clued her in on a full-fledged scandal.

Chapter Forty-One

SKIP SLIDER HAD always vowed he would never wear a suit-and-tie to any job. But on a windy Monday morning in early March he was walking down Michigan Avenue, head level, shoulders stiff, and back erect in his newly-purchased Brooks Brothers suit. The grey briefcase in his right hand included a resume for his interview at the *Windy City Times*.

Slider abhorred the thought of being normal. However, the stark fact was that he was a statistic. Seventy-five percent of the people who tried to make it as an independent trader failed. In Slider's three years as a CCE floor trader, he had fallen squarely into that majority. The scars ran deep. "I want to make it so badly," he had confided to his few close friends on the trading floor. "I wouldn't sit on my ass like most rich people. I'd explore places where no humans have ever set foot."

Alas, he had been forced to cry uncle after exhausting his personal savings, plus some family money. In humiliation, Slider fled to Alaska for the next couple years, surviving on odd jobs and living in flophouses. His parents tried all manner of cajoling him back to civilization. But their entreaties had fallen on deaf ears until Skip finally latched onto another dream: he would climb Mount Everest.

That required $25,000, which was 99.9% more than he possessed at any one time. Finally, his grandfather agreed to float him with one condition: he begin working on a career upon his return. Slider accepted without much thought; he had no idea if he would make it back alive. Fortunately, he proved to be a better climber than commodities trader and came through in flying colors. Others of equal ability bailed out, and one perished. Hands down it was the greatest moment of Slider's three decades on the planet, and he returned to Chicago for the first time in three years, flush with success. Since his earliest days growing up on the West Side, he had harbored a deeply-held faith that he was destined for greatness.

Unfortunately, after a few weeks back in his old environs, normality began to intrude. He dreaded the sight of family and friends, knowing they would ask him, "Have you thought about what you're gonna do next?" He decided to call the *Times,* hoping that his Alaskan adventure and Everest triumph qualified him for the Outdoor and Nature Section, a kind of modern day Teddy Roosevelt. Surprisingly, the *Times* focused on his commodities trading experience.

Today, Slider was scheduled to meet with the Executive Editor Ben Clayton for the third and decisive interview. He needed the job. The interview was at the Rookery building, a classic structure of art-deco design considered one of the choicest properties in America.

A bespectacled woman ushered his lithe form into Clayton's lush office, which featured a grand vista looking out to where the Chicago River flows out into Lake Michigan. The two shook hands and Clayton pointed Slider to a high-backed walnut-colored chair. He glanced around long enough to catch a glimpse of *All the President's Men* in Clayton's bookcase, along with various framed articles exposing local crimes.

"So, Skip," Clayton said, looking him in the eye, "your resume caught our attention. It's different."

Slider sat ramrod-straight and nodded.

Not missing a beat Clayton said, "We're beefing up the business section. The biggest business in town is that place where you used to work."

Slider felt sheepish.

Addressing the elephant in the room Clayton said, "I'm aware a lot of people—a helluva lot have rocky experiences on those trading floors." Fixing his eyes on Slider, he said, "I've seen those guys preening all over town like unicorns, making asses out of themselves in restaurants, clubs, or wherever. I guarantee you this, if you could buy 'em for what they're worth and sell 'em for what they think they're worth, you'd be a pretty wealthy individual."

That drew a spontaneous laugh from Slider who replaced his endemic suspicion of any large organization with an appreciation of the man's judgment.

Clayton studied Slider intently and shook his head. "I wonder what that business is really about. In my father's generation, the amount of money a person earned was at least a rough guide to what they contributed to society. Where is the value added in that business? Maybe I'm missing something."

"Yeah," Skip sighed. "I spent five years down there as a clerk and floor trader. And I was as confused about the place the last time I walked out as when I first got there."

"Let me ask." Clayton's eyes narrowed, and his voice slowed. "Do you think there is a story to be told?"

The old feelings of idealism and ambition began coursing through Slider. He leaned forward, his face flush with adrenaline. "You bet I do. I'd love to take a crack at it."

"Good," Clayton said. "We have one more person coming in. But you bring something to the table. You've seen those canines firsthand."

Late that afternoon Slider received a call from Clayton's secretary offering him the job as a junior reporter for the *Windy City Times,* specializing in the financial markets.

Chapter Forty-Two

CHRIS PARKER AND Jan Silverstein had been a natural fit from the beginning, even if it wasn't clear exactly what type.

They met in the elevator of the old high-rise where both lived. Chris had arrived in Chicago not knowing a soul, but excelled at elevator talk. Silverstein was more circumspect, but after a few months of occasional banter, she asked, "Chris, are you up for a pizza tonight?"

"Good deal."

Jan was eleven years his senior. Nonetheless, there was a certain undefined mutual attraction between them. Given that he had been dating a girl for three years without ever consummating the relationship, his eyes were open. Their once-a-month get-togethers had begun to have a loaded feeling. But then he introduced her to his friend, Frederick DuPree, who was five years his junior.

DuPree was a southern Californian, drawn to Chicago by the lure of big money in the commodity markets. But like most dreamers, riches had eluded him, and he survived on increasingly grudging infusions of capital from his father. Being tall, athletic, blonde-headed and blue-eyed, girls practically fell at his knees. Unfortunately, Frederick never could quit going on *ad-nauseum* about how much better looking the girls were in California than in Chicago. Every time he and Chris went to a gymnasium together, Frederick would point out a girl and say, "See that one over there. Any gym in California would have ten or twenty of those walking around."

But then one Saturday afternoon, Frederick and Chris were lolling along in Lincoln Park when they had run into Jan Silverstein. The vagaries of human nature again showed their hand. The naïve young Californian hit it off with the sophisticated lady sixteen years his senior. An all-afternoon chat in a coffee shop had ensued, followed by dinner at Jan's apartment.

"Did you see her ass in those blue jeans?" DuPree later enthused when he and Chris were out on the street in the cold nighttime air. "I really wanted to fuck her." He said it in a tone of wonderment.

Alas, it was not to be. Mr. DuPree rejected his son's umpteenth request for more money and repatriated him to the paradise of California. When Chris and Jan went out on their monthly Saturday-night outings, they were again a twosome. One snowy Saturday evening they returned to their apartment building after a night of sweeping conversation. Usually they exchanged pleasantries at the elevator and headed off to their respective apartments. But on this occasion Jan said, "Would you like to come up for an apple cider?"

"Sure."

Again, she walked around in her blue jeans. Tension welled up in Chris when she sat down next to him with two steaming cups.

"Jan, may I kiss you?"

"Sure," she hemmed. "What do you have in mind?"

"Well, I'm not blind."

Adrenaline flowed.

"What are you saying? That you are attracted to me?"

Adrenaline overflowed. The timing seemed propitious for a blunder.

"Oh yeah, Frederick and I used to talk about you. Wow, *he* really thought you were attractive."

"You're kidding," she said with ill-disguised elation. "He was pretty cool himself. Well both of you are."

And that's what Chris was to remain: a cool friend. Thereafter, Jan always found a way to slip in an inquiry about Dupree in their discussions. Chris and Silverstein's Saturday night POW-WOWs remained pizza and politics.

After her Saturday afternoon lunch with James Luxem, Jan knew exactly who to call. "Chris, could you come up right now? It's important."

"Be there."

When he arrived, she handed him a cup of tea with honey and pointed to the sofa. They took a seat and she leaned forward. "Chris, all those stories you've told me about that crap happening on the trading floor."

He nodded.

"Now I've got one," she said, raising her eyebrows. "And I'm assuming the same level of confidence I've shown to all your stories."

"To be sure."

"Because this is serious."

She went into a controlled explanation of the events resulting in Luxem's photocopies of Richard Sherry's letter to Stanislav. Chris was prone to daydreaming during long presentations, but sat transfixed. "I have the copies right here," she said, extracting several sheets from a manila folder and handing them to her silent interlocutor.

After scanning them for several moments he said, "Yep, uh-huh."

"What?"

"Look, Jan, there's nothing worse than somebody saying, 'I told you so', especially somebody who's wrong as much as me. But remember a couple months ago when that story came out about Hillary Clinton's cattle trading, and I told you the fix was in? Well, that's exactly what this is. They allocate good trades to favored customers, and all the others take it deep."

A sour look came across her face. One of the reasons Chris and Silverstein had gotten along so well was they both knew there were many more shades of gray than black and white. But this evidence they were looking at was pregnant.

"Is this not flat-out crooked?" she asked, her face turning an uncharacteristic shade of red.

"Well, yeah," Chris said, shaking his head as he drew a breath.

"Why do you think they're doing something like this now?" she asked. "And for so much money—I mean, look at this, $633,000. That's ridiculous."

"You're familiar with the moves toward electronic trading, aren't you?"

"Yeah, you told me about that." A quizzical look came across her face. "So, you mean, all the traders figure they're screwed if an electronic system catches on and that fat goose raining golden eggs down on them is put to rest?"

"Yeah, pretty much so."

"Why is that, again?" she asked in the tone of someone accustomed to having a handle on things.

"Millions of reasons," Chris said. "Consider these two. First, it's gospel in the Treasury Pit that when a broker like me gets a customer order, he's supposed to give first dibs to the locals trading for their own accounts, before letting another broker filling for a customer have anything. And then, anytime a trade goes against a local, the broker is supposed to come back to the local with get-well trades."

She shook her head. "Now see, that sounds like some sort of *cosa nostra.*"

"Trust me," Chris said. "It works grotesquely in favor of the big traders. And half the time it's like that game *Marco*

Polo everybody played as a kid, traders hearing and seeing customer orders coming into the Pit. You can't expect a trader to not front-run a big order any more than a ten-year-old is not gonna open his eyes in a swimming pool to tag somebody."

"Marco Polo." She giggled. "I'm becoming a fan of electronic trading as we speak." But then she looked distraught. "What I want to know...I mean, I work at this place, for God's sake. Who can blame the traders for playing the whole thing for all it's worth. But these people at the top putting the fix in—I can't continue working for them."

"Yeah," Chris said, nodding his head. "Your heroes have always been muckrakers like Woodward and Bernstein."

They sat in silence, probably wondering the same thing. *Was this just going to be a new bit of lore for their Saturday-night pizza dates, but something neither could do anything about?*

Chris suddenly lit up. "Hey, wait a minute. I ran into an old friend a couple weeks ago when I was leaving my kung-fu class. He recently got hired as a reporter by the *Windy City Times*. He used to trade at the CCE. Wow, he despises the place. The guy standing next to him in the Treasury Pit bit him in the nose."

"Bit him?" Jan laughed derisively. "Like a bulldog? Maybe they should turn the whole place into a fucking kennel.

"No, seriously," Chris continued. "He told me he's looking for scoops. Do I have permission to tell him this whole story?"

"Hmm." Silverstein sat there pensive. "Why not? A public official is effectively taking a huge bribe—that's what all this trade allocation sounds like."

Chris nodded. They looked at one another.

Jan broke the silence. "Let's send the circus on its way. I'll be happy to look for another job."

Chapter Forty-Three

IT WAS THE single most crowded golf course in the United States of America. It routinely took seven hours to play eighteen holes. But Chris and Skip Slider decided to meet at the Jackson Park Municipal Course on the South Side, just below Hyde Park, for their rendezvous.

One reason they had chosen Jackson Park was that 90% of the golfers were African-American, but they seemed to respect the ten percent who weren't. And given that the trading-floor population was less than one-percent black, despite Chicago being almost half-black, chances of being spotted by another trader were small. He and Slider, two middlebrows by nature, had played there on several occasions. Both loved the hot dogs served at a stand after the tenth hole, and Chris never failed to say, "Man, they could patent this sauce."

Now, four hours after beginning, they sat munching chili dogs on the eleventh tee. Chris reclined his head on his golf bag, knowing it would be a while before the hackers in front of them cleared the eleventh fairway.

He couldn't resist asking, "Skip, how's Darby these days?"

"Couldn't live without her," he answered plain as day.

Chris was referring to Slider's cat, named after Darby Shaw, a female trader in the Treasury Pit over whom he had developed his own unrequited fixation. However, unlike Chris's paranoia over his preoccupation with Barbra Lasky, Slider had always regaled any person who would listen to him wax poetic about Darby Shaw's queenly virtues.

"Is she still trading?" Slider asked.

"Yeah, but I hardly ever trade with her."

"Go ahead and tell me, though," Slider said, not hiding his eagerness. "Is she still to die for?"

Chris sighed, wanting to give him better information. But the truth was that other than a couple inane conversations in the hallway, Darby Shaw had never figured one way or the other in any of his matrices. "You'd recognize her," was all he had to offer up to Slider's palpable disappointment.

An exciting thought occurred to him.

"Hey, Skip, do you remember Barbra Lasky?" he asked, lifting his head from his golf bag.

"Not offhand."

"She was the short girl in the baby-blue Vortex trading jacket—stood over by Weakley in Coffin Corner."

Slider shook his head.

"Come on, you don't remember the girl I'm talking about? Really short, even more sexy? Dated Thomas Krone for years?"

"I remember Krone."

"And you never saw that girl he dated?"

"Man," Slider answered, dragging the vowels out in his signature fashion. "to me, there was only one girl down there."

"Got you."

"What else is going on?" Slider asked.

Chris filled him in on some gossip. "Divorce is the big thing down there these days. And man," he said dragging his vowels out like Slider, "these wives don't just want their husbands' money; they hate them and sue for everything they've got."

"Hell yeah," Slider responded. "Because they know them. Remember what people always were saying: 'He's an asshole in the Pit, but a nice guy outside of it'. What a crock. Hitler and Stalin were great guys at the pub, too—they were just dicks at their jobs."

"You should hear these stories," Chris continued, ignoring Slider's historical reference. "Schroeder, Chapman, and Dooley all left their wives for girls on the floor—Schroeder while his wife was pregnant with their first, and Chapman with their second. And Dooley's wife is in the hospital from a bad wreck when he was driving. Now he's tagging some young runner that everybody has been raving about."

"I never thought any of those were as great of traders as everybody acted like," Slider said. "It was always the same old story—rule by fear."

"Speaking of fear," Chris said, "I'm sure you remember Guritz."

"Who doesn't? What was that guy making—like $20 million a year. Everybody was scared to death of him."

"Maybe with good reason," Chris said with a laugh. "He just got kicked off the floor for a month for stabbing the trader next to him right below the eye with a pencil. You should have seen it—the guy bled like a pig in a poke."

"The only thing that surprises me about that," Slider said, "is he didn't get away with it."

"Normally he would," Chris agreed. "But he stabbed the chairman's youngest son. And the guy that's the second biggest gun in there has got a hearing next week for biting the First Boston broker after the guy got him in a headlock."

"Not the first time that's happened in there."

"But now this jerk, who's up five, if not $10,000,000 on the year, is pressuring me to testify—I stand right behind him—that it was the other guy's fault." Chris lowered his head. "The subtext is he'll find a way to screw me if I don't."

Slider sat nodding, not having taken a bite out of his hotdog. Chris lifted his head from his golf bag and checked out the fairway. Nothing had changed. He decided to broach the topic that had led to their golf game.

"Skip, I've got a story your paper might be interested in."

"Talk to me."

"You're aware of the need for absolute confidentiality?"

"Done. Talk to me."

"Because, man, the retribution I'd face in the Pit..." Chris bowed his head to emphasize the seriousness of the matter.

"Got it."

"Remember how we always talked about Karol Stanislav being wedded at the hip to the CCE?"

"Yeah, you had the politics down. I remember you going on about Stanislav."

"You kept wondering what he was getting out of it."

"Yep." Slider was starting to sound invested in the conversation.

"And obviously you've followed the Hillary Clinton cattle story?"

"Yes," Slider said, shaking his head with a mocking smile.

"It ends up she's a piker compared to Stanislav. Look at this." Chris pulled out a copy of Stanislav's trading statement. "Before I show you this, Skip, tell me how much you think Stanislav made trading last quarter."

He sensed his timing was good; the voluble Slider didn't say a word as he took the statement. Chris pointed to the front page. "Here is his initial investment—$10,000— followed by his gains and losses." He waited a few seconds before pointing out, "And here is his ending balance."

Slider, who never could be bothered for long with any one detail, seemed to be staring a hole through the paper.

"Pretty good trader, huh?" Chris said.

Slider emitted the first of three drawn-out 'holy shits.' Since he couldn't seem to articulate anything else, Chris continued. "Look here. This page lists all the trades he supposedly made." Slider's face stayed glued to the pages, looking like a twelve-year-old boy who has just swiped a copy of his father's *Playboy* magazine.

"You reckon Stanislav was calling in these trades from Capitol Hill?" Chris asked, goading Slider.

"Hell, no. Hell, fucking no," Slider responded in rebellious fashion, his face turning a dark red. "He doesn't even know some of these markets exist. Look at this trade. He made $29,744 in rapeseed." He stopped a second, and his voice tightened. "You know politics better than me. Why are they padding Stanislav so much right now?"

"Isn't it obvious?"

Slider was uncharacteristically mute, allowing Chris to fill in the answer. "Electronic trading."

"Oh, yeah. Yep, hell yes. Because it's obvious electronic trading will wipe out that whole jerry-rig like a neutron bomb, the split-second customers get any kind of option for relief."

Chris noted that Slider was unable to keep the bitterness out of his voice. Like so many Chicagoans, he had followed everybody in his neighborhood down to the Exchange. Unlike most of them, he had studied market fundamentals. But he lacked physical aggressiveness towards others. Worse yet, his high school class's ultimate reject, who had been expelled when he got caught red-handed mooning a group of eighth-graders, stood right behind Slider in the Pit. The guy was built like a bowling-ball, allowing him to crack anybody within reach. To

Slider's disbelief, he was one of the insiders, entertaining everyone non-stop with his raunchy humor.

"How did you get this statement?"

"This is where I've got to be careful." Chris pulled himself up to affect a firm persona. "Because the person who gave it to me works for the Exchange."

"Listen," he said fixing Chris with a stern look. "They could decapitate me before I divulged a source."

Chris took comfort that, in the case of Slider, that might be literally true. "It's a lady who is an executive assistant to Dean Beman, the chairman."

"Beman, eh? Yeah, I remember that guy," Slider said. "I knew he was a crook the minute I saw him."

"Do you think you will be able to print this story?" Chris asked, point-blank.

"Don't worry," Slider chirped. "Do not worry."

Chapter Forty-Four

"GOOD MORNING, SKIP."

"Hello, Ben," Slider said as he entered the plush offices of executive editor, Ben Clayton. "Thanks for meeting me on such short notice."

"Yes." Clayton's curt tone indicated the ball was in Skip's court.

Other than a few awkward salutations in the hallway, he hadn't spoken with Clayton since his interview. He was aware of the journalistic ethos that the more time a reporter spent in the home office, the worse job he was doing. He needed to make it count.

"One of my closest friends when I was a trader at the CCE came to me this weekend with a story that I think you should hear." Slider's quickening tone denoted discomfort. "He knows a woman who works in the executive offices for Dean Beman and Mike Kilpatrick. Do you know those names?"

Clayton returned a businesslike nod. "The Chairman and the President."

"Without getting into all the details, Kilpatrick has apparently arranged a special trading account for Karol Stanislav."

A questioning look came across Clayton's face, encouraging Slider to lean forward. "You're probably aware Stanislav has been doing their bidding in Washington for a long time."

"You can say that again."

"Well, this woman I mentioned got ahold of a copy of Stanislav's first statement. Mind if I show it to you?"

Clayton was beginning to look focused. He took the pages and spent ten seconds perusing the first page before breaking into laughter. "What the hell are they doing?" he asked, sounding like a junior high-school headmaster discovering a new form of mischief.

Slider decided to switch course. "Do you remember the Hillary Clinton cattle trading story a few months back, about how she made $100,000 in one trade?"

Clayton kept his eyes on the papers. "Uh, huh."

Slider kept his natural enthusiasm under control and recounted the details. "Same thing here. This is an obvious case of illegal trade allocation. The rules are so poorly enforced—largely from Stanislav's slashing away at the regulatory budget—that the commodity funds can get away with allocating the winning trades to their most important customers, at the expense of the rest."

Clayton reached over and grabbed the telephone. "Missy, could you reschedule Jankovich for another day? Who's after that? Becket. Move him also." Brief silence. "Yes, another day." He hung up and turned his attention back to Slider. "Skip, if this is what it seems to be..." He stopped. "Is this definitely Stanislav's account?"

"Yes. My source said they had an unscheduled meeting one Saturday night in February and agreed to set it up."

"Saturday night in February?" Clayton asked with an incredulous look rare for a veteran journalist. "Where?"

"Downtown at the exchange."

"On a Saturday night in downtown Chicago in February." Clayton worked to regain his professional tone. "I mean, damn. They've been coddling Stanislav big-time since before I first became a reporter. But why so drastic now?"

Slider smiled. "Apparently, the New York investment banks are developing an electronic system that the Chicago exchanges have gotten wind of. They consider it a mortal threat to the whole open-outcry method of trading. Have you ever seen it down there on the trading floor?"

"Yeah, I've seen it." Clayton shook his head as if a chill had filled the room.

Slider waited a couple seconds to let the gravity of the situation sink in, which prompted Clayton. "So the idea is they figure they're doomed unless Stanislav can eighty-six that electronic system?"

"That's what my source says."

"Tell me more about this source. How well do you know him?"

"He was one of the few guys down there I really considered a friend."

"But he got it from a lady friend of his that works for these pirates, right?"

"He swears she's one of the most honest people he's ever met," Slider said. "Look at this statement—how detailed it is."

"Yeah, it looks authentic, although I'd be a pretty easy lay on something like this." Clayton looked up. "We can't do this on some friend of a friend deal. We need to get closer. I'm just wondering if the lady will agree to meet."

"I'll have to ask."

"Get back to me," he said, shaking his head in dismay. "Because let me tell you, this Stanislav, he is the wrong guy to turn into an unnecessary enemy. I can't remember the last time he lost any battle to anybody."

***

"HELLO, MISS SILVERSTEIN."

"Good morning."

It was 8:00 in the morning and Ben Clayton immediately sensed he had met his match in Jan Silverstein.

She struck first. "You want to know if I'm some kook, don't you?"

Clayton looked back. "To be honest, yes."

She looked at Clayton appraisingly, before beginning a cool presentation of the facts, that matched Slider's story.

"Do you see any possibility this is all some mistake or just a coincidence?" Clayton asked.

"I don't."

The perfect witness, Clayton found himself thinking. "Let me ask, Miss Silverstein. How did you end up working at the Exchange?"

"I needed a job."

Clayton stuttered a half-second in his interrogation before noting, "It's just that the few times I've visited the floor, I couldn't make heads or tails of the whole thing."

That loosened her up. "Yes, when I first got hired, I visited the floor a couple times. Finally, I decided if I wanted to witness a bunch of primates carrying out dominance functions, I should just go to the local zoo."

Clayton laughed openly. Leaning forward, he said, "This story makes perfect sense. Because the first question that everybody asks is, 'Why in the world do they do business like this?' It all comes off as a throwback." He touched Stanislav's earnings report. "It would take something this ridiculous to keep the whole thing going." Clayton raised his chin and looked directly into her eyes. "So why come to us?"

Silverstein smiled. "Because you have the power of the press."

"Yes, ma'am." Clayton nodded. "But this is a big one and we've got to do our homework first. The obvious next step is to ask Karol Stanislav himself to comment on the story."

"Sure," she agreed. "He's an elected public official and deserves a chance to state his case before the first damning word is ever printed."

Clayton tried to keep from betraying raw curiosity. "I understand that you work up in the CCE executive offices with Dean Beman and Mike Kilpatrick?"

"Yes." A frown shone across her face. "I do."

Clayton got the impression he was looking at a deeply-conflicted woman. But he suspected it wasn't from any reluctance to voice her suspicions at the CCE.

"It's just," Silverstein squinted off to the side, "I'm used to being on the other side of a big, powerful institution, instead of working on the inside. And," she shook her head, "in almost every case like this, there ends up being a lot more than just the initial story."

Clayton nodded. "Yes, there does."

Chapter Forty-Five

BEN CLAYTON WAS accustomed to being the last person to arrive at meetings. Now, though, he found himself cooling his heels in front of a restaurant on the West Side, as he awaited Karol Stanislav.

Nonetheless, he wasn't put out. The Stanislav story had a rank whiff, bound to get any journalist's vital parts wiggling. Clayton considered abuse of power an immutable law of human nature and loved quoting Thomas Jefferson to his reportorial staff: *I'd rather have a press without a government, than a government without a press.* However, the Chicago, Washington, even American colossus he was waiting on reputedly had a very different attitude about the value of a free press.

He had personally called Stanislav's chief of staff, Joe Wolf, and requested a meeting.

"We have to know what it's about," Wolf demanded.

"I need to talk with him."

"Nobody meets the chairman without stating the agenda in advance."

"All I can tell you is that for Chicago's sake, the Chairman is the right person to hear first."

Wolf had reluctantly assented. "I'll get back to you on a time and place."

At 12:15 a black limousine pulled up to *Bentleys*, an upscale steakhouse Stanislav favored when in this part of town. The veteran congressman stepped out. "One forty-five," he said to the driver, before approaching Ben Clayton and offering his hand.

Undoubtedly there were thousands of places he would rather have been, so Clayton considered it seemly that Stanislav skipped a more felicitous greeting.

"Thanks for coming, Mr. Chairman."

"Karol will do."

They had met a few times before at public functions. But considering that one was the head of a popular urban newspaper and the other the major public figure in that city, they didn't know each other well. Unlike most politicians, Stanislav didn't seek headlines.

Clayton had arranged a table in the far corner with a view of nothing more than a Dempsey dumpster. A Fillipino waiter approached the table and asked if they would like a beverage.

"I'll take a Merlot," Clayton said.

"Ginger ale on the rocks for me," Stanislav said, which caught his dining partner by surprise. "And a shrimp cocktail."

I should have let him order first, Clayton thought. I'll feel like a fool sipping wine alone. He did have an icebreaker though.

"I was driving on the Dan Ryan Expressway to get here," he said, "and my thought was, 'Who says our government can't do anything right?'"

That drew an appreciative laugh from Stanislav, who took the bait, launching into what Clayton had heard through the grapevine was one of his favorite political war tales: Edward and Lyndon. As a young congressman, Stanislav had lobbied President Lyndon B. Johnson for the federal funds to construct the Kennedy Expressway running west out of the city. Finally, Stanislav received a call from the President reporting that he was going to get the funds included in the next transportation bill. Flushed with excitement, Stanislav had phoned Chicago Mayor Edward Riley to tout the success. However, the mayor was not nearly as buoyant at the news and cut the call short. A few minutes later, long enough for an irate Mayor Riley to call the White House, Stanislav received a second call from LBJ, reporting he had gotten the details wrong. It was the Dan Ryan Expressway, which ran near Mayor Riley's neighborhood on the South Side, not the Kennedy, which was getting the funds.

The chairman glowed with childlike joy from the umpteenth retelling of this tale of political intrigue. And he was able to round out the story with, "Of course, we eventually got the money we needed for the Kennedy, so it all worked out fine."

Stanislav enjoyed his audiences with the high and mighty. But now he was dining with the head of a local newspaper who was hoping to bring him to earth.

After the waiter cleared Stanislav's appetizer plate away, the two men sat in silence.

Does he have any idea what I'm going to bring up?

"Karol," he said, "please trust that I wouldn't randomly call you without a specific concern."

Stanislav kept his eyes on Clayton.

Clayton's felt his palms get clammy and his mouth drying up. What he was preparing to inject into the conversation was out of tune with the tenor of the conversation up to now. He took a long breath.

"One of my reporters has come across a brokerage firm's statement showing you have had large windfall gains in the commodity markets."

Stanislav tilted his face back, but remained silent. Clayton needed to penetrate deeper.

"Obviously your financial affairs are your own business," he continued, "but the thing that has caught our attention is where this statement was found—in the executive offices of the Chicago Commodities Exchange."

The Times lawyer had suggested giving Stanislav a copy of the statement. Indeed, he had one in his pocket. But he decided that would be too in-your-face. Instead, he asked, "Can you please give us some idea why a copy of this statement would be sitting in the office of the CCE President?"

Clayton knew Stanislav had built a reputation in the nation's capital as that rare person who never lied. He did what he did unapologetically.

"I've been working to clear the way for them down at the Exchange since Ed Riley assigned me to represent their interests in Washington, oh, thirty plus years ago," he said, sipping his ginger ale. "It's worked well for everyone concerned and created one heckuva lot of good jobs here in Chicago." He nodded in affirmation. "Obviously those folks down there are gonna see that I get treated fairly on my own business affairs."

Not surprising that Stanislav had veered to the safe harbor of the Big Picture. But Ben Clayton was a journalist; *pain-in-the-ass* was part of the job description.

"Let me ask," Clayton probed, "is my reporter correct about these huge gains you've had in the commodities markets?"

"Sure, it's been lucrative," Stanislav acknowledged, pressing his lips together.

"What I have trouble understanding is why Mike Kilpatrick would have a copy of your statement in his office at the CCE?"

Stanislav lowered his eyes briefly, before resuming his airy manner. "Mike has been telling me for years that there were opportunities in the Chicago markets. But," he gave a genuine laugh, "when you see the way they do business in those pits, you wonder if you should dive in. I finally did. So far, so good."

Throw him off stride, Clayton thought. *Hit him with it.*

"Our copy shows eighty-seven trades attributed to your account in the last quarter. Did you really make all these trades? Frankly, we're trying to figure out how a high public official had the time to do all of that."

"It was a managed account I invested in," Stanislav stated. "No, I didn't have any inkling as to what trades they would make. I put my blind faith in the fund manager."

That was also true. Clayton was not drawing any blood. But again, this got back to what he drilled into his paper's reporters, probe further. Be pesky.

"Do you think the fund allocated the winning trades to you and losing trades to the less important customers?"

Stanislav showed no sign the question had hit home. "I have no knowledge of any such arrangement."

"But you only put up $10,000 to open the account. My research shows that for the size trades credited to your account, a customer is required to post $214,500."

"That's news to me," Stanislav said with his lips pursed. "I cut a check to the broker for the amount he told me."

"But I'm confounded as to why the President of the CCE would have a copy of your statement in his office."

Clayton was proud of himself. He had started off as if addressing His Majesty. But the last few questions had been in the same tone he would have addressed any rank-and-file public official, despite Karol Stanislav's notorious intolerance for dissent.

"Well, Mike Kilpatrick is the one who originally made the introduction to the broker. Knowing Mike the way I do —he sweats every detail—I'm not surprised he would have a copy."

"And you think this is an acceptable way of doing business?" Clayton asked with a hint of disapproval.

Stanislav appeared to pucker up at the subtle change in tone. He fixed Clayton with a level gaze. "Look, you're a reporter. You make your living the way you do. Other people have got to make a living, also, so they can buy your newspapers. Now we've got a lot of people making a lot of money, sometimes a helluva lot of money, down at those exchanges. That means a lot of newspaper-buyers. Are you following me?"

Clayton met Stanislav's stern look. "Yes, I'm very interested."

"Believe me, it didn't just happen overnight. We've sweated a lot of stuff over the years with them." Stanislav went into a disquisition on various ways he had lubricated the way for the exchanges to clear regulatory hurdles and become economic powerhouses.

Clayton felt he had gone as far as he could, unless he was prepared to directly accuse Stanislav of taking a bribe. The two men passed the remainder of the meal discussing boilerplate topics: Chicago steakhouses, the White Sox, spring cherry blossoms in Washington.

Clayton motioned for the bill and signed off without a peep from Stanislav. The two men headed outside where Stanislav's limo was waiting.

"Karol, thanks for your time."

Stanislav nodded.

Let him know it's not over. "Before we go, Karol, I must tell you I have an obligation to report anything that the public may find relevant."

"You do what you've gotta do."

"It is unusual. We have to go forward with a story."

Stanislav climbed into his limousine without a response.

Clayton stood still on the sidewalk watching the sleek-black limo motor off.

Chapter Forty-Six

STANISLAV'S CHIEF-OF-STAFF Joe Wolf stood in his customary position, across the desk from his boss with a notepad in hand.

"The guy, Ben Clayton, from the *Windy City Times*," Stanislav told Wolf. "He's planning to run a story."

"A story?" Wolf's ears perked up.

"Yeah. About an investment I made in a commodity fund."

"A commodity fund?" Wolf was flummoxed.

"Yeah. Mike Kilpatrick recommended a broker in St. Louis. I opened an account. Sure enough, it's gone gangbusters."

"Is there anything wrong with that?" Wolf asked in the sympathetic tone of a courtier.

"No. But somehow the newspaper got a copy of my financial statement."

"Any idea how they got it?"

"I don't know and didn't ask."

"Well, damn."

Wolf knew his commiserating tone would set off Stanislav's basic instinct.

"You know," he said as if on cue. "I meet with corporate CEOs drawing gargantuan salaries and half the time they can barely find the bathroom. And I carry the water for those commodity exchanges for decades, so all these limber backs can run around living the life of Riley. Now when I finally make some real money, what happens? The newspaper decides they've got to run an exposé on it."

"I hear you," Wolf said, wondering what Stanislav meant by *real money*. Something told him it truly was real. But when it came to his boss and money, he knew to tread gingerly; it was a sore subject. "When do they plan to run the story?"

"Sunday."

"Let's see, the quick response from us...."

"Tell 'em the damn truth," Stanislav said. "We have worked hard to create markets the world can have confidence in. And we sure as hell don't exclude somebody here in Chicago from participating."

Another question occurred to Wolf. "Uh, is the account still open?"

"You bet your bottom dollar it's open."

"Got it." Wolf's tone was officious. But not enthusiastic. The main lawmaker in charge of the commodity futures and options industry was reaping windfall profits off it.

How much did Stanislav make? Wolf would have to wait until Sunday to find out like everyone else.

***

THE *Windy City Times* RAN the story on Sunday. Noise arose from the predictable quarters—watchdog groups, campaign finance advocates, and the like. One editorialist wrote, "We are shocked at this blatant conflict-of-interest. Can anybody say in good faith that this doesn't have the appearance of a huge bribe—$633,000 in one quarter? That's ludicrous."

Stanislav's office issued a terse statement drafted by Joe Wolf: "How can anyone have the audacity to question the Chairman's right to participate in the liquid markets he has endeavored so fervently over the decades to help create?"

Reporters noted the similarity in Stanislav's huge profits and Hillary Clinton's large gains in cattle futures. One asked, "Will the Chairman close out his account like Mrs. Clinton did after her windfall profit?"

"It's not a scandal," another newspaper wrote. "More of a brouhaha."

In any event, whatever the Chairman's knowledge of the commodity markets, he knew the politics cold. The controversy subsided to a curiosity amongst various insiders within a week. The critics began to sound shrill.

"Remember we like our politics hot and spicy in Chicago," one old wag opined. "And we sure as hell ain't gonna get rid of this one-man, billion-dollar industry we've got representing us in Washington."

Chapter Forty-Seven

JAMES LUXEM AND Jan Silverstein met again on a Saturday afternoon, six days after the *Times* article on Stanislav.

Luxem had cryptically approached Jan at work and again asked to get together. "How about *Ann Sathers* in Hyde Park?" Jan suggested. "I give architectural tours on the South Side on Saturdays anyway."

No one had openly discussed the article at work. But Luxem had noticed a grim-faced Dean Beman huddling first thing on Monday morning with Mike Kilpatrick. It hung in the atmosphere, having specifically mentioned that Stanislav's statement was found in CCE President Mike Kilpatrick's office. Everyone knew the most likely source of the leak was someone in the executive offices.

"How was your week?" Luxem asked Jan when she arrived at Ann Sathers. The question sounded unusual given they worked in neighboring offices.

Silverstein appeared to be in a sullen mood. When they got seated in a corner booth, she said, "It was eerily normal in there this week."

"Are you sorry you went through with it?"

"Not at all," she said, before throwing her hands up in surrender. "But they look like they've gotten away with the whole thing without breaking a sweat."

"It's not over."

"Oh, it'll just be another obscure story in a couple more weeks."

"Not so hasty," Luxem replied with uncustomary assurance.

"How do you figure?"

Luxem did a quick scan of the area. "I got to thinking, Okay, they've hit on this grand idea of having a commodities broker funnel winning trades to Stanislav. Big payday, to be sure. But think for a second, what about *before* this? Did he really do all the exchange's bidding in Chicago for decades without any compensation at all?"

"That's a good point," Jan affirmed with a roused look.

"So, what I did," Luxem continued after another glance around the room, "was go through the payroll sheet in Kilpatrick's office."

"Uh-huh."

"Guess who was on there."

Jan said nothing.

With a newly-acquired magician's timing, Luxem opened a large folder and pulled out a white printout with hundreds of names listed. He turned the list sideways for Jan to get a close view. On the second page, he had underlined two names:

Jeanna S. Parkins: 1431 Lunt Avenue
Sandra Druze: 2995 Paulina Avenue

"Do you recognize either name?" Luxem asked.

"No."

"Not that you should," Luxem said. "But they're both Karol Stanislav's daughters."

"Can't say I'm surprised to hear there's favoritism in hiring," Jan said with indifference.

"But listen," Luxem said. "I'd never heard of them either. And you know me, wanting to know everybody." Jan laughed, but Luxem kept on coming. "This sheet lists one as an employee in Accounts Payable and the other in Operations. I called both departments three times this week. Each time when I asked for Jeanna Parkins and Sandra Druze, various employees told me nobody by those names worked there."

"How did you know to look for a Jeanna Parkins and Sandra Druze?"

"The story goes back a while. About two years back, my sister was out with Jeanna Parkins, the oldest daughter. Apparently, everybody was out of their minds sloshed, when Parkins started bragging that both she and her sister drew paychecks from the CCE, without having to go to work."

"Your sister remembered their names?"

"No, but when I called her on Wednesday night, she offered to ask one of the other people that was out with them that night. Her friend gave her the names."

Silverstein looked back at the sheet in disgust. "Those losers," she hissed through clenched teeth. "The rest of us show up and work all day. And here are these two women getting paid for doing nothing because their father is a powerful politician."

"How about the same route as we did on the slush fund?" Luxem asked in a whisper that didn't hide his eagerness. "Will that guy push it again?"

"Forget that." She waved off the idea. "I don't give a shit anymore. I'm willing to go to the press myself. In fact, I want to walk up to Kilpatrick, Beman, and even Stanislav if I ever see him, and tell 'em all they're a bunch of low-lifers."

"I appreciate that, Jan", Luxem said, acknowledging her remarks. "Nobody has more integrity than you. But we've got the makings of something big here. The way this thing is developing, there are bound to be more stories."

"Yeah, okay," she said with a sigh.

***

THE CHAIN OF events repeated itself. Silverstein took the elevator two floors down to Chris Parker's apartment on the ninth floor, leading him to meet covertly again with Skip Slider.

This time, Slider walked past Ben Clayton's secretary and into the head-honcho's office. After giving him a ninety-second summary, Clayton lowered his chin in an analytic manner. "This sounds like a variation of the old ghost-payroll scam."

"I've heard of ghost payroll," Slider commented, "but I never really knew what it was."

"Oh, it's been going on from Chicago's very beginning," Clayton explained. "Putting ghosts on city payrolls who don't actually work there. Then some bigshot in the machine collects all the paychecks."

"But can he get away with it? It seems kinda pregnant."

"I don't know," Clayton said wearily. "I understand the advantage of having an ultra-powerful congressman represent their interests in Washington. But what you have here is a big man playing it small." Clayton looked as if he was letting some internal conflict play itself out, so Slider held his tongue. "This damn ghost payroll thing has stained Chicago's reputation for ages. To still be doing it this day and age..." Clayton shook his head in disgust.

"What do you reckon he does with it?" Slider asked. "Put it in Swiss banks or something?"

"No, that's the thing. The early Polish immigrants figured they were so down and out, they needed to put all their chips on the one *Big Man*." Clayton mimicked the description with his fingers. "But then that person is supposed to act grandiose and donate to all sorts of high-profile causes."

"Is the story suitable to run?" Slider asked.

"Hell yes, we're gonna run it," he said. "But this time he doesn't get a free lunch."

Chapter Forty-Eight

"KAROL."

"YEAH."

"AW, Karol."

"Tipper."

"Heeey, big man, Babe Ruth,"

"Oh, knock it off," Karol Stanislav said with a laugh.

For over a hundred years, St. Casimir Pulaski's Cathedral had been the epicenter of Polish life in Chicago. The ties ran deep. Karol Stanislav's grandfather, who had been the leader of the West Side Poles, jumpstarted the fundraising for it. A Polish immigrant, he never had a salary higher than $5,000. That had not stopped him from being the single largest contributor to the church, regularly donating $10,000 and upwards per year to the church's construction. No one had ever questioned how.

"Hello, Karol," the refrain continued from the constituents, true-believers, sycophants, and the like. The impressive thing was their smiles, which seemed to come from the diaphragm.

However, this morning there was some added titillation to the Stanislav family's arrival at St. Casimir's. The Sunday morning edition of the *Windy City Times* had featured an article by Skip Slider reporting that Stanislav's two daughters, Jeanna and Shirley, were on the CCE payroll but didn't actually work there. Yet here they were dolled up in flowery dresses, alongside their doting parents. Stanislav's wife, Sheila, was a blushing blonde and ex-beauty queen who hated politics. But she stood next to her husband, who knew the whole scene was bound to be a hit.

All during Mass, the parishioners gazed at the Stanislav family, a shining symbol of Polish-American success. Afterwards, Stanislav was at his affable best, attending to every friend and admirer until his family and longstanding-friend, Father Wojtekla, were the last people on the cathedral's property.

Later the Stanislavs made a stop further up town at *White Eagle*, the renowned Polish diner in northwest Chicago. Eighty-five-year-old Joe Koslak, who had worked in the field for Karol's father as a precinct captain, self-propelled himself in a wheelchair to the Stanislav table.

"Karol, Karol, Karol," he kept repeating. "Karol."

Stanislav got up and bent over to hug him.

"Karol. I knew him, I knew him," Koslak babbled.

"You can say that again," Stanislav reassured the man with something between an appreciative smile and a concerned look. "What can I do for you, Joe?"

Koslak continued. "Picture. My grandchildren. A picture. I know him."

"Oh, we're gonna do a picture. Sure. Let's do it."

Stanislav looked over where seemingly the entire 9th Precinct of the 5th Ward—his father's old ward—looked wide-eyed at them.

"Up, up, I knew him," Koslak hollered at everyone, at which point thirty-eight people, including grandchildren, took to their feet.

These were working-class people who had never done anything but toil with their hands to ensure a roof over their heads and enough to eat. The whole scene bespoke an atmosphere of plenty. Finally, the Stanislavs got around to lunch, which proved to be another protracted affair as one course after another was brought to them.

By the time Stanislav and Sheila had dropped their girls off and arrived home it was 7:00. The long day had been worth it. His mood, fragile at the outset, had morphed into buoyant, grateful, and proud.

Meanwhile, the CCE issued the following statement in response to the newspaper article: "We don't comment on employee compensation. However, it is worth noting that this story was written by a reporter who was an abysmal failure as a trader. Such vendettas are best disregarded."

The statement from Stanislav's office was even more pithy: "The Chairman will continue his long-standing policy of refusing to answer any questions regarding his family."

More titillation followed, but again a feeding frenzy failed to develop.

"You gotta wonder," one old-time reporter mused. "We had the Great Chicago Fire, Al Capone, the mob, the political machine, and, of course, ghost payroll. Maybe it's just our culture, kinda like the Cubs losing. We take pride in it."

Chapter Forty-Nine

CHRIS WALKED IN the dark towards Lake Michigan, hyper-alert to his surroundings and hoping not to have any unwanted company. He knew to keep heading in the direction where he could see nothing.

The previous evening Skip Slider had called from a pay phone. Chris sensed an urgent tone in his friend's voice. Rather than meet at either one of their apartments, Slider had suggested Waveland Golf Course on the near North Side. The two of them had a long-running debate over whether Waveland or Jackson Park was the most crowded golf course in America. Slider had once been accosted by a foursome on Waveland after hitting his ball into their group. In the middle of the rhubarb, Slider suddenly slugged the biggest guy in the group, followed by a high-speed getaway in which he outran the four of them all the way to the bus stop—golf bag in tow.

As Chris knew, Slider had an emotional attachment to Waveland that went well beyond that. Whenever he heard thunder raging in the sky, he had the habit of rushing in his bicycle to Waveland, which featured a pristine two-mile shoreline on Lake Michigan. There he would exult in diving into the choppy waters, as javelins of electricity traveling from the sky at a brisk 270,000 miles per hour raged at him. "It's the single greatest experience a human can have," Slider rhapsodized to the few whom he confided in.

Tonight, Chris had taken the bus up to Waveland Avenue, which ran west to Wrigley Field and east toward the lake. To maintain his bearings in the black-as-pitch night, he focused on the steeple of the abandoned church that served as the pro shop. Soon he was at the first tee where he continued until arriving at a low-cut stone wall.

As he looked out over the broad, watery horizon, Chicago's renowned skyline twinkled in the not-too-far distance. Intermittent waves of spray dusted over him like manna from heaven. Like many CCE traders from the packed Treasury Pit, Chris had begun suffering from mild claustrophobia. The nighttime scene felt rejuvenating, even if he was dubious about being here.

At nine o' clock sharp Slider arrived in a sleek gym suit, looking like a Nordic god.

"So, do you recognize this place without a heavenly-pyrotechnics show?" Chris cracked.

"Hardly," he said with enthusiasm. "Hardly."

Slider was wearing his buoyancy on his sleeve these days. Who could blame him after his bitter experience at the CCE? Chris's enduring image of Slider in the Treasury Pit was of him embroiled in an argument with a trader known as *Doctor Death*, who was reneging on a trade they had done. "I'm gonna kill you," Dr. Death kept repeating. "Do you hear me? I'm going to kill you." Slider had both hands up in an obvious attempt at reasoning. But in the end, Dr. Death had successfully walked away from the trade without breaking a sweat.

They began ambling along the empty course. A man of indeterminate age was hovering along the stone wall. He appeared to be stumbling drunk. Even so, Chris lowered his voice and suggested they reverse directions.

"No need to be spooked," Slider said with assurance. "Traders lack the imagination to be out here at night."

"Yeah, okay," Chris responded in terse fashion. Of late he had begun to fret over a fundamental imbalance in his relationship with Slider. Namely, Slider had much more to gain and a heckuva lot less to lose than he did from the stories.

"First, Chris," Slider said, "Ben wants me to applaud you for the great job you're doing. Ghost payroll is something people can understand better than the commodity fund story."

"They understand, alright," Chris agreed.

"Ben and I were talking," Slider said, showing more confidence than he ever had on a trading floor. "We really think this has phenomenal potential if we can keep the stories going."

We? Chris thought, ominously. *We is me!*

"Remember, I'm only as good as my source," Chris clarified. "Jan Silverstein came to me twice. That could be it. Don't you think Beman and Kilpatrick are bound to cover their tracks after that second story?"

"That's what we were discussing," Slider said, moving closer.

Chris again found himself scanning the periphery to make sure nobody was tracking them.

Slider stood still, looking up at Chris. "Ben thinks if you can start giving us some actual pit situations where the customer is getting totally ripped, we could begin a chain of stories. Think about it. That's what brought Nixon down, that day by day drip coming from Deep Throat."

There it was—*Deep Throat.* Chris had been wondering exactly that. He remembered from reading *All The President's Men,* that Woodward and Bernstein had described Deep Throat as a Nixon supporter, not, as was commonly assumed, a Nixon-hater. The book hinted that Deep Throat was trying to warn his boss about his errant ways. But he ended up mortally wounding the President instead.

"Look," Slider continued, "I stood down in the groin of that damn Treasury Pit, where you couldn't even tell what the hell was happening. But you're right up there where all those customer orders are flying around."

"Yeah," Chris said, drawing a deep breath. He stopped in his tracks and looked down at Slider. "Skip, come on. You were around that place long enough to know the minute any story hits the papers, every single person on the entire trading floor is going to be on a witch-hunt for the mole."

"I know there's some risk," he conceded. "But how many people have an opportunity to do something game-changing like that?"

Chris noticed the minor hyperventilating sound that always became palpable when Slider went on another of his flights of fancy. Another *Sliderism* popped into his mind, a favorite quote from Charles Manson: "*He was crazy back when crazy really meant something.*" Anybody who had been around Slider for any length of time had heard this line, always delivered with deliciousness.

"How would we communicate?"

"Ben and I talked about that. He says the old Chicago machine used to wiretap all kinds of people. Since Stanislav and Kilpatrick were once part of that machine, we shouldn't chance talking by phone. If they don't have me staked out yet, they probably will, especially once I start writing inside information about the Pit."

"What do you propose?"

"Remember in *All the President's Men...*"

"Here we go again," Chris said, only half-joking.

"It's the most practical way."

"Yeah, I guess," Chris sighed. "So are we going to start meeting in an underground parking garage like they did with Deep Throat?"

"We need a code."

"Nothing to do with *Helter Skelter* please."

Slider ignored the Manson gibe and pulled out a piece of paper. "Let's try this. If you've got a story, drop a copy of the *Chicago Tribune* off in my brother Freddie's mailbox. You remember where that is, right?"

"Yeah, the loft up there on North Avenue."

"Scrawl a large X on page three of the *Tribune* if you want to meet on Monday, page four for Tuesday, page five for Wednesday, and so forth. Whatever day you say, I'll meet you in the parking lot at Jackson Park that night at ten o' clock."

"Way down there?" Chris said, feeling situational anxiety. "Nowhere closer?"

"Everybody down there is black. If we see somebody who's not, we'll know they're probably up to something."

"Okay. We'll go with that. But Skip," He stopped, holding his hands to the side and speaking softly, "please respect that I work down there. If I get caught doing this, they'll probably take me gangland-style on the spot."

"Well stated." Slider laughed with abandon. "Well stated."

Chapter Fifty

"WELCOME BACK, CHRIS," Dr. Kater said.

"Hi."

He noted Dr. Kater had a different look on his face today, less that of just another appointment on his schedule. His counter-attack in their previous meeting at Dr. Kater's simplistic advice to quit trading with Barbra appeared to have struck home. Chris had cancelled his appointments for the next several weeks. But then he called in out of the blue asking for an appointment.

Dr. Kater looked squarely at him. "Chris, I have been thinking about you and your situation. How are things?"

"Well," he said, tilting his head, "there have been a couple changes."

"Very good," Dr. Kater responded with ebullience. "We therapists are ardent opponents of the status-quo."

"Now, please," Chris said, his cautious instincts at play, "I don't want to overpromise. Disappointment and worse are the rule on a trading floor."

Dr. Kater waved off his concerns and said, "I'd be interested in anything you have to say."

"For starters," Chris began, "believe it or not, and it just occurred to me the other day, I have become a little less fixated on Barbra Lasky." Chris watched Dr. Kater's eyes open wide, causing him to throw up a cautionary hand. "I don't want to make this sound better than it is. I still trade with her, but not as compulsively. Lately the trades have seemed, well..." he paused, searching for words, "almost like a couple that breaks up, but whenever they see each other they have sex again, almost by force of habit."

"Hmm," Dr. Kater purred at that analogy. "Chris, don't sell yourself short. As a practicing therapist for sixteen years, one thing I've learned is when a person gets the faintest glimmer of light, no matter what else happens, he doesn't go back to the status-quo. Not back there again. No!"

Chris lowered his head to digest that hopeful analysis. Dr. Kater asked, "Do you think the change you've made is because of the suspicions she voiced about you?"

"The insinuation that I'm an FBI stiff? She slanders me, and I recoil from her." Chris laughed and shook his head. "That would be far too rational."

Dr. Kater looked engaged. "I must say you are one of the most objective patients I've ever worked with."

"When you're this tall," Chris responded, "you'd better learn to look at yourself objectively." Dr. Kater kept looking into Chris's eyes. "Actually, my mind of late has become fixated on something different."

"Oh, yeah."

Chris began to recount the whirl of events that had him on the cusp of leaking information about his colleagues in the Treasury Pit to the newspaper. "This is the biggest decision in my trading career," Chris stated. "Actually," he said coming to a sudden realization, "it's probably the biggest decision in my entire life. One way or another it's going to lead to the end of my trading career."

"Would that be a good or a bad thing?"

"God knows," Chris said. "There is nothing more washed up than an ex-futures trader."

"You're in what—your early thirties now? You project lots of energy. I wouldn't be so glum."

"Yeah," Chris said, reflecting on the consequences. "Leaving this job would cut my lifeline with Barbra."

"How do you feel about that?"

"Three months ago, I would have considered that an occasion for sackcloth and ashes. But now I'd probably jump at any viable option to get away. "

"Has the relationship worked for you?"

He shook his head. "At first it was nice trading away from all those Neanderthals I'm surrounded by in the Pit. She's not a bad trader, either. But ultimately it led to my break up with Shannon and my Pit neighbors using it as an excuse to scrimmage on me. Throw in a tense arbitration hearing that could have cost me my job. No, it's all been a big misadventure."

"From this unique situation you just described," Dr. Kater said, "it sounds like you have a chance to use your talents in an innovative way."

Still, Chris remained reluctant. "I recently read a book called *Word of Honor*, by Nelson DeMille. The main character had commanded a platoon in Vietnam that committed all kinds of atrocities, murders, rapes, sadistic acts, you name it, expressly against his orders. But when it came time for the court martials, he was reluctant to testify against them."

"Why do you think that was?"

"Because they had all been through some pretty tense moments together."

"And you feel the same way about this crowd that surrounds you?"

Chris sighed. "In the book, the commander actually felt like it was Vietnam itself that had screwed the people up." His mind went back to his brother's recent visit to Chicago, when he had professed to be appalled to hear some of the racy humor and lurid tales that cascaded out of Chris's mouth. "You've got *CCE Syndrome*," his brother had concluded. "Just like all the people that came back from 'Nam."

"Let me ask, Chris. If you're feeling guilty about blowing the whistle on these people you've described in such barbaric terms to me, shouldn't you also be asking where the whole thing ends up if you don't?"

"That's true," Chris said, nodding. "I remember my college fraternity; you'd see a freshman showing admirable restraint, not giving in to this or that decadence. But two years later you'd go to some party and there's the same guy running around naked and breaking windows. And the CCE is even worse because it's like a fraternity house that you never even graduate from."

"It sounds to me as if it would do some folks a lot of good to leave that fraternity house," Dr. Kater said.

Chapter Fifty-One

"SHUT UP, FUCKWIT. You're starting to remind of dick-brain over here."

"Nice move, 'Shitfabrains'."

"Another brilliant statement, 'Einstein'. Let us know when the next brain fart is coming."

"Get the fuck off me, you cow-humping piece of shit."

On an otherwise ordinary June afternoon, the nation's financial markets were in a tizzy over the Rodney King riots in Los Angeles. And Buster Kinman was hard at work.

Kinman, who fit into the broad category of CCE *lifer*, held a Stop Order to sell 1,000 contracts of Treasury-Index Futures. The emergency sell order with a face-value of $100 million would be triggered if the market fell to 92-08. That had been far away from this morning's price when his customer *Cook Mercer* had given him the order. But then the Los Angeles police chief Daryl Gates announced, "We have been unable to restore order on the streets in Los Angeles. The National Guard has been alerted."

All hell proceeded to break loose on the trading floor in Chicago based on the street riots in Los Angeles. The market began crashing. The board flashed the FAST sign, affectionately referred to by brokers as the FUCK sign. Once it appeared on the board, the customer had to take pretty much anything the broker gave them.

Soon the Treasury market had fallen two full points. However, Buster Kinman was so busy raging at everyone around for their stupidity that he forgot about the order.

Suddenly, however, he looked up at the board; to his shock the market had already traded at 92-08.

In panic, Kinman reached back to hand the Stop order to his broker, Rob Petritz. But just as he was about to whisper to his boss, he caught another glimpse of the board and froze. The market had already rebounded up to 92-23. He had saved the customer money—approximately $450,000—by forgetting to put the sell order in at the dead low of the day.

Kinman made an immediate conclusion: *I'm a hero.* That was followed by an even happier thought: *I deserve a reward.* A rare smile washed over his poker face.

He looked over at the Cook Mercer desk. "Hey, Bugsy, Bugsy," Buster called to Bugsy Kendrick, the most junior Cook Mercer phone clerk.

Kendrick had a phone in each ear; he pulled one receiver away and held out a hand.

Buster knew he needed to be firm. For once, though, he didn't want to make a scene. "You're filled on your Stop Order," he shouted. "You sold 1,000 at 92-08."

Kendrick looked up at the board with a confused expression, trying to verify that the market had even traded as low as 92-08 during the prior pandemonium. He raised his eyebrows, indicating realization. For once his ignorance wasn't met with a snide remark from Buster, which itself should have been a tip-off that something was afoot. Kendrick hung up with one customer and picked up another line to inform the customer they had sold 1,000 contracts at the dead low of the day, 92-08.

Buster watched Kendrick's mouth closely. *Does the customer believe him?*

Kendrick kept looking at the board and Buster could read his lips: 'racing,' 'chaos', 'low,' '92-08.' Finally, Kendrick hung up with no further ado.

Now Buster Kinman sensed the opportunity of a lifetime to make some big money. In his left hand, he was clinching a $450,000 gold mine.

***

BUSTER'S BROKERAGE GROUP habitually fought like wild cats. As anyone could see, he excelled at this aspect of the job. Kinman gave one newly-hired clerk so much lip about his "much-fucked mother", that the clerk finally pleaded for a bathroom break, only to proceed straight out of the building and never come back.

Buster himself was a ruffian who had been kicked off the floor twice for fighting. But his brokerage group was impressed by it and always took him back. Added to that, his curly, dark hair, perpetual tan, and brusque ways were a hit with the young female trade checkers that ringed the Treasury Pit.

There was one problem: he kept making errors. To be sure, he was one of the most talented on the entire floor at blaming fellow clerks for these mistakes. But the errors made his brokerage group afraid to sponsor him for a trading membership. And now friends from his old neighborhood were getting cleared to trade. They continued buying him drinks, weed, and occasionally some blow, and Buster was good at acting like he deserved it. Lately, though, they had shown signs of becoming less enamored.

Now, though, he was seized with a chance to turn the tables on everyone. *I need a partner on this.*

"Here, take the deck," he said, stuffing the large stack of customer orders into the hands of a surprised clerk, who didn't dare question what Buster was doing. He tore around to the other side and shot through the clerk's entranceway into the Treasury-Index Pit.

"For fuck's sake, move it," he huffed to the line of clerks filling the passageway, before wedging himself between the aisle way and traders and charging into the Pit.

"Hey, asshole, off," one trader growled when Buster brushed up against him.

But today was not a day to fight. Buster had bigger fish to fry, hurrying his way through the crush of bodies.

***

"HEY STUTZ, STUTZ."

Terry Stutzel heard the voice of his longtime friend Buster Kinman and acknowledged him with a faint nod. But he didn't dare speak.

For Terry Stutzel knew he was likely in his last hours as a trader at the CCE. His clearinghouse, Kite Futures, required locals to have $50,000 in their account. Stutzel had begun trading four months ago with $70,000 in his account. But he stood four steps down from the top step in the maw of the Treasury Pit and rarely got anything but trades nobody else wanted. His precious last dollars appeared to be flowing through the hourglass. He had started the day with $52,000 in his account but was down almost $3,500 on the day. The clearinghouse management had been giving him eat-shit looks the last couple weeks. He knew they wouldn't let him continue past today's washout.

"Hey Stutz, look at me, come on," Buster called up, while tugging at the sleeve of Stutzel's trading jacket. "I got you covered, man; listen to me."

Stutzel bent down but didn't say a word.

"Stutz, dude," Buster said in a confiding tone. "We had a stop order to sell 1,000 at 92-08."

Stutzel turned and looked at the board with an uncomprehending look. "I didn't even see it trade at that price."

"That's just it; I was busy and never gave Petritz the order. Look, Stutz." Buster grabbed Stutzel by the shoulder and looked him in the eye. "I gave the customer the fill for selling 1,000 at 92-08."

Stutzel ceased looking at the Pit and locked his eyes onto Buster's. "You gave the customer the fill on selling 1,000 at 92-08?" he confirmed. "But your broker never sold them?"

"Yeah," Buster whispered with palpable enthusiasm.

"So, what do *we* do?

"I've got one of Petritz's cards here," Buster said. "I'll write down him selling you 1,000 contracts at 92-08."

"Will he go for it?"

"He won't even know about it until tomorrow, if that," Buster said with certitude. "And he'll get the commission on selling the 1,000 contracts; *everybody's* good."

"You're telling me I've bought 1,000 contracts from Petritz at 92-08," Stutzel confirmed.

"Yeah, dude," Buster said, having trouble keeping the ecstatic tone out of his voice. "Look, Stutz. Understand, you've got to sell them out right now before the market goes back down."

Stutzel eyed the board but still appeared hesitant. Nonetheless, he wrote down on his card that he had bought 1,000 contracts at 92-08 from PET, Rob Petritz's acronym. Buster wrote the inverse on his employer Petritz's card, selling 1,000 contracts to STZ—Stutzel's acronym.

Up until now, Stutzel's biggest trade his entire career had been ten contracts. He began scanning the pit trying to figure the best way to sell $100 million of Treasury futures. His heart was in his throat. But before he could get his hands halfway up, Buster placed a firm grip on them.

"Stutz, one more thing. You gotta know, we're partners on this one."

Stutzel looked at Buster. "Oh, yeah man, sure. You know you can trust me, Bust."

Buster turned his head to angle. "Fifty-fifty partners. Right?"

"Fifty-fifty," Stutzel confirmed.

Terry Stutzel took one more look around the Pit before commencing an orgy of selling that stunned anyone who had stood near him the last year-and-a-half. Hurling himself into the air, he screamed, "Sold, sold" at the top of his lungs while swatting down bids of the biggest brokers and locals in the Pit. He flagged down Pit legend, Don Guritz. "Sell you 500, Guritz." At first Guritz looked amused, before signaling he would buy two-hundred and fifty contracts. That night, in drunken slurs, Stutzel would regale Buster and friends about having stood down Guritz *mano a mano*.

"Hey STZ," people on the top steps who didn't know his name were calling down in pleading tones, "STZ, checking, I bought 100, hey, hey, checking."

The Treasury Pit had seen several rogue traders in the past; the glassy stare on everyone's face indicated this could all be a gigantic scam. However, the locals were also aware that, scam or not, it was not their problem; the rogue trader's clearinghouse would be financially responsible.

"Stutz," Buster said, grabbing Stutzel's raised right arm. "Hand me the cards; I'll get you a count."

"Yeah, yeah."

Buster counted Stutzel's sales and came up with a total of 770 contracts sold. "You've sold 770. Sell 230 more."

Stutzel did as Buster instructed him, although Buster had miscounted, Stutzel had actually sold 830 contracts, leading him to end up selling a total of 1,060 contracts. The market then dipped again, and they made an extra $25,000 on the sixty contracts he had oversold.

Stutzel's fifteen minutes of fame only lasted about ninety seconds. However, he had gotten a taste of the big time. The total profit added up to $483,874, which he had to split with Buster Kinman. But he didn't want to stop there, and began firing big trades around the Pit, at first making an extra $30,000 on top of his windfall gain, but then losing $75,000, convincing Buster that night to split the loss with him.

Leaving the floor after the 2:00 close, he heard a cacophony of obsequies. "Man, you were dominant in there." "That was something else." "A star is born."

It was highly intoxicating. Better yet, Terry Stutzel vowed this was the way it was going to be in the future.

***

BUSTER KINMAN DID not think anybody knew what he had done. However, standing three feet away from him was Chris Parker.

Chris had stood within a few feet of Kinman for the past six years. At first, he attempted to use his genteel southern ways—"So Buster, where ya' from? How long ya' been down here?", to build rapport with Kinman. "What gives, dude?" Buster had finally responded with barely-concealed malevolence to his entreaties. That was it for the next six years; nary another word spoken between the two, and Chris always stayed watchful and wary of him.

When Chris saw Buster report having sold 1,000 contracts at 92-08 to the Cook Mercer phone clerk, he smelled a rat.

"Did it trade much down there at 92-08?" Chris quietly asked a couple of the traders around him.

"I didn't even see the board print a 92-08 trade until the market was already back up at 92-15," the Goldman Sachs broker said.

Like everybody else in the Pit, he had stood transfixed as Terry Stutzel had bombarded the market with his rapid-fire selling spree. But he also noticed something else, the clerk standing at Stutzel's side, Buster Kinman.

Despite it being a busy market, Chris decided to step out of the Pit and meander around the trade checkers in Buster's brokerage group. He was looking for the Cook Mercer order slip to sell 1,000 contracts at 92-08. But after poking around a couple minutes, he did not see it and climbed back into the Pit.

Right then, Buster reappeared. He walked up to their trade checker. She was eighteen years old, but lived the life of someone twice her age, having first trysted with Buster, and then her married boss, Rob Petritz. She still held Buster in awe; he began whispering to her in confidence, while slipping her the customer order.

Chris extended his long neck and was able to make out what was written on the order. It showed the selling broker as PET, Rob Petritz's acronym. The big question was the buyer. Chris squinted and was just able to make out the acronym, *STZ*. He jerked his head around and looked down in the well of the pit at Terry Stutzel. His heart skipped when he saw Stutzel's badge—STZ.

Chris's first thought was what Stutzel's clearinghouse would say about a theretofore pigmy local making almost $500,000 in a few minutes. Or had the two pirates just pulled off the perfect crime?

Chapter Fifty-Two

CHRIS WAITED A day. Nothing happened, which meant it was time to go cloak-and-dagger.

After work he set off on a four-mile walk to North Avenue, where he drew an X on page three of the *Chicago Tribune* and inserted it into Freddie Slider's mailbox, before continuing three more miles to his Lincoln Park neighborhood. That night he traveled fourteen miles to Jackson Park Municipal, where Skip Slider sat waiting on the hood of his red Volkswagen Beattle.

"Christopherrrr.,." he trilled the words in a display of bonhomie, which contrasted with Chris's feeling of spookiness.

"What's up, Skip?"

"My brother found this in his mailbox," he said with relish, pulling out page three of the Chicago Tribune with a large X drawn across it.

"Do you think this is a good place?"

"Perfect," Slider cooed. "Perfect."

"Why don't we get in my car," Chris suggested.

"Sure." Slider said hopping off his car and getting into Chris's spacious Cadillac. "These things fit you well," he noted, once inside.

"They're the most popular car on the market to steal because you can fit lots of drugs and bodies in the trunk."

That fit Slider's mode of humor and he guffawed readily. "What's happening down on the good old trading floor, Chrissie?"

Chris shook his head in pronounced fashion. "I thought I'd seen it all. Until yesterday."

"Oh, baby." Slider rubbed his hands, savoring what was to come.

"I mean, damn."

"This sounds good."

For the next ten minutes Chris described the events of the previous day in the Treasury Pit, culminating in a gain that he estimated was around a half-million dollars. When he finished, Slider's eyes looked like saucers.

"A half-million dollars," he repeated after Chris. "And I hardly ever made a thousand dollars in a single day."

"You should see this Buster guy," Chris said. "Total piece of work, non-stop screaming at everyone about everything all day."

"Yep, that's the profile down there," Slider said, nodding his head.

"Imagine what kind of asshole he's going to be with his pockets lined," Chris noted.

"You think they got away with it?"

"I halfway expected to hear they'd been caught today."

"Yeah, from what I remember, those clearinghouses watch their traders like hawks. They'd have nailed me to the barn door if I'd tried to take a position like that, even if it made money."

"What I'm thinking—why they haven't gotten caught—is that this guy Stutzel clears his trades through Kite Futures. Some of their customers have left them because they suspect the managers and owners are winging their own trades in front of customer orders. Kite is used to seeing big swings from their traders."

"Man," Slider said, his voice dripping with anticipation, "Ben's gonna love this one. "

***

TWO DAYS LATER, the *Windy City Times* ran a story under Slip Slider's byline:

PERFECT CRIME AT THE CHICAGO COMMODITIES EXCHANGE

BY SKIP SLIDER

There have been many attempts at the perfect crime at the Chicago Commodities Exchange, which is not surprising given that $200 billion of contracts trades there daily.

Two years ago, an impostor with a fake-membership badge made a series of large trades in the Treasury-Index Pit. When the trades went against him he fled, only to be arrested at O' Hare International Airport—the so-called O'Hare spread.

A more elaborate plot was cooked up last year by two veteran traders. They brought Pakistani taxi drivers onto the CCE trading floor and introduced them as Middle Eastern oil sheikhs. Smelling big commissions, various floor brokers agreed to execute huge orders for the two men. One speculated heavily on the market going up; the other bet heavily the market would fall. The first trader made $4,000,000, while the second trader lost $6,000,000 and fled to Canada. However, when the first trader showed up at his clearinghouse to collect his $4,000,000 profit, the clearinghouse refused to allow the trader—who had never made over $60,000 in one year— to withdraw the money. He was later arrested by the FBI.

In the latest scam, a smalltime trader, in cahoots with a brokerage clerk, has successfully pulled off quite a caper. In a volatile market during the Rodney King riots on Friday, the clerk reported to his customer, Cook Mercer, that one of their customers had sold 1,000 contracts of Treasury futures at the very low price of the day—92-08.

However, the clerk, a mid-twenties male named Buster Kinman, had never even entered the order into the market. Instead, he simply wrote his employer's name on the order as the seller and put a friend's name—Terry Stutzel—as the buyer. Given that the market only briefly touched 92-08 before turning back up sharply, Stutzel is thought to have made almost $500,000 on the trade within minutes. Meanwhile, up to this point the customer is out over $1,000,000 for a trade that never actually occurred in the Treasury Pit.

The article proved to be a dead strike. The violated customer immediately sued Cook Mercer for treble damages on their seven-figure loss. Buster Kinman and Terry Stutzel heard about it when they arrived together at 7:00 in the morning. By 7:10 they had fled by taxi cab, only to have Buster apprehended by the police a few weeks later when he reappeared in town to torment an ex-girlfriend. The CCE issued a terse statement decrying the "egregious and unprecedented breach of etiquette to the liquidity of our financial markets here in Chicago."

Meanwhile, Slider floated on cloud nine. Ben Clayton came by and slapped his desk. "Great, story," he exulted. "You've really done a public service with this article." Indeed, nobody had disputed the story and it had led to a remedy. "This is journalism at its finest," Clayton concluded.

However, he wasn't satisfied. "Yeah, this was good, Skip. But these were a bunch of fringe characters. What we really need are some big fish to show the whole shebang is corrupt to the core."

"I couldn't agree more," said Slider, who was an unlikely person to be sounding like a company man. "I'll relay it to our source on the floor."

"Yes, tell him he's doing the financial markets a great service," Clayton said. "Oh, and one other thing, Skip. Come see me later this week to discuss your compensation and how we can make you more whole."

Chapter Fifty-Three

"COME ON, PARKER. Let's go. Breakfast."

Chris looked down at the foot of the Pit and saw John Weakley. He then glanced in the other direction and saw Barbra Lasky's sculpted figure turned around chatting up the brokers behind her. It was 9:00 and the market was dead. "Aw, what the hell." He handed off his deck of customer orders to Drew Solly's brokerage group and descended the Pit ladder. "Take forty-five minutes," he told Danny.

He and Weakley headed out the back entrance of the Exchange and across the street to *The Trading Goat*. Better yet for Weakley, one of the great raconteurs at the CCE, a whole gaggle of traders he knew was already seated. Chris and Weakley joined their table.

Breakfast in downtown Chicago invariably featured hard eggs, flavorless hash browns, crusty bacon, and watery coffee. The conversation was the standard fare of pit shenanigans and sexual debauchery. Ray Malley was again a featured topic. Weakley began regaling the table full of males in their thirties about his trip home on the Eisenhower Expressway the previous afternoon, when he had come upon a Rolls Royce traveling at twenty miles per hour, as it veered across several lanes.

"Finally, I decide I've got to get around this thing," he recounted with animation, "so I head into the emergency lane. When I look over, guess who is at the wheel of that $150,000 toy?"

"Elvis," Chris said, trying to expedite the answer.

"Your man, Malley. And guess what his problem is?"

"Blow job?" a trader at the far-end of the table ventured.

"Not quite," Weakley said, pausing for effect. In a low voice, he continued, "He's got a car phone in one hand, and the other hand is also occupied."

Everyone laughed on cue and Manory jibed, "I can't wait to tell my wife that story tonight."

Weakley craved the company of big traders. Sure enough, as everybody sat there eating, Ronnie Elin came rushing by. He looked to be in a harried state when he spotted his colleagues.

"Hey, hey, Weak," Elin asked, "have you seen Batesy come through here yet?"

"I don't believe so."

"How long have you been here?"

"Fifteen minutes."

"Good, he's dust."

"For what?" Weakley asked.

"Oh man, Blondie's got this new unit on her team named Rascha," Elin gushed, before reaching down with his mouth and making an exaggerated motion of kissing his hand. "I've been waiting all night for 9:00 this morning to get here." He rushed off before yelling back, "Tell Batesy to forget it."

"What the hell was that about?" Chris asked after Elin was out of sight.

"You mean you haven't heard about the Service?" Weakley asked, a delicious enthusiasm suffusing his voice.

"What service?"

"The service you call that supplies the women."

"How do you know they're not men?" Tony Manory remarked.

"Well, listen to this," Weakley said, lifting his forehead. "Ken Flippen told me these women really are perfect—good enough to keep you coming back, but not so fine you've gotta leave your wife."

"Where do they keep 'em?"

"It's headquartered over in Lake Point Towers; that lady, uh . . ."

"Blondie," Chris helped him.

"Yeah, Blondie; she runs it. Anyway, Elin and Batesy have a standing bet; whichever one is the first to get up $10,000 for the day makes the first reservation when they open at 9:00. And that girl he just said, Rachel?"

"Rascha," Chris corrected him.

"Yeah, Rascha. Anyway, she's some new import from Russia they're all raving about."

"That explains some things," Chris commented in neutral fashion.

Just as the waitress arrived with the bill, Ronnie Elin again came rushing through, looking more discombobulated than ever.

"Hey, Weak, Weak, have you seen Brett?"

"Brett?"

"Yeah, my trade checker."

"No."

"Goddammit. I call up Blondie and what happens— Rascha doesn't show for work this morning. Blondie can't even tell me when she's gonna get there. I get up in my office and," he shook his head in disbelief. "it was all over with. If you see Brett, tell him he's got some serious cleaning to do."

Elin hurried off, looking concerned. But after a few steps he stopped in his tracks, seized by an epiphany. In fact, it was a glimmer of decency. "Hey, wait, Weak, forget it—don't even mention it to Brett, okay. I'll handle it." He reached over and grabbed everyone's bill, along with all the napkins he could get out of two holders, before bolting again.

This time the laughter started before Elin was out of earshot. Chris knew Weakley was ecstatic to have another arrow in his quiver of stories. He briefly considered relaying the anecdote to Skip Slider, before deciding it was better to keep any rank perversion out of his stories.

Finally, Ricky Horne brought up the newspaper story as everyone was getting up. "How about those two idiots trying to rip off that customer like that? Can you believe they thought they could get away with it?"

"Yeah, that guy, Stutzel, stood right down from me," Manory said. "Worst trader I ever saw. On second thought, maybe it was worth a try."

"Any idea how they got caught?"

"No," Manory answered. "But it is strange how the newspaper gets the whole story before either the broker, the customer, or clearinghouse. Nobody knew anything until this article."

***

"CHRISSIE, HOLD ON there a minute, will you?"

"What's up, G-Man?"

"You got a second?"

"Yeah, but I gotta get back to the salt mines." Chris was feeling fidgety. He was standing in the CCE lobby with George Haskins, otherwise known as *George the Grapevine* because of his insatiable desire for gossip.

Haskins had always been a great *smiler* and incorrigible lickspittle. But today he was direct. "Chrissie, that article in the newspaper this morning about those two guys pulling off that scam—it was written by Skip Slider."

Chris gave him a questioning look.

"There was a Skip Slider that used to trade in the Treasury Pit. You remember him?"

"Oh yeah," Chris said. " I do remember."

Haskins looked him in the eye in a way that seemed foreign to all their previous gabs. "You two used to talk all the time."

No. Chris knew the split-second reaction to Haskins's comment was the key. "Yeah, but I think that's a different Skip Slider," he told Haskins. However, his throat constricted, causing his voice to trail off wrong.

"That's not what I heard," Haskins said with uncharacteristic firmness. "Somebody up in the *Vortex* office told me it's the same guy."

"For all I know, it is," Chris said with a furrowed brow. "He was one of those guys that just disappeared." Then he added, with a short laugh, "If it is him, we're sure gonna have something to talk about next time I run into him."

"When you see him, tell him it was a darn good article." Haskins never dropped his stare.

"If I get a chance," Chris said airily, before breaking away.

He tried to forget the conversation. Haskins had always seemed harmless. But he also knew George the Grapevine had long since earned his sobriquet.

Chapter Fifty-Four

Big fish.

SKIP SLIDER HAD relayed Ben Clayton's message that he wanted the scalps of Napoleons and Caesars. However, Chris remained occupied with his own struggles in the Treasury Pit. He especially dreaded the first Friday of every month, when the U.S. Labor Department issued its monthly unemployment report at 7:30 Chicago time.

On July 6th at 7:29, he again found himself pinioned up against the Pit dividing rail by a sardine stack of heated bodies. As usual, the entire left side of the Pit was cut off. *No orders please,* he silently wished, in a perversion of his normal thinking. Meanwhile Solly's large apparatus of brokers and assistants stood like a coiled spring waiting for orders.

7:30.

The west board flashed the report: the economy had created 185,000 jobs in March—in line with market expectations. The market stalled, and Chris breathed a sigh of relief. However, the locals who made their money off market volatility felt differently.

"This market blows," Henry Cash said.

"For fuck's sake, this is starting to feel like a job," another trader chimed in.

Nonetheless, nobody headed off for breakfast. The first Friday of every month was lifestyle-support day.

"Hey, hey," a phone broker stood and screamed at a broker's assistant. But before she could flash her order,

Marty Allman called over, "How 'bout some cheese with that whine?", bringing the house down in the maelstrom of packed bodies, as the girl looked on in confusion.

"Check out the tush on that runner in the yellow jacket," Dick Joyner said, referring to a blushing, late-teenage girl rushing along with an order in her hand. "I was talking to her the other day."

"Sorry to ruin it, gentlemen," the sexpert Allman piped in, "but if once again you haven't heard, that coke whore you just pointed out goes out with Pearl's brokerage group two Fridays ago. Five of 'em end up at Vince Fanning's house. He's got a big glass table in his living room where we play cards. Bottom line is this: four of 'em end up with their heads below the table watching her drop a payload at 'em."

"That's gotta be bullshit," Joe D' Abruzzo shot back amidst the laughs.

"No, that's real shit," Chris said, reflecting his light mood.

"But I don't even see the point," Allman's younger brother, Bill, standing nearby said.

"You wouldn't," Marty hectored him into silence once again.

***

THE LOFTY CONVERSATION on Buttfuck Row got interrupted when Dave Revord of Elliott House jumped up and called to Solly's clerk. "Hey, hey, sell a thousand at the market."

"Dammit, why didn't we get that order?" Chris yelled down at Danny. "A dead market is the perfect time for a big order."

Phone buttons began lighting up at desks around the trading floor. Phone brokers screamed to get the attention of brokers' assistants.

"Hey, hey, sell 200."
"Hey, 300, sell 'em now, now."
"Sell me 500 at the market."

Traders who had been complaining about the lack of volatility just a couple minutes before stood by with confusion drawn across their faces. Chris glanced up at the gigantic Reuters screen:

BUSH PASSES OUT AT TOKYO ECONOMIC SUMMIT.
SPECULATION OF HEART ATTACK

An ominous thought entered the nation's collective consciousness: *President J. Danforth Quayle.* The man who was the nationwide butt of comedians' jokes could soon be the most powerful person in the world.

Several phone brokers began screaming to cancel buy orders they had previously placed. "I'm out, I'm out, hey, hey, out, out, out." But the normally attentive broker assistants strategically lost their hearing.

"Anything on my sell order?" Dave Revord shouted at Solly's clerks. "Something, come on," he pleaded. But he could only look on helplessly.

Finally, after the market had plunged over two full points, Mike Patti of *First Boston* jumped up and shouted to Drew Solly's group. "Hey, hey, buy 1,000 at the market."

Perfect timing.

"Buy 'em, buy 'em, buy 'em," Tripp Cole screamed at his boss, Drew Solly.

Solly, who was still flailing away trying to sell a thousand contracts, hurled around. "Sold, sell you a thousand," he shouted at Cole. Just like that, a hundred-million-dollar trade between two brokers in the same group.

Chris's stomach sank. *I'm a nobody.*

"Have I got 'em?" Dave Revord continued screaming from the Elliott House desk.

"Yes?" Mike Patti also shouted from the First Boston desk. "Come on."

The look of fear on both Revord's and Patti's faces was palpable. The board showed a chaotic skein of prices— 95-09, 95-12, 95-19, 95-24, 95-19.

This should be simple enough, Chris thought. But then Drew Solly turned back to Tripp Cole. "Hold 'em," he whispered.

Hold 'em? Chris stood spellbound.

Revord and Patti held their hands high, trying to expedite getting the prices for their customers.

Chris watched Solly whisper something else to Cole, who leaned over and spoke into their clerk Jerry Stanton's ear. He looked back at Cole with a glum face, before buckling up to become a good soldier. "Dave, I've got it," Stanton called to Revord at the Elliott House desk. "You sold 1,000 at 95-09." He then turned to the First Boston desk. "Hey Mike, you bought 1,000 at 95-21."

How is the price different? Solly and Cole traded with each other!

Chris moved his neck over Cole's head to see what he and Solly had written on their cards. Just as he gained a vertical view, the pursuit from the Sleazebags cracked his top half over the rail and into Tripp Cole's head. He had a clear shot at Chris's exposed front-side, but he didn't react —a surefire sign that something large was afoot.

Cole took Solly's card, along with his own, and held them in his fingers like aces in a poker game. Chris finally gained enough traction to cork his head over Cole's shoulder. What he saw on both cards could be described as *revelation*. Both Solly and Tripp Cole had scratched out the other's acronym as the counterparty they had traded with. In its place, both had written PUM.

PUM was the acronym for Dale Turner, a journeyman local widely known for his stout head, thus occasioning his nickname *Pumpkin*. He stood directly in front of Solly and seemingly wore a different-colored trading jacket every month, as he got bounced around from one clearinghouse to another. Now Pumpkin seemed to have morphed into his most perilous role yet, *bagman*.

Chris did some quick arithmetic. Solly and Cole had stuffed twelve-thousand ticks of juice ($375,000) into Pumpkin's pockets.

Chris's heart was throbbing. "Danny, let's get out of here."

"Now?" The alert clerk looked around at the waving hands and roiling market.

"Yeah."

Chris followed him down the Pit ladder and began making his way back to the Elliott House desk to inform them that his arch-foes, Drew Solly and Tripp Cole, had royally screwed Elliott House's biggest customer. But just as he reached the Elliott House aisle way, he stopped in his tracks. *No. This is devastating. Why not inform Elliott House and everyone else through Slider?*

"Hey, Danny," Chris screamed over the heads of several clerks, "we're out of here. See you tomorrow."

"Oh, okay."

With the market in full uproar, Chris began to rush off the CCE floor, before again having second thoughts. A couple days from now everyone on his side of the Pit would be under intense suspicion. Don't be too obvious, he thought.

He did a U-turn, and came upon Danny as he was leaving the floor. "Sorry, Danny, I just needed a quickie. Let's get back in there."

"Alright," his confused assistant said, and they piled back into the Pit.

In spirit, Chris was elsewhere for the rest of the day. He didn't pay any attention to the Elliott House desk to encourage orders coming his way. When the closing bell rang at 2:00 that afternoon, he marched off the floor, barely acknowledging salutations from anyone. Once outside he remembered to purchase a copy of the *Chicago Tribune* and began loping up LaSalle Street until he stopped. I don't want to be seen by anyone, he thought.

The frugal Alabaman took the rare step of flagging down one of Chicago's yellow taxis.

***

"CHRISTOPHER."

"LET'S GET in my car," Chris directed Skip Slider in an uncharacteristically stern tone. It was their second nighttime meeting in as many weeks at Jackson Park, but he wasn't any more at ease.

"Do you remember Solly?" he asked once they got inside.

"Hell, yeah, I remember him," Slider answered without hesitation. "He was a god down there. He never traded with me a single time."

"How 'bout Cole, the guy he crossed the trade with?"

"I might recognize him."

"Solly's henchman. One of the guys on the back row of the Pit."

"Oh, those guys were the worst. They had their own markets back there."

"He's feared almost as much as Solly."

"I remember the way the place worked."

"I've gotta say this again," Chris said, taking a solemn tone, "if it gets out that I leaked this story, they will Jimmy Hoffa me."

That drew an appreciative laugh from Slider. "Well stated, buddy."

"Seriously," Chris continued in something approaching a browbeating tone.

"I know," Slider said. "But this isn't so much crazy as it's just stupid. Even in that shithole down there, somebody's bound to pick up on ripping off a customer that bad."

"Think of a pickpocket lifting a wallet," Chris opined. "It's a Pavlovian reaction."

"But Solly's got to have more money than he could ever need. Why do something like that?"

"Look at Milken, Boesky, and all the other inside traders on Wall Street. They were plutocrats to begin with. But next thing you know, they were meeting people in underground garages in Brooklyn to get inside information for the next killing."

"So, what do Solly, Cole, and this Pumpkin guy do now?"

"Oh, come on," Chris said, shaking his head with a mocking smile. "Just think of the proverbial wise guys getting together for a game of poker. Only there's plenty of swag for everybody to walk away a winner."

Chapter Fifty-Five

Schadenfreude. IT HAD ITS own subculture at the CCE.

Chris had always found it eerie how much raw pleasure traders gained from the downfall of their colleagues. As he walked to the coatroom, he heard one clerk whispering to another, "Biggest broker," while pointing excitedly to a copy of the *Windy City Times.*

Chris had not bought a copy this morning for fear of being seen reading it. Once he stepped foot onto the trading floor, he detected a delicate atmosphere. Treasury traders appeared to be tiptoeing around.

"Hey, did you read the article in the paper about Solly and Cole?" Marty Allman whispered to Chris.

Allman's covert tone alerted him because he had never been discreet about anything. "I heard about it," Chris responded, in his first deception of the day.

"I mean, damn," Allman continued, "crossing a thousand-lot trade with twelve ticks of juice."

"Not chopped liver," Chris agreed.

"Don't reckon we'll be seeing Pumpkin for a while."

Chris looked into the Treasury Pit where Pumpkin had been a permanent fixture, planted directly in front of Solly. Unsurprisingly, he wasn't there. Surrounding locals murmured nervously to each other.

"It didn't look like he'd had a winning trade in six months, anyway."

"Problem's solved," Allman said with a flicker of an evil grin.

"How much do you think he's blown in Las Vegas already?" one of the Sleazebags piped in.

"Blown?" Allman corrected him. "He's getting blown."

"It explains why people see him all over town spending like a drunken sailor, even though he can't hit the side of a barn here in the Pit."

Pumpkin wasn't there. But Solly and Tripp Cole were, attempting to show the flag. The normally poker-faced veterans stared straight ahead, unable to hide their grim moods.

The opening bell rang. Elliott House phone brokers rose from their seats and began flashing orders into the Pit. However, none of them went to Solly's group. Instead, everything was aimed at Danny.

Chris now had Solly's business, but not his central position in the Pit, and the familiar tormenting figure of Ray Malley clung to his backside. Chris continued jumping and pirouetting as he bought and sold large quantities. Locals quickly began focusing on him from the back row, over the head of Solly's group.

By 7:30, Chris had already cracked out twenty-five hundred contracts and was drenched with sweat.

"Sell ten, Chris," Danny called up. Finally, a small order.

Chris turned his neck to look at Coffin Corner where Barbra Lasky was bidding 94-18. But when she saw him, her doe-like eyes darkened and took on a hooded look. She jerked her head in another direction, not wanting to trade.

Ray Malley saw what Chris was trying to do. "Eighteen bid," he shouted, while pawing away at Chris's arms like a defensive lineman.

What the hell. Give myself a break. Chris folded and sold Malley ten at 94-18, hoping Malley might give him a crevice more of space.

Soon the market was 94-19 bid and Malley began roaring, "Sell ten at 94-20, sell ten at 94-20," hoping to take a quick profit. All Chris could do was shake his head.

By 11:00 Chris had executed 8,000 contracts, the most he had ever done in one day. "Let's take a break, Danny." He jumped out of the Pit and made the break sign to Jack Fitzgerald, as if snapping a stick in two. Fitzgerald raised his thumb, indicating good job.

As he loped off the floor, locals began jibing him. "Skyscraper, you're the man," one local yelled over.

"No, you'se da one," Chris sallied. "I was looking for you."

Even someone as wary of the whole business as Chris had to resist the headiness. One person, however, saw him coming down the hallway and swerved in the opposite direction. Barbra.

Always wishing to abide her, Chris breezed by with a quick salute, which she didn't acknowledge. Up until now she had always been the perfect weathervane, glowing when his business was good and offhanded when the cupboard was empty. But now the look that veiled her face was distant and alien. *What's going on?*

The person standing next to her, George the Grapevine Haskins, had the opposite reaction. "Hey, Chrissie," he said and began tagging along beside him. "Lots of biz in there today, huh?"

"Must have been some other tall guy you were looking at it," Chris responded in deflection.

"No, man, you were letting 'em fly all over the place." Haskins couldn't resist adding, "Except to me." He gave a mock elbow to Chris's ribs.

Haskins' mention of Skip Slider a couple weeks before had caused a temporary bout of paranoia. Chris had brought it up with Slider, who asked, "Who is he?" Chris had done his best to describe Haskins—smiley, frizzy hair, touchy and fidgety. But Slider responded, "That could be a thousand people down there."

"Hey, buddy," Haskins edged in on Chris. "All that business you had this morning might be here to stay. Woo-wee, your old buddy sure did a number on Solly and Cole in the paper this morning."

"I heard about the article," Chris muttered.

"Look, man," Haskins edged in with his eyes narrowing and his smile diminishing. "We were trying to figure out where he's getting these stories. It's gotta be somebody over there in your area of the Pit."

"Could be," Chris acknowledged.

"I was just up in the office," Haskins reported to Chris. "Guess what everybody's calling Slider's inside source."

"Got me."

"'Deep Pit', after the whole Watergate Deep Throat thing."

"Clever," Chris acknowledged.

"You don't talk with Skip Slider any more at all?" Haskins continued probing.

"Naw, I was actually gonna call him after that last story. Say, you're a golfer, G-Man. If I can ever find him, why don't the three of us get out there some day?"

Instead of a congenial response, George Haskins stood back a half-step and looked up at Chris longer than normal. He seemed to be trying to process Chris's denial of any recent contact with Slider. His expectant look of gleaning gold-plated gossip evaporated. He straightened up and said in a business-like voice, "Okay, Chrissie, be seeing you. Knock those big orders out."

Jesus, Chris thought as Haskins walked away. *Am I really that good of a liar?* Such a notion left him in a fragile mood.

Chapter Fifty-Six

CHRIS EXITED THE 156 LaSalle bus at 7:00 a.m., turned the corner to Madison Street and walked towards the news box in front of the CCE. He bent his extra-long frame to check out the front-page headlines of the *Windy City Express*. One look gave him a stiff jolt.

SHADOW TRADING RING IN MIDST OF WORLD'S LARGEST MARKET
CHAIRMAN'S SON INVOLVED

BY SKIP SLIDER

The Chicago Commodities Exchange boasts that its Treasury-Index Futures Pit is the most liquid market in the entire world. But now it seems that a handful of its participants have formed a shadow market to all but eliminate their risk. One such group is widely referred to as The Sleazebags.

This rogue brokerage group of five males in their early to mid-thirties, including CCE Chairman Dean Beman's son, survive off a deck of retail customer orders. Their modus-operandi is to give the right of first refusal on all their orders to the other members of the group.

"Whichever member of the group fills the customer order is actually the stooge," says one nearby trader. "All he gets is the commission, while the other members get the

fairy dust, because their customers—more accurately referred to as victims—almost always lose money."

The Windy City Express *contacted Dean Beman to ask for comment. However, his response was not fit for print.*

Chris scooted away from the newspaper box, again afraid to purchase a copy. A helpless feeling swept through him. He had complained incessantly to Slider about the Sleazebags, but not for the purpose of a newspaper article. Slider hadn't even told him a story was in the works. As for the Sleazebags, the naked truth was Chris feared gang violence from them.

Should I go in today?

He walked around the corner where he looked down another skyscraper-lined boulevard, before deciding his only viable option was to buck up and play it normal. Once inside the massive granite facade of the CCE, he hurried through the lobby, up the escalators, and straight to the clerk's bathroom, where he hid in a stall reading the scribbling on the wall. The racist invective dotting the bathroom walls during his first years at the Exchange had been replaced by sexual perversion—perhaps a modest step up.

The depressing thing was that during those early years as a clerk, the exact people he was now obsessed with—Molina, Grutzkis, D' Abruzzo, and Mutley, the Sleazebags—had pushed, shoved, and humiliated him with impunity. Chris had chalked it all up as the price to pay. But here it was several year later and all the Sleazebags were still there, contesting over the same piece of real estate, like the Arab-Israeli conflict. Maybe Slider was right to expose them.

He got up from the commode, washed his hands, and headed back into the hallway. There he ran into the elfin-like figure of Barbra Lasky.

"Hey, stranger," Chris said.

"Oh, hi," Barbra said in a voice that started off friendly, but with wariness creeping in. "So, more stuff in the paper today."

"Yeah," Chris answered, also trying to affect concern.

"Any idea what's behind it?" she asked, crossing her arms in front of her like a shield.

"This place is like Washington D.C, one giant ear."

"It's all going on right over there in your area of the Pit," she said, her hawkish eyes practically impaling him. "On both sides of where you stand."

"Yeah, well, we're overdue to get some living space around there."

"Is that so?" Mysteriously, she added, "I just hope everything is okay with you."

Barbra split off towards her locker and Chris headed to the escalator.

***

"CHRIS." JACK FITZGERALD summoned him in a confidential manner. "Did you see the article about the Sleazebags?"

"Just heard about it," Chris fudged.

Fitzgerald touched his shoulder. "Wouldn't it be nice to finally get them off you? And for fuck's sake," he added, "their customers deserve a break from the pasting those assholes have administered to them over the years."

"Yeah," Chris said, shaking his head. "But I reckon it's a cold day in hell before this gang gives them any relief."

He grabbed his trading cards and dutifully climbed the ladder to the Pit. For once he found himself hoping Ray Malley would be there to serve as a buffer. But he was nowhere in sight, so Chris edged into his familiar spot, between senior Sleazebag Mickey Molina and the wooden rail, making a show of scanning the board to see what was happening in the overseas markets. "What's the call?" he asked. But it sounded awkward.

"Don't know," Grutzkis answered, followed by a brooding silence.

Chris noticed the Sleazebags were passing around a large stack of customer orders. The game was still on. However, the minute the opening bell rang, Molina and Benjie Beman began calling out locals' names in the Pit and selling to them at the Bid-price and buying at the Ask-price on their customer orders. These long-lost traders down in the groin of the Pit were almost pathetically grateful. "Yeah, checking Benjie. Thanks, I bought five at...Thanks, thanks. Mickey, yeah, Mickey. I sold you ten at...Yeah, Mickey. Got it." The Sleazebags carried out the duty with grim faces, clearly tormented by the thought of all the cream getting away.

I've cleaned things up!

Chris tried to keep busy signaling market information to the Elliott House desk, and acting like he didn't hear. But he heard Molina ask, "He's the type, I'm telling you. How can we find out?"

"Benjie's father is bound to know somebody down at that paper," Jeremy Mutley said. "We can find out if Parker really is that Deep Pit bitch."

That got Chris' attention. By mid-afternoon the Sleazebags seemed less shaken up, and began trading with each other again on their customer orders. The promise to hunt down the whistleblower gave them extra mojo.

Chris left the trading floor that afternoon feeling like a lamb in the valley with wolves peering down from the hills. His overwhelming desire was to talk to Slider. The article about the Sleazebags was the product of two late-night storytelling sessions, with Chris at his flowery southern best. It appeared Slider had remembered every detail cold.

What was next? Chris wondered if he could even stop Slider at this point.

Chapter Fifty-Seven

BEFORE THE FIRST two articles on illegal trades appeared, Chris had tingled with excitement. But since the Sleazebags story six days ago, he had been creeping up to the newspaper box each morning with dread.

One Monday morning in mid-September he looked into the box and saw the following headline:

OVERSEXED TRADERS POPULATE TREASURY PIT AT CCE
TRADERS FLOCK TO 'LAKEFRONT MADAM'

Skip Slider

For the second time in a week Chris found himself seized up, while hovering over a newspaper box on LaSalle Street. He peered over the shoulder of the well-dressed man crouched in front of him, who appeared to spontaneously purchase a copy upon seeing the titillating headline.

From his sideways angle, Chris was only able to catch a few words. But that was all he needed to see. The name *Blondie* was referenced in the first two paragraphs. The man in front of him turned the page as if on cue, and Chris caught a glimpse of the name, Steve Moore, and then the number 96.

Oh, shit.

Chris was well acquainted with the Steve Moore legend. He was not only one of the biggest traders in the Treasury Pit, but apparently harbored one of the greatest sex drives.

During the time of the FBI investigation, when every trader shuddered at the thought of being questioned by the Feds, Moore had been called in. He arrived at the local FBI office in a petrified state, fearful of being investigated for illegal trades. His anxiety was exacerbated when he saw several agents and secretaries sticking their heads out from behind cubicles, straining to catch glimpses of him. He was sent to the office of the lead interrogator.

The man opened up the interview by saying, "Mr. Moore, we have come in possession of an appointment book held by a lady named Blondie Drake. She has you listed for appointments a total of ninety-six times during the past year." Moore had hemmed and hawed for a few minutes about some headaches he had been having, before the conversation came to an awkward halt.

Finally, the agent said, "Okay, that will be all."

In Moore's later enthusiastic retelling of the tale, the man did not ask him any questions, make any threats, or even suggest he cease and desist from future activity. "I think they just wanted to have a look at this souped-up guy," he exulted.

Chris would soon learn today's article was dotted with tales of *white-powder pigs* and wide-open hooker blowouts in trader's offices. He felt partly relieved because the stories weren't specific to his area of the Pit, although he did catch the name Ray Malley. But on second thought, Malley had passed the photos of his sexual exploits all over the Treasury Pit.

While this article didn't appear personally dangerous at first glance, Slider had once again written an article reciting verbatim the facts of a story Chris had told him, even though he had never acted like he was doing anything other than enjoying the tale.

***

ALL FIVE SLEAZEBAGS were packed up against Chris for the opening range, with Mickey Molina's hand in its usual placement on Chris's lower spine.

"Well, the guy tattled on some more traders," Molina said.

"The article, you mean," Chris obfuscated.

"Yeah, yeah," Molina grumbled in a weary tone. "And the same people in the article you're always talking about."

"The same people everybody talks about."

"I've heard you tell that Steve Moore story five times, and now here it is splashed all over the paper."

"Yeah, but I've heard the damn story fifty times," Chris said.

Danny called up, "Chris, sell twenty."

"95-14 bid," Molina shouted up. The other Sleazebags chimed in behind him. "95-14 bid, Parker. Come on douchebag."

Chris gazed around the Pit. All around, locals were bidding 95-14. It was bound to be a good buy for whomever he sold the contracts to.

"Are you filled?" Danny called up.

"One sec." Chris knew he had plenty of time because the 95-14 bid was so large.

"For once, don't be an asshole," Molina said, increasing the pressure on Chris into the rail. "95-14 bid."

What the hell. Do myself a favor. Chris gave in and doled five contracts out to three of the Sleazebags at 95-14, with five left over for Ray Malley. Immediately they all began screaming like banshees. "Sell five at 95-15, sell five at 95-15," trying to take a quick profit. Chris rolled his eyes. Soon they had sold out, each one making $157.50.

The old violated feeling was back. After the damning newspaper article, Drew Solly had recovered most of his business by lavishly entertaining the Elliott House phone clerks and assuring them he was in the clear. Chris was still stuck on Buttfuck Row with a bunch of provincials who had one overriding credo: *nobody in the neighborhood lifts his head above the tulip field.*

Of late, he had begun to hone in on a central fact of life at the CCE, and for that matter, probably every trading floor since time immemorial: nobody ever voluntarily left; never once had he seen or even heard of a profitable trader quitting. Everyone hung on for dear life in this pagan ritual, hoping to suck as much as juice as possible out of it.

And here he was doing the same thing, just another trading drone.

Chris bit his lower lip as he held the Pit-dividing rail to avoid another crotch-crush. However, this thrust was different from the countless reps that preceded it, because on the spot he made a solemn resolution: his trading career would soon go either straight to the top, or he was out the door. The status-quo was the great enemy; somehow, he was going to escape.

Chapter Fifty-Eight

"AY, SECRETARIAT," A reporter joshed, as the upstart Skip Slider buzzed by.

"Hey, Skip," a young woman who had been receiving inordinate male attention since her recent arrival at the *Windy City Times,* greeted him.

Slider couldn't resist a modest strut; the attention that had been denied him during his bitter tenure at the CCE was upon him.

On this September morning, he had a new visitor. A slight, middle-aged male approached his desk. The man's fidgety look indicated he was nervous.

"Hello, Skip," he said. "I'm Blaise Topol from Arts and Culture."

"Yes, Blaise," Slider said. "We've passed each other but never formally met."

Topol nodded. "First, Skip, I want to congratulate you on your recent reporting. Fine work."

"Thanks."

Something told Slider to avoid any gregarious chitchat.

Topol leaned forward. "Could you come into my office for a few minutes? I have a story you will want to hear."

"Sure." He gave a heads-up to the receptionist and headed off with this previously unknown reporter.

When they entered Topol's office in the rear of the building, the first thing that stuck out was the walls. Rather than framed copies of his published articles like most reporters, Topol's office was stacked with Impressionist paintings. His desk was spotless.

"Have a seat, please."

Topol folded his hands in a businesslike manner. "Skip, I have a close personal acquaintance who was a long-time member of Karol Stanislav's staff. He worked in Stanislav's Chicago office for fourteen years. He has taken great interest in your recent articles."

Slider again chose to say nothing.

"My friend firmly believes Karol Stanislav is the greatest legislator of our time," Topol said. "But he felt he could no longer continue working for him."

"Okay."

"Despite holding the Chairman in great personal affection, he was forced to leave for two reasons. The first was rank homophobia in the office amongst all the workers."

The atmosphere shifted from business to electric, as Slider waited for another shoe to fall.

"However, that was not the deal breaker," Topol said with a nod, as if agreeing with his absent friend. "His greater concern was what he discovered during his tenure."

Slider tried to remain expressionless.

"It will probably come as no surprise to you that the Chairman has a well-funded political operation."

"I bet."

"He hasn't had a serious opponent since being elected thirty-six years ago. He does not even have an official campaign headquarters." Topol stopped and shrugged at Slider. "But guess what."

"Well," Slider said, drawing the word out with a laugh, "I could take a stab."

"It's bound to be a pretty good one," Topol assured him. "Don't get me wrong; there are some official employees.

But what do they do?" Topol threw up both hands in mock surrender, drawing a snicker from Slider.

He reached into his desk and extracted two sheets from a folder, handing one to Slider.

"This first sheet, Skip, is a list of the names on the Stanislav campaign payroll around the time my friend left."

Slider stared at a list of eighteen names, along with familiar addresses he recognized from Chicago's West Side, as well as the accompanying salaries. Each employee drew a salary in the $40,000 per year range.

"Let me guess," Slider jumped in, "this is the old ghost-payroll thing, right?"

"That is correct."

"So, let me, I'm sorry," Slider stuttered, "Does that mean they don't exist?"

"No, on the contrary," Topol corrected him, "they are very much flesh and blood, these people." They receive one-hundred percent of their paychecks, and keep enough to pay taxes on the whole thing, along with some extra." Topol paused before adopting a solemn tone. "However, the balance of their paychecks is passed on."

"How long has this been going on?"

"Oh..." Topol's eyes took on a far-off look that drew another spontaneous chuckle from Slider. The two of them were exact opposites, but there was something he liked about Topol's sincerity.

"Could I meet with your buddy today?" Slider asked.

Topol put up his hand in a blocking motion. "I'm sorry, Skip. That is not going to be possible. He has decided to remain private for several reasons. But the last several evenings he has repeatedly said, 'This story belongs in the public domain.'"

"He's dead-right about that," Slider said, his enthusiasm breaking into the open. "That's what I plan to do." He edged to the front of his seat as a prelude to standing up.

Topol stopped him. "Please, just a few more minutes."
He spoke in a grave manner. "I have one other thing to
show you." Topol handed Slider the second sheet which had
a list of ten names, along with Washington addresses and
salaries. All were in the $45,000 range.

"These people were on the federal payroll as members
of Stanislav's congressional staff in Washington." Topol
looked closely at Slider. "But none of them actually worked
there."

Slider slowly repeated, "None of them worked there."

Topol gave a grave nod, allowing Slider to dive in.
"We're talking a serious felony, right? I mean, diverting
campaign money is one thing, but this is taxpayer money.
That's a doozy of a felony."

"Yes," Topol said with pursed lips. "But mind you,
diverting campaign money is as well."

Leaning forward as if ready to sprint out of the office,
Slider got down to the nitty-gritty. "So your friend will not
come forward. Which means I have to rely on these sheets,
right?"

"Yes," Topol said, "but this is all you need. It is
devastating."

Natural instinct took over. Slider jumped up and said,
"Dude, Blaise, you've done a great public service here,
amazing reporting job. I'm gonna find a way to make it all
worthwhile for you."

Topol looked embarrassed at that last pledge and
remained still as he fought off a small blush.

"I'm headed to Ben's office right now!"

Slider stood and was gone.

***

BEN CLAYTON MADE no bones about it; results trumped
fairness in journalism. A wet-behind-the-ears reporter like

Slider now had greater access to him than many of the paper's wizened veterans.

Slider walked unselfconsciously into Clayton's office and noticed the executive editor perk up. After a brief synopsis of his meeting with Blaise Topol, he handed him the sheets with the payroll information of the ghosts.

Clayton took to flipping through them like a teenager scanning baseball cards. "Yes, yes, yes," he said in a covetous manner, before quoting Shakespeare. "The treason I love, the traitor I hate."

"Do we publish it?" Slider asked.

"Are you kidding," Clayton snapped. "Just give us a few days to verify none of these people actually works for his campaign or congressional office."

Clayton stood and sauntered over to the window. Looking out on the river, he opted for a philosophical tone. "I believe Karol Stanislav should be studied in American institutes of higher learning. In political science classes, finance, and ethics. Definitely journalism, too. There is a lot for us to learn." He maintained a pensive manner, before adding with a surprised look. "And it's not all bad."

Chapter Fifty-Nine

KAROL STANISLAV HAD visited the White House countless times. Nonetheless, he still got frisky about the trip down Pennsylvania Avenue to the executive mansion the way a young boy loved going to the circus.

"I can't get enough of it," he unabashedly told his colleagues on Capitol Hill. "It never gets old."

His old friend, George Herbert Walker Bush, now occupied the Oval Office. The two of them couldn't have been more different. One was the Great WASP with lineage back to Mayflower descendants, while the other evoked the ethnicity of one of America's most embedded urban political machines. But politics always had made strange bedfellows, and the two men never failed to bring out the gregarious best in each other. When Bush had arrived at the White House on the day of his inauguration, he shunted aside all Cabinet officials, White House staff, and dignitaries, even family members, to meet privately with his old friend in the Oval Office. Once they were alone, Bush shook his head in disbelief. "Karol, can you believe it?" he asked. "I'm President."

"Damn right you are," Stanislav responded, holding nothing back as he grinned from ear-to-ear. He had then used his clout to convince the President to sign a bill breaking his campaign pledge not to raise taxes, which had Bush in hot water with conservatives. Now the President was trying to convince Stanislav to return the favor by pushing through a landmark bill reforming the nation's vast welfare system. He knew his only chance of passage in Congress lay through Stanislav.

They were scheduled to meet alone at two o' clock in the Oval Office; Stanislav had already popped out of his office twice to ask his staff about the timing of the limousine ride down Pennsylvania Avenue. He was to be picked up in the circular driveway behind the Capitol at exactly 1:47. But at 1:35 his chief of staff, Joe Wolf, knocked on his door and entered. He looked stricken.

"Mr. Chairman," Wolf said, sounding winded, "I just received a call from *The Windy City Times*. They..."

"Joe," Stanislav cut him off. "I'm off to see the Big Fella in ten minutes. Let's hear it afterwards."

"Mr. Chairman..."

Something about the frozen look on his chief of staff's face gave Stanislav pause. He stopped his preparation for the presidential meeting and looked at Wolf.

"Mr. Chairman," Wolf continued, "a *Windy City Times* reporter just faxed two sheets of paper to us. One's a list of people on our Chicago campaign office payroll; the other shows our Washington congressional staff."

Stanislav didn't say a word as Wolf handed him the two sheets. He scanned them for no more than a few seconds before looking up. "They're running a story on this?" His voice sounded like his solar-plexus had been walloped.

Wolf, the ultra-confident enforcer, nodded.

"I see," Stanislav said, his lips pulled into a tight circle as he looked out the window onto the back terrace of the U.S. Capitol. His face looked sunken and older than just a few minutes ago, the solemn picture of a man whose deepest beliefs were being called into question.

His decency instincts kicked in. *My friend, the President.*

Stanislav spoke quietly. "Maybe the best thing for everybody, including the President, is for you to call the

White House and say we're gonna get whacked pretty good in the papers tomorrow. He's got his own re-election to worry about."

"Do you want me to cancel the meeting?"

"Uh, if that's what they want," Stanislav answered in a humble tone, nodding at his desk as if still trying to convince himself. "Let them decide."

The ever-confident man with the surefooted ways in the halls of power sat immobilized. *Will people ever believe me when I say that I never thought of this as stealing?*

Chapter Sixty

"THE FIRST RULE of politics is survival," CCE Chairman Dean Beman pronounced. It was an early-autumn Friday night and Beman was sitting in his office with a worried-looking CCE President Mike Kilpatrick at his side.

The *Windy City Times* and *Chicago Herald* had both published stories today indicating the CCE's greatest-ever ally, Karol Stanislav, was being investigated by a grand jury for a fraudulent ghost-payroll scheme. Stanislav had issued a defiant statement declaring he was not resigning and planning to seek re-election this November.

"Mike," Beman said, while reclining his neck backwards, "we could get hurt bad here. I mean bad. Unless we protect ourselves."

Kilpatrick looked at his feet and remained silent.

"Think about it," Beman continued, unwinding from a reclining position and stretching his neck forward over his large desk. "Yeah, Stanislav cratered that silly electronic-trading system in New York. And he did it in a way that showed a brilliance all his own. The whole thing has been put to bed, as long as," Beman ratcheted up his voice, "as long as we take care of ourselves."

Kilpatrick remained frozen, emitting a barely-audible assent that sounded like a child agreeing with a parent.

Beman's face flushed and he raised his hands high like a linebacker blitzing a quarterback. "As the chairman of this great American institution, it is my responsibility to ask where our future lies."

Kilpatrick looked medically ill, palpably fearing what the man in front of him was planning.

"Mike," Beman went on, "the lesson of Watergate is you've got to get in front of a scandal. Nixon stuck by Haldeman and Ehrlichman too long and let it bring him down."

"But, but," Kilpatrick finally cut in, "Karol Stanislav doesn't work for us."

"Mike, look at me," Beman said, striving to project the image of a man liberating himself from a long-standing dependency. "We're funding Stanislav's re-election campaign through all of our political action committees, member endorsements, you name it. We've been wedded at the hip to this man ever since I got to the Exchange. But we're entering a whole different political environment; we need a new horse to ride."

"Dean," Kilpatrick muttered in a voice evocative of depression, "can we really just walk away from Karol? Nobody will ever trust us again."

Beman looked at Kilpatrick, his confidence waxing as Kilpatrick's appeared to wane. "Mike, look here. I grew up way, way over there. And if you really get down to it, there is only one lesson I carried out of there. You know what that is?"

Kilpatrick remained silent, unable to fill the vacuum. Beman was plenty happy to do it; he reached to the far left of the large walnut desk and grabbed a frame that faced him all day. It contained a quote by Freud, which he felt compelled to read:

Men are not gentle creatures who want to be loved. As a result, their neighbor is for them someone to use sexually without consent, to seize his possessions, to humiliate him, to torture him and to kill him. A savage to whom consideration towards his own kind is something alien.

Once finished, Beman replaced the frame, his face flushing with pride at his own brilliance.

"Mike, I'm not going to sit by like Nero and fiddle while Rome burns," Beman said, leaning forward. "You know what we need?"

Kilpatrick didn't respond, so Beman pushed on. "We need a new rainmaker. I recently met Stanislav's opponent. His name is Raymond Haack; if you ask me, he looks like the new Chicago." The chairman began laughing aloud, before catching himself. "And he's a Republican. I never saw a Republican that didn't welcome the support of a big business like ours."

He pressed his lips together. "I want you to get our PAC fully behind him. In fact, double whatever is in there, and we'll take it out of the General Fund. We're still gonna have our man in Washington. But it's gonna be a new one."

Kilpatrick's felt like he was holding back tears, while Beman chuckled.

"Oh, and another thing," Beman said. "Tell Richard Sherry to close down Stanislav's trading account."

That spurred Kilpatrick to a quick recovery. "But it's the Chairman's, uh, it's Karol's own trading account," he rebutted Beman. "We can't just close it down for him."

Beman's old trading-floor glare surfaced. "Yes, we can," he said. "If Stanislav wants to play the futures and options markets on his own, he's welcome to go ahead. But we're not using our clout to get him any more of these astronomical returns. Besides, we put up most of the capital to open the account."

Kilpatrick again felt cold-cocked, as if he were struggling for oxygen. He had been a member of the Chicago political machine since graduating from a South Side high school, riding Karol Stanislav's coattails shamelessly. He knew he never could have reached these heights without him. But the man sitting in front of him was the only person in position to knock him off his current pedestal. He forced himself to nod at Beman. "I'll get on it right away." He pulled himself up and headed toward the door to begin pulling the plug on his oldest ally, Karol Stanislav. However, just as he was almost out, Beman stopped him in his tracks.

"Mike, hold on."

Kilpatrick stood still, bracing himself.

Beman began nodding his head, as if working to convince himself. "Yeah, Mike. Now looks like the right time to go ahead and clear the deck. That case for crossing trades against Drew Solly that we've soft-soaped so far." He paused to form his words. "No two ways about it, that was a direct hit by that newspaper reporter. Christ, Solly's the chairman of the Treasury Pit Committee." Beman paused a second before saying, "Go ahead and have that case expedited. We're gonna have to suspend him, or that rag at the Times will be all over it again."

What about the Sleazebags? Kilpatrick wondered inwardly. *They also got exposed by the newspaper. His son is one of them.*

"Got it?" Beman pressed with a hint of harshness.

"Yes, okay," Kilpatrick said, realizing he was in personal damage-control mode.

But it appeared Beman was still charging forward. Kilpatrick could sense his boss was looking to set the dagger.

"Now, Mike. About that reporter."

Reporter! The silence of horror enveloped Kilpatrick.

"Mike," Beman continued, sounding like an adult leveling with a child over something silly they have done. A knowing smile covered his face. "This thing, this fella, has gotten completely out of hand. Surely, you're aware we've got to do something about it? We've lost $27 million in membership value since the whole thing started." His voice rose, suddenly tinted with rage. "Goddammit, I've lost a million in the value of my own personal memberships in the last three months alone. Don't go telling me we don't need to take action now."

He leaned his chin forward, as if confiding in Kilpatrick, but said no more. These long silences of Beman's disturbed Kilpatrick. He felt the need to cut this one off. "Okay, yes, it will be taken care of."

Kilpatrick remained standing at the door, itching for a split-second chance to make a getaway. But the chairman was still looking at him from one side of his face to the other, as if Kilpatrick were hiding something. "What else, Mike?"

What else?

A smile little shy of ridicule washed over Beman's face. Is he humiliating me? Kilpatrick asked himself. Of the seven chairmen he had served under, Beman was the one he was least comfortable with. But for the first time, he began to feel another emotion, naked fear.

Kilpatrick—and many other veterans—had never been able to completely forget the dark tale of the sizable fortune Beman had made in one week during the so-called Great Soviet Grain Robbery in1972, when he supposedly pimped his biggest customers in a Faustian bargain with the most powerful traders in the Pit. Where would this man draw the line?

Finally, Beman broke the silence. "Mike, whoever this subversive is in the Treasury Pit, whoever he is, surely considers himself a genius. But to state the obvious, his days are numbered here at the Chicago Commodities Exchange. Look." He shifted to a more workmanlike pose. "Let's go with this. You pledge to give me the traitor's name by the end of the week, which shouldn't be any problem once you've got this reporter taken care of. And once we get the name of that weasel, I'm gonna...." Beman stopped talking. Again, a dangerous silence reigned.

Kilpatrick did not trust his mouth to form the right words. Nodding deferentially seemed less incriminating.

"Okay," Beman said, his face glowing but not smiling. "That'll be all for now."

Like a kid dismissed from the headmaster's office, Kilpatrick jackrabbited out of Dean Beman's office.

Chapter Sixty-One

FEW PEOPLE REALIZED how important CCE President Mike Kilpatrick was. In his staggering ascent to the president's office, he had stunned both friend and foe with backbreaking work habits and ruthless infighting.

As Kilpatrick sat in his office on this early autumn morning, he realized he was going to have to call on some old cronies from *the machine*. It killed him to think about, so proud he was of his exalted role in a premier financial institution.

Kilpatrick picked up the phone and rang Scottie Gallagher. He and Gallagher had been together from the first grade and started in the Chicago political machine the same week almost thirty years back. A whole generation of public employees could fairly be said to owe Gallagher their careers.

Nonetheless, Kilpatrick figured he had outwitted Gallagher. Chicago's modernizing economy had become steadily less dependent on patronage upon the demise of the political machine after Mayor Riley's death. His old pal found himself coming hat-in-hand to Kilpatrick looking for a new revenue source, although he never seemed to understand the business of "those damn exchanges."

Kilpatrick still needed Gallagher for errands. One perennial headache for Kilpatrick was the city fire code, the CCE being in violation of every conceivable fire-code regulation. With several thousand bodies crammed into an old wooden building with only one exit and a rickety fire escape, the trading floor was a hazard that could rival Chicago's Great Fire of 1871. Kilpatrick had long relied on Gallagher to make arrangements with the fire department.

He cringed to think about his most recent call to Gallagher. Kilpatrick's eighteen-year-old son had been involved in a late-night wreck on Lake Shore Drive, killing the driver of the opposing vehicle. He had failed the drunk-driving test by a wide margin and was put in jail. At Kilpatrick's request, Gallagher reached deep into the bureaucracy to prevent a long jail sentence. "I won't be calling again soon," Kilpatrick had promised his old colleague. But now, in the biggest crisis in the CCE's 140-year history, there was only one logical person to contact.

"Scottie," Kilpatrick said when he got an answer.

"Mike, how are you?"

Kilpatrick let out a sigh. "Tough business over here."

"Apparently so." Gallagher's dry tone said it all.

Kilpatrick knew he couldn't hold back. "We've got a problem," he stated intently. "I've got to put a lid on it."

"Uh-huh."

"This reporter is killing our image," Kilpatrick confessed in a whispered tone that he realized sounded more like a shriek. "If he keeps it up, he has the power to capsize us."

Kilpatrick paused to let that sink in, but Gallagher was playing hard to get and remained mum.

"What we really need to know is *who* he's getting his data from." Kilpatrick said in a practical manner. "Once we have that name, we can contain the whole thing."

"Um," Gallagher grunted. He was not known for asking many questions. But Kilpatrick could sense one coming. "Now, are we talking any *wet stuff*?" Gallagher asked.

Kilpatrick's stomach plummeted; he felt like crying. Here he was President of one of the world's largest financial institutions, yet involved in a conversation fit for a Mafia operative. But the question was unavoidable. "It's your judgment on that," he rasped. "We really need to do something to stop the whole darn thing." After pausing for a few seconds, he felt the need to add, "No floaters, please."

"Yeah," Gallagher agreed.

They both seemed embarrassed by that last reference to the age-old Chicago term for bodies of troublemakers being found in Lake Michigan.

"Okay, Mike. We're on top of it."

"Thanks, Scottie."

***

SCOTTIE GALLAGHER HUNG up the telephone and sat staring at it for a full minute.

He had to resist the urge to laugh. He had noticed that Kilpatrick, almost in spite of himself, had been unable to resist a swagger at his exalted station in life whenever he ran into anybody from the old neighborhood. Yet beneath the coded language, the CCE President had just made an unmistakable request—Gallagher was to bring in *the heavies.*

Awe, shit, he could understand. That one guy, Skip Slider, was killing them. Twenty-seven million dollars in collective membership value evaporating in two months. Hell, in his father's day, people killed for quite a few zeros less than that.

Nonetheless, he was determined not to set loose a bunch of rogues. It was to be results-oriented, not revenge-driven. His wife's brother had just lost his job as a security guard at Marshall Fields for theft. Despite these periodic screw-ups, Scottie had always gotten along well with him. But there was no mistaking the crowd of local ruffians he hung out with at a neighborhood bar. Last time Scottie saw him he had a scar angling off his face from a recent brawl, and his persistent limp from a high-school football injury had become more pronounced. He was surviving off odd jobs.

Gallagher picked up the phone and dialed a number.

Chapter Sixty-Two

"I HAVE ALLIES, not friends," Skip Slider liked to say.

His closest ally was his youngest brother, Fred. Skip liked to swing by Fred's West Side law office at 5:00 in the afternoon and roust him, barely acknowledging his pleas that junior associates in a law firm were expected to work into the night.

"If you're gonna work in a sweatshop, then go to Chinatown," Skip rebutted him. "All lawyers do is sap the productive economy, anyway."

Fred bore it, never quite knowing what to make of his eccentric brother. After all, Skip had shown he could be right on occasion.

The afternoon of his latest article, the two brothers were walking up Milwaukee Avenue, Skip still high from his latest scoop. "The chickens are coming home to roost," he shouted. "Those commodity exchanges are dead. Dead." He jumped in the air, turning sideways to pester his brother. "You know what I was thinking today?"

Fred said nothing, allowing his brother to keep going. "There is only one analogy for what is happening," Skip said. "You know what that is, don't you? You gotta know this one." Slider was jabbing his finger at Fred's chest, waiting for a response. "Come on," he prodded. "It changed history on a dime. Think Reagan, Gorbachev, the Pope. Just like that, the three of 'em blew up the Soviet evil empire."

"Yeah, I see," Fred responded, not comfortable with the conversation.

"If it only took a few people to crush an evil system that controlled half the world," Skip said, "don't you think one man can bring down those commodity exchanges? And while I'm at it, put the world's financial system on a sounder footing?"

Ignoring the megalomaniacal tone, Fred said, "You *have* proven there is corruption."

"Aw, man, corruption stalks that whole place from the chairman down to the lowest clerk," Slider contended.

"Yeah, but it's mostly at the top." Fred was feeling dubious about the whole discussion.

"You've never traded in one of those pits," Slider corrected him. "Have you been reading my articles? You don't have to be Charles Darwin to see that whole breed of floor traders is doomed."

"I hear you."

"Fred, listen." Skip stopped walking. This was the part Fred hated, where he had to stand on a sidewalk and nod his head like a puppet. "Take a look at the obituary section. People are only remembered for one thing in their life, if somebody's lucky, two. The rest is water off the duck's back." Slider stopped and bent his upper body aggressively in the direction of his brother. "When that moment arrives, you've got to be ready to put everything on the line to bend the arc of history. People like Mandela, Gandhi, and Martin Luther King—those men were willing to pay the ultimate price."

"You're right," Fred acknowledged, allowing him to escape a stationary position. But then he spoke for himself. "Skip, there's no reason you can't control your personal risk. If these people are as corrupt as you say, couldn't they just come out here and do a hit on you?"

When Skip didn't comment, Fred added, "I love you, Skip, that's all."

They stopped at a familiar Himalayan restaurant for kebabs that Skip said reminded him of the food in Nepal, then continued up Milwaukee Avenue at an accelerated pace of four miles-per hour. At the corner of North Avenue, a newspaper box featuring the *Windy City Times* blared its Slider-driven headline.

"That surprises me to see a paper still available," Skip said, pointing at the news box. "Ben told me we're printing 30,000 extra copies a day to keep up with the surge in demand."

"I'm happy for you," Fred said softly, as he reached the corner where they went separate ways. "Just take care, will you?"

***

AFTER HIS HEATED monologue, Slider felt a need to decompress. He sloshed his way through the oak trees along a bike path in Blair Park. Young couples in various degrees of coitus populated park benches. Slider didn't even want to look. *Just wait until this thing culminates; there won't be enough benches.*

Once again, he began thinking about Darby Shaw. Specifically, he wondered whether she was aware he was the author of the articles shaking the Exchange. The thought weighed on him, realizing she might not even remember him.

He followed a side path leading through a more sylvan setting. He was so deeply into his reverie that he didn't notice a group of white males had been hurrying along on both sides of him the last couple hundred yards. They were distinguished by their barrel chests, gold chains, half-buttoned shirts, and heavy breathing from trying to maintain the same pace as the fleet-of-foot Slider.

The stumpy one walked with a limp and was trailing behind to Slider's left. He took a quick look in all directions. When the coast was clear, he gave a chopping motion like the conductor of a symphony. The men on each of Slider's flanks made a beeline for him. He didn't even know what was happening until two goons had locks on both of his underarms.

"Hey, what you doing?" Stumpy barked in a raspy voice.

"Walking," a confused Slider croaked.

"No," the man said with gritted teeth as he grabbed hold of Slider's collar. "I asked, *what* you think you are doing?" A jolt of pain rippled down Slider's spine, his confusion instantly morphing into an elemental fear. The man's hands moved up his back to his throat, and suddenly Slider lost the ability to answer. However, he was able to rotate his face enough to see he was surrounded by burly white males.

The lead interrogator wore a t-shirt stretched tightly across a broad chest. He had thick, stubby fingers made for a barroom brawl, but no neck to speak of. His most intimidating feature, however, was his head. It was muscular and immense, like a bull's, exuding power. A deep-red scar ran diagonally from one ear to the corner of his mouth, and his wide nostrils flared when he breathed. "I'm gonna ask this question one more time," he bellowed, spraying Slider's face with an awful mist. "Or else this neck of yours ain't ever gonna move as freely again. What are you doing?"

He released his hold just enough, allowing Slider to answer, "Walking through the park."

"You wanna throw ten thousand people out of jobs, huh?"

"No," Slider gasped, embarrassed at the pleading sound of his voice.

"Well, that's what you're about to do."

"I'm just a reporter."

"You think you'se a hero?"

He started to respond, but the man's grip around his neck tightened. One of the three assailants surrounding the lead thug flashed a switchblade in Slider's face. Looking at his tattooed head was enough to make Slider tremble.

"Since you like newspaper stories so much, how would you like being the subject of one in tomorrow's paper?"

Slider made no attempt to hide his white-knuckled terror. "No, please."

"We've seen enough of your game, candy boy."

The guy's lips were now less than a foot from Slider's mouth. He couldn't help focusing on the prominent varicose veins in front of his eyes. "You have to understand."

"I gotta do what?" He fired a punch into Slider's gut, forcing him to go limp in his interrogator's arms.

Stumpy, who appeared to be the group's principal spokesman, put up a hand signaling to lay off. For thirty seconds, nobody said anything until Slider bucked up, allowing the principal interrogator to open a new line of questioning.

"You say you're just reporting, huh?"

"Yes." Slider's terse answer showed he was a quick learner.

"This liar who is feeding you all this tripe you've been writing." The man stopped, and stared Slider directly in the eye.

Slider had always loved this type of television scene. This was when the heavy-base music started, signaling the protagonist was in deep doo-doo and needed to act heroically. But now he was immobilized and helpless.

However, he did retain enough self-image to know he wasn't a squealer.

"Well," Stumpy said, an impatient tone building in his voice, "are you gonna share this loser's name? Or," he paused in workmanlike fashion, "are we gonna get personal here?"

An alarming thought flashed through his mind, the infamous cornhole scene in *Deliverance*. Apparently, his thoughts were transparent. The man got in front of his face and lowered his voice. "I see what you're thinking." He paused for several seconds, in full control of the tempo. "Whatever it feels like now, it's gonna be a world different in a few minutes."

Slider heard a reserved, even shy voice from his back left. "Is this the right time?"

"Are you ready to meet this gentleman?" the man in front asked Slider. "He just got out on parole and would like to share an intimate experience with you."

Slider's horror was relieved only when he felt a stabbing pain in his back from the elbow of an unseen assailant. Again, Stumpy held him up from collapsing.

"You're starting to bore us," Stump said. "Looks like we need to provide some leadership."

Slider realized he had to give them an answer, or else... "Okay, what you want now," he muttered as drool involuntarily spilled from his mouth, "is the, uh, name?" He felt the man's grip lessen. The next step would be like climbing in Everest's *Zone of Death*—the ballgame. He slowly began to lift his head as if to answer the interrogator. Suddenly in one seamless motion Slider released his entire body weight to a squat, jerked his arms loose like a running back breaking a tackle from a huge lineman, and shot to the right. He accelerated down a hill where two of the heavies closed in on him at an angle.

"Hey, fucker," they screamed in unison.

Slider knew he had to cut sharp left or right and then outrun them. But in mid-stride he noticed an oak tree in front of the intersection where his pursuers would cut him off. Natural instinct took over. Like a squirrel, he didn't hesitate at the base, placing his left foot on the trunk and catapulting himself to grab the first limb which was about nine feet off the ground. By the time the attackers reached the tree, he was walking on the branch and nobody could lay a hand on him.

Shouts of "Get that asshole!" emanated from the ground.

Slider leapt to haul himself to a second limb.

"I'd like to know where this genius thinks he's going," an obnoxious voice called out.

"I've got a gun. I'll shoot your sweet ass," another man shouted.

Gun? Maybe. But stopping didn't seem like a viable option, so Slider kept climbing. The branches protruded outwards and he skillfully executed a rappelling move onto a second tree. Unfortunately, all the tree hopping did was move him about forty feet laterally, which the four pursuers easily covered on foot.

"Punk, you're a joke," one man called up, followed by murmurs of approval.

Nonetheless, Slider saw value in movement even if he had no idea where he was trying to go. *At least I'm doing something I'm good at.* After valiantly traversing two more trees he was negotiating a long limb when he began to hear a cracking sound.

"Tiiimberrr," someone shouted up in ecstasy.

SNAP! With the instincts of an acrobat, Slider leapt head-first from the cracking limb and in mid-air caught the next branch down. He hung in suspension, fifteen feet above the four men. But hung he was; his margin of safety was nil. After a few seconds with lactic acid building in his limbs, he girded himself for a maximum ebb, creating enough torque to hurl himself safely onto the limb. He was breathing heavily, but far from spent.

"Hero man." He heard Stump's voice. "The longer this goes on, the worse it's gonna be."

Slider remained mute and continued climbing. As best he could tell in the dwindling twilight, the tree line ended in a few more trees. Finally, he got to the last tree.

Stump seemed to sense this was where Slider might make his play. He edged over into the bushes, halfway disappearing into the dense foliage. From a distance Slider had thought they were weeping willow trees, but a close-up revealed a mixture of laurel and sticker bushes. However down below a fate worse than any sharp bush awaited him. It was *McGyver* time.

Slider catapulted himself off the last limb well beyond Stump, disappearing into the middle of the thick bushes. The first twenty feet went perfectly, with the furry trees slowing his descent. But then he hit heavy foliage and was buffeted helplessly; ten feet off the ground his right leg got caught, leaving him suspended head-first. *Is this the way it ends?*

Wildly swaying his head and arms left and right, Slider kicked his feet up to release himself. Another razor-sharp sticker bush sliced the right side of his body on the way down, causing blood to spew. But that was the least of his problems, as he heard pursuing voices that reminded him of bloodhounds. Like a Marine trainee at Paris Island, Slider burrowed into the jagged bushes, every so often diving to the ground to avoid a header with limbs. He quickly realized the more obstacles the better, and morale began to surge.

After several minutes of jungle-like navigation, Slider emerged into a residential neighborhood. He considered screaming for help, but quickly became embarrassed at the thought. Besides, he knew these streets like the back of his hand. He sprinted past one couple pushing a stroller, the parents too occupied to notice blood gushing out of the fleeing passer-by.

He cut across the back yard of several different houses, before arriving at the corner. All that remained was a three-hundred-yard sprint to Milwaukee Avenue. Sixty seconds later he was jumping and waving for a taxi; a yellow cab promptly pulled to the curb. Fortunately, the driver didn't notice his customer was bleeding profusely until he was safely ensconced inside. Slider could see the man's face freeze in the mirror, but it was too late to eject him.

"Windy City Times," he gasped.

Chapter Sixty-Three

JIM MCKINNEY, THE night editor for the *Times,* had his feet propped on his desk at 9:00, while perusing an article on a new White Sox pitcher. The press room was populated with the standard night-crew of a beat reporter and production people finalizing the next morning's edition.

Suddenly he heard a buzz by the entrance. When he looked up, McKinney saw what appeared to be a bloody apparition wending in his direction. As the person got closer, he recognized him as the young reporter who had been on the hot streak with the Karol Stanislav and CCE stories. The man walked up and hit a knee beside him. "Jim, I'm Skip Slider," he said, holding out a blood-stained hand.

McKinney shook it as an aside, peering at Slider's scarred face. He wiped his hand on his desk. "You sprint through a glass factory to get here?"

Ignoring McKinney's remark, Slider mumbled through heavy breathing. "Are you the right the guy to tell? I've got a major story to report."

It was hard to imagine two more different reporters. McKinney was known inside the building as *Dr. No,* the joke being that his favorite two words were *too late.* His low-key manner belied a tough Irishman who had grown up on the South Side. He was naturally skeptical of Slider's dramatic arrival. But given the kid's recent red-hot streak, along with his ravaged physical appearance, there was no denying him the right to be heard.

"Yeah," McKinney answered, reaching for his pack of Marlboros and holding one out. Slider seemed confused by the offer, before holding up both hands in refusal. McKinney then remembered an old rag he kept in his desk. He reached in the drawer and held it out. "Maybe a tourniquet?" He was not able to hold back a smile. Slider accepted it without a word and wrapped it around his still-gushing right bicep.

Noting his kneeling position, McKinney cocked his head towards a rolling velour chair. "How about a seat?"

Slider crawled to the chair and resumed leaning towards McKinney. For the next fifteen minutes, he delivered a spellbinding account of the evening's harrowing events, leading to this strange nighttime encounter at the newspaper.

While Slider was describing his high-wire act in the trees in Blair Park, McKinney thought to interject, "You're a climber, right?"

"Everest," Slider answered. He seemed to want to say more but stopped himself.

After McKinney had stubbed out his second cigarette of their encounter, he said, "Yeah, that's an amazing story. My first question is why you didn't go to the hospital and police before you came here?"

"Because I knew you had a deadline to meet," Slider answered.

That confirmed what McKinney suspected. After twenty-three years as a journalist, one of the main truths he had discerned was that when somebody—a reporter, athlete, public figure, whoever—gets on a roll, they rarely stopped on their own. Even worse, they often became messianic.

"Skip," McKinney said in a confiding tone, "helluva story, no two ways about it." But then he fixed him with a stern look. "You do know we've got a 10:00 deadline."

Slider said nothing but continued staring at McKinney with an endorphin-suffused face. "Jim, first you would probably agree that since I'm the subject of the story, I shouldn't write it."

"You would be correct."

"But," Slider said, "this thing is going to have more shock effect if tomorrow morning people are reading about something that happened in their own city just twelve hours before."

"That may be so," McKinney responded. He nodded at the wall. "You see the clock. The fastest we could write this up and get it in would be past midnight. Then we would have to move everything around from where it's blocked in now. It could take hours."

Slider spoke in a confiding tone. "Jim, I've worked a lot with Ben these last few months. He loves this string of stories."

"Are you saying this attack was related to those stories?" McKinney asked. But the veteran reporter quickly realized he had made a tactical error.

"There's no doubt about it," Slider said, adopting a more confident tone. "Let me also say, Ben would want to hear about one of his reporters getting attacked by people that evil."

"Yeah, but . . ." McKinney said, before cutting himself off. "What are you saying, that we call him at home?"

"I'll be glad to call him if you'd like," Slider offered. McKinney caught the subtle context: this guy had free access to the executive editor.

McKinney realized he was on his heels. "No, I'll call him," he said, noticeably picking up his pace.

***

SLIDER WATCHED MCKINNEY'S weathered-face tighten, as he spoke with their mutual boss. Then the veteran turned and handed the telephone to him.

"Hi, Ben."

"Skip, I'm sorry to hear this," Clayton said. "Yes, we can run the story in the morning's edition."

Slider dove in. "Ben, I've just witnessed the devil's spawn with my own eyes."

Clayton halted him. "Skip, as I said, we can run the story tonight. But the next few hours are going to be complicated for Jim who is going to write it." The phone went silent; Slider realized he was drawing down the capital balance he had built up with his boss. "One other thing," Clayton said. "This is all very unfortunate. But under no circumstance should you embellish the story. The readers will fully appreciate the danger you faced. We should not indulge in any speculation as to who the perpetrators were. That's the police's job, which is where you need to go next. It sounds like the hospital, also."

"Yes, okay," Slider agreed, feeling chastened.

It was well after midnight when Slider left the *Times* building from a side exit, warily scanning the sidewalk. Soon he saw a yellow cab, which he flagged down and took to the emergency room. There, he rejected all but the most basic treatment of his wounds. Within an hour, he was outside hailing another taxi, this time to the Chicago police department.

At the front desk, he explained that he wanted to report a violent crime. The receptionist asked him to sit in the waiting room.

A few minutes later, a man with a powerful athletic build approached. "Skip Slider?"

"Yes."

Slider hopped up and followed him down the hallway in the mostly-empty headquarters building. His office was spare, featuring a photo of a police-graduation class, as well as headshots of his wife and young children. Slider was glad to see the man appeared to be mixed race, which meant he almost surely wasn't some ex-machine apparatchik. Or for that matter, not at all like the thugs who had attacked him earlier in the evening.

"Kinda ironic that you get more crimes at night, but most police work during the day," Slider said.

"Isn't it the truth," the detective agreed.

Slider recounted the assault for the detective, including facial descriptions, physiques, tones of voice, and clothing. When he described his attackers as "the modern-day equivalent of Al Capone's gang,", the detective toned him down, although Skip noticed the veteran couldn't help but smile at his description of Stumpy as some aging, unemployed member from the television show, *The Little Rascals.*

Finally, the detective reclined in his chair and looked at Slider. "What do you think is the motive for those four males to follow and attack you?"

Slider fancied himself as an independent operator. But the man's practiced-interrogation method engendered enough confidence that he decided to tell him about the scores of articles in the *Windy City Times.*

A crack appeared over the detective's stolid features. "I was wondering if that was you. Yeah, I've been following your stories. I must admit to wondering how the heavy hitters would react."

"They've responded," Slider said with certitude.

The officer remained noncommittal. "Do you think they know where you live?"

"My brother is subletting an apartment, so it's not in his name. I could move there."

"That sounds like a good idea—at least for starters."

They got up and shook hands. The detective stood with his arms by his side. "Skip, those exchanges have been there a long time. So has that congressman. You've got to be careful." He continued looking at Slider. "If they keep up the harrassment, we may have to make some plans for you."

The thought of cloak-and-dagger lifted Slider high as a kite at 3:00 in the morning, as he skipped out to hail a cab to his brother's house.

***

WHEN SLIDER FINALLY woke at Fred's apartment, it was 11:00. He had one thing on his mind, today's headlines of the *Windy City Times*. Did he make it? Without combing his hair, he rushed onto the street. Soon he came up on a neighborhood-looking geezer. "Excuse me, sir. Any idea where I can get a newspaper around here?"

The man pointed to his left towards Halstead Avenue before beginning what looked like would be elaborate directions. The frisky Slider bounded off before the first sentence was complete, yelling back, "Thank you."

After trotting a couple-hundred yards, he got to the corner of Halstead and Diversey, where two men in business suits were bent over a newspaper box.

"Excuse me," he said with a heavy pant.

The men edged aside, allowing Slider to insert four quarters and extract a paper. He stood to the side and beheld the day's headlines of *The Times*, wondering if the men recognized who was standing next to them.

TIMES REPORTER SKIP SLIDER MAKES DRAMATIC ESCAPE
FROM ATTACKERS

Skip Slider, the reporter at the center of the scandal rocking the Chicago Commodities Exchange and U.S. Congressman Karol Stanislav, was physically assaulted early last night by four unknown attackers.

Around 7:30 in the evening, Slider was following his customary walking route through Blair Park when he was suddenly cornered and grabbed by four white males estimated to be in their mid-to-late thirties.

The story included a recitation of the facts, heroic to be sure, but nowhere near the drama he would have written himself. As it was, he could barely focus on the article, so entranced he was with the front-page photo of himself looking like a prize-fighter after a championship bout.

He turned and ran back to Fred's apartment. Within thirty minutes he had showered, dressed, eaten a banana on the run, and caught a taxi to the *Times* building. As he entered the office, he was magically overtaken with mental renditions of Beethoven's Piano Concerto Number Five, *The Emperor*. For him, it was these rare highs, like his triumph over Nepal's Everest, that made life worth living.

The first few secretaries he passed couldn't hide their blushes. "Hello, Mr. Slider!"

Once he arrived in the reporter's section, all action ceased. He felt pats on the back and innumerable voices saying, "How are you?" and "Oh my God."

A couple reporters began asking probing questions. Rather than recount the details of his great escape, he opted for the big picture. "It doesn't really matter about those thugs, does it," he proclaimed to his impromptu audience, "until you go after the power structure behind them."

A popular female in the Arts Section who had never showed more than passing interest in him, walked up and asked, "So who do you think did it?"

Hesitating, in order to demonstrate gravity, Slider said, "Well, we know who did it, don't we?"

That brought everyone in listening distance to the intended hush, allowing him to announce, "Excuse me. I need to have a word with Ben."

Chapter Sixty-Four

"HEY, YOU'RE GETTING better at those leaps," Ron said with a pregnant smile as Barbra Lasky hopped off the dock onto his yacht in a light-green swimsuit.

"Practice makes perfect," she responded in level fashion.

"You might make an Olympic hurdler one of these days," he gushed.

"You think so?"

"I'll be in the stands for the finale," he enthused.

"Okay, we'll see."

Unfortunately for Ron, he was not Barbra's date this afternoon. He was merely lending his yacht to her boyfriend, Tim. She had to put up with his nauseous flirting.

"Thanks. Enjoy your afternoon, Ron," Barbra said. She and Tim waved as the yacht set out into Lake Michigan, Chicago's towering skyline coming into better focus the farther they sailed from shore.

Barbra had always been determined to suck as much juice out of her weekends as possible. This morning she had gone roller-blading, and gotten psyched up when she overheard a group of college students marveling at her passing-by figure.

Normally she didn't display her bathing suit until she was out on the water. But today she had donned it entering the marina and couldn't escape the aphrodisiac of power, with one male after another eyeing her on the dock. What's there to sweat?

Barbra had recently confided to her therapist, "Something critical is missing in my relationship with Tim." Down at the CCE, he was just another trading drone. And outside of there, she could force him to do pretty much anything she willed, including supplicating his friend Ron to lend them his yacht on weekends.

Barbra had begun to realize what she coveted most deeply: a tidal wave of being, an intense existence, the sheer surging of life. Truth be told, she was beginning to look back nostalgically on the no-holds barred shouting matches with Thomas Krone on his $400,000 yacht. At least she got to hear stories of the huge swings he and the other pit gods took.

It was consolation that her income was up sharply the last couple years. As much as she hated to admit it, having a broker willing to trade all the way to her isolated corner of the Pit was propitious. But even that nagged at her. Chris Parker? What is his real story?

Lately, her father's repetitive words had been echoing in her mind: *Fate comes clothed in veils and approaches from behind.*

***

BARBRA ALWAYS CONTROLLED the tempo on the yacht. Sometimes she and Tim would go down in the well where there was a rectangular rubber mattress. But today she preferred staying on deck and displaying her ultra-healthy physique to any passersby on the water.

"Tim."

He looked her way.

She looked distracted. "I'm wondering about Chris Parker."

Again, he said nothing.

"I know you were skeptical when I used to say he was trading with me because I was the shortest person in the Pit and he was the tallest."

Tim nodded.

She breathed deeply, before shrugging. "And I guess you never believed me that most of those trades are losers for me."

Tim lost his self-possession for a brief second and let a faint smile break through. Barbra began to rebuke him, but then caught herself. Who can blame him, she thought? Her annual income had rocketed from slightly larger than his to three times higher.

"Tim, I've started to worry."

He said nothing; silence was dominant.

"This Deep Pit that everybody is speculating about." Barbara looked at the floor of the yacht with a pained look. "I swear, the last couple days I've started to think it's him."

Tim affected the necessary grave look, which encouraged her to continue. "Think about it. If he's Deep Pit, I could get in a lot of trouble."

Tim continued staring at her as if she was the only person on the planet.

"What do you think I should do?"

After a suitable interlude, he said, "Stop trading with him is the first thing that comes to mind."

Barbra sighed. "Yeah," she said looking out into the distance. "We don't trade as much anymore. I just wonder if it's too late."

"But suppose he is Deep Pit. What would he have over you?"

"Nothing," she said, slacking her perfectly-proportioned shoulders. "Absolutely nothing. I swear haven't done anything wrong. But you've seen what happens in these things, the way innocent people get taken down."

"Maybe you should go to Herman about this?"

"I think I'm gonna have to." She hesitated. "He doesn't seem like a bad guy—a nice southerner." She shook her head. "But, wow, he's different from most guys down there, the way he just hangs back. I mean, I hate getting him in trouble. But Daddy always taught me, when the chips are down you have to take care of yourself."

Again, Tim nodded. He continued looking squarely at her.

Barbra stretched her arms high over her head and took a long inhalation and exhalation. She saw the solemn look on Tim's face, as he focused on her slightest move. Spontaneously, she stood up.

He sprung to his feet and followed her to the stairs.

Chapter Sixty-Five

"CHRISSIE."

CHRIS TURNED and and saw George Haskins.

"Hey, G-Man."

Normally Haskins walked with the light prance of a born courtier. Now, though, he appeared self-conscious treading towards Chris in the CCE lobby. These run-ins with Haskins were beginning to make him uneasy.

"Could we have a little chat?"

"Sure," Chris answered in a low voice, picking up on Haskins's self-conscious look.

Haskins's eyes darted around, checking to see who was nearby. "Let's go to the clerks' break room," he suggested in a low voice.

Chris followed him into the small room at the far corner of the lower level, where clerks sat consuming sodas, snacks, and bag lunches. He recognized many of them, including one trade checker who sat near him on the city bus in the mornings.

"Over here," Haskins said, pointing to a vacant table in the far-right corner.

Chris was bending to sit when he noticed a heavyset middle-aged man in a baby-blue Vortex trading jacket. That meant he probably knew Barbra.

"Hey, George," Chris whispered, and gave a glance at the man. "Somewhere else."

Haskins picked up on his concern and nodded, before following Chris down the hallway. They entered the CCE library.

"How about behind the shelves?"

They tiptoed past the seated patrons, mostly traders savoring a respite from the madness on the floor just above. Chris spotted two vacant chairs in the far corner. "Here?"

Haskins took a seat without a word, which only made Chris more anxious. He noted the squirrely veteran trader again checking to be sure the coast was clear.

"Chris." He spoke just above a whisper. "I was just upstairs in the office."

"Yeah," Chris nodded in apprehension.

Haskins tightened his lips. "Well, anyway, Barbra was in there talking with Herman."

"Barbra Lasky?" Chris confirmed, but immediately reprimanded himself for being deceptive.

Haskins nodded, but this time with a hint of sternness.

"And?" Chris asked, abandoning his careless pose.

Haskins took a deep breath. With a measure of gravity, he said, "they know."

Chris started to feign ignorance by asking, "Know what?" But he caught himself. "About the newspaper?"

"Yeah," Haskins said. "They think they know the identity of Deep Pit."

Chris couldn't resist asking, "How do you reckon they found out?"

Haskins looked down for a split-second, enough to rid his face of any cues. "Well, you know how things get out around here."

Yeah, I do know, Chris thought.

"Okay," Chris grimaced, wondering if he should walk straight out of the building, never to return. But as was his wont, he looked at Haskins in a leveling way. "Honestly, George, what do you think of the whole thing?" Effectively, he was admitting prior deception to Haskins.

Uncharacteristically, Haskins struggled for words. "I'm aware that the articles made some great points about all the shenanigans here." He stopped and opened his hands, before adding, "At the same time, I don't want the baby thrown out with the bath water."

"But you know this place," Chris dug in. "They're no more likely to reform themselves than the Roman Empire. It takes outside pressure."

"That's true," Haskins agreed, although shaking his head.

"Let me ask," Chris said, hoping to get some buy-in. "What do you think I should do—stop trading?"

Haskins shook his head and turned his eyes away; he wasn't gonna take that hook. "Chrissie," he said, recapturing his affable form, "you're an interesting guy. I gotta give you that. And you may be onto a winner here." Edging forward in his chair as a prelude to standing up, he said, "You can count on me to not blow your cover to anyone. I just wanted to let you know what I was hearing."

"Do you think Herman Mann will spread it around?"

He shrugged. "That was not the impression I got." But then he held up his hands as if in defense. "But you know how it is. Herman is gonna do what it takes to protect his business."

"Yeah." Chris said. The sound of his grave tone depressed him even further.

Haskins patted him on the arm. "Take care of yourself, fella."

Chris remained pensive as he watched Haskins walk away.

Chapter Sixty-Six

HERMAN MANN HAD long counseled Vortex locals, "If you aren't sleeping, you're trading too big." His strictly-enforced trading rules had allowed him to avoid the ruinous catastrophes that had befallen so many other clearinghouse owners. But now he was having trouble sleeping himself. Per his own advice, that meant he had to do something about it.

Mann had gone on high alert two days ago, when an alarmed-looking Barbra Lasky had rushed into his office and closed the door to announce, "Herman, I think SKY is Deep Pit."

"Why do you think it's him?" he asked, not hiding his concern.

"Because I do."

Mann knew the redoubtable lady in front of him was a student of the male gender. On a few occasions, he had even caught himself permitting her to trade larger positions than justified, given the amount of money in her account. He would go home and sigh at the mirror, resolving not to do it again. Despite very different backgrounds, Mann and Barbra were kindred souls. Both were bottom-line people. Barbra's fears had him jittery, knowing SKY traded with Vortex locals all over the Treasury Pit. Having a mole doing business with his traders could spell trouble.

"Oh, then one other thing," Barbra said. "George Haskins walked up the other day with this look on his face. He knows SKY pretty well."

"Doesn't surprise me," Mann said with a knowing smile. Actually, the only real surprise was Haskins and Barbra talking. Mann had noticed that they seemed to circle warily around each other.

"Listen to this. He said SKY used to hang out with that Skip Slider guy who is writing all those articles."

"Are you sure?"

"Yes, he remembered all these details about how they used to talk." Barbra nodded to emphasize her point.

"Now, that's something," Mann agreed.

Barbra had been uncharacteristically mum when she had exited his office.

He remembered how she had come to him in a similar situation a few years back in the wake of the FBI investigation paranoia, worried that one of the brokers standing behind her was wired for sound. Mann had focused on the broker like a laser beam for several months, even poking a little into his background. Nothing had come of it. Nonetheless, he took Barbra's alarm with deadly seriousness.

Mann had spent the last twenty-four hours obsessing over what to do. Reluctantly, he had concluded there was only one logical course of action.

***

LIKE EVERY CCE old-timer, Mann had gotten his start trading in the agricultural pits. Thirty years later, those same traders were running the Exchange. Unfortunately, Mann didn't trust this old-boy network any more than he had three decades before. Worse yet, he was going to have to call on the one individual he trusted less than any other. He picked up the phone and dialed Chairman Dean Beman's office.

Soon the chairman came on the line. "Herman, how are you?" he asked in the familiar baritone that had caused Mann so many sleepless nights decades ago.

"I'm having trouble sleeping," Mann responded in a stab at candor.

"How can we improve that?"

"Something has come to my attention," Mann said, feeling strange confiding in Dean Beman.

"Let's hear it."

"My traders in the Treasury Pit are getting all worked up over that infiltrator everybody's calling 'Deep Pit.'" He added, "Throw in a clearinghouse owner as well."

"Add an Exchange chairman to that," Beman piped in.

"Have you got any idea who it is?" Mann asked.

"Oh, we've got plenty of people floating names." Beman stopped a few seconds, before planting his flag. "But guess what."

Mann remained silent.

"Guesses aren't the way I play." Beman dug in. "I need two things and I'm gonna get them—the name of this rascal, and that he's gonna be out of this place for good." He couldn't resist adding, "That's just for starters."

Beman's authoritarian tone brought back unpleasant memories for Mann from their own trading days. With his huge deck of customer orders, Beman was fond of forcing independent traders to take bigger trades than they wanted. Several times Mann had tried telling him, "But I was only bidding on ten contracts," to which Beman fired back, "I was selling a hundred. Get out of my way if you're not gonna trade." Like most locals, Mann had feared getting blackballed by the biggest broker on the floor, and several times he took sizable losses on trades he never had wanted. Now it was sounding like Beman had brought his strongman style to the CCE executive suite.

"Dean," he said in a confidential tone, "I've been given some information about a particular individual in the pit."

"Go ahead."

Mann was horribly afflicted about this next step. He had grown up dirt-poor, and couldn't stand the idea of keeping anyone from pursuing his or her hopes and dreams. What's more, the impression he had gotten from observing, and briefly chatting with, Chris Parker, was that he wasn't anybody's bad guy. He couldn't get himself to utter Parker's name over the telephone. Finally, he said, "Dean, could I come up to your office?"

"I'm here."

Ten minutes, two elevator rides, and a handshake later, he sat in front of the one and only person in his career with whom he had never been able to develop the least level of comfort. Beman stared at him with a face that said, "Play your cards." This was not Herman Mann's type of game, but he was in.

"Uh, Dean, do you know the real tall guy who brokers for Elliott House in the Treasury Pit?"

Beman looked at him, not offering the slightest cue of comprehension.

Mann shuffled in his chair, wondering whether to elaborate. "Extremely tall," he emphasized, raising his hand as right high as he could.

All Beman did was stare.

Mann turned his head to an angle. "Do you know the guy I'm talking about?"

After several more uncomfortable seconds, the chairman said, "The tall guy?"

"He works for Elliott House," Mann repeated.

Beman continued staring in a disconcerting fashion.

Does he know who I'm talking about?

Finally, Beman said, "You haven't told me his name."

"Chris Parker."

"Chris Parker," Beman repeated slowly. "Who is he?"

I just told him. Mann again thought back to the old days, when Mann was infamous for sticking locals like himself with errors. Most had accepted the explanation that Beman's frequent errors were unavoidable due to the sheer volume of his business. However, after years of dealing with him, Mann and his closest friends had all come to a different conclusion: Dean Beman was dense. However, the feudal political system at the CCE had been a perfect fit for his ruthlessness, allowing him to annihilate all internal opposition.

"Well," Mann said, raising his eyes to the ceiling, "as I was saying, I mean, Christ, he's the tallest guy on the whole floor. He wears an Elliott House navy-blue jacket."

"Now," Beman said, leaning his head forward, "you're telling me he's the guy that is leaking all these lies to the newspaper?"

"My source says Parker knows this reporter well and thinks Parker is the reporter's source."

"Who are you talking about?" Beman asked with the look of a man ready to take action.

"Chris Parker."

"Chris Parker," Beman repeated.

"Yes," Mann responded with a nod, the full capacity of his diplomatic skills now being tested. "Why, hey, why don't I—if you will, let me use one of your pieces of note paper. I can write it down for you."

He stretched forward and snatched a small piece of white paper from of a tray on Beman's desk. He wrote: Chris Parker, 7-feet tall, navy-blue jacket, Elliott House, before placing it in front of the chairman. Mann suddenly felt an overwhelming urge to get out of this man's presence. "Dean, thank you."

Beman said nothing as Mann rushed out.

Chapter Sixty-Seven

CHRIS LOPED ALONG the sidewalk in his gym clothes and windbreaker on a drizzly early-fall evening. His apartment building was conveniently located at the northern boundary of Lincoln Park, within walking distance of the gym and grocery store.

He anticipated calling up Frankie Hope and swapping war stories from the trading floor, as well as listening to any colorful commentary Hope might have on Skip Slider's escape. Lately, Chris had been feeling an undefined anxiety about not filling his close friend in on his extracurricular activities. Besides, he wanted to hear the story of Frankie's latest coup that had everyone buzzing, in which he had short-sold the Treasury market all the way down on a government auction, leaving those who had taken him on, in trader parlance, *tits-up*.

Chris opened the glass door to the foyer of the old high-rise and started through the hallway. The receptionist, an older lady named Vera whose friendly manner led many to refer to her as the *house mother,* called at him. "Chris, who in the world is that guy looking for you?"

"What guy?"

"He was here just a few minutes ago, asking to go to your room."

"Rail-thin little guy with freckles?" Chris asked, hoping it was Frankie.

"No," Vera answered. "He was short, alright. But huge, and walked with a limp."

Limp? Chris froze and looked at Vera, before rushing to the counter. "Vera," he spoke in a hush, "did you let him in?"

"No," she said with indignation. "You know I'm not letting in some man I don't know." She added, "Especially somebody that looks like that."

Chris leaned over the counter, feeling his heart throbbing.

"What's the matter?"

"The guy you just described," Chris said, "if he's the one I've been hearing about—did he have a scar?"

"Oh, a horrible scar running across one whole side of his face," Vera said, looking pained.

"Vera, that man, I'm almost sure it's him, just assaulted a good friend."

"What?"

Chris put his finger to his lips. "Vera," he spoke quietly, "they're an organized-crime group of some type. Should I call the police?"

Her forehead wrinkled in concern.

An awful thought occurred to Chris...*could the police be in on this?*

"Can you call Kaz to come down?"

"Kaz?" she repeated in dismay.

"Yes," Chris said with uncharacteristic firmness, "he carries a gun."

"But the man walked back out..."

"He could easily go up the service elevator from the back hallway."

Vera looked at him, conflicted in a way he had never seen. Finally, she stretched over to the phone and pressed some numbers. Within a few seconds, she had her connection. "Kaz, Chris Parker is down here and needs you for an emergency."

A few awkward minutes passed as Chris ricocheted around the lobby cold with fear. Finally, he heard the elevator and saw the lean, friendly face of Kaz Mihalevich rounding the corner.

"Kaz," Chris greeted the Yugoslavian immigrant who worked as the maintenance man. He spoke slowly. "A criminal wants to attack me."

"A criminal?" Kaz repeated, mirth and worry showing on his face.

"Yes, he already attacked a friend. Vera says he was here earlier."

"I told him someone with a limp was looking for him," Vera interjected. "I don't know who he is."

"It was him," Chris insisted. "I'm sure of it." He bent down and said, "Kaz, could you help me look around the building?"

Kaz had had many joking conversations with Chris over the years. Now he looked at him quizzically.

"Okay," he said. "I go upstairs first."

A few minutes later, Kaz reappeared wearing a jacket. "Let's go check it out," he said, regaining his amiable ways as they headed for the back door. Chris took a quick look to see if anything was bulging out of the jacket but was too unschooled in these matters to know.

They entered the poorly-lit back hallway, which featured overhead pipes and greenish lacquered walls darkened by soot. Kaz fired up a cigarette and pulled out a flashlight. Chris watched as he scanned various nooks and crannies. After several minutes, they arrived at the service elevator and took it to the ninth floor, where he accompanied Chris to Room 905.

"Don't see nothing," Kaz said.

"Sorry to bother you," Chris said, feeling guilty. "It's just that this group of men is carrying out attacks on their enemies."

"Sounds like Yugoslavia," Kaz commented, which lightened up Chris. As he turned to leave, Kaz volunteered, "I'll walk the stairwell, all twelve floors."

"Let me do it with you."

"No, I take care of it," Kaz said with a reassuring smile of Slavic steel.

It occurred to Chris how much he had always enjoyed this working man's company. He earned his money. Chris made a mental note to buy him a bottle of vodka.

Chris opened the door to his efficiency apartment. His initial glance revealed nothing other than a sheet of paper slid under the door. He grabbed it on the way to the trashcan, assuming it was a routine message from the building management. But when he took a glance, he froze.

It was a map with writing above it in bold print:

Chris Parker
Sweet Home Alabama

The map had an arrow that ran from Chicago to his hometown of Montgomery, Alabama. A message on the arrow read: *"Capisce?"*

Chapter Sixty-Eight

SKIP SLIDER WAS in a breakout phase. Every neuron and dendrite in his body was lit up seemingly every waking moment of the day. His credo of taking bold, even extreme, action had been vindicated.

A couple years back, he read that baseball legend Joe Dimaggio had been sending a dozen roses to Marilyn Monroe's grave every week for the thirty years since her death, in spite of their marriage lasting less than a year before being up-ended by her repeated extramarital dalliances. Taking that as his cue, Slider had made the same arrangement with a local florist, sending flowers every Saturday afternoon anonymously to Darby Shaw. Right before leaving for Nepal to attempt Everest, he mailed a $300 check from Alaska to the florist, that ended up cutting into his celebratory budget upon his great moment. But Slider never had any second thoughts. The knowledge of his weekly contribution to that goddess's lifestyle kept him in a state of low-level ecstasy.

Now, though, was his real moment. He had recently walked into the florist's shop and changed the order from once a week to every day. Both the florist and he seemed embarrassed. "Oh, okay," she responded, taking the money with her lips pursed. On the way out, it occurred to Slider that florists see their share of stalkers and creeps.

He had been dying to ask, *What does she say when you deliver them*? He never signed the card, although he had begun to wonder if that should be his next bold move. Does she remember me? he asked himself for the thousandth time.

Slider had last seen her on his final day as a trader; he vividly remembered the moment. His account was teetering just above the $50,000 limit that would force the clearinghouse to pull the plug on his trading privileges. He bought ten contracts—a large position by his standards—at a price of 97-14. It looked good for a second as the market briefly traded at 97-15. But when large institutional sellers came into the market, Slider lurched towards the Salomon Brothers broker to sell ten contracts at 97-14 and scratch the trade. He was the first person by a full two seconds, but the broker didn't see him. A minute later he was forced to sell out at 97-10 for a loss of $1,250.

Slider had stood in a trance for several minutes, knowing he was never going to step foot in the Pit again. In most jobs, there was at least some minor festivity on a person's last day. But all one got on a trading floor was a one-way ticket to Skid Row. Oblivion. Now it was his turn to make the long-dreaded *perp walk*. His psyche was in such a ruptured state that he didn't realize Darby was standing by the Pit exit in her customary upright pose. Slider suddenly realized he was next to her, but for the first time, he wasn't self-conscious. Their eyes locked. "Darby," he said spontaneously. Darby seemed to lose her vaunted poise for a moment; somehow she sensed the occasion was momentous. "Goodbye," she said in what he remembered and cherished as her most authentic voice.

***

ON A SATURDAY afternoon, four days after being chased through the park, Slider was struggling to maintain his equanimity. Things looked better than ever for his career, yet he was feeling down.

He had gotten his customary daily high in the early afternoon, around the time the flowers were ordinarily delivered to Darby. Then he met with brother Fred and friends for chicken wings in Lincoln Park where he had gone off on a tangent about Middle Eastern oil, everyone fawning over Slider's apparent expertise. But he needed *more*.

By late afternoon, he was back at Fred's apartment and feeling sullen, edging on treacherous. Without any internal deliberation, Slider bounded down the stairs onto Halstead Avenue and started south on foot. It felt good to be moving briskly in the *right* direction. He turned right onto North Avenue and hurried in the path of the sinking sun. Before him lay an urban milieu, replete with gas stations, repair shops, and small stores. The drab setting gave him impetus to pick up his pace to four-miles-per hour. He began squinting his eyes in the waning light, as he looked for a particular street. It was a name and number that had been etched in his imagination for years, and which he knew by heart from the CCE directory. Up until now he took personal pride in *not* going there.

Finally, he came upon a Gulf oil station with a street sign turned at an angle away from his approach. He broke into a sprint. In the near-darkness, he read *Thousand Oaks*. Which direction was *#188*? Without slowing down, he cut right and saw 312, followed by 316. Wrong way. Slider pivoted and retraced his steps towards the descending numbers; now he was closing in on 188 Thousand Oaks Street. He slowed just enough to read #194, #192, and #190; all were rectangular houses with small plots of grass. Then he saw #188. It was different, a red-brick multi-storied condominium complex at the end of the street with two tall pines between it and the road. Perfectly proportioned, just what you would expect.

Knocking on the door was out of the question. Never would he knowingly do anything to make a woman's life worse. But what was wrong with being curious.

He rushed to the far side of the house, slithering between the bushes and a pine tree. The setup was favorable, with plenty of ways to make himself unobtrusive, concealment being too strong of a word. He was looking for #301. The first and second floor apartments were dark. But the light on the third floor beamed brightly. Which meant *she* was home. Even more entrancing, the windows were open. Then like a rifle blast to his chest, Slider was staggered. Sitting on the windowsill was a vase of white roses. *God!* Slider quickly castigated himself for this sac-religious impulse. Barely able to contain himself, he ricocheted left, then right, before standing stationary on his tiptoes, longing to see that veritable species of womanhood.

Tinkling sounds filled his ears. It was unmistakable, Rachmaninoff's Piano Concerto #2. It made sense; she preferred the romantic Russian composers. He ached for greater proximity to drink in her classical beauty.

At a time like this, it was important for Slider to remember the single most important thing. Namely, she needed him infinitely more than his yearning for her. That bedrock belief he would never abandon. The problem, as he saw it, was that her beauty gave her cushion from the most savage depredations of a trading floor. Even the lucky ones who made a living became mysteriously unhappy and they never seemed to know why. But he did, he had it figured out.

The so-ethereal lady was now sitting or standing, maybe even lying, three floors above him. He stood behind the large tree, his neck craned at the open window above him. *Don't scare her.*

Nonetheless, he had an overwhelming desire to achieve some measure of physical proximity to this Venetian goddess. Only seventy-five feet, and not a single human lay between them on a Saturday night at 8:00.

***

THROUGHOUT HER TEENS and twenties, Saturday night had always been Darby Shaw's favorite time of the week. But as she entered her thirties, it became her least favorite.

Darby had grown up in a modest neighborhood in Des Moines, with broad streets, stately architecture, and well-tended yards. At St. Pius Prep, she cleared 5'10" in the ninth grade and began hearing rogue commentary from the cheap seats. She was relieved to never hit six-feet, tall enough to start on the basketball team, but without the dubious feat of dominating games.

The preppy East Coast held allure for this heartland girl, and she enrolled at Radcliffe, quickly adapting to the ethos of being a *Cliffie*, including prancing around campus in skirts and loafers, but no socks. English Lit would have been a suitable major for a Cliffie. But the Reagan era had begun, and she became increasingly interested in economics, taking a degree in finance. Specifically, she started reading the *Wall Street Journal*.

Like many Midwesterners, Darby had heard tales of fortunes being made and lost in the Chicago commodities business. When she mentioned an interest in trading, her mother reacted negatively. "I've seen all those people shouting on television," she told her daughter. "Those aren't people like you."

"It's getting big, Mom. Really big."

"What about Chicago?"

"It's my kind of town," she replied with unexpected brio.

If there was such a thing as a normal career in the chaotic Chicago commodities business, Darby Shaw had lived it so far. She got a job as a phone clerk for First

Boston, a white-shoes Wall Street firm. Quickly she learned to laugh at the forced humor of her bosses, but also how to artfully shut them down.

After a couple years, one thing became glaringly obvious —the ambitious types hankered to get in one of the pits and trade. She had saved her annual bonuses, which gave her seed capital. Again, her parents were skeptical.

"What happens if you are wrong about the market?"

"You lose," she answered plainly.

"What kind of business is that?"

"I plan to be professional in every way," Darby promised.

Her first year she made $64,000 in the Treasury Pit. The next five years she made between $100,000 and $150,000. That was enough to support a high-maintenance lifestyle. But she wasn't getting rich. Wasn't that the point of getting in the Chicago commodities business?

Like everyone who ever stepped foot on the CCE floor, she had originally thought of it as a glamor business. Lately, though, she had begun telling anyone who would listen something different: "You wouldn't believe how boring the whole thing is most of the time. Everybody is so predictable—more, more, more. Never anything more imaginative than *more*."

She had dated two different guys each year in Chicago. The pattern was eerily similar. The first month was a halo. Sex and euphoria characterized the second month. The third and fourth months saw ennui and drift. She had started to wonder if that was the rhythm of cosmopolitan dating. Now thirty-one years old, she had begun to hear that ticking sound. All the lattes, expressos, nail polishes, massages, psychotherapy appointments, wine bars, shows, and restaurants seemed to be blurring together. The brokers at the CCE who had fed her juicy trades all these years seemed to be less infatuated these days. Her income was down; she might not even make six-figures this year. She was beginning to question the point of the whole business. Still, she needed the money.

Tonight, a group of Darby's friends were meeting up at a jazz bar. She knew the routine well: wry jokes by the women about strange dates and male neuroticism, with males listening and laughing too hard, all followed by an inconclusive ending for the evening.

She was content to stay home, listen to classical music, take a long bath, followed by a nineteenth century European novel.

***

WHEN SHE HAD moved into this building four years ago, she always kept the blinds drawn and window closed while bathing. Finally, she summoned the nerve to leave the windows up on summer nights. Recently, she had become risqué enough to also roll up the blinds and let in some fresh air. After all, this was Chicago, not Des Moines.

She ran her thin fingers over her long limbs, taking special time to knead her limber muscles. Like most people, sex remained a mystery. If she had to guess, she was in the middle of the Bell Curve in the number of different partners for a single woman her age. She was typical in another respect, as well; she enjoyed sex, although her male partner seemed to savor it at a different level. More damning though, it wasn't a panacea. Closing her eyes while listening to Rachmaninoff, she thought, *I need a change. Either more or fewer sex partners,* instead of always allowing the guy his moment on the sixth date. In fact, the more she thought about it, the more obvious was the conclusion: a totally different kind of man.

Which brought up another question altogether: *who the hell was sending the flowers?* At first, she had found it a little bit spooky. But her friends all told her to not worry too much. A true creep would have written something alarming by now. Besides, she had gotten accustomed to the roses adorning her house. She'd like to find out who it was if for no other reason than to thank the guy. But despite several brainstorming sessions with her closest friend, she had drawn a blank. The males at the exchange all seemed too coarse. In any event, her friends assured her that sooner or later the truth would hit her over the head.

On full moon nights like this one she was afforded a tantalizing view of Chicago's distant skyline through gaps in the tree branches. Chicago—millions of people doing and thinking an infinite number of things.

She heard something stir. Reflexively, she looked over and saw an object high up in the large pine tree outside her window. At first, she assumed it was one of the infinite shapes nature can take. But then she noticed the object blink. Something was alive up in the tree. It was too big to be a cat, so for just a split second she wondered if it was a dog. *I didn't know they could climb like that.* She giggled and waved, before dipping her head in a prolonged rinsing under the showerhead.

A few months before, she had gone outside one night to make sure passing cars could not spot her bathing so openly. She had gladly concluded that was not a problem, and thought nothing as a car rolled by on the street below. But as she gazed blankly out the window, the car lights illuminated something in the tree. Suddenly tremors of horror ransacked her body. A *human* was in the tree.

Screaming and panic were not Darby's style. But preparedness had always been her motif. When she moved in five years ago, she had placed the phone numbers of the fire and police departments on the kitchen and bathroom walls and put the telephone on the table beside the shower. *Execution is the key, like on the trading floor.*

She didn't want to alert the stalker. Darby stretched her long physique to grab the phone and dial the police. Within five seconds, she heard a man's voice. "Police, hold on please," he said, "unless it is an immediate emergency."

"It is," she said in a hushed tone. "I am home alone. An intruder has climbed a tree and is next to my bathroom watching me take a shower. If the police are here in the next few minutes, I promise he'll still be up there. Please come to 188 Thousand Oaks right this minute."

"I'll see if we've got anybody in your area," the man said.

"You've got him if you come now," she persisted.

"We'll try."

She hung up and reassumed her showering position, trying not to alert the person. But when she lowered her head to soak her hair, she caught a glimpse of him making a slight adjustment to his position. His eyes were trained on her like an animal in the wild. Just the thought of how he got up there was enough to frighten her; she wondered how in the world he was going to get down.

She heard two cars tear around the corner onto her street. Within ten seconds, blue halogen lights flooded the immediate area. The man in the tree jerked his head away from her, risking his life in the process.

"Attention, attention," a policeman shouted into a megaphone. "We know an intruder is hiding in a tree on this property. Come down this minute, or you will be endangering your life."

Darby watched the man propel himself off the limb and onto the tree trunk at whippet speed. He began shimmying down at a pace that made her again wonder if she was seeing things. She jumped out of the shower and in the nude yelled out the window, "He's escaping down the tree."

The entire property was lit up like a stadium. She watched in rapt attention as the policemen converged at full speed onto the trunk of the tree.

The intruder attempted a Houdini-like leap from thirty feet above the ground and landed on all fours. He tore away from the police and the street. But Darby knew the fugitive wasn't going far, because of what her neighbors referred to as *Little Wrigley,* an ivy-covered wall at the rear of the property.

Below, she heard, "Down, down, I'll shoot. Get down; I'm shooting now. One, two, three." Darby braced herself for a hideous act of violence. "Stay on the ground. Don't move." The locust was corralled.

She hurried to put on some shorts and a t-shirt, before tearing out the door and down the stairs. When she got into the courtyard she saw neighbors streaming out with expectant looks toward the scene of the crime. The police had the man handcuffed and up against one of their cars.

A policeman rushed up. "Ma'am, are you the lady who called us?"

"Yes, I am."

"Ma'am, please. He is obviously dangerous. It is best for him not to see your face."

"I'm afraid he's already seen it."

Darby proceeded to walk to within ten feet of where the suspect was detained. The same policeman approached her once more. "Ma'am, if you insist on being here, could you please tell us if you have seen this man before?"

She stared at a curly-headed man with brown locks, slightly less than medium height, and an athletic build. He appeared to be around her age. Then she zeroed in on the face and it hit her at once. She threw her hand over her mouth the way little girls learn to do. It was *him,* the guy who everybody at the CCE told her liked to go on ad-infinitum about her. Darby continued honing-in on the man, as he was being handcuffed by two policemen. The look on his face was of someone who had done his all in something he believed in devoutly, yet failed disastrously.

She didn't say a word, and he didn't either. But he didn't hide his face in shame like some kind of child molester or sex offender. In fact, a certain ineffable peace was written across his face that she found endearing.

Chapter Sixty-Nine

CHICAGO TELEGRAPH
SEPTEMBER 20, 1992
JOURNALIST TURNS PEEPING TOM
Star Reporter Caught Spying on Female Trader

IN A STUNNING turn of events, Skip Slider, the journalistic star of the Chicago Commodities Exchange (CCE) and Karol Stanislav scandals, was arrested by the Chicago police Saturday night for climbing a tree to watch a woman take a bath. Before becoming a reporter, Slider had been a trader himself in the CCE Treasury-Index Pit, where the woman in question, Ms. Darby Shaw, is currently a trader. Both he and Ms. Shaw refused to comment.

Slider's employer, the Windy City Times, *was asked whether this discredits the investigation that has rocked the world's largest commodity futures and options exchange, as well as the most powerful member of the U.S. Congress.*

"We have no comment until we speak with Mr. Slider," a Times spokesperson said.

The CCE was none so reluctant. "This explains a lot," spokesperson John Mackey said. "This guy is the ultimate dead-ender. He'll do anything for a thrill. Look at the facts. He loses all his money trading. Then he goes on hysterical rants with specious, half-wrought stories about our markets, obsessed with discrediting the place where he was such an abject failure.

"As for this latest salacious role, such perversion forfeits any rights Mr. Slider might have to public respect. Surely a reputable newspaper like the Windy City Times *will terminate this whole sorry episode before it wastes any more credibility."*

***

THE WORST PART of Saturday night's debacle for Skip Slider came on Monday morning. Grudgingly, he put on the gray business suit he so despised to go hat-in-hand to his boss.

He normally reveled in gliding two miles down Milwaukee Avenue to company headquarters. However, the business shoes were so uncomfortable he opted for a taxi this morning. Walking up the stairs he had ascended so triumphantly in recent months, he felt like he had a water tank strapped onto his back.

Slider had spent the entire previous day straining to put his actions in a larger context. His brother Fred, who had bailed him out of the clinker on Saturday night, stayed silent when he kept saying, "She waved at me, I swear to God. If I hadn't been hanging by both arms, I would have waved back."

"But why did she call the cops?" Fred asked in a measured tone.

"I'm just telling you. Listen to me. Please listen," he kept repeating, "The look on her face was different when she walked up to the police car. I struck her dead center."

Today was the hard part.

"Hello, Skip." "Morning, Skip." The salutations came as he skirted the bullpen of reporters. *They're all gonna wait and laugh behind my back.*

He approached Ben Clayton's secretary.

She adjusted to a formal pose. "Yes, Mr. Slider."

"I'd like to meet with Ben as soon as possible."

"You can go right in," she said, giving him a gut poke.

Everest—the Zone of Death. He had spent half of Sunday drilling that mode of thought into his head.

He entered Clayton's office and was overtaken by the sweet smell of pipe tobacco. This time last week he would have refused to enter a room with such a toxic smell.

Clayton sat reclining in his chair, looking at the disgraced reporter as if studying him.

Slider started into his game plan. He walked around Clayton's desk to offer a handshake. "Good morning, Ben."

It appeared to catch Clayton by surprise; he jerked his hand out front to clasp Slider's hand.

"Hello, Skip."

Slider decided to press for momentum. "I've got some explaining to do."

Clayton said nothing.

"Saturday night I was walking..."

"No," Clayton interrupted with his hand held out like a traffic cop.

"I just want you to know it wasn't quite as spooky as it probably sounds."

"No," Clayton said again in a pinched, angry tone, as if following some internal command. Slider had built up such clout recently that he couldn't even remember hearing Clayton say 'no'. But now he couldn't even get him to listen to a pedestrian explanation of events.

"I knew you were eccentric, Skip," he continued. "But this is Cuckoo-Land. It's damaged our newspaper."

The look on her face for that one fleeting second.

"Ben," he said, struggling for full breaths. "It was so strange. Honestly, I decided to do it about two seconds before I began scaling that tree. Believe it or not, she actually waved at me when I was up there."

"What?" Clayton cut him off, sounding like a mad hornet. "I can't believe what I just heard. You're telling me she liked what you did? Oh my God." He jumped out of his seat and walked over to the window to let out a big sigh. "This sounds clinical."

"Sorry, sorry," Slider pleaded, his face reddening for the first time in embarrassment. "I shouldn't have said that."

"Are you sure?" Clayton asked in an attitude-drenched tone.

"No, you're absolutely right," Slider answered, shaking his head profusely. It was groveling time. "I never should have been anywhere near her."

"You might do it again," Clayton shot back in a tone that had a hint of pleading himself. His mouth looked gnarled.

Slider realized he needed to give the man a wide berth and held his tongue.

"I've seen a lot of people in my time," Clayton continued. "Alcoholics, addicts, and hell's bells, gamblers. They're the worst. They always say they're not gonna do it again."

"I'm not an addict. A creep is not what I am," he said, managing to sound stoic and pleading at the same time. "I give you my most solemn word I will never do something like this again."

"I don't know that," Clayton cut him off. "It's too risky."

Slider felt the momentum trending against him. But he also knew he had an ace-in-the hole. Per journalistic convention, he had never divulged the identity of his source, Deep Pit.

"Ben, this is my story," he said, adopting a principled tone. "Without my source, the Times wouldn't have had any of those gold-plated articles about either the CCE or Karol Stanislav. You've sold a lot of papers that you otherwise wouldn't have. If you fire me, it will bring discredit to everything we've done." He breathed deeply and swallowed, before leaning forward for his final parley. "Our source is working on snaring some more big fish." Clayton seemed intent on his words, which allowed Slider to go for the kill. "One other thing, Ben. I'm pretty sure I could find another newspaper to continue these stories."

That brought a few moments of silence; Clayton's eyes did a full rotation out the window towards the lake and back to him. Slider sensed he was trying to make up his mind.

"Skip," he finally said, his anger evaporating "You've shown you have the fingertip instincts of an investigative reporter. No two ways about it, the stories have lifted our boat. But the bottom line is this: I am the executive editor of a major metropolitan newspaper. I have to act to save our brand."

Clayton reached into his desk and pulled out a copy of a rival newspaper, the *Chicago Telegraph*. The bold headline read: **Has 'Peeping Skip' Ruined CCE and Stanislav Stories?**

Slider remained mum.

"Skip, I have to combat this headline," he said, like a parent explaining the facts of life to a child. "There is only one way to do so. We have to have a counter-headline announcing we are terminating you, effective immediately."

Slider was speechless. From the beginning, he had felt Clayton had a sense of fair play, despite the cutthroat business they were in. He despaired for some reed of hope.

"What I can do," Clayton said, in a leveling tone, "is offer you a side deal, if you are interested."

Slider lifted his chin to cue Clayton.

"I give you my solemn word—call it a blood oath—that if you get some new scoops, I will endeavor to print them, and under your byline."

Slider's eyes narrowed, trying to digest what his erstwhile boss was saying.

Clayton elaborated. "You would have an open pipeline to me for discussing any potential articles, just like you currently have. We will pay for each article of yours we publish. But you will no longer be on our payroll." His tone softened as he tilted his head. "Let's face it, public figures disgrace themselves all the time. In America, we are perennially fascinated with comebacks."

Slider knew the conversation was over. His trading career had ended in ruins and it had taken years to recover. Through innovation and undaunted courage, he had fashioned himself into the golden-boy journalist. But now he had crashed and burned, to the point of dishonoring himself.

As he walked out, his mind was dominated with one line of thought: *How in the world can I ever recover from this? How?*

Chapter Seventy

"CHRISTOPHERRR," CAME A familiar voice from behind as he jumped on the CCE escalator heading to the coatroom. "How are we?" It was Batesy.

"A seven," Chris responded.

"Come on, dude."

"What's so bad about a seven? Especially at seven in the morning."

"Throwing down some huge size in there these days, are we?" Batesy remarked, referring to Chris's latest surge in business.

"Even blind pigs find acorns," Chris said, downplaying the compliment.

"I just wish I was on the other side of some of your marshmallows," Batesy continued, "instead of those Attila-bitches you like to throw at me. Those 94-18s you hit me with late yesterday destroyed my whole day and then some."

Chris didn't take the bait. "First losing trade you've had with me in a year," he said, taking it in stride.

"No, it's Kaner here that gets all the gold," he argued, pointing at Jeff Kaner, who had sidled up to them on the escalator.

Solly and Tripp Cole had been suddenly and surprisingly suspended a month ago, allowing Chris to finally occupy a fertile piece of real estate in the Treasury-Index Pit. Business was way up, and he had all kinds of new friends. He had even begun to wonder if it was fortuitous that the Slider pipeline had been disrupted. He was making more money than ever in open-outcry trading.

Grabbing his trading jacket, Chris started up the final escalator. Despite having the single lowest error rate of any broker in the Treasury Pit, he still got butterflies right here every morning. It never failed to amaze him the number of different ways he had seen traders blow up.

Chris arrived at the Elliott House desk at 7:10. His trade checker Jason was waiting.

"How'd that entrance exam go?" Chris asked. The recent upsurge in business had given Preston Beatty impetus to put up his two assistants, Danny and Jason, for memberships.

"Still waiting to hear," Jason answered his boss.

"You're getting there," Chris encouraged his clerk, who like all the rest was willing to suffer for years in a menial job to get his shot at the gold.

***

AFTER TOILING FOR so many years on the back row, Chris felt just shy of ecstatic each morning walking un-accosted to Solly's old spot on the front row. However, this morning when he climbed the ladder, a new person was planted there.

Actually, there was nothing was new about Nickie Zambowlie. Known as *Wrecking Ball*, his sawed-off stature and expansive girth were perfect for the slash and burn tactics for which he was renowned. The last time Chris had seen him, Zambowlie was engaged in a Mexican standoff in the well of the Pit with a rookie trader, when he suddenly round-housed the newcomer. The stunned victim had rushed away with a bleeding nose, as sounds of euphoria echoed around the Pit.

Zambowlie wasn't in his exact spot, but he might as well have been. His wide frame veered well into Chris's horizontal space, forcing him to edge up to the front row sideways. Just as he got wedged in diagonally, Wrecking Ball made a jerky lateral movement, sending Chris veering into Dennis Leonard.

"Woops," Chris said.

"Watch it," warned the territorial Leonard, who had occupied the same spot for ten years.

Chris found himself oscillating back and forth between Leonard and Wrecking Ball, using all his energy to avoid careening into either man. Fortunately, all the customer orders off the opening were small and medium-sized, but even those required abnormal energy from a contorted position. By 7:30, Chris was drenched with sweat. *Déjà vu.*

"Hey, Chris, sell 500 at 95-13," Danny called up to his boss.

Chris struggled to get squared up to the Pit, but Wrecking Ball maintained steady pressure on his left thigh. "Sell 500 at 95-13," he shouted, straining to maintain his balance with both hands held high.

"Buy nine," his old nemesis Ray Malley shouted.

Damn you.

"Sell you nine, Ray," Chris acknowledged the trade.

"Sell 491 at 95-13," he yelled, wondering if the rest of the Pit realized the odd quantity he was offering for sale. Suddenly, from the far side, Chris heard the sound he was trained to listen for: *Buy 'em, Buy 'em, buy 'em.*

He looked over and saw Pat Sheridan signaling to purchase the balance. *Pat Sheridan!*

"Sell you 491, Pat," Chris shouted to Sheridan, while giving him as clear of a hand signal as possible.

"Filled," he called down to Danny. "I sold 500 at 95-13."

A few seconds later, Danny called up, "Hey, Chris, sell ten."

Practically the whole Pit was bidding 95-13. He looked
to the far corner at Barbra Lasky, who also had her hands
up trying to buy. But when they locked eyes, she jerked her
head away, not wanting to trade.

What the hell?

Jay Rickey, a couple months removed from his bitter
arbitration defeat to Chris, was also bidding 95-13. When
Rickey saw what happened, he pumped his hands to
emphasize his 95-13 bid. Chris spontaneously decided to
sell the ten contracts to Rickey. However, the whole scene
left him feeling unbalanced.

"Let's take a quickie, Danny," he called to his assistant.

Weaving his way out of the Pit, Chris brushed up
against the Sleazebags, packed in on the back row like cords
of wood. He couldn't help but feel empathetic toward these
indentured humans stacked up in his old neighborhood.

But then Jeremy Mutley spoke up. "Hey, Parker. How's
your peeping friend?" Mutley didn't try to disguise the
ecstasy in his voice.

"Cool dude, huh?" Chris responded in his best offhand
manner.

"Let's hear your take on this world-class perv?"

"That says it all," Chris said plaintively.

"You sound defensive," Mutley dug in.

"Not," Chris said, trying not to sound defensive.

"All I got to say is the two of you sure like different types
of girls," Mutley said, drawing round laughs from his fellow
Sleazebags. "How tall is he?" Mutley persisted.

"What, the tree climber?"

"He's probably short," Mickey Molina analyzed.
"Freakishly tall guys want a munchkin and vice-versa."

"Thank you, Dr. Freud," Chris gibed.

Mutley changed tack. "You do know that if you're lying
about being the rat for that perverted reporter, you're

finished down here." His words hung in the air, as Chris continued down the ladder and out of the Pit.

Chris remembered he had just made a large trade with Pat Sheridan. Knowing Sheridan's treacherous history, he called down to his trade checker. "Hey, Jason, check those 191 contracts I sold to Pat Sheridan right away."

***

CHRIS AND BARBRA came up on each other in the hallway.

"Hey, Barbra."

"Morning, Chris." Again, she sounded circumspect. "Looks like you've got company in the Pit."

"Hell yes," Chris said. "Wrecking Ball. Did you send him over there?"

She ignored his question. "Why does it seem like things are always happening to you over there?"

"We could use you to come over and straighten all us guys out."

"Whatever," she said in weary fashion and shuffled off, any hint of flirtatiousness long gone.

As Chris watched her walk away, Jay Rickey turned up at his side. "Chris," he said, looking him dead in the eye, "thanks for the trade this morning. I was short and needed them."

Chris gave a quick nod.

Fixing him with a level stare, Rickey said, "I want you to know I don't hold a thing against you about the arbitration case. That's business."

"Good deal, yeah."

He trudged back to the Pit, strong emotions roiling his concentration. To his relief, Wrecking Ball passed by, headed in the opposite direction.

"Jason," he called over, "are we checked up with Pat Sheridan?"

"Yeah," Jason answered, holding a thumb up. Not that Chris was too worried. The market had rallied, and the trade was a winner for Sheridan. Maybe he's gotten better, Chris thought.

Chris climbed the ladder and squared up to the Pit on the front row. Relief. Right away he got two orders to buy 50 contracts and banged them out with dispatch. *Piece of cake.*

"Sell 500 at 95-14," Danny called up.

"Sell 500 at 95-14," Chris began shouting, glad to not be jostled while offering $50 million worth of contracts for sale.

After a few seconds, he heard a voice from his left. "Buy 'em, buy 'em." *What the...* It was Pat Sheridan again. Chris placed five fingers on his forearm pointed outward to signal selling Sheridan 500 contracts. Sheridan did the opposite.

"Filled," Chris yelled back to Danny, and immediately began waving at Sheridan to check the trade.

"Hey, Pat, Pat, hey Pat," he yelled at the top of his voice. But Sheridan was staring off in the other direction. "Pat, Pat," Chris continued shouting, holding both hands high. Unfortunately, Wrecking Ball returned to the Pit. Immediately Chris felt his physical integrity vanish, as Zambowlie muscled Chris' lean frame to a sideways position. Now Sheridan was blocked off from Chris's view.

Chris swiveled on his right foot, hoping to aim his body in Sheridan's direction without bumping up against Wrecking Ball. "Hey, Gary," Chris shouted at Gary D' Arco, standing next to Sheridan. "Get him." D' Arco tapped Sheridan on the shoulder, but all Sheridan did was shrug. Chris kept waving and D' Arco again said something to Sheridan. Finally, Sheridan turned to Chris.

"Come on, Pat," Chris chided him. "Checking, I sold you 500 at 95-14."

All he got out of Sheridan was a Cool Hand Luke stare.

Meanwhile, Merrill Lynch began selling 95-13s, followed by Goldman Sachs selling 95-12s.

"Looks like Sheridan's hot streak didn't last long," Marty Allman noted with ill-disguised delight.

The market soon traded down to 95-10. Chris heard Danny's voice. "Sell 500 at 95-10."

Chris again rotated for traction, allowing him to raise his upper body. "Sell 500 at 95-10," he screamed. *Not gonna be easy to sell 500 from this position.* He was wrong. Someone from his blind side started screaming, "Buy 'em, buy 'em." He jerked his neck around and saw Pat Sheridan again signaling to buy 500 contracts. Chris reciprocated with a sell signal.

Does his clearinghouse know he's trading this big?

Chris felt a twinge of guilt, because he remembered—a lot of people did—the horror tale for which Sheridan had become infamous. A few years back, Sheridan had stood in the way of a falling market, buying everything that the wave of sellers could throw at him. Ultimately, he had accumulated a position of 3,000 contracts before word reached the owners of his clearinghouse, who rushed down the elevator and onto the trading floor. They were forced to physically eject Sheridan from the Pit, all the while him laughing and attempting to make final suicide trades before they had been able to subdue him. Their final loss on the 3,600 contracts that they had to sell out in an emergency was $4,800,000, bankrupting the clearinghouse.

The incident made Sheridan a laughingstock, and he had disappeared from the Exchange for a couple years. Improbably, though, he was back, wearing a purple jacket for BDB trading—a clearinghouse owned by CCE Chairman, *Dean Beman.* Now, it appeared he was long at least a thousand contracts, which meant each tick was worth $31,250.

The market continued dropping like a rock.

Chris got a few more medium-sized orders, which would have been easy just one day before, but Wrecking Ball was adept at keeping him off balance. This asshole hasn't done a single trade, Chris thought. *What's going on here?* Besides being a perennial loser, Zambowlie—like Sheridan —had murky connections to the CCE chairman.

Soon the market crashed through the key support level of 95-00, which was sure to trigger more sell orders from technical traders at desks around the world.

"Wow, you went deep on Sheridan," Marty Allman exulted. "Did you lube him up first?"

Batesy jumped in to add, "Damn, I should move over next to Sheridan. Every time he opens his mouth I'll take the other side of the trade."

"You'd better go over there right now," Ray Malley advised him with a smirk. "He may not be around long."

That prompted Chris to jerk around and call down to his clerk. "Jason, are we all checked with Sheridan on those trades?"

"No, I've got all these people wanting to check trades," he said, pointing to three trade checkers surrounding him.

"Forget them," Chris shouted in a rare peremptory tone. "Go find Sheridan's trade checker right now."

Two minutes later, Danny jumped to whisper in Chris's ear, "Jason says Sheridan doesn't have the trades."

In one whirling motion, Chris shouted, "Which one? The first or second trade?"

"Both."

Chapter Seventy-One

My entire career right here.

CHRIS STRUGGLED TO disengage from the dense pack of bodies. Just as he was extracting himself, he got bumped into the Sleazebags.

"Hey, asshole," Mickey Molina growled, before body-checking him into the rail. "Where are you going—to the newspaper again to tattle on someone?"

Chris didn't respond, as he lurched from the thicket of traders and hurled himself down the Pit ladder.

The market was plunging; traders who had bought contracts at higher prices were in panic-selling mode. If he really was out the trades with Sheridan, it was already a $400,000 error. He rushed around the arc of the Pit, with Jason chasing behind.

"Which one is Sheridan's trade checker?" Chris asked over his shoulder.

"That girl," Jason answered, pointing at a young female everyone in his area of the Pit had been microscopically analyzing.

Chris rifled a question. "You don't have the two 500-lots I sold Sheridan?"

The young girl looked unnerved to be talking to a trader. She jerked up the cards as if balancing them on her chest and began sifting through them. When she got to the end, she shook her head.

"Dammit," he said, jolting her. "How about asking him if he's got them?"

Then Chris thought better of it; this was a career-changing situation. He hauled himself up the Pit ladder towards Pat Sheridan, but reams of brokerage assistants stood in the way.

"Pat, Pat, Pat Sheridan," Chris called over their heads. He got no acknowledgment. "Hey, Pat," he continued shouting, beginning to sound helpless.

Finally, one of the assistants tapped Sheridan on the shoulder. He turned around as if performing an unwanted task.

"Pat," Chris called forward, "your trade checker says she doesn't have a card for those two 500-lots I sold you at 95-14 and 95-10."

"Whoa, whoa," Sheridan said to halt the line of discussion. He then turned back to the Pit as if readying to make a trade.

"Hey, Sheridan, goddammit," Chris shouted, "I sold you two 500-lots. Write down the fucking trades. I'm coming up there."

That got his attention. Many cornered traders would have opted for a high-pitched showdown on the spot. But Sheridan had always been more of an eel; he turned and motioned out of the Pit which satisfied Chris's inclination for a reasoned discussion. In retrospect, he would wonder if he should have opted for a face-to-face encounter on the spot, given the number of witnesses to the two trades.

After both had descended the ladder, Sheridan pointed to the far wall, where they walked silently and separately. Once they were by the fire escape, Sheridan furrowed his brow. "What is this—we're out two trades?"

"No, we're not out any fucking trades," Chris clipped his words. "You bought 500 contracts from me at 95-14 and 95-10, but you didn't write them down." Chris bent to get his face in front of Sheridan's eyes and spat, "Or maybe you did, but tore the cards up when the market went down."

A look of concern drew across Sheridan's face; he made a show of taking a few steps to look up at the board. Chris had long suffered from naiveté, but the way Sheridan feigned surprise as he scoped-out the board was a dead giveaway.

"You know we did those trades," he shouted, stabbing a finger in Sheridan's face. "You signaled buying 500 from me at 95-14 and 500 more at 95-10." Chris mimicked Sheridan's buying motion, with five fingers placed inward on the back of his forearm.

"Did you check them?" Sheridan asked without expression.

"Yes, I checked them, and everybody saw it."

"One person didn't see it," Sheridan said with a level expression.

He's not worried, Chris realized. That alarmed him. He had noticed over the years that a small percentage of unprofitable traders could not accept the slow death that was the inevitable fate of most traders, culminating in the anonymous final perp walk. Rather, they savored the darker, more orgiastic music of self-destruction and ruination. Chris's mind flashed back to Sheridan's sordid history. Amazingly, he had gotten clearance to return to the CCE trading floor despite his prior atrocity in the Treasury Pit. How? Chris knew there could only be one answer, Dean Beman. The implications of that were ominous.

Then there was Wrecking Ball. Why had he turned up out of the blue this morning, standing in Chris's spot? What was going on?

"You screamed buy 'em from me at both 95-14 and 95-10," he continued haranguing Sheridan. "Write up the damn trades. Everybody has heard all the shit you've done."

Sheridan looked at Chris dreamy-eyed. "We're out the trades," he said in a meek voice that might have been endearing in another situation.

Right then Chris heard a thudding sound. Heavy selling by Dean Witter was driving the market below another support level—94-28, 94-27, 94-26. His primal anger was beginning to morph into white fear. Stop-loss orders were being triggered at this key level, guaranteed to trigger more technical selling.

"You need to get out of them," Sheridan said. Indeed, Chris had no other choice other than to do what Sheridan suggested.

For the first time in his life, he grabbed another person by the lapels and leaned down at Sheridan's face. "I'm taking this to arbitration."

Another loud clap from the Treasury Pit, "Morgan Stanley sells all the 94-26s," a broker's assistant shouted.

Chris tore back towards the Pit, careening into a rotund exchange official. "Sorry," he said, throwing up his hands, before turning back to Sheridan to point his finger and shout, "I've got proof we did the trades."

Sheridan was expressionless.

***

CHRIS CHARGED INTO the Treasury Pit, knowing it might be the last time he ever entered it. He needed to sell a thousand contracts in a plunging market.

He wasn't concerned about anybody else's feelings. His ravenous mood seemed to transmit outward; everyone moved aside to let him slide up to the front row. Everybody except Nickie Zambowlie. When Chris began to assume his spot, Wrecking Ball gave him a hip check into Dennis Leonard.

Infuriated, Chris shoved Zambowlie back, but it didn't budge him. Wrecking Ball promptly sent an elbow into Chris's ribs, knocking the wind out of him. It was the best he could do to maintain his spot turned sideways.

"Hey, hey, Chris, sell 300," Danny yelled up.

"No, no, tell 'em to give everything away," Chris shouted back to his loyal assistant. This was becoming surreal. He had spent his entire career trying to get business, and now he was giving it away. Perhaps even worse, the error was beginning to reach a quantity that didn't seem to matter, like someone freezing to death in the Arctic in a Jack London novel.

Chris forced himself to buckle up. "Sold, sold, sold," he began screaming, while waving and swatting at whoever was bidding. He knew there were buyers to his left, but Wrecking Ball had him blocked off. Finally, he effected a sharp pivot off his right foot that would have made his high school basketball coach proud, giving him free motion. "Sold, sold, sold." And that is when the disaster began to turn into a farce the likes of which were seen only in Shakespeare's darkest tragedies. For Pat Sheridan, armed with the knowledge Chris needed to sell a large quantity of Treasury futures, had re-entered the Pit and began lunging at other traders, screaming, "Sold, sold, sold."

"You fucking asshole," Chris screamed at Sheridan at the top of his lungs. "You scumbag." He got the attention of one of the brokers who had bought from Sheridan. "Wake the fuck up, you idiot," Chris berated him. "I offered to sell first." In what was looking like the final act of his trading career, Chris had at last adopted the ethos of the CCE.

Sheridan acted like he didn't see Chris, and kept on selling. The market continued plummeting, 94-24, 94-23, 94-22... Worse yet, his showdown with Sheridan had alerted other traders, and they smelled blood. Chris was having trouble selling over 25 to 50 contracts at a time. When Ray Malley saw Chris yelling "Sold" at a RefCo broker, he practically got the guy in a headlock to force the broker to buy thirty contracts from him, instead of Chris. A hushed thought occurred to Chris: the error could exceed a million dollars.

Finally, Lehman Brothers broker Jeff Mullins hollered, "95-20 for 500."

"Sold, sold, sold," Chris screamed at Mullins in mid-air, trying to sell 500 contracts. Mullins snapped his head towards Chris. But just as he came into Mullins' focus, Wrecking Ball squatted for maximum torque and launched Chris's body five feet laterally, into the midst of the Sleazebags.

It took a couple seconds for the woozy Alabaman to realize what had happened. "Get the fuck off me, you piece of shit," the big Sleazebag Dick Grutzkis bellowed, grabbing Chris's featherweight body off the floor and flinging it in the direction it came from. In mid-flight Chris collided like a piñata with Mickey Molina.

"Hey," Chris said helplessly.

"Hey, fuck you, too," Molina mocked Chris before shoving him away. Chris went doubling over the sawed-off Sleazebag figure of Jeremy Mutley and splatting onto the ground. "You scumbag," Joe D' Abruzzo screamed, before commencing kicking away at his shins. "It *was* you."

The sharp kicks reminded Chris of dogs barking at a car. He was trapped. His mind shot to a concert in 1980 of the musical group, *The Who,* in Cincinnati, Ohio, where hundreds of anxious fans had careened over at once, eleven of them being trampled to death.

Get up. He contracted into a ball to push off the ground. Just as he was almost erect, another body blindsided him back into a crouch; the Sleazebags began swinging from the waist with open fists and pushing his head to the floor

"You sorry piece of shit, telling the paper all those lies," D' Abruzzo screamed in a black rage. "Deep Puss. That's who you really are."

"Wait," Chris gasped.

"Wait for this," Grutzkis shouted as he and his fellow Sleazebags pounded at his helpless physique like he was a two-dollar whore. Chris drew into as tight of a fetal position as he could muster, but kept getting whacked from one into another. Perhaps most alarming, his will to defend himself began weakening as he lay strewn on the steps of the Pit, while surrounding traders alternated between looking down at the human roadkill beneath and making trades.

Chicago. His earliest memories of the city while growing up in Alabama had featured dark overtones. *Could I die right here?*

Right then, Chris heard a noise that sounded more like a primal force than any decipherable words. Two monstrous forearms reached around his throat; he was powerless to resist. *Is this it?* Chris suddenly realized these were the same two meaty arms he had battled every day for the last several years and the thunderous roar came from the person who had kept him awake many a night.

"Get the fuck away," the man shouted at the Sleazebags, "or I'll knock you into yesterday." That was followed by the truncheon-like sound of an elbow walloping a chest. Chris glanced next to him on the ground and saw the dazed face of head Sleazebag Mickey Molina.

"Come on, Chrissie," Ray Malley said. "Let's get out of here." He used his massive pipes to lever Chris off the floor and onto his feet. Blood was gushing from a wound on the left side of his face. "We gotta get out," Malley commanded and hauled Chris out of the Treasury Pit for the last time.

Traders, trade checkers, and phone clerks all watched in silence as the tallest guy on the floor was carried off by the biggest guy. When they got to the First Aid office on the first floor, Malley said to the confused-looking attendant, "We had a dustup upstairs. He took it pretty good."

The young lady in a white nurse's uniform stared at Chris in disbelief.

"I'll be back after the close to check on him," Malley said. "Give him whatever he needs. We'll take care of the bill."

"Thanks, Ray," Chris croaked in disbelief at the juxtaposition of Malley from villain to savior.

"No sweat, mate."

Chapter Seventy-Two

PRESTON BEATTRY WAS all set to unleash an Irish temper tantrum. Jack Fitzgerald had given him the broad outlines of the massacre, both financially and physically, of Chris Parker in the Treasury Pit the previous Friday. Beatty couldn't wait to come out swinging on behalf of his longtime broker.

The telephone rang at 8:45 a.m., fifteen minutes before Parker was scheduled to arrive. It was Mike Kilpatrick.

"Hello, Preston," the CCE President began. "Mike Kilpatrick."

"Yes, Mike. What can I do for you?"

Beatty was well versed in the ways of kings. However, he had never developed a working relationship with this arguably more important operative, and felt uneasy.

"Have you got a few minutes to discuss something important?" Kilpatrick asked, although it wasn't really a question.

"Yes, but I have someone coming in at nine."

"It shouldn't take that long," Kilpatrick assured him. "First, though, I really do have to ask for a pledge of confidentiality regarding this phone call."

"Amen," Beatty responded in amicable fashion.

"Preston," Kilpatrick began, "without getting too much into the how, it has come to our express attention, and now been confirmed, that your Elliott House employee Chris Parker is Deep Pit."

Beatty had long been the boss; part of the gig was to always act in control. But now someone with a higher rank in the pecking order was telling him that he had a rogue elephant in his ranks, which he knew nothing about. He was dumbfounded. An embarrassing silence ensued as Beatty groped for a dignified-sounding response. Finally, he opted for the pedestrian. "Are you sure?"

"Yes," Kilpatrick answered. "One hundred percent!"

Beatty felt his Irish skin flush. He found himself thankful that the conversation was occurring by telephone, keeping his humiliation from full exposure.

"I've spoken with Dean (Beman) about this," Kilpatrick continued. "He says the next move is up to you."

The normally voluble Beatty was apoplectic. But suddenly, this reader of John Le Carre novels was interrupted by an ominous thought. *The error—were they behind it?*

"Preston," Kilpatrick broke in, "I don't need to tell you how damaging—not to mention illegal—this has all been to the Exchange, and frankly to Elliott House. I'm sure your superiors in New York would agree."

Beatty found himself disliking this hatchet man more by the second. "So what are you trying to tell me?"

"We want to know if you can fix the problem."

"There are a lot of problems with this place," Beatty retorted with thinly-disguised impudence.

""I spend sixteen hours a day dealing with all of them," Kilpatrick volleyed back. "But this is a big one, and the ball is in your court."

Beatty's old football instincts to go crashing head first into this man's entire thesis were warring with his executive bias. As annoying as he found this functionary, he knew Kilpatrick held the trump card. Assuming Kilpatrick was correct, exposure of Chris Parker as *Deep Pit* would not only be the end of Parker's career at Elliott House, but probably ruin his own as well. The stark truth was that Beatty could economize on casualties by heeding this unpleasant man's suggestion.

"Give me the bottom line," he responded in clipped fashion.

"Parker goes right away," Kilpatrick matched him.

Beatty lost his resolve a split-second, before spitting back, "Done." He added, "You folks remember this one up there."

"Done."

***

CHRIS SPENT MUCH of the weekend in bed, too sore to do anything but walk to the bathroom. That gave him plenty of time to plan for the pivotal encounter with Preston Beatty. But regardless of what he said, one statistic trumped all: $1,170,232. That was the final amount of the loss from the two out-trades with Pat Sheridan.

He did not get the final figure until visiting the trade-processing department a half-hour before his appointment with Beatty. The Elliott House floor staff had spent the last two hours Friday afternoon attempting to reconstruct how many contracts he had sold before getting pulverized. They came up with 480, before selling the balance of 520 contracts at lower prices. Elliott House would give the customers the lower prices and had until the close of trading today to cut them checks totaling $1,170,232 to make up the difference.

Chris, who had spent his entire career in the inglorious task of controlling risk, was devastated. When he walked into Beatty's office, the Elliott House head of futures and options trading bounded out of his seat and proffered his hand to the lanky southerner he had hired eight years before. However, Beatty's customary wide grin was replaced with a more circumspect look.

"How are you, Chris?" he asked in a voice a couple octaves lower than normal.

"Aw, I never wanted to be a hockey player to begin with," Chris drawled, shaking his head. "I feel better this morning."

"They tell me you have a concussion."

Chris found his eyes watering up. "You warned that pit trading was a contact sport, before ever putting me in there."

Beatty nodded.

There was no possible way to whitewash this meeting, so Chris decided to take a standup approach. "I just went by Ronnie's office down in clearing," he said, traces of wooziness lingering. "He gave me the final tally—seven figures. Wow." He shook his head in awe. "You hear about those kinds of disasters, but I never thought I would be involved in one."

"Chris," Beatty said in an official tone that made him uneasy, "the report I received painted a picture of total anarchy. Do you mind taking me through the sequence?"

"Sure."

In a sober voice, Chris recounted the improbable series of events in the Treasury-Index Pit the previous Friday, straining not to sound defeated. Nonetheless, a palpable feeling of doom overlay the atmosphere. Chris knew his back was against the wall, and decided his only hope was to go on the offensive.

"Preston, let me say two things. This Pat Sheridan, he's a con man from the word 'go.'" Chris hesitated a second, turning his head sideways. "And Dean Beman himself is almost surely involved in this. Great to have a chairman like that, huh?"

"What makes you think that?" Beatty asked.

Chris had spent the weekend torn whether to inform Beatty about his leaking activities to Skip Slider, suspicion that his phone had been wiretapped, along with the unknown visitor to his apartment and the threatening letter. Ultimately, he decided to stick to the subject of the huge fraud he had been a victim of the previous Friday.

"Dammit, Preston, why don't you run against this piece of shit Beman next time he is up for re-election. This whole place is going the way of the milkman with that bunch of low-lifers in charge."

Beatty appeared taken aback by his haughty tone, which encouraged Chris to continue. "Because the only possible way a sorry piece of protoplasm like Pat Sheridan could re-gain trading privileges after all the calamities he has wrought with other people's money is through the direct intervention of Beman."

"Who clears his trades?" Beatty asked.

"BDB," Chris answered. "That's Beman's company, you know. At the very least we should take Sheridan to arbitration," he suggested. "He's always broke, but then we sue his clearing house, Beman's company, to regain the money."

Beatty rocked back in his chair as if suffering from temporary whiplash. Soon he regained his composure. "I can see why you're upset, Chris. But right now, I've got a seven-figure error to explain to the folks back in New York."

"I'll be glad to fly out there and give it to 'em from the shoulder."

"Do you have any witnesses that will testify for you?" Beatty asked.

Chris's spirits sank. Beatty had always used *we* to the point of nausea. But the way he said *you* in this instance left him feeling forlorn. He shook his head. "Sheridan has got this deck of customer orders that he also probably got from Beman. The traders around Sheridan aren't gonna want to antagonize him."

An inquisitive look came across Beatty's face. "Chris, uh, what do you think caused all those people to attack you like that?"

Chris again noted the distant tone this erstwhile raconteur was adopting. All he could do was attempt to reason. "Preston, don't you think it's strange the way that guy Wrecking Ball turns up out of nowhere that morning and parks himself next to me? You should have seen it. I mean, he didn't even try to make a trade; all he did was hammer at me."

Beatty lifted his brow in acknowledgment, but demurred on his usual colorful commentary.

What's going on here? A dreadful thought occurred to Chris. *Has someone gotten to my boss?*

"Chris," Beatty said, "I will have to talk to Stuart Richardson about this; I'll get back to you."

Beatty was putting the onus on his own boss in New York. That was not good news. One way or another, his commodity trading career was probably history.

They shook hands and Chris looked at Preston Beatty. "This is strange, Preston." He squinted in physical and emotional pain. "Preston, it's wrong."

Pain shone on Beatty's face.

PART IV

Chapter Seventy-Three

JOE WOLF BARELY knocked before barging into Karol Stanislav's office. He noticed his boss seemed taken aback at his forwardness.

"Mr. Chairman, I just got a call from Bucky Avant over in finance. He's got some news."

Stanislav said nothing.

Wolf knew Stanislav was bored with the mechanics of campaign finance.

"Bucky tells me the CCE has done a full U-turn and is reneging on all financial commitments to us." Stanislav looked at him in apparent incomprehension, allowing Wolf to add, "They are going to go double-down on Raymond Haack."

"Raymond Haack," Stanislav said in confusion, as if it was the first time he had ever heard the name of his opponent this fall. "Are these people serious?"

"You betcha," Wolf said in cocksure fashion.

"Judas Priest," Stanislav blurted.

Wolf couldn't rid himself of a certain deliciousness in informing his boss that his political support was beginning to cave. He secretly fantasized about replacing Stanislav in Congress.

"We know how to take care of them, don't we?" Stanislav said.

Wolf wondered if Stanislav realized his pat solution—to kneecap politically anyone who got in his way—was rapidly becoming obsolete. "Mr. Chairman, the CCE is our biggest financial supporter. Bucky says they're leaking their U-turn to everyone around town. Our gunpowder could soon be running dry."

That got Stanislav's attention. "Those folks at the CCE think they're pretty smart, huh?

Wolf turned his head as if wincing. "All I'm saying is it looks like they've hit us where it counts."

"We'll see who gets hurt," Stanislav fired back.

***

"HEY, I'VE GOT it," Skip Slider said.

Another Slider idea, *that* was enough to make Chris skeptical. He reclined in his chair, while Slider leaned way forward with his fingers grazing the rug. They were sitting in the increasingly-rundown apartment of Fred Slider, which featured Skip's mountain bicycle leaning on its side across the middle of the room. Chris noted the feline smell of Skip's cat, Darby, was getting more ingrained in the surroundings.

Chris had walked up to the apartment without the usual cloak and dagger routine. Preston Beatty had called him three days ago to report that the higher-ups in New York considered the seven-figure brokerage error a deal-breaker. Having been outed, savaged, and excommunicated, he was liberated. But also miserable. Sitting around bandying fanciful ideas with another disgraced idler in the middle of the day made Chris feel like a member of the infamous *Bleacher Bums*, a mile further north at Wrigley Field.

"Why don't you go straight to Stanislav and form an alliance?" Slider suggested.

"Me, go to Stanislav?" Chris repeated incredulously. "I'm one of the major reasons, along with you, that he's facing ruin."

"Exactly," Slider gushed. "Remember what the Chinese say: an enemy of my enemy is my friend. You and Stanislav now have the same foes."

Chris took a breath in frustration, knowing he and Slider would never be on the same wavelength in some matters. But then he turned his head sideways and had a second thought. Maybe *Slider* was the one being the realist here, and he was the one slow on the uptake. He was kaput in the Chicago commodities business, which had been the purpose of his move to the city in the first place. It was time to think anew. In the most unlikely way, Slider's idea of a Stanislav gambit made some sense.

"You know," Chris said slowly, "I *have* long wanted in on the political game. And think about this, Skip. What if Stanislav—now that the CCE has pimped him—announces he has seen the light and wants to take the lead in promoting electronic trading?"

"Aw, man." Slider's eyes widened like a child hearing about a new toy. "That's a great idea. He could blow the CCE out of the water!"

" Remember, Nixon was an old commie-bater before he made the historic peace with Red China," Chris continued, feeling himself becoming Slideresque. "Who could better spotlight the corruptness of open-outcry trading than Stanislav, himself?"

"Brilliant, brilliant," Slider said.

Chris became pensive. "I've got to figure out a way to approach Stanislav."

"I could ask Ben to arrange it."

"That would win him a Pulitzer," Chris said. "The newspaper that has played the key role in taking down a legendary politician then arranges for him to meet up with one of the secret agents in his destruction." He stopped and gave Slider a skeptical look. "Skip, be real. Is Ben gonna do that for you, after, uh?"

"You might be surprised," Slider said with a knowing look. "Ben is a realist himself."

Chapter Seventy-Four

THE WEST SIDE of Chicago was classic *urbania*.

Small merchants and family businesses blended in with boxlike brown homes featuring postage stamp lawns to form the landscape. The main artery was Milwaukee Avenue, its façade scarred by a half-century of wear, neglect, and graffiti. The dominant theme throughout was the glacial but inexorable struggle to ascend from lower middle-class to solid middle-class.

When Slider had relayed word that Karol Stanislav was ready to meet, Chris anticipated a viewing of the legend ensconced in the trappings of power. But the building he arrived at off Milwaukee Avenue looked just shy of crumbling. The main entrance consisted of a single unmarked door off a sidewalk full of cracks, broken glass, garbage, and dog turds. He followed the dimly-lit hallway with a low ceiling that had him stooping, as his footfalls echoed off the cracked-tile floor.

Chris looked for the elevator to get to the third floor, but all he could see was a sign that read STAIRS. Feeling an undefined anxiety, he climbed two flights of steps. At last he stood in front of a brown wooden door with paint chipped off and a metal sign that read GRUZINSKI HOME REPAIRS. He hesitated, wondering if the larger-than-life figure really was behind the door. Or could this be a setup?

After a few seconds, he knocked. As if on cue, someone opened the door. Standing in front of him was a middle-aged man with a clipped moustache who surely had never been the most powerful member of the U.S. Congress. Rather, his clipped tie, white shirt, and expressionless face made him look like a poster child for middle management. What hair remained on his balding head stuck out untidily, and the drab blue suit looked like it might have been donated to the Salvation Army and rejected.

"May I help you?"

"Yes," Chris answered in a tone just above a whisper. "I'm looking for Karol Stanislav."

The man looked at Chris with blazing eyes. "Your name?"

Chris shifted his weight. "Chris Parker."

"Very well. Come in."

Chris entered the anteroom, whose beige walls and standard-issue tables and desks gave it the look of an elementary school classroom.

"One minute, sir," the man said before filing down a hallway.

Chris soon heard a deep voice, followed by two sets of footsteps, the latter heavier and more decisive. The man re-entered the reception, followed by a much more imposing and recognizable figure.

"Karol Stanislav." He offered his hand, but didn't bother with a smile.

"Chris Parker."

They stared at each other for a couple seconds. The improbable setting goaded Chris to take a stab at humor. "You've really upped your digs here, Mr. Chairman," he cracked, raising his eyebrows.

Stanislav felt no such need for camaraderie. "George is letting us use his office." His tone indicated he saw it all as an unfortunate mess, with no need to pretend to be ecstatic meeting Chris Parker in a place like this.

The two men continued looking at each other; this time Chris held his tongue. He noticed the lines working their way around Stanislav's noble-looking face and eyes. The veteran power-broker had always been the model of supreme confidence in the marble citadels of power in Washington, but now he appeared at a loss. Finally, he cocked his head at a chair on Chris's side of the desk and said, "Have a seat." But he still had a sour look on his face. "I trust you're not wearing any sort of recording device."

Chris threw up his hands. "Absolutely not." He was innocent there. However, Stanislav's remark brought to mind the question he had been obsessing over since Ben Clayton set up the meeting, namely, did Stanislav suspect Chris's involvement in the leaks that had knocked him off his perch?

"Okay, let's hear this proposal you have," Stanislav said, sounding like he was chairing a committee on Capitol Hill.

Chris shifted in his seat. He could talk *ad-infinitum* about the idea in the friendly confines of Skip Slider's apartment. But now he was gripped by a strangling fear, and Stanislav didn't offer any non-verbal cues. However, Chris knew he needed to strike quick.

"Mr. Chairman, it seems like you are in one of those rare sweet spots in history to effect sweeping reform and score huge political points at the same time." Stanislav didn't respond; Chris decided to keep on coming. "Imagine the loop you could throw your opponents with a sweeping proposal to move all trading from the outdated open-outcry method to electronic trading."

Again, the congressman didn't budge.

Chris knew it was asking a lot for him to turn on a dime and embrace something he would have considered heresy his entire career. He decided on a quick feint to Stanislav's vanity. "Mr. Chairman, who could possibly move Chicago's largest industry towards the twenty-first century better than you?"

Stanislav still said nothing, allowing Chris to swing for the fences. "Heck, I'd bet that if the Chicago exchanges don't get out in front of that fast-moving train, the city will lose the entire business to New York, or maybe even overseas. One way or another, it's all gonna be electronic in five or ten years. You know better than anybody how many careers are at stake."

Chris remembered his own personal admonishment on the way to the meeting *Don't talk too much.*

Stanislav stirred in his seat. "Chris, Chris Parker," he said as if straightening himself out, "how is it you suggest I go about such a proposal?"

He's asking me? There was a hint of embarrassment. Effectively, the ultimate powerhouse insider was soliciting political advice from a nobody. But Chris, who had long thought he should be advising political candidates, dove in.

"Mr. Chairman, nobody could possibly have your megaphone. However you decided to roll out the proposal, a press conference, television ads, interviews, you would have a captive audience."

That was an understatement. Here was a man who represented the old way of doing things more than any other person since the late Mayor Riley. Now, in one bold stroke, he could attain an aura of leading-edge progressive and leave his opponents behind.

Let him talk.

"Chris." He adjusted to a more upright position. "No two ways about it, that's a helluva proposal. I'm gonna consider it," he said, pressing his lips together. "What role do you see for yourself?"

Chris hated asking for things. *But I'm out of a job.*

He girded himself. "On this one issue, I think I can be an effective point man for you."

Stanislav turned his head to the side, seemingly lost in thought. Finally, he pursed his lips and looked at Chris. "Okay. Come to my office tomorrow morning at 9:00. I'll have my chief of staff go over details, position, money, all that."

"I'll be there."

They stood simultaneously to shake hands when Stanislav pinioned Chris with his eyes. "One thing. This electronic-trading proposal—you don't say anything to anybody until talking to me." He turned his head sideways in a way that said they were allies, but could quickly become mortal enemies.

"For sure," Chris agreed and met his stare, before turning to leave, giving a nod to the intermediary who sat in the corner.

Once back on Milwaukee Avenue, he sensed a rare lightness of being as he skipped up the potholed street through the urban decay. *I'm jumpstarting reform of the Chicago commodities business!*

Chapter Seventy-Five

"HELLO, MARGARET ANNE," Stanislav greeted his secretary of twenty-one years.

"How was your meeting, Mr. Chairman?"

"Fine. Have Joe and Glenn come to my office."

"Together?" She knew that the Chairman preferred one-on-one meetings to facilitate his crisp commands.

"Yes."

Sixty seconds later Joe Wolf arrived, with Glenn Lipsky on his heels.

Stanislav knew that a critical political calculus was the illusion of power. He prepared to drop a bombshell.

"Guys," he opened, "we've got a chance to make history." He immediately felt odd. Nonetheless, he continued. "It is clear the open-outcry trading method on the Chicago commodity exchanges is obsolete. The time has come to change."

He looked at his two senior staffers for any sign of mutiny. All he saw was two hushed listeners. "You don't always get to choose your timing in this business. Long ago I learned that if you get a chance to make something happen, you take it. Yep, the exchanges have had a lot of good years with everybody packed in there on the trading floors. But it's undeniable; the computers are coming."

Both Wolf and Lipsky appeared dazed at what they had just heard, the mother of all political turnabouts.

"How do you plan to do this?" Wolf asked with a hint of hostility.

Stanislav didn't hesitate. "With so many livelihoods at stake, we've got to do a big rollout here in Chicago. People have to know what's in it for them." One couldn't help but note the quasi-populist tone that master of the smoke-filled room was adopting.

The two staffers had spent the last dozen years trying to one-up each other in front of the Chairman. But now Lipsky turned to Wolf and asked, "What do you think?"

The ultra-confident Wolf did something even more uncharacteristic, throwing up his hands and saying, "Christ, I'll have to think about it."

That gave Stanislav the opening to broach the most sensitive topic of all. Wolf and Lipsky seemed to sense this, and both went rigid. "There's a trader down there," Stanislav said, gritting his teeth. "Well, he's not trading anymore; they've blackballed him. I've met with him and he would like to help us roll out our new proposal."

Confusion spread across his two assistants' faces. Lipsky asked, "Uh, this guy, is he somebody we can trust?"

Stanislav didn't give a decisive answer, allowing Wolf to blurt, "Are we sure this trader isn't involved in those leaks that have torpedoed us?"

Stanislav felt his white face helplessly blush. He was going directly against his own political DNA, allying himself with a *deus ex-machina* against the powers-that-be.

"To be honest," he answered Wolf, "he may be. Let me ask—is that really what matters at this point?"

"I see what you're saying," Glenn Lipsky said. "We've got to get on offense again, however possible."

"Damn right," Stanislav responded to Lipsky, who had always been his most loyal assistant. "Lonnie Herbert as committee chair." He shook his head. "He'll look decrepit when we uncork this blockbuster."

"Actually," Wolf spoke up, "this plan does make some sense. If we execute it properly, we could crater Herbert and get back on top."

A thin smile broke out on Stanislav's lips, followed by his top two aides. All three men had wielded fearsome power, to the point of feasting on it. They wanted it back.

Chapter Seventy-Six

CHRIS STRODE BRISKLY through the grid of streets in downtown Chicago in a charcoal-gray suit. He felt declasse. For somebody who had moved to this Midwestern metropolis to become a floor trader, wearing a suit was a step down.

He wound his way south down LaSalle Street and had to consciously remind himself not to turn right to the CCE, instead diverting east to Stanislav's Madison Street headquarters. A channel of autumn wind kicked some leaves up into his face, and he savored the tangy sensation. At least he wasn't stacked up against masses of sweaty bodies in the Treasury Pit.

His autumn idyll received a sharp jolt when two people in trading jackets turned the corner onto Madison Street, coming his way. The male was wearing a purple jacket, while the female had a svelte physique that could not be disguised by her baby-blue trading jacket. There on the streets of downtown Chicago, two wary rabbits came eye to eye.

Barbra Lasky gave her purple-clad companion a dismissive nudge in the elbow; he dutifully headed off in the direction of the CCE.

"Hey, get back into the Pit," Chris tried joking.

"Look who's talking," she came back.

"*Touché*!" Chris feigned dismay.

"Are you not coming back to the floor?" Barbra asked; her look was neither sympathetic nor hostile.

He started to answer, but could only sigh.

"Where are you going?" she asked.

Chris had grown up in a family that held no secrets; he abhorred keeping them. But Karol Stanislav had specifically enjoined him from telling anyone about their meeting. "I'm meeting with some folks," he answered, pointing down the street.

"It must be important," she said, glancing at his suit.

Chris shrugged. "I wish."

He sensed things were falling flat. *I may never see her again.*

"Barbra," he said, straightening himself, as she focused her vivacious eyes on him. "Let me say one thing. I know you thought I was trying to entrap you in some way. The God's honest truth, though, is that I was not."

"I can't know that for sure, can I?"

"You just heard it."

She appeared to look in his eyes for a split-second in a way she had not before, as if appreciating him defending himself. But she knew how to stick up for herself. "There were those newspaper articles."

"They weren't aimed at you."

"I have to be careful, don't I?"

No longer in the throes of a crippling fixation, Chris looked down at this doughty woman trying to get a better read. Neither had anything new to offer. To Chris, *that* was the most depressing thing of all. If the purpose of life was to know people well, to know them fruitfully, know them soulfully and fulfillingly, Chris couldn't escape the thought that he and Miss Barbra Lasky had failed miserably.

"The market's been terrible," she said, pulling away. "Nobody's making any money."

"Good luck," he offered in salutation.

***

CHRIS WAS SUPPOSED to enter the Douglass Federal Building through the back entrance. He wound around the side of the gray-slab edifice, before arriving in a truck-loading area. An officious-looking man in a light-blue shirt and yellow tie eyed him as he approached.

Once within earshot, he inquired, "Chis Parker?"

Chris nodded, but said nothing.

"I'm here to take you to the Chairman's office."

Chris followed him down a tile-floored hallway, neither speaking. They took a service elevator to the fourth floor where a beefy, fortyish male with a dark mustache stood waiting in the reception area. The man's crossed arms gave him the appearance of a sentinel. "I'm Joe Wolf, the chief of staff."

"Chris Parker."

They shook hands.

"This way."

Wolf started down the hallway with Chris in tow, hanging a left at the end of the hall into a modest-sized office. Wolf took a seat without offering Chris a cue. He chose one of the two opposing wooden-backed chairs, while stealing glances at the numerous framed-photos adorning the shelves. The largest was a shot of Stanislav with Ronald Reagan at a black-tie dinner, both men wearing ear-to-ear smiles. Like many observers, Chris couldn't help but note that Stanislav looked equally presidential. Another photo that stuck out was a younger and slimmer Joe Wolf positioned between House Speaker Tip O' Neill and Senate Majority Leader Bob Dole. Wolf was beaming with joy, while Dole appeared to be critiquing his tie.

"Okay," Wolf opened, "you've been at the CCE eight years, you were a broker for Elliott House, and your friend is this *Times* reporter that has been writing all those articles. How do you fit in with us?"

How does he know I'm Slider's source?

Chris decided to try to match Wolf's salvo with directness. "I was on the top steps of the Treasury-Index Pit —couldn't get any more-Grand Central Station than that. At first I thought open-outcry trading was a great way to do business and understand why the Congressman supported it so strongly."

He felt that last sop was necessary to assuage what was obviously a prominent ego. But Wolf wasn't having any of it.

"Yeah, I got all that," he clipped Chris with cadences of arrogance. "How is the Chairman supposed to convince everybody that this new way is better?"

Despite the inhospitable environment, Chris felt liberated. "It's pretty simple. Open outcry is horse-and-buggy. Electronic trading is leading-edge. One way, Chicago maintains its dominance in futures- and-options trading; but stick with the trading floors and tens of thousands of jobs will vanish to some electronic exchange."

His crisp response silenced Wolf for a few seconds, allowing Chris to continue making his pitch.

"It seems like what the Congressman—the Chairman— needs is somebody capable of making a credible assault on open-outcry trading. I'm willing to take on that role."

"Let me ask this," Wolf responded, a bit of respect creeping into his voice. "Do you feel capable of laying out this case in detail at a press conference?"

Chris had read countless political biographies. In his best analysis, one thing stood out. Those who made it to the top had never hesitated when they got their chance. Kennedy, Johnson, and Nixon had all been elected to Congress in their twenties. He was thirty-two, high time to get in the game.

"Yeah sure. I'd love the opportunity!"

***

AT FIVE MINUTES to two, Chris found himself cooling his heels in a frigid holding room. He kept looking at the door for Stanislav to burst through and join him. Press Secretary Jack Messina poked in his head, and Chris jumped to his feet. But to his disappointment, Messina fled around a corner. Finally, a man he had never seen before approached. "Sir, let me show you the way."

"Sure," Chris said, displaying a self-assurance he didn't feel.

Chris followed him to a door, where the man muttered an embarrassed-sounding, "Good luck in there," before turning in the opposite direction.

Chris ducked his head under the door and entered the packed press room at the Midland Hotel. The bodies of reporters sandwiched together immediately reminded him of the trading floor. Even as a babe-in-the-woods, Chris knew that Chicago journalists adhered to the international code of ambush. "How tall are you?" "Are you afraid?" came the questions as he loped onto the platform. "Are you friends with that Peeping Tom?" Cameras were lighting up from all sides.

A lumpish middle-aged man was standing up front by a long table. Chris thought he was one of the organizers and looked for a cue. But the guy quickly showed himself to be just another frothing-at-the-mouth reporter. "Why are you coming out alone?" he spat. "Is Stanislav hiding from you?"

Chris didn't answer and hurried around the table to collapse his long frame into one of the two metal chairs. He steeled himself to appear in control, but the questions continued in staccato fashion. "Are you bankrupt yet?" "Why are you here?" "Is Stanislav going to prison?"

All at once the questions stopped. Everyone looked to his right. Chris turned and witnessed the imposing figure of Karol Stanislav striding onto the stage in a handsome-checkered suit. The undeniable impression he emitted was of bedrock confidence. But a closer look, which Chris took, revealed a man trying, not very successfully, to rein in a smirk.

"Okay, let's get on with it," he announced in his committee-chairman's voice. "I'd like to make a statement, followed by a word from Chris Parker."

Stanislav began reading: "The Chicago commodity exchanges have created countless high-paying jobs for my constituents over the last thirty-five years. The exchanges need to immediately switch from open outcry to electronic trading or those jobs will vanish."

A young reporter raised his hand and shouted, "Congressman, why are you suddenly changing your position on electronic trading. Is it political desperation?"

"Son," Stanislav came back, "I'm sure that somewhere here in downtown Chicago there is an otolaryngologist. I suggest you seek him out. Meanwhile, Chris Parker here is going to tell the rest of you *honorable gentlemen* about electronic trading."

The reporter looked like the neighborhood bully had smacked him. Nobody else followed up on Stanislav's statement, and all eyes turned to Chris.

He fumbled through his suit pocket for the statement he had worked on with the chairman's staff. For the next five minutes, he gave a *tour de force* of his journey from ardent supporter of floor trading to staunch advocate of electronic trading.

"It has been a great pageantry on the trading floor. Seemingly half the world is out there. Heck, I moved up from Alabama to throw myself in the fray. But the longer you are on the floor, the more you see grotesque inefficiencies—anarchic pricing, non-competitive trading, and front-running of customer orders."

He ended his statement by pronouncing, "None are so blind as those who can't see. It is entirely predictable that the exchanges will be the last to realize the need for great change."

The questions came hard and fast.

"Did you get fired from your job for making a million-dollar error?" asked a pot-bellied fiftyish male, whose prominent varicose veins made him look like one of the CCE's many washed-up traders.

"Yes," Chris admitted, feeling the old pride for his low error rate coming to the fore. "Because somebody—I won't give his name, but he has suspicious connections down at the Exchange—walked away from two large trades I did with him."

"You're blaming it all on him?"

"He walked away from the trades," Chris repeated.

"Isn't that what everybody says when they have an error?"

Chris changed tack. "By the way, we can all agree on one thing. Nobody could walk away from any trades in electronic trading."

A question went to Stanislav. "On countless occasions in your prior public statements, you have said electronic trading was a pipe-dream. Are you now saying that was all a lie?"

"Look," Stanislav said, while lowering his head in a way that connoted gravity, "every major piece of legislation in my time has faced the same obstacle, the small, pedantic, finger-waving Lilliputians who can't lift themselves up beyond all the tittle-tattle and focus on the larger issues at hand. So, I'm not surprised to see the likes of you out there trying to derail electronic trading. There is only one worthwhile headline to come out of this charade—10,000 jobs. That is, if somebody who writes for a living understands what a real job is."

After that rejoinder, Chris could see the reporters consciously decide to divert their attention back to him.

"Hey, hey," a man shouted from the back row, sounding like an obnoxious lout from the trading floor. He rushed around the other reporters and began waving his hands. "Look, look," the reporter continued with blood rushing to his face, and began pointing at Karol Stanislav. "Tell us— and tell the congressman—whether you are this character from the shadows, Deep Pit, that tried to destroy the congressman's career."

Chris's first instinct was to cringe. The situation was so unlikely, his mind raced for context. *I've been surrounded by bullies for the last eight years, and lacked the body mass to strike back. But at least I've got a chance with this group of loudmouths. It's now or never for me in Chicago."*

"Ding-dong," he shot back at the reporter, mimicking a popular trading-floor insult. "I'm gonna do something I'll regret and wager you're smarter than you let on. You produce a substantive question, and I'll be glad to oblige you."

Hisses came from all around; Chris pointed at a different reporter. The game was on.

"Do you think Stanislav is a crook?"

"Nothing has been proven in court."

"Are you being paid to back Stanislav?"

"More than you're being paid."

"Is this all just a way to get revenge because of being fired for a million-dollar error?"

"Dude, even blind Homer can look at one of those trading pits and see that you're going to have errors and dishonest people. Instead of ranting, why don't you muster the courage to take one visit. You'll become an ardent supporter of electronic trading on the spot."

Now, though, came the one thing he could never have imagined.

A reporter shouting over everyone's voices, began repeating, "Mr. Parker, excuse me, Mr. Parker." Something about his formal tone concerned Chris. "Mr. Parker, do you have anything to say, do you have anything to say, anything, anything at all, to say to this gentleman *right here* about the propriety of his actions?"

He pointed at a young man standing near the back entrance wearing a ten-gallon cowboy hat, along with dark glasses and an apparent rodeo suit. Upon hearing the question, the unidentified man bolted out the door. But not before Chris was able to take note of the gliding stride he knew so well.

"Who? Who? Is it him?" came babbles from the audience.

"It's that Skip Slider, goddammit," the reporter yelled at his colleagues.

"What the hell is he doing here?" another shouted.

"Peeping again," a different person shouted in ecstasy.

A furor of noise enveloped the room. A reporter charged through the crowd, throwing elbows at his fellow members of the press, before planting himself in front of Chris. "Are you still friends with this pervert?" The saliva flying out of his mouth reminded Chris of some of the more uncouth traders on the CCE floor. "Do you think Stanislav should go to jail? How much are you being paid?"

"Out of my face, underwear sniffer," Chris shouted.

"What does somebody from Alabama know about electronic trading?" the man screamed, spraying Chris again, as he kept on charging until he was leaning over the table. "How can somebody with all that height have been such a failure on the trading floor? Can you count to ten?"

"Ten!" Chris shouted. "You heard the chairman—ten-thousand jobs. Do you know a headline when it's in your face?"

"What do you know about a job these days?" the man fired back. "Have you signed up for food stamps yet?"

A roar of laughter shook the room.

Never in his entire life had Chris done anything to belittle someone because of their height. But instinctively he stood and shouted down at the sawed-off reporter. "Listen up, Napoleon. The circus left town last week, what are you still doing here?"

The house came down. The man's face flushed a dark-unhealthy purple; he rared back to swing. Chris drew his elbows to his center, per his kung-fu training.

From his side, he heard Stanislav's approving voice. "Yep, the circus is over. Let's go."

He stood and bolted the press room, followed by Chris.

When they got in the hallway, Chris was surprised that none of Stanislav's staff was anywhere to be found. The quiet was surreal.

Chapter Seventy-Seven

"LET'S NOT GO that way," Karol Stanislav said in droll fashion. He was peering down the hardpan of Broadway, scene of much X-rated Chicago drama over the years.

"It's not in our district, Mr. Chairman," Glenn Lipsky spoke up.

"A shame." Stanislav suddenly looked skeptical about the whole thing.

Chris felt anxious. The whole gig had been his idea in the first place. At the last staff meeting, he had suggested a walk around Lincoln Park to showcase the veteran congressman as a man of the people. Lipsky had wholeheartedly agreed, fantasizing about creating a wave effect on the streets. However, chief of staff Joe Wolf had been dead-set against the idea. "You don't get it," he hissed at Chris. "That's not the way we do things here in Chicago. You folks play politics different down in Alabama, don't you?" He stormed out of the meeting.

Stanislav had sat there like a sphinx, before saying, "I guess you want me to show some ankles, huh?" Ultimately though, he agreed to the idea, indicating he was aware he was in deeper trouble politically than he let on.

Chris, Lipsky, and Stanislav stood in sports blazers at the northern end of Lincoln Park on a brisk autumn day. Turning away from Broadway, Chris said, "Clark Street is a good scene during the lunchtime hour."

The three of them schlepped along the sidewalk of the busy North-Side thoroughfare, Chris and Lipsky's jackets adorned with *Stanislav—Now More Than Ever* buttons. Their boss went unidentified. Nonetheless, they began drawing stares, which Stanislav didn't acknowledge. "Is that Karol Stanislav?" several people whispered, to which Chris and Lipsky replied, "Sure, join us." The trio began picking up stragglers.

Soon they came upon the renowned *Weiner Circle* hotdog stand. Without saying a word, Stanislav headed to the counter and ordered a *char dog with the works*, consisting of a grilled Vienna Beef hot dog on a warm poppy-seed bun, topped with mustard, relish, onions, and a splash of celery salt. On the side, he had their renowned cheese fries and a large orange drink.

He took a seat at one of the wooden-picnic tables out front, and was ringed by a dozen-and-a-half people.

"Mr. Chairman," a late middle-aged man asked, as he licked a dollop of mustard off his finger, "are you aware you are eating at one of the most famous hot dog stands in the United States?"

"Give my staff credit," he responded between hungry bites.

"Take some credit yourself," Chris pitched in. "If you had ordered a hamburger, we'd have lost the election on the spot."

Stanislav guffawed along with the others.

The owner, a corpulent redheaded man in an apron came out to shake hands with Stanislav. "Sir, most of us look at Washington D.C. as some far-off alien land."

"You're getting warm," Stanislav commented to snickers.

"Well anyway, it's great to have a real, live politician sitting here having lunch with us."

"Any martinis on the menu?" Stanislav cracked.

"No, that orange drink is the best we carry."

Chris couldn't resist. "I bet they don't serve anything as good with your dinner at Morton's."

The crowd erupted, but Chris froze, knowing the newspaper had run exposes on Stanislav's expensive dining tastes. Fortunately, Stanislav's face soon turned beet-red from laughing.

"Cheers," the congressman said with cup held high, before taking to his feet and leaving everyone with a smile.

So far, so good, Chris thought.

The entourage headed off, its numbers multiplying. Two hundred yards later they were at *Frances* deli, which had been Chris Parker's favorite eating spot since his first days in Chicago. Better yet, Steve Herring, a reporter for the *Chicago Herald*, was on hand per prior arrangement. Chris made the introduction. As they shook hands, he noted Herring appeared star-struck gazing at the political legend.

"How are you enjoying street life?" he asked Stanislav in good-natured fashion.

"It's an acquired taste."

"Is this the way your campaign will be going forward?"

"We'll see."

"Mr. Chairman," Chris interrupted, "I would never take you to most of the places on my eating rotation."

"Don't pamper me," he said before barreling inside, leaving dozens behind on the sidewalk. Chris followed him into the restaurant.

Stanislav said something to the hostess before approaching the nearest table. Its occupants looked up and ceased their dining activity. It was not a gawking crowd, but soon everyone had taken note of the congressman's arrival. Chris stood by the cashier's counter, feeling like a fixer who had arranged a blind date, as Stanislav engaged the occupants of a few tables in conversation. Everyone appeared delighted to be meeting the longtime public figure. He's pretty good at this, Chris thought; too bad it took a scandal to get him out of the smoke-filled rooms and into the arena.

After about ten minutes, Stanislav abruptly headed for the exit. "Let's go, boss man," he said while brushing past Chris.

The crowd outside had grown anew. However, Stanislav felt no need to plunge in, and continued up Clark Street.

Steve Herring sidled up to Chris. "How do you like politics compared to your previous career as a trader?"

"Off the record?"

"You got it."

"The element of ego is in-your-face in both avocations," Chris said. "But whereas a trading floor seemed to bring the worst out of people about ninety-percent of the time, it does so only 49% of the time in politics."

Herring seemed surprised at the answer, allowing Chris to add, "Gives you hope for the future of our republic, huh?"

***

THE THREESOME STOOD at the curb on Clark Street, as the crowd began to scatter. Stanislav thought the campaigning day was over and looked relieved. However, Chris was readying to break his final proposal, the one he and Lipsky had strategized as their *Hail Mary.*

"Mr. Chairman, so far so good. But Glenn and I think you need to press the biggest issue in the campaign, your electronic-trading proposal." He hesitated, knowing it was really the second biggest one, behind Stanislav's legal problems. However, it was their only potential winning issue. "If you agree, we have a reporter waiting on the sidewalk in front of the CCE at 2:00, when trading closes. You could hold a press conference."

Stanislav focused his laser eyes at the tall, thin southerner who was still a new acquaintance by the standards of his own career. "You trying to get me lynched or something?"

Chris shook his head. "The thing that would surprise you, Mr. Chairman, is how morbidly unhappy many traders are. More than half are losing money and blame it on the gross favoritism shown to the big traders. And we won't have to worry about any of those turning up because their egos would never allow them to do anything as pedestrian."

Stanislav appeared annoyed. It occurred to Chris that his pejorative description of the trading floor prima-donnas was probably not very different from Stanislav's magisterial ways back in Washington. The legendary power-broker was clearly out of his comfort zone. But after a few moments his face turned pensive, then accepting—the look of a man staring political defeat straight in the eye. Without a word, Stanislav pointed in the direction of downtown.

Chris stuck out a thumb; thirty seconds later the three of them were in a yellow-cab, driven by a Pakistani. Just before two o' clock they alighted, with Chris flipping the driver a ten-dollar bill. They approached the imposing stone structure that had played such a large role in their lives, albeit in very different ways.

A muscular man in his early thirties with a notepad spotted the three of them walking up. Alongside him was an older Asian man holding a shoulder-held camera like a bazooka. The younger one sprung forward. "Hello, Mr. Chairman. Luis Kuhlman of the *Chicago Telegraph*."

Stanislav nodded.

"How does it feel to be standing in front of this large financial institution that you worked so hard to build up?"

"My personal feelings are irrelevant," he responded.

"What are voters to make of your shocking turnabout from staunch advocate of floor trading to its biggest opponent."

"This is about keeping jobs here in Chicago, instead of losing them to New York—or somewhere worse. Don't expect the people running this place to understand that."

Traders were pouring through the revolving doors on the way out of the Exchange. Chris was heartened to see many gravitating toward the klieg lights. One was Rickie Mancuso, who Chris had stood packed up against as a broker assistant during his first year in the business.

"Hey, Chris," he whispered, standing on his tiptoes. "What's this?"

"Did you see the proposal he made to switch to electronic trading?"

"Hell yeah," Mancuso said. "He's dead-right."

Chris knew Mancuso was barely hanging on as a trader. He leaned down and whispered, "How about a softie?"

Mancuso smiled.

"Mr. Stanislav," Mancuso said, raising his hand. "A quick question. Most of us on the trading floor witness blatant inefficiency and rampant favoritism every day. Will electronic trading remedy that?"

Stanislav didn't flinch. "Once you see how efficient the new trading system is, you'll be embarrassed to have ever been associated with the old way."

Politician's hyperbole, Chris thought, but his audience of traders gave fulsome nods of approval. A mid-thirtyish woman that Chris recognized as an options trader, raised her hand. She looked nervous.

"Do you have a message for the powers-that-be that run this place."

"Yes," Stanislav deadpanned. "Hire lawyers."

Chris held his breath. When spontaneous laughter erupted, he blew a sigh of relief.

With an actor's sense of timing Stanislav moved towards Lipsky and Chris, as if they had other places to be. The three of them crossed the street, where Chris used his old trading-floor form to hail another taxi and make a quick getaway. Once inside, Stanislav stretched his arms out. "Are the two of you giving me the rest of the afternoon off?"

"Yes, you knocked it out of the park," Lipsky enthused.

"Best of all, you did it your way," Chris added.

The taxi dropped them off at Stanislav's office. As they rode up the elevator, Chris couldn't escape a sense of building camaraderie amongst the traveling threesome. Almost as important, Chris and Lipsky had saved face in their internal battle with Wolf.

Lipsky said, "That reporter Luis told me to look for coverage on the six o'clock news."

"Hope they got one of me with the hot dog and orange drink," Stanislav quipped, showing unusual gusto.

They entered the office reception where a stern Joe Wolf was waiting. "We have to talk, right now," he told his boss.

Stanislav was not going to let anything break his bluff manner. However, he dutifully followed his chief of staff, followed by Lipsky and Chris. But when Wolf saw Chris tailing behind, he barked, "No, nope. This is official state business, not campaign stuff. Turn around."

Chris disciplined himself to not look to Stanislav for help. But after a few seconds, the congressman intervened. "Joe, he's with us."

Wolf turned in a huff and continued marching down the hallway. When they got in Stanislav's office, Wolf and Lipsky filled the two chairs on the opposing side of Stanislav's desk, leaving Chris to lean against the wall. He couldn't help but think Wolf was enjoying ruining their moods.

With a sense of gravity, Wolf brandished a sheet of paper. "This just came down from the grand jury." Wolf looked at his boss, Karol Stanislav, like he was some sort of brigand. "You've been indicted for defrauding the American taxpayers. It is being publicly announced at 4:30 this afternoon."

Chapter Seventy-Eight

FOR SOMEONE WHO had spent his entire career in politics, it was ironic that Karol Stanislav had never experienced a nail-biting election night. The night of November 4th was to be no different.

Stanislav's opponent, Raymond Haack, was a neighborhood barfly. On a dare from his drinking buddies, Haack had gallantly thrown his hat in the ring. With five-hundred dollars to his name, he was the only challenger, and one more than Stanislav usually faced. It was all a wet dream.

But then, in front of the nation's eyes, Stanislav had crashed and burned. The split-second he became toxic, the special interest money that had floated his entire career reversed directions. The Chicago Commodities Exchange set up a separate political action committee with the express purpose of burying their former patron, allowing Haack to dominate the airwaves. Several ads featured live shots of the trading floor, with a voice-over saying, *Raymond Haack will protect tens of thousands of jobs right here in Chicago.* Then referring to Stanislav's turnabout on electronic trading, it said, *What happened to the Karol Stanislav we thought we knew?*

Stanislav had taken the unprecedented step of stooping to retail politicking. At times he even seemed to enjoy it, almost in spite of himself. But news of the indictment made it all a quixotic effort. By 9:15 on election night, all the national networks had projected Haack as the victor by double-digits.

The soon-to-be ex-congressman arrived in a black limousine to campaign headquarters where the vultures were out in fine fettle. Pundits and reporters were promoting the storyline of *The Fall of the Last Power Broker*. He emerged from the limousine alone, having told his wife and children to stay home. Stanislav viewed the occasion as an unpleasant task to be carried out, and fully expected to be exonerated and working as a high-priced Washington lobbyist within a few months.

"Mr. Chairman, Mr. Chairman," reporters called as he passed through the white lights. "Do you still maintain your total innocence? Can Congress function without you?"

Stanislav didn't bother to acknowledge the questions. He entered the building and shook hands with Glenn Lipsky and Joe Wolf, but made no effort to extend himself into the crowd at large, instead heading to holding room in the back.

His staff had prepared four speeches: long and victorious, short and victorious, long and defeated, short and defeated. "Gimme that one," he said, pointing at the latter script. Looking at Lipsky, he asked, "Are we ready?"

"Yes, sir."

"Let's go."

He almost trampled over his press secretary on the way into the ballroom. Within seconds, two-hundred people in the ballroom were on their feet, giving the defeated legend a standing ovation. Stanislav returned an embarrassed-looking smile, without breaking his decades-long personal ban on waving back. After fifteen seconds, he put a lid on the crowd. "Okay, okay," he boomed in his old chairman's voice. The applause continued. "You heard me. I'll raise your taxes if you don't stop."

That drew a laugh, and the audience went silent. He began to speak:

"I have called Raymond Haack and offered him my congratulations on his accession to the U.S. House of Representatives. It is his turn.

"I had mine. We've had a great run, and I've enjoyed it. I hope many of you choose to go into public service. It is worthwhile."

The crowd took a few seconds to realize the speech was over. Stanislav gave a small cue with a dip of his head before starting for the door. Spotting a trash can, he lofted his speech into it on the way out.

Staffers, volunteers, and audience members sprung forward and offered their hands. He shook each one without a word. Chris Parker, exhausted from canvassing neighborhoods from dawn to dusk the last two weeks, stood by the door. He had learned the best thing a campaign aide can do is physically stay away from the candidate. "Everybody wants a piece of him," Chris lectured other campaign workers. He remained silent as the defeated giant passed.

Stanislav turned to him without missing a beat. "Chris, let me know how things work out."

Chris stiffened, before nodding.

Stanislav was soon out the door, smiling at someone's remark about a long-ago political persona, while getting in his vehicle. Then he was off, fourteen minutes after arriving.

An era was over.

Chapter Seventy-Nine

IT WAS 11:00 AT night and Chris was sound asleep. Ironically, he had been sleeping better than in years since being fired. The trading floor had been a constant buzz-saw of anxiety, for which he always felt under-armed.

Gradually he became aware of a steady knock on the door. He surprised himself by not springing bolt upright. Rather, he took his time getting out of bed and walking to the door, feeling wizened about the inner workings of the Chicago machine in a way not possible just a few months back. The old machine might do *it* out of force of habit, but the newer powers-that-be were results-oriented.

He looked through the peephole where a middle-aged man in a brown suit and wide tie stared back.

"What do you want?" Chris called out.

"I have a summons to serve."

"Have you got identification? Who do you work for?" He couldn't help noticing that his voice sounded disembodied.

Chris heard the man extracting something from his jacket; he held a badge up in front of the peephole: **District's Attorney.**

Within seconds, Chris's mind did a schizophrenic somersault. At least the guy wasn't part of an organized-crime gang; but Chris was now a target of the government.

"Sir," he called out, "meet me in the lobby in ten minutes."

But before the man could answer, Chris reversed himself. "No, wait. It's okay. We'll meet in here." He didn't want to be known around the building as a person under suspicion. Besides, the individual who was peering back didn't appear immediately threatening.

"One second," Chris said, before turning on the lights and hurrying to get dressed. Sixty seconds later he opened the door and waved the stranger in. The man made a small bow of courtesy and entered.

They stood about five feet apart and Chris noticed the faceless official seemed to be trying to contain his surprise at Chris's height. His eyes, the color of toffee, were blanks. Methodically, the man opened the briefcase and removed an envelope. Chris sensed the surreal feeling of the last several weeks engulfing him.

"I guess I should open it," he said in a jittery voice, not wanting the man to go anywhere.

He tore into the envelope, throwing the cover on the floor. Inside was a letter written on County D.A. stationary. It read: Christopher W. Parker is hereby ordered to appear for his arraignment on December 8th, 1992 at 9:00 at Marovitz Courthouse in Daly Plaza to answer to the following charges:

• Intentional fraudulent libel against the Chicago Commodities Exchange, including spreading damaging and false information about its members, directors, and managers.

• Deliberate passing of confidential customer information to news outlets.

A toxic brew of fear and dread flooded the near-seven-foot-tall southerner. Not the least of his concerns was what this piece of paper meant financially. The legal fees in a protracted struggle would decimate his carefully-built net worth.

"Let me ask," he said, looking at the man. "Actually, would you have a seat for a second and explain what this means for me?"

The functionary deliberately placed his briefcase to the side and took a seat on the sofa.

Chris began to pepper him. "Is this a criminal action?"

"Yes sir, it is."

"Has someone gone to the D.A. to press criminal charges against me."

"Yes, that is correct."

"Am I allowed to know who filed these charges?"

"Well," he said looking at the charge sheet in Chris's hands, "usually it is pretty clear."

Yep, it was clear, Chris thought with trepidation. And if the powers-that-be, namely the CCE with its political connections, could get a prosecutor to trump up charges against him, they could probably nail a conviction.

"Is this case already decided against me?"

"I am not qualified to answer a question like that."

Chris noted the man's answers were all very even, giving them an Orwellian quality. He also began wondering if the man was taping the encounter, and decided it was best to cut it off. "Alright sir, that is enough for tonight," Chris said, pointing to the door.

The man showed no emotion as he picked up his briefcase and headed for the door, which Chris held open. The odd thing was he took a left out of Chris's door in the direction of the service elevator. Chris shook his head and let out a deep breath. What vile characters, Chris thought; even one as civilized-acting as that person.

It was almost midnight, but Chris's instinct was to do something right away. However, his three closest friends were traders and probably asleep. Besides, his phone was almost surely tapped.

As was his wont, he hit the floor and cranked out an exercise routine. Then he lay back in bed and disciplined himself to practice deep breathing with closed eyes. His mind was a torment. *Do something. Flee to Mexico? Alabama? Maybe they would just declare victory, perhaps with headlines of ridicule about the disgraced whistleblower on the run.*

None of those were serene thoughts, and Chris was soon writhing in a cold sweat. After fifteen minutes, he chalked the falling-back-to-sleep effort as a failure and sprung from his bed. He walked to the window, where he stared into night. No help.

Finally, he had a better idea.

Jan!

Chris and Jan Silverstein had always had a symbiotic relationship. Nonetheless, he had never called on her at 2:00 in the morning. He felt the need to get dressed up, brushing his teeth and throwing on a button-down shirt and dress pants, before taking the elevator up to her apartment on the 11th floor. He knocked firmly.

Soon he heard the pitter-patter of steps approaching the door, followed by the rhythmic sound of a woman bending down to the peephole. She opened it without a word. Before he had a chance to begin explaining, she said, "I'll make the tea."

A few minutes later Chris was heaving the facts on her.

"Should I just get the hell out of here right now," he asked, "to as far away as possible—maybe even Mexico."

She threw her hand up. "No, don't go doing that male-asshole thing and take off on some flight of fancy that makes it worse," she harangued him. "You've got a serious problem. First thing in the morning, get yourself a lawyer and fight back. I know these people persecuting you better than I ever wish I had; you can't give them one damn inch."

Chris looked down and sighed with resignation. He realized he was lucky to be discussing the problem with her instead of Slider, who would have stoked his fantasies of some great escape.

Not wanting to loiter in the middle of the night, he stood and began for the door. She followed. Before he reached for the handle, they looked at each other. Her posture was so erect it again surprised him how much he towered over her 5'4" physique. He started to embrace her with a hug, but she didn't lean forward. Instead, she took his fingertips lightly and tilted her neck, looking into his eyes.

"Now is as good of a time as any," she said in a warmer voice.

What? Chris's heart skipped a beat. Could it be? In one instant, he felt his tectonic plates making a tidal shift from the shadows and fear of the last couple hours, overcome by the sensation of surging rapids and approaching sunlit uplands.

Jan glided her fingers down to the very tips of his, which instantly had him aroused. After a few seconds, the shapely, early-middle-aged lady turned and led the slim, athletic southerner by hand through the hallway.

When they got to her dimly-lit bedroom, she silently began undressing. He followed suit until they stood apart, looking at each other like Adam and Eve. The vague sight of her luscious alabaster skin shining through the dark brought on a primal hunger.

"Are you comfortable?" she asked in a sincere fashion to her much younger and taller companion.

Chris felt he should match her solemn tone. But then he couldn't resist. "It's been so long, I've forgotten who's supposed to tie up the other."

Right away, he wondered if he had blundered. He focused on her eagle eyes, which appeared to be processing his remark. Suddenly, she sprung to her tiptoes and pulled his head down with both arms to lock her mouth on his. For a full minute, they remained embroiled in an unbalanced position, before she took him by the hands and placed him in a supine position on her bed. She readily assumed a prone posture.

For the next few hours, neither spoke a word. The undulations, alterations, light groans, heavy moans, and crescendos, were punctuated with intervals of lying side-by-side, listening only to their respirations. The seamless rhythm of sexual congress reminded Chris of listening to nighttime waves at a beachfront house, despite being in an urban high-rise apartment building surrounded by millions of people. Even more surreal, he felt a wartime-like liberation, as if the world was coming to an end in the morning.

At first light, he got up to dress, while she lay in bed watching. Finally, she broke the silence, speaking in a meek tone he had never heard before.

"Chris, knock 'em dead."

He looked down at her and gave his shoulders a shrug. "I guess I'm off to a decent start."

The sound of her giggling like a little girl while he was on his way out served to psych him up for the tense struggle that lay ahead.

Chapter Eighty

CHRIS MAINTAINED A brisk pace walking along *the Magnificent Mile,* Chicago's bejeweled shopping area. The place had always held out a certain magic for him, but now his ever-curious nature seemed banished from his person. He didn't look at a soul.

It was 1:00 and his introductory appointment with his attorney was set for 1:30, another mile down Michigan Avenue. He had insisted on an appointment for today, so it was imperative to be on time. But after the roller-coaster ride of emotions all evening, he was struggling to maintain equanimity. Walking was his best hope, so he continued galloping.

At 1:20 he cleared the Chicago River where it flowed into Lake Michigan, and at 1:25 he passed 362 Michigan Avenue, where he had been scared to arrive six months ago for fear of being spotted going to a psychiatrist. Given the imminent danger he faced, the thought brought a smile to his face.

Two blocks later he came to 184 Michigan Avenue, and hurried inside. Per his kung-fu training, he disciplined himself to practice deep breathing until the elevator arrived on the third floor. A sign above office 314 said KNOCK SOFTLY. Within a few seconds Chris was looking at the bespectacled, bald-headed face of Barry Butman.

"Hello, Chris," Butman said, abstaining from any demonstration of camaraderie. That struck Chris as just as well. As best he could recall, in the thousands of times they had presumably passed each other on the CCE trading floor, never once had they exchanged so much as a greeting, despite occasionally making very large trades with each other across the Treasury Pit.

"Hey, Barry." They shook hands.

Despite their lack of kinship, Chris had followed the outlines of Butman's career. One thing stuck out: Butman was different.

Barry Butfuckman, he was unaffectionately known as amongst exchange cronies. He had been an attorney before ever stepping foot on a trading floor. When he became a trader, he had naturally gravitated to the CCE's rules and disciplinary committees where he rapidly developed a reputation as a pain-in-the-ass.

Traders had long been making covert trades with each other after the 2:00 closing bell to close their positions. However, Butman began walking through the Pit after the close as people traded on the sly and outing them. *That's an illegal trade*, he would inform them. *I'm taking it upstairs to the disciplinary committee.* They stared at him like he was some invading alien. But word traveled fast, and traders stopped doing business after the bell.

Butman next took on dual-trading, which allowed brokers to trade for their own accounts, while also filling customer orders. *It's a license to steal*, he repeatedly stated. Soon big brokers were retaliating by avoiding trading with him.

His Waterloo at the CCE, though, had come when he commenced disciplinary action against his own customers. He noticed that his customer Blinder-Mason's phone brokers were not time-stamping customer orders, allowing them to time the entry of certain preferred orders to the disadvantage of less important customers. When he managed to get them hit with a $100,000 fine, they promptly dropped him as their filling broker. His customer business dried to a trickle and traders from the back row began shoving the scrawny 54-year-old off the top step. One dark-headed ruffian who had been standing within four feet of him for years collided into Butman, knocking him onto his knees and down to the second step. As he scrambled to gather up his trading cards, the brute screamed out, "Get out of this neighborhood, Jew Dog."

Butman had been forced to face bitter reality; his trading career was effectively over. He returned to practicing law.

Chris had always been impressed with these stories, even if they were told by people who spat his name with revulsion. After returning from Jan Silverstein's apartment at 6:30 in the morning, he had thumbed through the telephone book and found Butman's listing, ringing the number until finally reaching Butman.

"Come on back," Butman said and led Chris into a no-frills office with little in the way of a view. Chris felt comfortable enough to plop down without permission in one of the cushioned chairs across from Butman's mostly empty desk. Looking around, Chris saw a picture of Butman in a suit-and-tie, receiving an award on the CCE trading floor. Next to the photo was a bumper sticker: NEVER UNDERESTIMATE THE POWER OF STUPID PEOPLE IN LARGE GROUPS.

"Your political career at the CCE went further than mine," Chris commented.

"Yeah, but I got impeached," Butman responded with a puckish grin.

"How many years did you trade?"

"Ten."

"Do you feel like you got your money's worth?"

"You ask the hard ones."

"And I gotta ask," Chris said, grinning, "what was it like standing over by Guritz?"

Butman got a far-off look for a couple seconds, before responding, "Do you prefer cobras or boas?"

Chris nodded with appreciation. "Man, it would have been easier to sneak daylight past a rooster than that guy."

Butman shook his head warily. "He had it going, didn't he? Guy was meaner than a shithouse rat."

Chris decided enough camaraderie for now. Besides, he had never been to a lawyer and didn't know if clients got charged for the preliminary chitchat. Butman quickly resolved that mystery. "Okay, Chris," he said, "we make our living in this business by time, instead of volume. If I'm going to represent you, then I have to turn on the clock now. It will cost $310 per hour."

Chris solemnly nodded. He had his conservative father's phobia of lawyers, and the idea of bleeding financially by the hour left him nauseous.

It was Butman's turn for pointed questioning. "Let me ask, Chris, are you still a broker at the CCE?"

"Not as of thirty-three days ago," Chris said. "That's why I'm here."

He quickly decided to tell the entire tale with the bark off. Every time Chris mentioned names such as Ray Malley, the Sleazebags, Pat Sheridan, or Mike Kilpatrick, Butman seemed to almost physically absorb the words.

"Did you take that million-dollar out-trade case to arbitration?" Butman asked.

"No. Elliott House fired me four days later." Chris shook his head. "You could tell the tide had turned. My guess— and it's just a guess—is that Preston Beatty, the head guy at Elliott House, received word from on high. He became the good soldier for the Exchange by cashiering me."

Butman looked as if he was trying to piece together the sequence of events. "You say that the minute you found out you were out the trades with Pat Sheridan, yeah, I remember that harlequin alright," he said, "and Zambowlie, the large hunk of flesh, starts wailing on you and next thing you know they all come at you like flaying Mongols, and you're on the ground. Then Malley of all people hauls you out of the whole pileup?"

"Exactly."

A grin countenanced his face. "Yeah, the main thing I remember about you is every time I was trying to get your attention to make a trade, Malley would be shaking you like an apple tree trying to steal it."

"Leaning Tower of Pisa I was?" Chris concurred.

"But," Butman focused in, "it always seemed like there were other invisible people back there, subterraneans let's call them, hacking at your lower extremities."

"Lower extremities, indeed," Chris agreed, feeling vindicated in his choice of lawyers.

"But you're saying the attack that last day was different than all that other flailing around?"

"Yeah. What you witnessed was everyday bullying," Chris stated firmly, "That last action was of a different character. It had the hallmarks of a premeditated attack, walking away from huge trades, followed on its heels by a gang assault."

"Okay, okay," Butman said, throwing out a hand as an overture. "So, we're talking a setup here, right?"

"I think so.'

"Do you see any way to prove it?"

The question made Chris feel sick. "Barry," he bleated. "You remember how tribal those types were. Unless one of the apparatchiks gets screwed himself and goes rogue, then I don't know." He shook his head.

Butman pointed to the legal notice. "Let's look at this, then."

"Is it legal to serve someone an arraignment at 11:00 at night?" Chris asked.

"No, but yes." Butman's owlish visage turned dour. "They can say anything; they've been visiting frequently, but you're trying to elude them. That is not our most fertile defense."

Given his reputation as a pit bull in procedural matters, Chris glumly accepted the answer.

Butman felt compelled to add, "Trust me. As a member of a minority group, I find the late-night knock on the door highly offensive."

He tilted his head. "So, they get one of their cronies to stiff you on a couple of big trades, then sic the heavies on you, and now have hit you with a late-night arraignment notice," he summarized. An inquisitive look came across his face. "Why do you think they picked you?"

Chris knew *it* was coming. Effectively Butman was giving him a prompt. He was aware that his problem was as much political as legal.

"Barry," Chris said, breathing deeply, "I found the daily routine so corrosive and the violation of both my physical integrity, as well as career path, so blatant that I tried to do something about it. You've probably followed the stories in the *Windy City Times* enough to know what course I decided on."

They stared at each other for a few moments, the silence taking on an electric quality. Adjusting his wire-rimmed spectacles, Butman asked, "So you think this is all retaliation for your leaks to the paper?"

"It seems obvious that it is."

"Yeah, I read the stories," Butman said. "In fact, I feasted on them. How do you think they figured out it was you?"

Chris felt the old puckered-up feeling of the trading floor coming on again. *This is my last act in Chicago.* He steeled himself. "Do you remember Barbra Lasky?"

"Barbra Lasky," Butman repeated. "The little girl on the far side of the Pit?"

"Yes." Chris's voice sounded drained of force. Butman said nothing, so Chris continued. "Well anyway, I used to trade with her a lot."

Butman looked quizzical. He started to say something, but stopped.

"Yeah," Chris sighed. "Quite a bit."

Butman stared keenly, as if the plot were thickening.

"She must have become suspicious," Chris said, sensing the same hurt in his voice as when he tried explaining the perverted situation to Dr. Kater. "Apparently, she voiced suspicion to the owner of her clearing house that I was Deep Pit."

"Herman Mann," Butman clarified.

"Yep."

Butman was no longer writing, but rather listening like a psychologist with his client in confession mode. The air was heavy with the obvious question: *What the hell were you doing trading with that tiny girl in that far-off corner of the pit?*

"My guess is, to protect himself, Mann reported her suspicion to a higher-up, either Dean Beman or Mike Kilpatrick." Chris let the words settle before continuing. "Once they suspected I was the one feeding the stories to Skip Slider, it was just a matter of how they were gonna get me out of there. It was bound to not be pretty."

Butman stared to the side of Chris's head as if trying to digest the labyrinthine tale that had played out in the world's largest futures market, less than a mile from where they were sitting.

Chris shifted restlessly. "Does it make any sense?"

The veteran trader-lawyer swallowed. "Well, sure. I worked at that place long enough to know the base instincts of both the people and the institution itself."

442

Chris dropped his voice. "What could they do to me?"

Butman pursed his lips. "If they decide to marshal every bit of their might, they can probably gin up enough evidence to get a grand jury indictment for defrauding customers."

Chris heard Butman's words, but he could barely contemplate them. His emotions felt deadened. "And if indicted, what are the chances for conviction?"

Butman bent over the arraignment letter. "Looking at this, the first charge about defaming the CCE." He shook his head in dismay. "What would you expect out of a hidebound institution? I'd be surprised if that charge goes anywhere." He hesitated a moment while re-reading the summons. "It's this second charge—deliberate passing of confidential customer information to news outlets and other traders—yeah, if they can arrange some jackal in the Pit to stiff you on some huge trades and another pack of wolves to attack you, then yeah, they can probably make some kind of case there."

Chris leaned forward. "Just to be completely clear, this *is* total bullshit. If you look at those articles, you will see I told Skip Slider about what had already happened in the Pit. To me, those crossed-trades were illegal as hell and belong in the newspaper just like all the scandals on Wall Street with Boesky, Milken, and the rest."

"I got you." Butman stabbed his pen into his desk. "To make the case, the prosecutor is going to need your old company Elliott House to serve up your customer orders."

"As I said, they *did* like me. By the logic of that place, they were pretty good guys." He stopped and thought for a second about his former life as a trader. "But we all got in this business to make money, not fight for justice. If the CCE leans on Elliott House, they will probably come to heel."

Butman's elbows were on his desk with his hands clasped. "Because, yeah, once they get copies of those orders, they can come at you from all kinds of crazy angles, claiming you were pre-arranging trades and leaking confidential customer information."

They sat there, both looking grim. Suddenly, Butman blurted, "Would you consider a plea bargain?"

"What kind of plea bargain?" Chris shot back in a hostile tone. "What the hell have I done wrong?"

"It's just my responsibility as your attorney to investigate options." Butman quickly responded.

"God, I don't know." Chris's mood had been schizophrenic since the knock on his door at 11:00 last night. His eyes welled up and emotions into a freefall. His mind went back to the childhood image of Chicago as a place inhabited by hoods and gangsters. Here he was sitting in a lawyer's office in that same city, on the verge of his life being ruined.

Butman bucked up and tried to smile. "I tell you what. I'm gonna get on the horn and try to find out how determined they are down at the CCE to pursue you. Let's see what they really want."

They stood to shake hands. Chris uttered, "I'm looking at going to jail in Chicago."

Butman held up a hand. "Way, way, too early, my man."

Chris slinked out of the lawyer's office. Once back on Michigan Avenue, his thoughts were dominated by the thought of urban prison. Could he survive? The horror stories he had heard about the County Corrections Institute would make Ray Malley and the Sleazebags seem like altar boys.

And it had all seemed like such a good idea.

Chapter Eighty-One

THE INTERNAL PHONE from the downstairs lobby rang, jolting Chris. Chris received very few such calls and they always had a 2:00 in the morning sound.

"Yes," he answered, not disguising his anxiety.

"You have a visitor," the operator said.

"Who?"

"Skip Slider."

"Send him up."

Normally when Chris had a surprise guest, he went through a frenetic ninety-second cleanup before the person arrived on the ninth floor. But Slider was the only person he knew who lived even more informally, so Chris saved himself the trouble.

He heard a knock and peered through the peephole. Nobody was there. Between the *Sweet Home Alabama* note and late-night arraignment notice, Chris had been living in paranoia of late. But then he heard the humming to Steely Dan's rebellious tune, *Deacon Blues,* and Slider's favorite lines about *laughing chance* being his *true romance.*

He opened the door and Slider bounded into the apartment in his trademark Fonzie-like style, looking no less confident for the humiliating exposure of a month back. "Dude, talk to me."

Chris didn't share Slider's enthusiasm. "I just hope my next home doesn't make this place look like the Taj Mahal."

"Aw, man. Let's get the hell out of here," Slider said, jerking his head toward the door.

"Yeah, anything."

They caught the elevator down with three female residents, Chris making small talk but Slider not even seeming to notice. Once outside, they bore into the blustery November weather, Chris straining to keep up with Slider.

"How bout' lunch at Yak-Zies?" Chris asked.

Slider flipped his right hand over carelessly.

It was mid-afternoon when they entered, and the place was empty. They took a seat at the same table he and Shannon had sat the night they met more than three years ago.

"You ever been here on a Saturday night?" Chris asked.

"No."

"Quite the scene."

"Uh."

Chris noted Slider was being true to form, either emoting on a topic to the point of hyperventilation, or indifferent.

A girl in her early-twenties with a notepad walked up. "You guys ready to order?"

"Chicken wings are the thing here," Chris pointed out to Slider's shrug.

"Twenty chicken wings," he said, and she scampered to place the order.

"What's new?" Chris asked.

Slider's face reddened, and he shook his head. "I don't mind the public criticism. I never thought I'd live this long anyway. The one thing that makes me sick is she might think I'm a serial killer or some creep."

"Have you considered writing Darby a letter?"

Slider's eyes bulged.

The waitress brought a plate of chicken wings, and they spent a few minutes devouring them before the conversation resumed.

"I guess you're the guy to tell," Chris mumbled. "But every good meal I've hovered over since getting that arraignment notice has gotten me thinking what the food would be like you-know-where."

A pained look shone across Slider's face. "Dude," he said, his face tightening, "it will be a cold day in hell, if I have anything to do with it."

Chris broached the heaviest subject of all. "I swear to God, Jay Anunzio's wife—remember her, a total flaming liberal-activist lawyer."

Slider gave a blink in acknowledgment.

"One night, a dozen or so of us are sitting in some Italian restaurant when somebody draws her out on the prison inmates she defends. She launched into a tirade about the societal injustice of them being there. But then she points around the table at every one of us and says, 'I'm telling you, every single one of you guys would get raped in there.' Even Slider seemed taken aback at that and held his breath. Chris added, "I've always thought the whole thing was bullshit. But to think of my fate being completely out of my hands, well...." He shook his head and suddenly his stomach felt like a lead balloon.

Slider sat upright on his stool. "If there's one thing I've learned as a climber," he said, "it's that there are plenty of places in this world where nobody can find you." He held up his glass and gave a mock toast. "South America, here I come."

"Easy to say," Chris commented.

"Easy to do," Slider rebutted.

Chris decided he'd said enough on this morbid topic. "Sorry. I really shouldn't be exposing you to my deepest fears."

"No," Slider said. "I can see where you're coming from. Let's face it—with your height you would be target number one in there. But there is a whole lot between here and there." His face turned morose; he shook his head. "Chris, you're a special friend. Heck, you've given me an idea just since we sat down."

He gave Slider a questioning look. But then he remembered and shook his head. "Skip, I did suggest it. But writing her a letter could get you in a helluva lot of trouble. All she'd have to do is go to the police and you'd probably beat me to the clinker."

Slider nodded, but Chris noted he didn't look convinced. He leaned towards Chris. "Remember, Ben and I have an agreement. I still think the CCE is a gaping target. How about them corrupting the District Attorney's office to prosecute you?"

Chris raised his eyebrows. "You know how to give a drowning man hope."

He then grabbed the check despite being unemployed, paid up, and they headed out.

Chapter Eighty-Two

DARBY SHAW STOOD in the well of the Treasury-Index Pit, finishing her second crossword puzzle of the day. It was 11:45 and she had already taken three breaks. Worse yet, she was dying to get out of the Pit again.

Nonetheless, she still had strict financial goals. She needed to make at least $35,000 this quarter to salvage a decent year. Darby traded the contracts with the furthest-out expirations; on a day like this one there might be only a few customer orders. She needed to get the Bid-Ask edge off those orders and eke out a profit of five-hundred or a thousand dollars.

She was planning to go on break again at noon.

At 11:58, a broker named Vince Patondra yelled down to the bottom steps of the Pit where all the late-expiration traders stood. "Hey, hey, what's the market?"

"93-17 bid," John Coleman screamed. "Sell 'em at 93-19."

Darby joined everyone in the idiorhythmic routine. "Seventeen bid," she joined in. "Sell 'em at nineteen."

We're sheep.

Patondra was standing at the top of the aisle way, when a runner brought him a piece of paper. He took one look at it and his eyes narrowed, knowing that every trader of the late-expiration contracts was focused like a laser beam on him. Next, he bent down with his *left* knee, allowing him to bang on the railway three times with his left elbow.

Strange.

Right then, Patondra's older and much fatter brother, Louie, who stood two people away from Darby, cried out, "What's everybody got?"

Again, everyone screamed, "93-17 bid, sell 'em at 93-19."

Louie was a local. Nonetheless, the corpulent veteran stood on his tiptoes and commenced a fusillade of selling to every single person who was bidding 93-17.

"93-17 bid for 25," Darby shouted.

"Sell you 25," Patrondra said, showering her with spittle. In one motion, Darby acknowledged him with a hand signal for buying twenty-five contracts and wiped her face with the sleeve of her trading jacket.

Altogether Louie Patondra appeared to have sold several hundred contracts. *What's going on here?* A local giving up a wide edge like that to other locals looked too good to be true.

But the split-second Louie Patondra finished his orgy of selling, there was *revelation.* Like a thunderclap, his younger brother Vince began waving his customer order in the air for effect. "Sell 'em at 93-17," he bellowed. "Sell 'em all. I'll sell 'em at 93-16, sell 'em at 93-15..." He began pumping his hands as if in panic-selling mode, which in the thinly-traded late-expiration months had a disproportionate effect. The market began to tank on this one customer order.

Darby—and everybody else but Louie Patondra—were screwed. Her first lesson upon becoming a local six years ago was to cut her losses. "Sell 25 at 93-14, sold," she screamed, but to no avail. "Sell 25 at 93-13..." When the market finally reached a floor at 93-10, Darby sold out her twenty-five-contract position for a 175-tick loss—$5,750.

She stepped out of the Pit, steamed at having suffered one of the worst losses of her career. Worse yet, something nagged. Why had Vince Patondra bent his left knee and started banging his left elbow on the rail before filling the huge sell order? A couple weeks before Patondra had done the opposite, with his right knee and elbow. On that occasion, brother Louie had gone into a buying frenzy, just before Vince had sent the market soaring with a large buy order.

They pre-arranged the whole thing.

She stood on the rim of the Pit watching Louie Patondra screaming, "93-09 Bid, 09 Bid, come on, baby," buying back all the contracts he had sold short at 93-17. Everybody else's loss was his gain, an easy $50,000. To top it off, she knew the two brothers would meet up tonight and gloat about the success of their brilliant plan.

Face-to-face confrontation was not in Darby's arsenal. She had only one urge and acceded to it, heading downstairs to change out her trading jacket for a windbreaker, before taking the escalators to the lobby where she fled out the front door of the CCE. *I'm never stepping foot in this place again.*

She usually headed due west when leaving the Exchange and caught a taxi after crossing the river, not feeling comfortable walking alone beyond that. But feeling ran high, and Darby continued at full speed. Normally she would replay losing trades in her mind to the point of torture; but this time her thoughts veered away from the bad trade toward the Big Picture. Specifically, she was thinking about *the letter.*

A couple weeks back she had found an unstamped envelope with a forty-two-page letter in her mailbox from her erstwhile stalker, Skip Slider, along with his return address. The police had advised her on multiple occasions that if she saw the slightest bit of evidence that Slider was attempting to make contact, she should urgently notify them. She knew an unstamped letter would bring immediate arrest of him.

Indeed, she had opened the letter fully expecting to alert the police. As she kept reading, however, she began to sense some coherence in Slider's mindset. "The cost of anything is the amount of life you exchange for it," he had written. "Darby, have you thought of the true cost of spending so many of your best years on a trading floor?" It was like he had read her mind. "Is it not a dance through meaninglessness towards death?"

His *mea culpa* for the episode was unflinching. "It was perverted. Yes, I apologize for it. But let's face it, that's part of who I was, even if I didn't know it until then."

At the end of the letter, he captured her imagination. "The ancient Greeks defined happiness as full use of your powers along lines of excellence. Darby, does spending all day in that grubby Pit represent your greatest possibilities?"

She had laughed reading that he had an ironclad deal from the executive editor to publish any new inside scoops, despite his termination. "Darby, if you became my new source in the Pit, you could help jumpstart sweeping reforms in the Chicago commodities business. Now THAT would be something, wouldn't it?"

She found herself barely paying attention to the street traffic; before she knew it, she had walked all four miles home. Upon entering her third-floor condo, she made a cup of tea before pulling out an empty notebook. Four hours letter she had polished up a twelve-page letter that she sent to Skip Slider.

Chapter Eighty-Three

BARRY BUTMAN STUCK out like a sore thumb in the waiting room in Karol Stanislav's West Side office. Every fifteen minutes, the receptionist droned a name: "Wocjeckowski, Hohenadel, Veckione, and Dragojevich." Most of these blue-collar types seemed content with their turn in the queue. In contrast, the bespectacled Jewish lawyer looked like a bulldog girding to smash through the door.

The last two weeks he had schlepped all over his old haunts at the CCE. "Okay, you've won," he tried reasoning with Exchange directors. "How about leaving the kid alone?" Many sympathized with him, but all pointed upstairs. "You have to talk with Mike."

Alas, Butman had run into enough dead-ends trying to contact Mike Kilpatrick to turn his bald head into a watermelon. Finally, Larry Weller, his closest friend on the board had sidled up to him. "It's a no-go, Barry."

When Butman had thrown up his hands and said, "No way to talk, negotiate, nothing?" Weller had replied, "Basic instinct, Barry. Let me tell you—he's incensed about that press conference on our front step with your kid running around stirring people up. We've got our sources, you know."

This was when Butman decided on a Hail Mary, going to Stanislav himself. He had shown up at Stanislav's office three days running, claiming he had an important matter to discuss with the congressman. Each time they had told him the same thing: Chairman is not taking visitors. Finally, a chunky red-headed woman with oversized glasses told him, "Sir, to what does this refer?"

"I'm an attorney representing Chris Parker. This concerns the Chicago Commodities Exchange."

She gave him a peculiar look, which Butman met with an earnest stare. "Okay," she said, "you can speak with Joe Wolf, the chief of staff."

Butman grimaced, because Chris had told him Wolf was a hatchet man that he needed to get around. But he had no other option. "Yes, that would be fine."

She led him through a door and down a hallway, before turning around. "Please wait here."

He watched her go down the hallway and tap on an office door before entering. A few seconds later she came out followed by a husky man in a gray suit and white shirt, with dark bangs covering his forehead and a clipped black mustache dominating his upper-lip. He walked up to Butman and stood with his arms folded. "Yes?"

"Mr. Wolf," Butman said, "if I could have a little of your time I'd like to discuss Chris Parker's case."

Wolf remained stationary in the middle of the hallway. "Go ahead."

Butman fought an inclination to shift weight and consciously firmed up. "Chris Parker has been falsely charged by the District Attorney's office with illegally disseminating customer information at the CCE. Since he worked on Mr. Stanislav's recent campaign, I would like to get some insight from the congressman about the best way to defend my client."

"Not gonna happen," Wolf said in a curt tone. "We're busier than ever around here."

Busy trying to save your own asses, Butman thought. He retreated to basics. "Chris is still a constituent of Mr.

Stanislav's, and these charges are an egregious violation of his rights."

"Mr., uh," Wolf had forgotten his name and Butman chose not to supply it. "We've got 875,000 constituents we're still serving. I'm sure at least half of them have special matters to discuss."

"Chris worked in your campaign loyally all the way to the end. Does that not merit at least a meeting for us?"

"Send us something in writing," Wolf cut him off. He pivoted loudly on his heels and headed back towards his office.

"Can you guarantee a timely response?" Butman called after Wolf. The only response he got was heavy footsteps followed by a slammed door.

Butman exited Stanislav's congressional office steaming at the display of arrogance. He loitered outside, feeling punch-drunk. What next?

He had long believed that certain occasions require a person to shove aside all ego and pride. With that in mind, he walked to a nearby pay phone and called his client, Chris Parker.

***

CHRIS APPROACHED THE glass door of Congressman Karol Stanislav's home office, decked out once more in business attire. He was wearing a *Stanislav: Now More Than Ever* campaign button. However, at the last minute he stuffed it into his suit jacket, deciding it was too cheesy for what could be the critical encounter of his life.

Barry Butman had called the day before to report the news on his case, all bad. Further, he had been staggered at his manhandling by Joe Wolf. When Butman said, "Chris, you know these people, you worked with them. You have a better chance of getting me a pipeline to Stanislav," Chris had blanched. Then Butman said, "Chris, to be honest, we're running out of options. Don't get me wrong, I'm not suggesting a plea bargain yet. But if they've compromised the DA's office, then the situation is deadly serious. Our best hope lies through Stanislav."

"I'll get you an audience with Stanislav," Chris had replied in an uncharacteristic husky voice. "Give me a day."

He had frantically tried to locate his campaign ally, Glenn Lipsky, only to find out he had gone on a month-long trip to visit his grandparents in Poland. Worse yet, Stanislav was nowhere to be found, probably at the counsel of his attorneys. That left the intransigent Wolf.

Last night Chris had darted around town in his Cadillac, ultimately tracking down someone in a nightclub on the North Side. He was determined to dig up some ammo to rock Wolf. Now, Chris walked past a half-dozen constituents in the waiting room up to a familiar face—the receptionist. She raised her head as he approached. "Why, hello, Chris Parker."

Rather than greet her right away, he walked around the desk and bent onto one knee. "Margaret Anne. I've gotta speak with Joe Wolf right away."

She turned her head and sighed. "Sorry, Chris, but we've got a backlog."

"Yes, I'm sure." He fixed her with a stare. "Joe's gonna wanna hear this now. And I seriously doubt he's gonna want anybody else to find out." He stared into her eyes and leaned closer. "Tomorrow will be too late for both of us. Trust me."

She looked breathless, which Chris took as his cue to stand and tiptoe past her to the inside door. Once he got into the hallway, he stopped to collect himself. The words echoing in his mind were from his recent reading of *The Bonfire of the Vanities*. "Turn fucking Irish," Sherman

McCoy's lawyer had counseled him before facing a municipal mob. Chris decided he needed to do just that.

He marched to Joe Wolf's closed door with his heels clicking prominently and gave a loud knock. A few seconds later the surprised chief of staff opened the door.

"Yeah, what?" Wolf asked.

"My lawyer needs to meet with Stanislav," Chris said.

"Your lawyer has cognitive dissonance. I told him the chairman is not meeting anyone these days other than his own damn lawyers."

Sucker-punch him. "You'd better get with your own lawyer, don't you think?"

"What the hell are you talking about? How did you get back here, anyway?"

"You wanna hear it from me first? Or how 'bout in a summons from the D.A.?"

At first, Wolf looked like he was gonna fire one below the belt. But then Chris could see his mind change. "Are we gonna stand in the hallway like two mannequins? Come sit down and tell me whatever it is you're confabulating. But make it quick. I've got a line of people out front."

"Ghost payroll," Chris blurted. "A felony, or not?"

"We all know that," he said. "That's why he's meeting with his lawyers. From what I've heard, you should be with yours." Wolf tried to project aggression, but his eyes betrayed concern.

Chris leaned forward. "Dude, here's your one chance to head off a much bigger problem. Karol Stanislav benefited illegally from the ghost payroll, no two ways about it. That's his tragedy for ruining a brilliant career." He stopped a second for effect, before continuing. "But he didn't run the whole scheme. He was not the person who compiled the list of ghosts and arranged checks to be sent out and for the money to be re-routed. Not just to himself, but," Chris raised his eyebrows in a knowing way, "perhaps somebody else."

When Wolf started to talk, Chris threw up his hands like a traffic cop. "Hey, chum, I'd rather not show my hand here. A court of law would be more appropriate. Agreed?"

Wolf looked cornered. "Dude, it's not gonna work," he said in machine-gun fashion. "It's not gonna work. You hear what I'm saying?"

"Does the name, Bryant Bucher, mean anything to you?" Chris said, clipping Wolf's words. In a frantic series of phone calls last night, Slider had tracked down Blaise Topol, who had originally tipped him off to the ghost-payroll story. Finally, Topol had broken down and agreed to arrange a meeting between his friend Bucher and Chris at a gay nightclub.

Wolf hesitated. "Yeah, I remember Bucher. Why?"

"You might recall Bryant drew a paycheck from this office for years. But he got tired of doing his gig every day and watching paychecks go out to all these folks he never saw a single time. And he has a very detailed memory of just how the checks went out and *who* the person was in charge."

Wolf appeared to be girding for a counter-attack when a look of resignation drew across his face. "So, what is your bottom line, a meeting between your lawyer and Stanislav?"

"Fast learner," Chris shot back. "Why the hell did you have to waste so much of my time with another one of your power-play masturbations?" He handed Wolf a card with Butman's contact information, and jumped to his feet. "Within forty-eight hours. Yeah?"

Wolf nodded.

"Be seein' you around. Let's hope it's not as roommates at County Corrections." After a brief hesitation, he gave Wolf a wink and said, "Or maybe that just maybe that's what you're angling for, pal."

Chris slammed the door on the way out.

***

"BARRY BUTMAN?"

"YES!"

He jumped up with the eagerness of a schoolboy headed to a baseball tryout and followed the gatekeeper for Karol Stanislav through a swinging door. Halfway down the tile hallway, the man stopped and looked down at Butman. "You want to talk to the Chairman about Chris Parker?"

"That is correct."

The hulking fuctionary studied Butman's face a few seconds before saying, "Okay, this way." He ushered Butman into the corridors of waning power. Butman heard the door shut behind him and stood face-to-face with the dethroned Karol Stanislav. The balding lawyer knew up front that in some important senses they weren't on the same team and never had been. Stanislav was a man known to have shown sporadic flashes of a provincial anti-semitism of his working-class forebears.

"Have a seat."

Butman followed suit.

"So."

"Congressman," Butman began, eschewing the chairman label as nonsense at this point, "I represent Chris Parker, who worked on your most recent campaign."

"Yes, Chris," Stanislav said, his eyes brightening.

"It was reported in the newspaper, and you are probably aware, that he is facing indictment."

Stanislav nodded as if someone was discussing a family illness.

Butman knew he needed to make it count. "I was on the CCE Board of Directors and traded in the Treasury Pit for ten years. However, I have learned in the last week that

Chris's case is being handled at the top." He held his hands up and let that sink in, hoping to goad Stanislav's instincts for higher-up matters.

"Without engaging in flattery, Congressman, let me just say you carried our water for a heckuva long time. A lot of us have had our livelihoods, and frankly our personal nest eggs, significantly enhanced by your industry on our behalf. I don't need to tell you that two of the biggest recipients of that gravy train are parked at the top of the whole show."

"Beman and Kilpatrick," Stanislav intoned.

"Which brings me to the purpose of this meeting," Butman said. "The case by the DA against Chris, who is still a constituent of yours, alleges that he divulged secret customer information and spread damaging information about the Exchange. Sir, the whole thing is obviously being engineered by the CCE to strike back against someone they consider a political enemy."

Stanislav tightened his lips and nodded enough for Butman to continue his presentation.

"Congressman, I am wondering if, despite the severely-strained relations you have suffered with the Exchange, you could convince them to drop it for no longer being in their best interests."

Stanislav stared transfixed. Something in the lawyer's audacious proposal appeared to have thrown him for a loop, causing him to look away and inhale. When he turned back, he had a twinkle in his eyes. "Severely-strained relations, huh? You *are* a lawyer."

"Sir," Butman said breathing deeply. "I am aware that nobody can fathom the depth of emotions you must have towards that institution you went to bat for on so many occasions, only to see it all turn pear-shaped in the end."

"Pear-shaped, huh?" Stanislav chuckled. "Yeah, that isn't pretty, is it?"

Butman could feel the congressman loosening up and his mind making calculations.

"What do *you* think of the whole thing?" Stanislav asked.

He's asking me? Butman knew the subject was fraught. Nonetheless, he tilted his head back and decided to gamble. "You wanna know the truth? Having beat my head up against the wall trying to move that hidebound institution forward into the twentieth century, I came to the conclusion that the Israelis and Palestinians have a better chance of resolving their differences. They simply lack the willpower to act collectively and impose some standards of decency in the pits. So, I won't be shedding crocodile tears if they meet their own ugly fate." He stopped to see what kind of reaction that drew out of Karol Stanislav, who seemed engrossed in what he was hearing.

That gave Butman impetus to play a wild card. "The truth is, I am impressed—mind you, in a ghoulish way— that such an inbred, elephantine institution as the CCE was tactical enough to switch horses like that so quickly when they saw you heading down politically."

Stanislav's lips puckered, and Butman wondered if he had gone too far. But the wondrous look that emerged across the congressman's face appeared like that of a student rapturously attending his professor.

"Yeah," Stanislav finally said, "I guess you could say that."

Butman sensed he had to move quickly here. "The striking thing, Congressman, is that, yeah, okay, they've made this fancy pivot. But it seems obvious that *you*, despite having lost so much, while they continue riding high, still have the whip-hand here."

Butman thought he saw a reminiscing look cross Stanislav's face.

"Boy, oh, boy, you should have heard the attitudes I've faced in Washington over the years about those commodity exchanges. Lyndon Johnson liked to chide me about 'those casinos' in Chicago.' And Tip O'Neil always said it reminded him of 'voodoo worship'." He laughed, before firming up his chin. "The exchanges had all kinds of regulatory and tax issues, and I had the wherewithal to help them. The commodity exchanges give the city a special cachet."

Butman let him go on, hoping to extend the comfort zone. An emotional look came across Stanislav's face. "Let me tell you something. When I'd go down on those trading floors and have kids from the old neighborhood coming up and saying, 'Hey, Mr. Stanislav, my parents went to your wedding at St. Casimirs,' I'd look down at their badges: Wocjeckowski, Zavorski, Nocek, Romanovski. That meant something."

He looked at Butman in a matter-of-fact way. "I was gonna do everything I could to give those folks an opportunity to move up from their hardscrabble backgrounds. It wasn't just Poles, mind you. They've got all kinds of Italians, Irish, Jews, you name it—wish the hell there were more blacks—trading in those pits."

"I commend you for a job well done," Butman said. "That gets back to the CCE. I'm sure that the lily-livered folks up in those executive suites are trying to cover their tookuses these days." Butman steeled himself for the big finish. "All this stuff in the newspaper that has been so damaging to your political career, I don't want to get into any of the details, other than to state the obvious: These people were your *partners* in many of these enterprises. So," he put a determined look on his face, "as Chris Parker's lawyer, I'd like to emphasize: You still have plenty of leverage in the very highest places at the CCE."

What Butman left unsaid was that leverage wouldn't be around long, given the narrow window a man has when facing the Big House.

"I tell you what," Stanislav said, recapturing his magisterial air, "whether the folks at the CCE like it or not, it looks like we've got a meeting at the river coming soon. I'll keep Chris in mind."

"Such a good deed would be greatly appreciated," Butman said.

Stanislav appeared embarrassed that he had enjoyed the conversation so much. There was no smiling farewell as Butman stood and darted from the office.

Chapter Eighty-Four

CHRIS PASSED UNDER the neon-signs marking the entrance to the Chicago Health Club at the northern end of Lincoln Park. He never failed to get a buzz, knowing young people engaged in peak effort were just ahead. At 6:00 in the evening, a person could be trampled by twenty-somethings piling in after work.

Since being fired, he had been attempting to maintain morale by arriving at the club at 8:30 in the morning for the first of two daily workouts. That had given him a tailwind for a couple weeks, but then he felt himself sinking again. His latest idea was to move the morning session to 7:15, to replicate his old life on the trading floor. Nonetheless, his overwhelming sentiment remained disillusionment.

He finished his workout at 9:00 and trod morosely through the early morning mist to the McDonalds located a couple hundred yards down Clark Street, where yuppies in business suits were jumpstarting the day. Chris noted this was about the time traders who were lucky enough to get ahead left the Pit, when the rest of Chicago had the day in front of them. *What an unusual business.*

Chris's mind went back to some words of wisdom from a veteran broker who had stood next to him in his early days in the business. Whenever Chris got bummed at missing a trade and feared losing a customer, the man would always assure him, "No worries, mate. Trust me, there are plenty more lined up out the front door of this place, grabbing their ankles and begging for more." At various times over the years, Chris had found himself thinking back to those same words; they had been prescient. Indeed, he had concluded that a sizable portion of the wealthiest people in the country were simply degenerate gamblers, never able to get enough. For this realization alone, the eight years were well spent.

But it went beyond that. The Chicago years had been an advanced case study in that timeless subject—*money*—that has inspired and haunted so much human behavior since at least biblical times. Chris had never been able to forget what happened to the big brother in his college fraternity, Jack Stanton, who had also been the biggest bookie on campus. Upon graduation, Stanton had garnered awe from everyone with grandiose tales of the riches to be had in the Chicago commodities business, as well as his unstinting decision to move to Chicago and go for the gold. A few years later when Chris decided to dive in himself, he had called on Stanton. "How's it going?" Chris kept pestering Stanton, but only got vague responses. When Chris visited Stanton on the trading floor, he noticed something unusual. Stanton appeared reluctant to step foot in the Pit; instead, he stood on the edge and whispered orders to a nearby broker, in a way that reminded Chris of placing bets with a bookie. Two weeks after that, Chris had taken the bus to Stanton's apartment, where he had recently met Stanton's roommate, Frankie Hope. A shaken Hope informed him that Stanton had moved everything out. A few days later, they heard Stanton had returned to Alabama. Chris soon learned that Stanton had taken a sizable loan from Frankie to maintain floor-trading privileges, only to blow through it in short order, before borrowing even more money.

Chris had run into Stanton several times in succeeding years when visiting home. Each time a gnarled look came across Stanton's face, followed by preemptive strikes at

Frankie Hope: "That guy screwed me over. I'm telling you, he screwed me." Chris had never gotten over the image of that former Greek god brought to such tawdry depths. Worse yet, Chris was to witness that exact reaction countless times in the following years, as destitute traders launched knee-jerk attacks on friends who had lent them money.

Money's reputation as the ultimate truth serum, capable of seducing, corrupting, dividing, and destroying humans without breaking a sweat, had been revealed in a profound way to Chris Parker on the trading floor in Chicago.

***

AFTER HIS FAST-FOOD fix, Chris trudged at an even pace back to his apartment. He flipped on the television to the local news, where Karol Stanislav's case dominated. All the speculation centered on a plea bargain, the prize being shorter jail time. Chris was glad to hear the coverage sensationalizing the fall of the legislative giant was not overwhelmingly negative. But then he had a pessimistic thought, would Stanislav really use his dwindling clout on behalf of a former campaign worker who had leaked damaging information about him?

Chris cut off the television and turned on his radio to the classical-music channel, where Rachmaninoff's piano concertos were in full flower. If nothing else, the Russians best understood gray days and melancholy moods.

He plopped down on the sofa and happened to look at the side table and see a thin, white book. An elderly black man living down the hallway, who Chris often debated Chicago politics with, had insisted on giving it to him. His stomach had sunk, thinking that every time he saw the man he would want to know what Chris thought of the book.

It was the gnostic *Gospel of Thomas,* which was a handy compilation of Jesus's less well-known sayings. Chris pulled it open, hoping to extract a couple talking points for his next elevator ride with the gentleman.

Saying 64 read: "Buyers and merchants will not enter the places of my father." Not radical by any stretch for a religious figure of any faith, Chris noted. Nonetheless, he found the pithy sentence from this apocryphal gospel to be comforting, given his exiled state from a financial institution.

He thumbed back a few more pages, until he got to Saying 42. Two words jumped off the page at him: *Be passersby.*

Be passersby? *What does that mean?*

It seemed clear enough. If this gospel was authentic, Jesus was dead set against any earthly pursuit in which a person stayed in one place for too long. The juxtaposition to his life on the trading floor, where he had been bottled up for eight years in a space the size of a phone booth, was startling. Sure enough, as the years had passed, Chris had become suspicious that such a static routine was fundamentally unhealthy to a human's psyche.

He had just finished reading Bruce Chatwin's travel epic, *The Songlines*, in which Chatwin postulated that nomadism was humanity's most uplifting state. Chatwin cited numerous examples of groups ranging from the Aboriginal tribes in Australia, to the ancient Israelis, Bedouin, Kurdish, and Moorish peoples with lengthy histories of perpetual movement. When they stayed in motion, better yet while singing, they rarely experienced conflict. Likewise, accumulating possessions was undesirable for a nomadic people, for the most obvious reasons. But life on a trading floor was just the opposite, all about claiming territory and accumulationism. Savagery was simply a natural by-product of this mentality.

Immediately Chris felt a burst of idealism coming to the forefront. *We were all proof of that. The only passersby were the people who went broke and were forced out the business. The rest of us stayed ad-infinitum trying to accumulate as much as possible, and it only got uglier and uglier.*

He stood and looked out the window at the bleak urban setting from his matchbox-sized studio apartment. Speaking from the soul to himself, he intoned, "I've got to get out of here."

The tragic irony of his own fate brought him back to the here and now. Just as he had discovered the imperative of eschewing a static lifestyle in favor of mobility, he was facing an incarceration far worse than anything the Treasury Pit could throw at him.

Chapter Eighty-Five

AS HE RODE in a limousine to the Fraternal Order of Police (FOP) Lodge for his meeting with CCE President Mike Kilpatrick, Karol Stanislav felt schizophrenic.

His latest meeting with his lawyer had felt like a death sentence. He knew this might be one of his last trips in any automobile. At the height of its powers, the machine motto had been *Guilty as hell, free as a bird.* But the winds of change were blowing, and Karol Stanislav was a man playing an outdated game. All signs pointed to this legislative Cyclops heading to prison, just like all the machine grafters and hustlers he had spent his life striving to rise-up from.

He found himself both irate and humble. Mike Kilpatrick and Dean Beman, two of the agents in his demise, couldn't so much as have carried his jock on Capitol Hill. To have these two pusillanimous individuals drive the final stake into his career was almost too much to bear. Back in the day, his ancestors would have dealt with such treacherous minions the old-fashioned way.

Ultimately, though, revenge did not have the whip-hand here. It was a higher emotion. *Love. Sheila.* Stanislav was a man's man, vulnerable in the extremis to the feminine species. He couldn't quit thinking of the lady in the cloth coat who had been at his side from the beginning, with her shy, but hopeful smile, along with their toddlers dressed in their Sunday best. His Polish-American family could have fit in a Hallmark-card advertisement of the American dream.

He had never let them down, never strayed from his wife in a business in which colleagues swapped out women like socks. He was bound and determined to take care of his family.

***

WINTER WAS BEGINNING to show its hand as Stanislav emerged from his limo on a late-November day. Instead of the magnificent nobility of the U.S. Capitol, he was facing the side of a building where the plaster façade was eroding, and the ventilation system sounded like it was belching up mustard.

Joe Wolf held the door open for his boss, who was wearing a navy-blue windbreaker.

"Have we got company?"

"Yes, he's here," Wolf said. "Unless he's escaped out the back entrance."

"Then he's more rational than we know," Stanislav remarked.

The first thing Stanislav saw when he turned the corner to the main floor was the very unremarkable figure of Mike Kilpatrick, standing in a gray suit on the far side, past the opposing basketball goal. With his back up against a wall, it looked like he was expecting a firing squad. Stanislav had to resist the urge to hurry and steeled himself to maintain a steady pace.

Kilpatrick sprung forward with his hand out. "Thanks for coming, Mr. Chairman," he said ten feet before their hands touched.

"Where?"

"I have the keys to both the precinct office and the captain's office."

Stanislav's first instinct was to keep Kilpatrick on the ropes with the silent treatment. But then he remembered what he had been counseling himself: *things have changed.*

"Let's go there," he said, motioning with his head to the bleachers on the side.

They ambled over to the stands where Stanislav plopped down on the second row, with his feet resting on the first. Kilpatrick moved to place himself beside Stanislav. However, he quickly decided they would be better off with some space and hopped down to the first row at a diagonal angle from Stanislav.

Kilpatrick and Beman had strategized extensively over how to handle the meeting with this wounded Goliath. *Take the initiative, get out front,* Beman had advised him. *He can hurt us.* As always, Kilpatrick had sweated out and memorized a detailed strategy for how to proceed. Nonetheless, he was dreading the encounter.

"Mr. Chairman," he began, peering at Stanislav's fearless eyes. "I want to offer our sincere thanks for the critical role you have played in turning the Chicago Commodities Exchange into the world's premier financial institution."

Before the words had settled, Stanislav mouthed a response. "Do you want me to vomit here or in the men's room?"

Kilpatrick felt sucker-punched. But after a brief hesitation, he forced himself to continue. "You will be remembered as a great legislator."

Stanislav responded deadpan with the line he would use the rest of his life. "The first thing anybody will ever say about me is that I went to jail."

Kilpatrick could not come up with a fit response, leaving a horrible silence to reign. The veteran operative knew he needed to change strategy and fast. "The truth is," he finally said, "we did what we thought was best for the CCE."

"There's no doubt about that," Stanislav said. "But remember, at least Brutus and Cassius were farsighted enough to go ahead and kill Caesar. I'm still sitting right here."

That rocked Kilpatrick, who knew exposure of the fund alone would rock the Exchange and ruin himself.

"What have you got, Mike?" Stanislav asked, opening the negotiations.

The CCE President appeared relieved at the question; details were his bailiwick. "We can continue the assistance plan for Jeanna and Sandra."

"What are we at there?" Stanislav asked, sounding like he was asking a committee-staffer for a detail.

"Twenty-five hundred a month for each," Kilpatrick answered.

"Sandra is fighting alcoholism that's gotten worse because of all this," Stanislav said about his oldest daughter. "Double hers."

Kilpatrick hesitated.

Stanislav knew that meant he was going over marching orders from Dean Beman. But after a couple seconds, Kilpatrick said, "Yes. We'll do it. Of course."

"Let me be clear," Stanislav went on in the tone of a boss to an employee, "we're talking about until I get out," before adding, "After that I should be making a lot more than ever in the private sector and we'll all be fine."

Kilpatrick nodded, content to have a deal. Just as he was gaining some comfort, Stanislav struck again. "Sheila is another story."

Kilpatrick tightened his lips as if steeling himself for further bleeding.

"She has suffered all these years taking care of the kids while I was away in Washington," Stanislav said. "Nobody could have borne the sacrifice any better. She has to be taken care of." Kilpatrick flushed, allowing Stanislav to add. "Since I'm the fall guy and everybody else skates."

Both men sat expressionless, as his remarks settled in. Finally, Kilpatrick spoke. "Obviously, you have every reason to expect Mrs. Stanislav to be taken care of. But when we set up your trading account with Richard Sherry, our assumption was that the very successful results would provide the necessary security for your family."

Stanislav fired back. "I haven't talked about my legal bills, either. Hundreds of thousands and still galloping. Do you want to talk about *those?"*

Kilpatrick lowered his head. "Mr. Chairman," he replied, sounding like a kid who had been knocked down on a playground and gotten up, "you have a good point. This must work for everybody. Obviously, we want to help within reason."

"And?"

"Well," Kilpatrick said, then stifled himself. "How about half your congressional salary?"

Stanislav couldn't help his mask from coming off for a second. Not only was this generous, but made eminent sense, as they would only need half a salary for the next few years, given his expenses would be nil. He then said, as if attaching a rider to a congressional bill, "Throw in a stipend for health insurance and everybody should be able to live with it."

More silence, although this time there seemed to be a subtle shift. Up until now, the pauses had weighed on Kilpatrick. But Stanislav had permitted a tinge of exuberance to trickle into his supremely-confident voice.

Kilpatrick's demeanor had started off obsequious and morphed into dutiful. But now he appeared annoyed. He looked like a man who felt he had been suckered. "Okay, you got the stipend. But that's it from us." He made a flipping away motion, before abruptly taking to his feet and starting toward the exit. Stanislav appeared surprised, but slowly got up to follow Kilpatrick.

Chris Parker.

Stanislav's ironclad rule on Capitol Hill had always been to make his word good to friend and foe alike. He had promised Barry Butman he would make a plea on Chris's behalf. However, the tide had unmistakably turned against him late in the encounter, leaving his pride under massive assault. Nonetheless, he knew his psyche—he had to remain true to himself.

Despite being ten steps behind, he decided to hesitate. Kilpatrick took the cue and stopped in the middle of the floor, well ahead of Stanislav, who caught up. They again came face-to-face.

Stanislav drew his eyes up slowly from the floor to give his words extra import. "Chris Parker," he said. But the man who had always been a natural politician was clearly out of his comfort zone and the words sounded awkward. Tension appeared to be running both ways, and neither man dared to look at the other. "What's he to you, Mike?" Stanislav asked in a funereal voice.

He focused on Kilpatrick. Nobody had ever thought of the high-level functionary as

colorful. But here and now Kilpatrick's internal struggle was on full display. From his very first day of hire thirty years back, the machine had drilled into him the *Rule of five:* the absolute necessity of meting out punishment at least five times worse than the transgression suffered. By that logic, Chris Parker was remained a mortal foe to be crushed.

For the first time in their decades-long relationship, it was Stanislav standing by hinging on Kilpatrick's words. However, rather than speak, Kilpatrick jerked away in anger towards the door, leaving Stanislav standing like a potted plant. But after a few heavy steps, Kilpatrick stopped, his eyes appearing on fire.

"No, you can't always have it your way," Kilpatrick spat. "You set that guy loose on us." He shook his head in disgust, as if seeking some sort of liberation from a negative dependency. He resumed his march to the front door, leaving his erstwhile mentor to trail well behind.

Joe Wolf held the door open and Kilpatrick went huffing past him towards his waiting limousine. When he got into the back seat, the veteran operative was still in a barely-controlled rage. But then he looked out and saw Karol Stanislav leaving the FOP Lodge for the last time.

His mind shot back to the very first event he attended as a machine *shoeshine boy* at age eighteen at this exact location, when he had first glimpsed Karol Stanislav. It quickly became clear that night that a person's position in the machine could be measured by his proximity to Stanislav, who literally seemed to overshadow everyone, even the mayor. Despite the crumbling surroundings of the building Stanislav was now exiting, Kilpatrick knew this would be a country club compared to where Stanislav would be in a few months. The image of the old master as a fallen lion tugged at his heart.

Uncharacteristically, Kilpatrick made a spontaneous decision to jump out of his limousine. He headed towards Stanislav who was ambling in the direction of his own limousine. The two men stood appraising each other.

"Mr. Chairman, we'll never forget you."

"I wouldn't have anything any different," Stanislav responded without hesitation.

Wow. The stoic nature of his remarks again rocked the unsentimental Kilpatrick. The man he was looking at had long shown he knew how to handle victory. But here he was facing the most bitter-possible defeat and the direst plight, yet he was still a rock.

Kilpatrick strained to not show emotion, but was on the verge of quivering. He didn't like drama, but was overwhelmed by the feeling of being in the middle of a passion play and a need to perform his role. He knew Stanislav wasn't going to say anything, which meant the ball was in his court.

"Mr. Chairman," he blurted. "A great man should always be granted his last wish."

Stanislav stood still like a sphinx, not tipping his hand.

"Your kid's off," Kilpatrick said with as much authority as his shaken-self could muster. He nodded for emphasis, which Stanislav returned.

They silently shook hands, before heading to their respective limousines, with Stanislav's departing the FOP Lodge first, followed by Kilpatrick.

Chapter Eighty-Six

THE PHONE RANG. Chris was shaken from his mid-afternoon philosophical idyll on nomadism and rushed to pick it up.

It was Barry Butman. "Chris, I need to see you."

"Have I got time to get there on foot"

"3:30?"

"I'll be there."

Perfect timing. At 2:25, Chris exited his Lincoln Park building into the blustery air. At 3:25 he knocked on Butman's office door, pleasantly winded, and almost having forgotten where he was going.

"Good afternoon," Butman said with an exuberant smile that reminded Chris of the rush chairman in his college fraternity. The flowery greeting allowed him to enter his lawyer's office with less anxiety than normal. Butman made an uncharacteristic sweeping motion of his hands.

"So," Butman began once they were seated, "don't ever say politicians never do any good."

"I never said that," Chris responded, "except, of course, about Chicago politicians."

Butman's eyes twinkled. "You might even have to reevaluate that judgment."

Chris felt pangs of encouragement but didn't say a word.

"Chris, I just received a phone call from Larry Luxemberg, who is one of the CCE board members. He has reliable word from on high, you know, as in high, high up,"

Butman raised his hands in theatrical fashion, "that the CCE will ask the DA to drop all charges against you."

"Talk to me," Chris said, feeling his breath catch. "Talk to me."

"Yes, it is true."

"But I thought these things were supposed to have bad endings," Chris said, only halfway in irony.

"Not if I'm your lawyer," Butman responded with a pixyish lilt.

"You're sure? This is from Kilpatrick? And the prosecutor will follow the CCE's directive to drop charges?"

"Yes, I'm confident," Butman said, glowing like a leprechaun.

"As in free at last."

"Freedom is yours."

Chris restrained himself from breaking into a jig and looked earnestly at his attorney. "Are you surprised they're dropping it?"

Butman tilted his head. "Not totally. Let's say I thought this angle—unconventional to be sure, going to a politician headed to prison—held a certain promise."

"Because of Stanislav?"

Butman leaned forward. "Look, that phrase you always hear in low-budget crime flicks, *He knows too much.* Greatly overused, to be sure. But in the case of Stanislav, why hell yes." He punched his fist on his desk. "He damn well did know too much."

"And the rest of us too little," Chris commented.

"God knows how many directions the money has flowed in that relationship," Butman said.

"A question—do you think of Karol Stanislav as a crook?"

Butman started to answer, then lowered his chin towards his chest for a second. "Look, my man, you will see along the way—and you've learned a lot these last several months—that humans have an infinite number of shades. Our mutual friend, Mr. Stanislav, is a glorious case of just that." He paused a second before continuing. "Now to answer your specific question, yes, Karol Stanislav is a crook. You need go no further than the ghost-payroll thing that the Chicago political machine ran for decades. But Karol Stanislav is also the greatest legislator of our time. Without him, everybody at that Exchange could sell their second homes and downsize the first one."

Chris sat still, taking in his lawyer.

Butman seemed jolted by another thought. "One other thing. If you ask me, Stanislav isn't such a bad guy." The gleam reappeared. "You've seen a few of those."

"Barry, that brings up a theoretical question my ex-girlfriend and I used to debate. Is it the types who get in that business to begin with, or is it just a normal cross-section of people and the pell-mell daily pursuit overwhelms their cores?"

Butman raised his eyes toward the ceiling, then brought them down. With a small laugh, he said, "Wow, that's what you used to talk about with your girlfriend?"

"That's why she's my ex," Chris said, drawing a chuckle out of Butman. "Honestly, what did you think of the people in that business?"

Butman shook his head and raised his arms wide. "Christ, it's so difficult to say. Just think of the tens of thousands of people who have worked on those trading floors. And a sizeable fraction of them would have gladly trampled over their own grandmothers for her last dime. So, it's bound to be unpleasant."

"But did you notice a general downward spiral of behavior the longer people were there?"

"Yeah, I understand what you're saying," he acknowledged with a soft smile. "Actually, what I noticed most was the more money a trader made, the more detestable that person became, almost like they morphed into caricatures of their original selves."

"Yeah," Chris latched on. "All those trading gods walking around, posing as self-possessed. The more I watched, the more obvious it became they were the ones who were most possessed of all."

Butman nodded. "We have the rest of our lives to try to make sense of our years on that trading floor." He gave a brushing-away motion. "Chris, where do you plan to go from here?"

"Good question," Chris said, before adding, "I can tell you where I'm not going."

Butman looked genuinely interested. "Do you think you will return to the South?"

"I sure as heck don't have anything against my native region. But while I found the commodities business to be mostly a gigantic hustle, I was quite taken with the Chicago magic. The people are authentic. I consider the city to be the best-kept secret in the country."

"Oh, you're on to something there," Butman said emphatically. "Those people that blow out of here to become beached whales in Arizona and Florida have got it all wrong."

Chris drew in a grateful breath. "Just in the little time I've been out of the business I have realized how downright morbid it is to stand in the same place, without full freedom of motion, for so long. I may have to fly the coop far-and-wide to exorcise the demons."

Chris put his hands on his knees. "But before I hit the road, I need to know the damage."

"I'll have to add up the hours."

"Ballpark figure?"

Butman wrinkled his nose. "Tell you what. Sometimes I charge a premium for a successful result. But in this case, I got to meet a legend, one it doesn't look like we will be seeing much more of. Call it eight thousand."

"Alright." Chris, who liked keeping things simple, pulled out his wallet and extracted a check, which he wrote for $8,000, and handed it to the diminutive man who had represented him. He noted, "I bet Karol Stanislav wishes he could gain his freedom that easily."

"He's gonna have to write his own checks now," Butman commented in a dry tone.

Chris suddenly felt a rush of claustrophobia, as well as a sense of pity for Butman for being confined in an office. "I'm going, Barry," he said, extending his hand.

"Good luck, Chris."

Chapter Eighty-Seven

CHICAGO IS THE Windy City. Some days the draft slices through its inhabitants like a knife. But on other occasions it is glorious.

When Chris exited Barry Butman's office at 4:15 on an overcast Tuesday afternoon onto Michigan Avenue, an Indian-summer breeze was wafting off Lake Michigan. Christmas lights were up and shining as shoppers, business people, and the like went about their activities. The whole scene fed into Chris's mood; he felt more liberated than any time in his life.

To be sure, he was unemployed, and his whistleblower effort was dust. He had made his best effort—for both selfish and unselfish reasons—to ratchet the commodity business forward into the modern era. He had failed, at least temporarily; nonetheless, Skip Slider's newspaper articles had told an indelible tale.

Chris saw a box for the *Windy City Times*. Despite his ill-fated effort, he still held the publication in affection. Chris leaned down to glance at the headlines, only to receive a blast, not of wind, but shock. The Marvin Gay-inspired banner read:

'Brother, Brother, Brother', What's Going On?'
By Skip Slider

Miss Darby Shaw, a veteran trader at the Chicago Commodities Exchange, and recently the victim of a humiliating peeping incident perpetrated by this writer, myself, has boldly come forward to report a fraudulent trading scheme by two brothers in the Chicago Commodities Exchange's enormous Treasury-Index Pit. What's more, Miss Shaw says that she has been witnessing variations on this scam for "at least six years."

Miss Shaw is renouncing her trading privileges and

The metal from the box cut off the rest of the article. Chris rifled through his pocket and was relieved to come up with four quarters. He stuffed the paper in his jacket, deciding to wait until he got back to his apartment to fully enjoy imbibing the contents.

He crossed the bridge over the Chicago River and came upon the Art Deco Rookery Building, where Miss Shannon Daly, she of the perpetually bright, smiling eyes, would be diligently pursuing her daily tasks. In a fairy-tale ending, Chris imagined that he would go rushing into the Rookery Building in tears and cry out his epiphany as a prelude to regaining that Irish princess's hand. Alas, it was not to be. In a profound way, he felt the curtain closing on the Chicago years. Seals and Crofts lilting tune, *"We Will Never Pass This Way Again,"* echoed in his mind as he walked along the Magnificent Mile and up Lakeshore Drive back to his apartment.

What did a person do after a career in the Chicago commodities business? The question filled him with a sense of mission. He had noticed over the years that ex-traders tended to hang around the Exchange, like old soldiers, recycling war stories from their days in the Pit and just sort of fading away. He was determined to do anything but that.

The key was to continue walking. Keep on moving. Be a passerby.

Epilogue

Chicago Political Giant Dies
November 12, 2010

KAROL STANISLAV, FOR many years considered the single most powerful member of the U.S. Congress, died yesterday at age 81. Stanislav, who came from a leading political family that long represented Chicago's West Side, was seen by many as embodying the city itself. Much of the landmark legislation in the late-twentieth century bore his hefty fingertips.

"The country has lost a great patriot," his erstwhile pal, former President George Herbert Walker Bush said. "He knew how to make sausages in our nation's capital like no one else. And one other thing: he loved Chicago all the days of his life."

Others were more equivocal in their praise.

"A truly Shakespearean character," veteran Chicago reporter, Jack Corrigan, said. "It was almost like it all of humanity was on display, in both its glory and vice."

In the early 1990s, a theretofore unknown reporter for the *Windy City Times* named Skip Slider began a series of sensationalistic exposés showcasing how the Chicago Commodities Exchange, long Stanislav's biggest financial supporter, arranged for him to invest a token amount of money and—in an obvious fix—gain enormous returns within months. Slider then ran a report that Stanislav's daughters were on the CCE payroll, despite not being required to go to work.

Stanislav seemed to shake off these charges. But then Slider reported that Stanislav had phantom employees on his campaign and congressional payrolls, whose paychecks he raked into his own personal account. That ultimately proved to be his undoing, forcing him to plead guilty to the felony of defrauding American taxpayers. He served two years in the federal penitentiary.

The CCE's purpose in its lavish support of Stanislav was a desperate attempt to fight off the specter of an electronic-trading system, which it saw as a mortal threat to its renowned open-outcry style of trading. In retrospect, its anxiety seems understandable.

Veteran clearinghouse owner, Herman Mann, reached at his suburban Winnetka home, said yesterday, "We owe Stanislav more than we ever imagined. All these young people from around town were making more money than they knew what to do with. But the minute it finally did go electronic, it was the damndest bloodbath. I mean a true horror show. Right in front of my eyes, my very best traders lost everything. Everything."

The *Chicago Herald* reached out to Skip Slider for commentary. However, his widow, Darby Shaw Slider, informed us that he died at the summit of K-2 in Pakistan in 2003.

We did locate Chris Parker, the trader who was eventually exposed as Slider's source, *Deep Pit*. Speaking by remote connection from Asuncion, Paraguay, Parker said, "It's impossible to imagine my time in the Chicago commodities business without Karol Stanislav. Heck, tens of thousands of people made their living down there, including me. And let me say—it wasn't all bad. Really. Not all bad."

The funeral will be on Tuesday, November 17th at St. Casimir Pulaski's, the renowned West Side Polish Cathedral the Stanislav family helped to construct in the nineteenth century.

About the Author

Bill Walker worked and traded in Chicago and London at the three largest commodity futures and options exchanges. Since leaving the business, he has hiked some of the world's longest trails, including the Appalachian and Pacific Crest Trails, losing 33 and 43 pounds, respectively. He later wrote the popular adventure narratives, *Skywalker—Close Encounters on the Appalachian Trail* and *Skywalker—Highs and Lows on the Pacific Crest Trail*. He developed the habit of walking long distances on the streets of Chicago.

Acknowledgments

I had long suspected that writing a novel was a more far-reaching process than non-fiction. That has been borne out the last couple years.

Stephen King describes the lonely task of writing fiction as "like crossing the Atlantic Ocean in a bathtub. There is plenty of opportunity for self-doubt."

Fortunately, I had good support along the way. Andy Livingston of Honolulu, Hawaii, Paul Pomaski of Detroit, Michigan, Joe Slott of New York City, and Gini Smith Walker of Macon, Georgia all offered helpful remarks and encouragement.

Mary Ellen Gavin, a literary agent from Ashburn, Virginia, proved to be an all-weather believer in the project. Like many who grew up in the Windy City, she had long heard strange tales about the high-stakes business in downtown Chicago.

Russ Nelson, a literary editor from Decatur, Alabama, maintained his enthusiasm when the manuscript was in its anarchic early stages. "Show me, don't tell me," was his unyielding motto. Thank you, Russ.

Marie Amerson of Macon, Georgia showed impressive resourcefulness and tenacity in creating the cover photo, as well as formatting the manuscript to fit book form.

Manufactured by Amazon.ca
Bolton, ON